THE DIVINES

Born and raised in England, Ellie Eaton lives in Los Angeles with her family. Former writer-in-residence at a men's prison in the United Kingdom, she holds an M.A. in creative writing from Royal Holloway, University of London. *The Divines* is her first novel.

THE
DIVINES

ELLIE EATON

HODDER &
STOUGHTON

First published in Great Britain in 2021 by Hodder & Stoughton
An Hachette UK company

1

Copyright © Eleanor Eaton 2021

A CIP catalogue record for this title is available from the British Library

Hardback ISBN 978 1 529 34012 9
Trade Paperback ISBN 978 1 529 34013 6
eBook ISBN 978 1 529 34014 3
Audio ISBN 978 1 529 34016 7

Printed and bound in Great Britain by Clays Ltd, Elcograf S.p.A.

Hodder & Stoughton policy is to use papers that are natural, renewable
and recyclable products and made from wood grown in sustainable forests.
The logging and manufacturing processes are expected to conform to the
environmental regulations of the country of origin.

Hodder & Stoughton Ltd
Carmelite House
50 Victoria Embankment
London EC4Y 0DZ

www.hodder.co.uk

FOR TOM AND IRIS

γνῶθι σ᾽εαυτόν

THE
DIVINES

PROLOGUE

Gerry Lake looked like a bird with a broken wing—something small and green and feathered, lying there in the middle of the lawn—a budgerigar. One of her knees was bent, the back of her hand cast across her brow in the closing moment of a routine. Very dramatic. Typical Gerry. Her tights were ripped, her plumes ruffled, sequins scattered, her ice skates landed beside her on the grass.

The younger years thought it was part of our dares. A joke. A prank.

"Marvellous," they called out, clapping.

They hung out of dorm windows in pyjamas and smoked, waiting for the punch line.

After a while we crawled from our various hiding places: the bushes, the boiler house, the ha-ha, the groundskeeper's shed, the vestry, the orchard, the gym. Cloaked and hooded, as tradition dictated, our dresses slashed at the seam, barefoot.

We formed a circle around Gerry like a coven.

Gerry was in her leotard, of course, her ponytail still rolled in its neatly gelled bun. Hand across her forehead in that panto-mime pose. *Woe is me!* Playing dead. By then we were sick of the endless tantrums and sulking, her door-slamming histrionics, the crying wolf.

No one thought to call an ambulance or alert our housemis-tress.

In our defense, there wasn't a drop of blood.

"Very funny, Geraldine," we said, arms crossed beneath our cloaks, our voices high and clipped.

We looked at her doll-like limbs, her tiny feet and small nose, flicking up at the end like a ski jump. The blue and gold glitter she wore in the rink, smudged down each cheek. Damp confetti. Instead of the sullen pout we'd come to expect from Gerry, her mouth was an open hole. She stared up at her window, uncharacteristically quiet. A budgie who'd flown into glass. Near her skates was a hairpin, a good luck charm she wore during competitions, a forget-me-not sprig made from fake sapphires, cheap and gaudy, snapped in half.

Later, when Gerry was front-page news, journalists hiding in all the bushes, some of us speculated she'd done it on purpose. Out of spite. To spoil our fun. All that time on the ice had given her a thirst for the spotlight. It was just like Gerry to cause a scene. She was an attention seeker, a spoilt brat, prone to telling tales. Gerry's nickname back then, one of many, was the Poison Dwarf.

We rolled our eyes, yawned loudly.

Feathers fluttered in the breeze.

Some of us noticed, for the first time, the clump of ivy in her fist.

The unusual bend to one knee.

The dark circle that had surfaced between her thighs like ink on our blotters, creeping slowly across her leotard gusset.

"For goodness' sake. Get up," we said, less confident now.

We nudged her with bare feet. Giggled self-consciously.

"Gerry?"

Our cloaks—thick black wool—were suddenly heavy. Our torn summer dresses, tattered and thin. Toes numb with cold. Our brown lace-ups, strung from the weeping cedar, twisted in the wind, clacking their heels. Strange what one remembers, even now, after all this time. Our housemistress, for example, careening across the lawn, bellowing like a cow. The blue flashing lights, the backboard, the neck brace. The handful of hostile locals already standing watch by the gate. The way, sheepishly, we picked up Gerry's broken hairpin from the grass and hovered near the stretcher, despite the obvious annoyance of the paramedics, one of them a man in a turban, who stared frostily at our shredded uniforms, the cloaks, the hoods. How, as they wheeled her away, a cortege of us filed behind the stretcher carrying her good luck charm. Some of the small gold leaves were bent, a gem lost during the fall.

"Here," we said.

Gerry's hands and shoulders were strapped to a board, her chin jutting up above a thick white cervical collar, a chorister's ruff, beatific looking, completely quiet.

How her body stiffened.

Her nostrils flared.

"All right, girls, that's enough."

We shuffled back, still holding the pin.

And finally, our last memory of Gerry Lake, so unlike the pictures in the Sunday papers—Gerry beaming on the ice, hugging a trophy, a plastic doll with a beauty pageant smile—our last glimpse as the ambulance doors swung shut. Her fists crumpled into small white balls, her face distorted, lips pulled tight, exposing the fangs she normally tried to hide.

1

I am Divine.

My mother was Divine and her mother before that, which isn't uncommon. Though that was at a time when being Divine meant something; it had cachet, as my mother still likes to brag; it opened doors, got you places. Though it's hard to see specifically where being Divine ever got her, other than married. Perhaps I'm missing the point.

I haven't spoken to another Divine for fourteen years, maybe more, despite there being ample online opportunities these days to reconnect with my former peers should I so wish. I don't. Every Christmas and Easter I fly back to England to visit my mother, who, in her sixties now, keeps backdated copies of our Old Girls' newsletter for me in her downstairs loo, next to *Country Living*. Births, deaths, marriages, the rare athletic achievement, horses for sale, and, of course, reunions. Endless reunions. Not one of which I have attended. Until, as a newlywed, I take my husband on an impromptu detour from our honeymoon destination, veering off the dual carriageway so unexpectedly at the road sign that he thinks for a heart-stopping moment I might have morning sickness.

"Just to have a look," I say. "It won't take long."

A trip down memory lane, then we'll be on our way.

I crawl our rental car round the Oxfordshire town, circling closer to where I remember my former school once stood, folding forward over the steering wheel, trying to get my bearings. This is harder than I think it will be. Nothing is as I remember it. Most of the grounds have been flattened. The gym is gone, the maths

block, the redbrick science labs, everything except those buildings deemed to hold significant historic value—the Old Hall and
a couple of boarding houses, subdivided into flats for young pro-
fessionals. I park outside the chapel, which is now, by the looks
of things, a private dental practice. My husband of two days is
bemused. Keen to get some miles under our belt on the long drive
to Scotland, he hadn't factored this pit stop into his calculations.

"This is it?"

"Give me half an hour," I say, squeezing his hand.

I point him in the direction of the White Horse. When he is
gone, I walk into the dentist's, slipping past a young receptionist
into the sanctuary-cum-waiting room, repainted a minty ortho-
dontic green. I sit for some time listening to the ominous clinks
and skirls and high metallic whines of the hygienist at work.
Along the nave, cubicles have been fashioned from low mov-
able walls decorated with huge toothy faces of smiling children.
The wooden bench I am sitting on looks like, perhaps even is, the
exact pew that the robed altar servers slumped on during our
Sunday service, obscured by puffs of incense. The organ pipes
are still in situ, way back up in the balcony behind the choir stalls,
which seem quite small, barely room for a handful of girls. On
the immovable stone pulpit where Fat Fran, my headmistress of
six years, made her daily proclamations, a series of dental brochures, women's magazines, food and lifestyle glossies have been
stacked, some of which, at one time or another over my career, I
have contributed to. I rest my head against stone and look up at
the arched ceiling. It is very surreal, the dental nurses padding in
and out of the vestry in their soft-soled shoes like nuns. Everything so familiar yet nothing quite as it was.

Behind my head is a sequence of very narrow and long stained-
glass windows reaching all the way to the beams. What shocks
me as I sit there is that—unless I actually sit up and twist my neck
to look—I can't remember what they depict, not even if you put
a gun to my head. I spent the entirety of my adolescence facing
those windows, staring at them every single morning for close to

five years, Saturdays excepted, and don't remember a single detail, not one saint or disciple or even the big man himself, which only goes to show the astonishing depths of teenage self-obsession. Or maybe, more accurately, it says something about me back then. Or my memory of my school days, selective at best.

As I am sitting on the pew a patient comes out of a booth, her jaw clamped down on wadding, her hand holding her cheek. Unsteady on her high heels, dazed, she is guided to a spot next to me. A dental assistant goes to retrieve something important, a prescription perhaps, and the patient's eyes roam around the arched ceiling and the fluted ironwork. It is an unnerving setting for a dental practice—the angels and the pulpit and stained glass—perhaps she thinks she is hallucinating. Blood catenates slowly from her empty socket down the gauze in her hand. We are probably the same age. She could have been a King Edmund. She stares vacantly at the neon exit sign as if she is waiting to be collected. Above the vestry door is the Divine school motto carved into a rectangle of wood.

MEMOR AMICI

Remember friends.

"Ha," I snort out loud.

The patient slowly turns towards me, medicated, her hand still firmly pressed against her cheek. She blinks.

I try to swallow it down, doubling over, in the grip of the kind of stifled laughter that catches you off guard, leaping up your throat during sombre moments: funerals, sermons, your fiancé's art exhibition.

My shoulders shake and the pew judders. The patient stands up suddenly, her handbag falling to the floor, its contents spilling.

"Shit, I'm terribly sorry." I see her lipstick rolling towards the lectern. "Sorry, sorry."

I put a fist to my chest and thump it. Swallow.

"Sorry."

I scramble to pick up her bag, holding it out to her.

"This used to be a school," I blurt, just to say something. "St John the Divine."

The poor woman's numbed head nods slightly, as she takes her purse. She looks down at a message illuminated on her phone and then over her shoulder at the door, checking for her lift. I assume she isn't allowed to drive.

"The private school," I keep going. "The one that shut down; it was in the papers a long time ago, remember? There was a scandal."

She stares at my face as if I am slowly coming into focus. Enough years have passed for me not to sound completely Divine. I have lived abroad on and off, my accent is sometimes hard to identify, but still, she looks me up and down and her eyes flash. She knows.

"Yeah," she says. As she talks her wadding unplugs momentarily, exposing ghoulish bloody gums. "And? My mum worked in the kitchen." She thumbs behind us in the direction of the old refectory. "Sixteen years scrubbing fucking pans, if you must know."

The right side of the woman's lip is drooping; her speech has a drunken slur.

"Bunch of stuck-up fucking toffs."

She plugs the gauze back in, clamps down on it, waiting to see what I'll say next. She's right, of course. But what does she expect me to do, defend my honour, wrestle her to the floor?

I think about my husband, Jürgen, waiting for me in the pub. Jürgen knows how to let moments like this roll over him. He is a pacifist, not someone who can be easily provoked. Despite the fact he's the artist in our relationship, things that make me flare up with rage don't bother him at all. When we met I had just come out of a turbulent, itinerant period of life and, exhausted, I suppose you could say that I found his particular brand of considered quietude seductive. That was what I had fallen in love with. Lately I have been trying hard to adopt some of Jürgen's sangfroid. Plus we are newlyweds. On our honeymoon. I don't take the bait.

Thankfully a bald man sticks his head around the chapel door, whistles and gestures at the woman with his thumb. She departs, her high heels clicking sharply on the tiled floor, marching down the nave, past the vestry and through the arched door.

MEMOR AMICI

I wait a decent amount of time, hovering on a Communion step, then I leave as well. My husband—that word feels so exotic— is waiting for me outside, hands in his pockets, resting on the hood of the rental car, chewing slowly. I feel a burst of relief to see him standing there, solid looking and straightforward, not in the least Divine. On our first date he rolled up his sleeves at the sight of the leaking pipe in my kitchen, requesting a spanner. He is a pragmatist, a maker of lists.

"All good?" he checks.

I nod. I turn my back and lean against Jürgen's chest; he loops his arms around my waist, his chin on my head, and I try to put the incident in the chapel behind me. I should never have come back. I'm embarrassed to have brought him here, to have wasted even an hour of our honeymoon on something so inconsequential. A moment of nostalgia, now gone. We gaze up at the stone statue of King Edmund in the centre of the town, close to the bus stop. Five pigeons spar for space on top of his helmet, bobbing and ducking, feather elbows. They flick their shabby grey tails and shit down Edmund's cloak. An elderly woman tugging a tartan shopping trolley shuffles past us into the market square. Traders hold bananas aloft on hooked fingers, hollering deals. Three old boys in tweed jackets stand outside the bookie's smoking. I am acutely aware of how particularly English all this must seem to him, my husband, an Austrian.

Jürgen pulls a piece of fudge from a paper bag and puts it into my mouth.

"Okay. Big drive. Let's go."

He checks the fastenings on his bike that is tethered to the boot of our rental car, and as he tugs the frame tight a bald man driving a red Mazda swerves across the road towards us and stops abruptly, blocking traffic. A window hums down, and the woman from the dentist's leans across the bald man, actually crawling across his lap, the lower half of her face distorted, stiff with pain.

"Hallo there," my husband says jovially, squatting slightly, "can we help?"

Austrians, particularly country bumpkins like him, are pathologically nice. I've seen him dig a car out of the snow for a stranger and drag each of our neighbour's bins out every week without a word of thanks.

The woman in the Mazda gives him the finger.

She glares at me, her real target, and pokes her swollen head farther out of the window as if there is something urgent she forgot to tell me back there in the chapel, her tongue fat and lisping.

"*Cunth.*"

"Ha." I laugh nervously. "Ha ha ha."

Then she spits at me, her gob landing at my feet, and they speed off.

So, this is the way it is. Fourteen years and nothing has changed. She is a townie. I am Divine.

"My god," my husband says, "Sephine, who was that?"

Hands on his hips, he looks up the road after the Mazda.

"Was that some kind of joke, my god?"

"Forget it," I say, humiliated, "let's go."

I give him a gentle shove towards the car in case the banshee decides to come back. I don't want her to jinx our honeymoon. Two days ago we were exchanging vows at the town hall, grinning at each other like imbeciles, euphoric.

"But I don't understand; do you know her?"

"No, nothing like that."

I slip my hands down his hip, taking the keys from his pocket.

I unlock the rental car quickly and get behind the wheel. Jürgen sits in the passenger seat, shaking his head.

"Was she from your school then, an old friend?"

I start the car.

"I don't have any school friends."

He frowns, as if he's only just found this out about me.

"You don't? Why not?"

I have friends, of course, but the oldest and truest friendships I have are the ones I forged at university or soon after, when an element of choice was introduced to the selection process. Plus my husband's friends, such as they are, though generally not their wives for some reason. Thanks to his extreme niceness, genial blue Austrian eyes, his obvious likeability, Jürgen has always been the social one in our relationship. Though these days he's just as happy to spend an evening at home, working in his studio or tinkering with his bikes. Occasionally we go to a gallery opening or drive visitors around whatever city we are living in, or meet an old editor of mine for brunch. I can count nearly all these friends on one hand. But not one of them is Divine.

"I don't know," I tell him with a shrug and turn the key in the ignition. "I just don't."

We break the journey in Yorkshire, spending the night in a bed-and-breakfast where we barely leave our four-poster bed. In the morning we scramble into clothes, unwashed, stumbling into the dining room moments before the end of service. The landlady, a stern matronly looking woman, reminiscent of a former housemistress of mine, stands with her hands on her hips, scowling at the clock. We slip sheepishly into our seats, trying not to laugh. Across the room two women, dressed in shorts and walking boots, barely glance up from their maps. A middle-aged man butters his mother's toast. Next to us an elderly couple smile and raise their glasses of orange juice.

"Congratulations," the wife says, leaning over and patting Jürgen on the back of his hand.

"Is it that obvious?"

The couple smile knowingly at each other.

Jürgen's T-shirt is inside out, my hair unkempt. As we brush against each other under the table, there's a stench between my thighs, musky and sour, like overripe fruit. I cringe, thinking of our attic room, the paper-thin walls and creaking bed frame, and bury my head in Jürgen's shoulder. The landlady slams a teapot on the table in front of us.

Jürgen asks the couple how long they've been married.

"Forever," the old man groans.

His wife flaps her napkin at him.

"Fifty-four years this September," she says.

I can feel Jürgen's fingers as they weave through mine, how his wedding band grates over my knuckles as he squeezes, causing me to wince.

"Any advice?" Jürgen asks.

The elderly pair gather their room key and newspaper and spectacles from the table. The husband gets up and pulls back his wife's chair so she can stand.

"Be kind," the wife says.

They nod at us.

"Good luck."

During checkout Jürgen stops in front of the landlady and kisses me, a hand slipping down the back of my trousers, and then we pack up the car and are back on the road. I begin to think that the unpleasant incident at St John's is forgotten, that the whole ugly scene is behind us. But then, unexpectedly . . .

"No school friends," Jürgen says, sliding his hand up and down my thigh as I join the motorway. "That's interesting, you know?"

I can see that my new husband finds this baffling. I wish I'd never mentioned the word *Divine*. He can't let it alone. He taps one finger against the glass as we cross the border into Scotland, staring out at the uneventful landscape, green fields with yellow pocket handkerchiefs of oilseed rape, culs-de-sac, warehouses and roadside cafés, snack vans parked in service stations. We have another four hours of driving ahead of us to get to Skye, not to mention the ferry.

"Not one?" Jürgen checks, uncharacteristically pushy.

"No."

"How come?"

The four men that are his best friends all come from the same Salzburg village where he grew up. Andreas, Hansi, Thomas B, Thomas F. Two of them were christened together, they went to the same school, shared their first cigarette in Hansi's woodshed, stole their grandparents' schnapps, chased their first girlfriends on Krampusnacht, pretending to be the Christmas devil, masked and growling, nipping their sweethearts' ankles with leather whips, threatening to carry them to the underworld. They have shed blood together, hunted together, drunk-wept at each other's weddings, actually staggering around the dance floor like bears. They are his family, closer than his actual brothers (one older, one younger, who I have to remind Jürgen to call on their respective birthdays). He is loyal to the core and would do anything for these four men, including jumping on a plane at the drop of a hat, or loaning them money without any expectation of return. A private annoyance of mine.

"Were you bullied?" Jürgen wants to know as we pull over to fill up with petrol.

"No. I don't think so."

"Unpopular then?" He pokes me. "*Eine Streberin.* How do you say, a geek?"

"No."

I grip the pump handle, my knuckles blanching.

"So you loved school?"

"Who loves school? It was fine," I snap, instantly regretting my tone. "I mean, I don't remember. Can we just drop it?"

Back behind the wheel he curls his hand around the nape of my neck to soothe me, rubbing his thumb up and down below my ear. He has calluses, little circular pads on the base of each finger from cycling that are rough as pumice.

"You don't know if you liked school or not? You must remember something."

"Not really," I say, wriggling out of Jürgen's grip, flustered, trying to concentrate on the road.

"Try," he says.

I don't answer.

Why won't I talk to him? Is it just that I'm embarrassed? The boarding school education, the implication of wealth and privilege, the Old Girls' network. When I met Jürgen (a sculptor I was sent to interview for a Sunday supplement, a rising star), he was still sleeping in a tent in his studio, washing in a sink, subsisting on grants and sporadic commissions. A self-made man, the descendant of mountain people, literally peasants—cattle herders and cheese makers—he described to me during the course of that first meeting how he'd paid his way through art school felling trees and slaughtering goats.

Jürgen turns his whole body to face me.

"Seriously, you're kidding, right? You won't tell me this?"

Ashamed, I say nothing.

He can see that I'm not going to budge.

This does it. Silently thunderous, Jürgen takes out his guidebook and reads the history of Skye. His stare bores down into one page then the next. We're not the kind of couple who bicker. I sit behind the wheel, gnawing on the inside of my cheek, trying not to cry.

On the ferry to Armadale we stand apart, his hood up, my scarf wrapped around my head against the spray. He has his camera around his neck but doesn't take one photo. When we get to the island, there are midges, huge biblical clouds of gnats. We cover our mouths with our T-shirts and run into the croft house we have rented, cornered together inside the tiny kitchen.

"Oh my god," I say, looking out at the bugs creeping all over the window frame, trying to find a way in. I try to make a joke about it but it falls flat. Jürgen is still furious with me, his new wife, for keeping secrets. He sits with the map spread on the floor, his precious road bike propped up against the wall. I open the bottle of single malt I bought on the mainland. I may have taken a few swigs already on the crossing. Dutch courage.

My throat warm, I place the whisky dead in the middle of his map. Jürgen barely looks up. I take off my clothes—it is our honeymoon, after all—and straddle Loch Hourn. Legs spread shamelessly. Afterwards, we lie on the floor and drink the rest of the bottle, picking midges from each other's skin.

"Please, Sephine," Jürgen begs. "Remember something. For me."

"Why are you so interested all of a sudden?"

"That woman, she hated you. She called you a cunt."

"So?"

"I want to know. I want to know about you back then."

"No, you don't."

I curl under his armpit, press against his warm ribs.

"*Liebchen*"—he circles the birthmark on my shoulder—"please."

I think of the elderly couple at the bed-and-breakfast. Be kind.

"Fine," I mutter. I believe, or so I tell myself, in the apotropaic power of marriage. That witch hasn't jinxed us, we are invincible. Golden even. What harm can it do?

"Memor amici," I begin.

Remember friends.

2

We sat, some of us early birds, on the ha-ha, legs dangling above the grass ditch, watching the Peck twins, Dave and Henry, play a so-called friendly game of tennis. It was mid-April or around then. The first day of the summer term, my fifth year at the school. What would turn out to be our last as Divine. A few weeks before the Gerry Lake scandal.

Dave Peck wiped her wristband over her top lip where she was pooling sweat, squatting slightly, shifting from foot to foot in a slow, hypnotic rock, waiting for the serve. Henry, the prettier and leggier of the Peck twins, at least according to my memory, tossed the ball high. She jumped, her racket arm primed, so that it looked for a moment like she was suspended in the air, levitating, truly divine. Then she plummeted down on top of the ball, which her sister somehow managed to return, firing it into the distant corner, just inside the line. Henry frowned and picked up a new ball without saying a word to her twin. The Peck sisters were in the midst of a spat. Henry had spent the Easter holidays giving blow jobs to their private tennis coach in the swimming pool changing hut of their Hampshire house, leaving Dave alone on court to practice with a ball machine.

"What happened to the Moose?" I asked the group.

This was the name we'd given the much-talked-about coach, a former pro, whose real name was something exotic sounding to us, like Moussa. By then the phrase "the Moose" had already morphed amongst Divines into a code word for blow jobs and big dicks, and eventually just dicks in general.

"Monaco," someone said. "The Moose went to Monaco."

"Or, like, Abu Dhabi?"

"Au revoir, the Moose."

"Yeah, no more moose."

"Brunei," Henry corrected, taking a break as the sisters switched ends, leaning against the court fence, the flesh on her shoulder squeezing through the mesh of small diamonds so that she looked vaguely upholstered.

"Hi, Joe," she said to me. "How was Hong Kong?"

My father was a banker; my parents had recently moved for his work.

"It was passable. Sorry about the Moose."

"Thanks, I mean, I don't know." She bounced her racket against her heel. "We're going to write to each other and stuff, it'll be cool. I'll see him at half term."

The Moose had it made. St John the Divine, a private boarding school, was staffed almost entirely by women, with the exception of Padre, our school chaplain, and a couple of ancient art and maths teachers; the Moose had had zero competition. The chances of us giving out blow jobs during the eighty-four days of that summer term, not counting exeats (weekend leaves) and a half-term holiday, were highly unlikely. Sebastian Moussa was probably thirty-two or -three, drove a convertible, and had a French accent. He was a god. We knew nothing about his life off court. This was preinternet, remember; no one could google anyone. For all we knew he could have been married with six children. The man was an enigma.

I remember that whenever I thought about Sebastian Moussa, who had the muscular knees of a long-distance runner and hard, dark brown thighs, I always started to feel my palms clam up and had to rub them across my school tights before anyone noticed because, at sixteen, I had never actually seen in the flesh or touched, let alone sucked, any moose. In this respect I was somewhat behind my peers. Divines were known for being sexually precocious. I had an extremely vivid imagination but couldn't for the life of me visualise having a part of someone else, especially not that part, in my mouth, or what I'd do with it once it was there. (In Second Year I was dared by my best friend, Skipper, to suck another Divine's thumb and, despite still being a resolute thumb sucker myself at that age, remember the repulsive, alien sensation of George Gordon-Warren's knuckle jammed against my lower teeth, her long nail nipping my roof cavity, so retch-worthy an experience that soon after I gave up the habit. If George's thumb made me gag, how, I wondered, could I possibly manage a penis?)

Which isn't to say I was frigid—an accusation we used to toss around back then—or unattractive, not a total disaster at least. True, I didn't have much in the way of breasts and had something of a mousy, forgettable face, but I had grown my hair long to master the flick, a single swipe of the hand, our signature move, that folded one's hair into a side quiff. We never tied our hair up back then unless it was for sports and were constantly tossing our heads from one side to another throughout the day. I'm surprised we didn't get whiplash. I had the same slippery fine hair I have now, which made this style hard to maintain and so I got in the habit of tilting my head to one side, inadvertently giving me a Princess Diana kind of coyness. Not exactly a coquette like Henry Peck, but still, it seemed to appeal to the boys. At least the kind of boarding school boys we knew back then: Harrovians, Etonians, Radleians, Old Stoics. Except that by the Fifth Form the closest I'd come to sex was some cack-handed fumbling through a tuxedo zipper at a school dance. Skipper, one of the most popular girls in our year, a safe bet for head girl, knew this, as did the other Divines and so all this moose talk back then made me feel vaguely fraudulent, as I often did during that period of my life, riddled with insecurity. Still, I continued to smile at Henry Peck that day as if I was in on the moose joke, kicking my legs against the crumbling stone wall of the ha-ha, and changed the subject before Henry returned to the question of my Easter holidays. No moose then, either.

Jürgen lifts his head to interrupt my story.

"Coquette?"

"Jane Eyre was one of our set texts, we were fifteen and sixteen years old, we knew all about coquettes."

"Okay," Jürgen concedes. "Go on."

He lies back down.

"Wait, the Peck twins, where are they now?"

"I don't know. That's not important. Are you going to keep on butting in?"

"*Nein, nein.*"

I cuff him on his thigh.

"Pass me the whisky."

My husband rests the bottle on my naked hip. It's obvious the effect my story is having on him—the teenage girls, the uniforms, the long manes of hair.

"Do it."

"Do what?"

"The flick."

"The flick? I don't remember."

"*Ja,* you do."

He leans forward and pulls the clip from my bun.

"Go on. Show me."

I pretend to scowl but stand up, catching sight of myself in the sitting-room mirror, my naked torso above the fireplace, small white breasts, my nipples mutinous in the cold and hard as bullets. I enjoy looking at my wide, milky coloured bottom, more than a handful, slightly dimpled at the edges. So different from how I was fourteen years ago when I was all edges and bone. I rub my hand across my soft belly. Absorbed by my own flesh. I almost forget Jürgen is waiting.

"So," he prods, "go on."

I comb my fingers through my knots, flattening my palm, and I do it. It turns out I haven't forgotten; in fact I perform it perfectly, my hair cartwheeling over, the apotheosis of the flick. I look at Jürgen as I used to look at those Radley boys, head tilted sideways, draped in gold, Hellenic.

"*Güt,*" he says.

He kneels before me, cupping my breasts in his hands.

"Do you want to hear this or not?"

"I do," he rasps, squeezing a nipple, "I do."

"Jürgen."

"Keep going. Tell me about the scandal."

3

A long-standing Divine tradition was to toss our brown leather lace-ups into the branches of a weeping cedar at the front of the school. My grandmother and mother had both done it, as would I a few weeks later in a moment of post-GCSE exam euphoria. On that first day of summer term I watched as a funeral procession of cars came peeling off the road and up the drive, looping round the Circle with this shoe tree in the centre. Cars paused by the entrance while royal blue school trunks with brass buckles and our names painted on the sides were solemnly heaved onto the grass by the long-suffering maintenance staff, grave as pallbearers, then the parents went gliding on in search of a parking spot beside the boarding house.

St John the Divine had a campus of two halves, conjoined twins, linked by a large metal bridge. This bridge, an eyesore of a construction, straddled the two splintered parts of our school grounds like some vast metal stick insect. Built at the behest of concerned parents, its intent was to stop Divines having to cross the road below on foot, putting an end to us playing chicken with townies who had been known to accelerate on sight, honking their horns, cutting so close we could hear the snorts of laughter, the spray of puddle water against our calves. Which says something about the civic sentiment back then. Long before the scandal.

We all loathed the bridge. In winter we clung to the frozen banister, bobsleighing down the near vertical set of steps. In the summer it radiated an unpleasant tarry heat underfoot, hot enough to burn through white plimsoll. That said, the view from the top was the best in the school. Standing in the middle you could see, to the east, pairs of strung shoes, polished as conkers, spinning at the top of the cedar tree in the centre of the Circle and next to that the laundry, sports halls, tennis courts, orchard, and the red-brick boarding houses where we junior years slept—formerly the property of a wealthy Victorian landowner, now renamed after saints, St Gertrude, St Hilda, et cetera. These various buildings were spread across the town, like a tumour, partitioned from disapproving locals by an imposing brick wall.

The Other Side was what we called the remainder of the school and included pretty much everything you could see to the west of the bridge: the chapel, classrooms, science labs, refectory, the headmistress's office and an oval vestibule known as the Egg (a kind of prechamber of the headmistress's office, where Fat Fran's henchwomen liked to congregate in large wingback chairs), and finally, the Sixth Form accommodation, Lower and Upper. These Sixth Form dormitories—two modern-looking brick bungalows, once a retirement home for Divine nuns, long dead, though their chalky odour still lingered—had the benefit of being set back from the road, away from the other buildings. This gave the occupants the illusion of privacy. Something Sixth Formers felt rather superior about.

The life of these Sixth Form girls seemed unimaginably sophisticated to us. Gone were the unflattering Edwardian school uniforms (blue tweed skirts, beige shirts, and ankle-length black wool cloaks in winter, striped cotton tunics in the summer months). Gone were the weekly dorm inspections, the endless monitoring of tuck boxes filled with snacks, and mandatory lights-out. Instead these Sixth Form girls wore their own clothes, lounged around the bungalow during free periods, drove their own cars home at half-term, and—the thing we coveted above all others— slept in private bedrooms, some of them rumoured to be en suite.

Another perk of being a Sixth Former, I remember, was unsupervised and unlimited access to the town, on the strict condition that they travelled in groups of two or more. This was due to the long-running grudge between Divines and townies, who tended to think of us all as a stuck-up, supercilious bunch of trust funders (not unfounded) with a pretentious tradition of calling each other by boys' names. It didn't help, of course, that so many of the locals were beholden to the school for their financial security—the allowance money we splurged at their corner shops on sweets and cigarettes and magazines, the minicab fares we racked up to the nearby city, the cinema trips and extravagant birthday cakes ordered from their bakeries. Moreover, the school was one of the few remaining employers that offered locals regular work. Townies scrubbed our floors, cleaned our toilets, painted lines on our tennis courts, washed our underwear, served us our meals and disposed of our scraps. No wonder they loathed us.

A townie could spot a Divine a mile away and vice versa. Shark-eyed girls from the local comprehensive with faces pulled tight by gelled buns, eyes glinting, sucking their teeth at us at the bus stop as we went past. Their grey King Edmund skirts hitched up their thighs, little school ties on elastic, and gold earrings.

"What the fuck you looking at, you posh twat?"

The loathing townies felt for us was visceral. Disgust radiated from these KE girls like white heat. They would spit on our backs the moment we passed, or swarm around us, as in the case of Henry Peck, dragging her behind the White Horse, where they shoved her against redbrick and flicked ash on her head. When I later relayed this incident to my mother, she shrugged and wafted her hand through the air as if it was nothing. This kind of hostility had gone on for as long as she, or any Divine, could remember, over a hundred years or more. There had been some halfhearted efforts over the years by our respective headmistresses to bring about a cease-fire, which came to nothing. Townies hated Divines. End of story.

By early afternoon the Peck twins had given up on their game of tennis and flopped on the grass beside the rest of us, sweating, red faced. We sat on the ha-ha watching the cars as they arrived, the grown-ups giving one another jovial salutes and hand waves and *hello there*s. They looked excited as puppies while, by contrast, their progeny were slumped in the back seat listening to a Walkman, so really, you had to wonder who all this performance was intended for, mothers leaning in to double kiss each other through lowered windows, fathers braying at one another across the grass. Beneath the shoe tree, girls, two at a time, were tugging the contents of their trunks inside and up to their shared dorms via the long-standing Divine technique of using bedding material as a holdall, twisting the ends of their duvet covers and hoisting the cadaver-like weight over their shoulders. A new bed each term, fourteen different dorms in my time as Divine, I calculated out loud, anything from two to eight girls crammed in one room depending on the year, a total of seventy-two different dorm mates since we'd started at the school.

"Not including Gerry Lake," Dave said, lifting her head up from the grass and grinning at me.

My stomach lurched as if I'd been shoved hard from behind.

"Bloody hell," I said, groaning.

The others snorted with laughter.

"Bad luck, Joe," they said, elbowing me in the ribs. "Nightmare."

Gerry Lake. The Poison Dwarf. The least popular girl in our year—loudmouthed, crude, famously temperamental. Instead of sharing a room as usual with Skipper and the twins, somehow I was stuck on my own with Gerry. After the dorm list had gone up on the board at the end of the previous term I was stunned, trying to work out why Gerry had chosen me, above all the other Divines, to be her roommate. It made no sense. We had barely exchanged more than a few words in her entire time at the school. A serious ice skater, she spent all her time either training or at competitions. But eventually it became obvious that Gerry was just as horrified as I was by our sudden cohabitation, which must have been the brainchild of my housemistress, Miss Graves, or one of her deputies, thinking we would be good for each other. It wasn't either of us who wrote our respective names on the dorm request slip, that's for sure. I discovered much later—in those hazy days after the scandal—that Gerry went to visit Miss Graves's flat in person to request to be moved. She would have happily picked one of the Chinese or Russian girls, though they understandably kept to themselves. Or Kwamboka Mosupa, the African exchange student, whom everyone liked, even Skipper, who treated Kwamboka—good-natured, smiling shyly, baffled by the attention—as if she was the classroom pet. But for whatever ill-fated reason, the housemistresses ignored Gerry's pleas. Skipper shared a room with the Peck twins that term, I was stuck with Gerry Lake. They might as well have put me with a townie.

Miserable, I changed the subject.

"Anyone coming for a fag?"

George, the girl whose thumb I had once sucked, leant over and exhaled so I could smell her Tic-Tac and tobacco breath.

"We've just been."

"Sorry, Joe."

You rarely see teenagers smoking now, not on the streets where I live at least, but Divines were notorious chain smokers. I squinted up at the orchard where we normally smoked, eyes thick with jet lag. I estimated that there were too many parents arriving by then, I'd have to go elsewhere. A father walked past us towards the trees with an arm draped around his daughter, a final mournful lap before he surrendered her to the Divine.

"Chin up, angel," we heard him say, "not long."

"Sod it." I took my time sliding off the ha-ha and into the grass ditch below. "I'm going."

4

"Townies," Jürgen says slowly to himself after I have finished.

It is as if he is learning a new word.

"Townies?"

"Yes."

He scratches his stubble. I feel, as I often do, chastened by Jürgen's overwhelming decency. He is the sort of man who can't tell a lie. He won't look at my emails if I leave my laptop open, not even a glance, or read a postcard that comes through the letterbox if it isn't addressed to him. A postcard, for god's sake. I, on the other hand, have been known to steal his phone when he takes a shower, strumming down his list of made and received calls, looking for signs of ex-girlfriends. I check his unopened email then quickly flag it as unread, flinging it across the bed, ashamed to have given in to my old bad habits, the insecurity and paranoia. Jürgen, on the other hand, finds my jealousy entertaining, endearing even. If I asked him—and I haven't—he'd delete every one of his exes from his telephone without a second thought. Jürgen isn't always a saint—of course, he has his shortcomings—but he has an inner moral compass that is finely tuned, the kind of person who leaves notes on car windscreens if he reverses into them. I am hit and run.

"Townies," my husband repeats.

"Jürgen, stop saying it."

"It just sounds so funny. You know. Like commoners. Very feudal. What did you call yourself? Divine, walking amongst us mortals?"

My cheeks begin to burn. Jürgen, who has always admired my

independence, sees me now in this new light: spoon-fed, entitled, Divine.

"Whose side are you on?" I say defensively, even though I know how silly it is to pick a fight about something so trivial, overreacting about something I haven't thought about for years.

"What side?" he teases.

"Exactly."

I scramble about looking for something to cover myself.

"Sephine, it's a joke."

I'm drunk. We should never have started this. Jürgen twists his legs around mine to stop me rolling over.

"Sorry, sorry, come here. I was kidding, don't go. You still haven't told me what happened to that girl, Gerry Lake."

Flustered, I tug a checked blanket from the sofa and wrap it around my shoulders. Flailing about, I scramble underneath the chair to retrieve my tobacco, not caring what I look like with my white arse raised in the air, legs spread, unzipped, everything on show. We are married; he can take it or leave it.

"Sephine, stop."

"I need a smoke," I say.

I pull the blanket around me like a toga and stick my feet in Jürgen's enormous cycling shoes as I march outside, aware how clownish I must seem. I sit on top of a picnic bench. It is dark. Inside the croft house I can see a light come on in the tiny kitchen. Jürgen peers out, stooped over, knocking on the window with his knuckle, mouthing platitudes.

"Come inside, *mein Gott*. Are you crazy? The bugs?"

I pretend to be squinting intently at the waves. It is too dark to see a thing. The blanket is itchy and, to be honest, I had forgotten about the gnats. Still, I stubbornly roll myself a cigarette, and I listen to the waves slapping against each other out there in the night, gulls squabbling. I am drunk enough that the first cigarette is a clumsy, loose effort, it gives me head spins. Not unlike my very first time, crouching in a smoking den with Skipper and the twins, a butt passing from hand to hand round the circle, the whispered secrecy of a séance. This might be what gives me the idea. I hitch up the blanket and inspect the back of the cottage where the property runs alongside a dank mossy wall. There is enough crawl space to sidestep if I hold my cigarette aloft, so I inch along the wall, one hand in the air, clumsily making my way with the cycle shoes on my feet like clogs. There are empty flower containers I trip on, a spade, a cracked shower door and some plastic garden chairs. I wedge myself between a drain and the chairs. It is perfect, just like old times. When I look up, the cottage walls seem to lean towards me amicably.

A light.

There are no bathroom curtains in the cottage, no need, the window looks out onto moss and stones. I see Jürgen gaze at himself in the mirror above the sink. He grasps his chin and pulls down on his bristles, pondering whether I need more space or if he should come out and make peace. I feel a rush of love. Gut churning, nauseating almost. He is, and will always be, an extremely handsome man. Perhaps a little too pale for some people's tastes, his clear blue eyes and the white nape of his neck that he keeps closely shaven, with the rest of his hair grown long on top and sun bleached. He has a cyclist's thighs, thick with muscle, brawny knees as sturdy as ham hocks, a sharp suntan line two inches above his patella where his Lycra shorts end. He rides multiple times a week, sometimes for four or five hours at a time when he needs a break from the studio. His shoulders are hunched from bending over his bike handles, his stomach almost concave. He is too good looking for me by a long stretch. The best person I know. I feel idiotic, lurking out here in the dark. Licking my wounds.

I wait as he splashes his cheeks with water, slurping his cupped palm to sober himself up, then runs his fingers through his hair to slick it back. He appraises himself in the mirror, purses his lips a little. He is not above a little vanity I see. I try not to giggle and give myself away. Then, still naked, he slumps down on the loo. Pecks his penis between his hairless thighs, rests his elbows on his knees, bending forward as if he is on his racer.

Oh my god.

Something about his effeminate posture, sitting to piss like this instead of standing, horrifies me. He tears himself a single square of loo roll as if he is going to wipe himself with that rather than shake.

I've seen enough.

I shrink out of sight, press my back to the wall, and slide to the ground. What else don't we know about each other? I roll myself another cigarette, and when that is done, another. Knees tucked up by my nose on my honeymoon, smoking like a Divine.

5

The smoking den was a narrow burrow between a hedge and the school boiler room, next to the laundry. Neglected over the Easter holidays, the beanbags and the rag rug and the legless sofa we had dragged in there carried a ripe doggy smell. On that first day of the summer term, trying to find somewhere quiet to smoke, I flopped down behind my boarding house, sinking into one of the damp beanbags, knees to nose. The other side of the wall maintenance men, taking a break from hauling trunks out of cars and being ordered around by parents, sat on an old church pew, their legs splayed, drinking sweet, milky tea, smoking.

A wave of jet lag came crashing over me, so heady that I could feel myself swaying. It was the middle of the night in Hong Kong. I had probably been awake close to twenty-eight hours. I closed my eyes and my bones began sinking into one another, chin into chest. I picture my mother in her silk sleep mask, the wooden blades of the ceiling fan humming overhead, my father still in his office. Just as I was nodding off there was rustling from behind the hedge, and a click and a flash. My first thought was that it was one of my friends playing a prank on me. The night of our Fifth Form dares was looming—a decades-old St John tradition that marked the end of exams, when housemistresses appeared to turn a blind eye as girls streaked naked through the rose garden, or glued hymnals to church pews, or sneaked out at night to paint the town statue red.

I jumped up and a sharp piece of card came over the fence, catching me on the cheek. Another inch and it would have impaled me in the eye.

"Bloody hell." I held my face. "That's not funny."

I scrambled up on the legless sofa to see who was there but heavy footsteps were already pounding across the adjoining car park and out onto the High Street. Whoever it was wasn't Divine.

"Bloody hell," I repeated, my heart thumping. I prodded the scratch on my cheek, not more than a small paper cut, but still, there was some blood. I swore loudly to make myself feel less pathetic, worried that there might be a gang of townie girls—King Edmunds—hidden somewhere I couldn't see, ready to pounce on me, to claw my skin with their long artificial nails and pull out my hair.

"Piss off," I shouted, "cows," then looked down to find whatever is was that had nearly pierced my eye.

A Polaroid photo lay facedown on the rug.

"What the fuck?"

I stooped down, picked it up.

Blank.

Out of the milky patina, I watched a faint pink creep in, a blush so slight I brought it closer to my face, and then held it right back, wiggling it in the air. What was this meant to be, a joke? Out of the creaminess I could make out the crest of a hill, or maybe a hat, or a figure of some kind wearing a hat, it was still impossible to tell. Relieved that there didn't seem to be a pack of townies waiting in the shadows to ambush me, I stood there, swaying with jet lag, waiting for the picture to develop, wondering what the image could be.

"Oh my god," I said.

I dropped the Polaroid on the floor, made a squealing noise, my face so scrunched up I could feel my top lip curling up into my gums.

It was a dick.

Actual moose.

I picked it up to examine it more closely. This was the first erect penis I'd ever seen.

A thumb pinned it down, a fist gripping the stump the way you see animal handlers holding geese or swans by the neck, to stop them flapping. A top-down shot taken in a hurry, trousers pulled down to knees behind the fence, the actual fence I was standing next to. It wasn't as turgid or pink as a dog, nor as pendulous as a horse (the only two points of reference I had): redder and angrier, the head bruised and shiny, like a boxer's face postfight.

It was the ugliest thing I'd ever looked at. Hands down. Except, I couldn't stop staring at the top, which had minute white dots speckling it, and the balls, which were far less hairy than I'd imagined, wispy and near bald in patches, like the ancient stuffed teddy bear Skipper still slept with. All I could think about was that Henry Peck had had one of these in her mouth. *In her mouth.* It was grotesque. I slumped down on the beanbag and kept holding the photo up close until I forgot that what I was looking at was even a penis and more like a weird fungus you might find in a street market in Hong Kong. I chewed my lip, examining the soft little nick at the top. I had my nose so deep in moose that I didn't even hear the King Edmund as she snuck into the den and it was too late.

My shoulders lurched up in shock, my head whiplashing back. "What's that then?" she asked.

6

Together Divines were indomitable. We strutted around the town during Saturday excursions in groups of five or six, or at the very least a pair, arm in arm, taking up the entire width of the pavement. We flicked our hair, making sly comments about the townies we passed—their makeup, the cheap clothes they bought from the market, their weight—often before they were out of earshot. We couldn't abide fat people. Also, this was the nineties; townies were clad head to toe in cheap denim while we, governed by our own trends, wore black leggings and large argyle cardigans, which we sourced from a shop on the King's Road; or we stole pink-striped shirts and V-neck jumpers from our fathers. In winter we wore black biker boots or sometimes cowboy boots before we switched to Docksider in the summer, the kind of shoes you'd find at a regatta, their leather laces wound into toggles. I had a new pair of penny loafers with a Hong Kong ten-cent coin tucked into the tongue instead of a penny.

Divines were also compulsive thieves. Dickie Balfour in particular, whose parents owned a stately home in Cornwall and gave her a hefty monthly allowance, was always stuffing Pick'n'Mix in her pockets at Woolworths or lifting hoop earrings from the market. Her father was an earl. She could have bought anything she liked but that wasn't the point. Managers began banning us, or they imposed a strict limit on how many Divines were allowed in their shop at one time. The rest of us prowled around outside, flicking our hair, ululating loudly, our arms chained together. (We were always touching one another, tickling each other's inner elbows and linking fingers, or sitting around the base of the statue of King Edmund in the market centre, resting back between each other's spread thighs.)

But cut us from the pack and we were nothing.

"You dropped your fag," the King Edmund said.

She nodded at the floor.

I slid the Polaroid so the dick was shielded under my thigh.

"If you're not going to smoke it, I'll have it," the KE girl persisted.

Her arms were crossed, one thumb hooked into her fabric bag strap. When she stooped to pick up the cigarette, the pouch flailed towards me and I flinched. I may have even put my hand up to shield my face. I bet she enjoyed that.

The King Edmund held the fag up in front of my nose.

"So, do you still want it or what?"

The top of the cigarette was soggy from lying on wet carpet. What did I care if this girl took it or not; I had an entire carton in my dorm, which I had duped a co-passenger into buying for me from duty free.

"It's wet," I muttered.

The girl shrugged, snapped off the damp tip, put it in her mouth and lit the remaining half stump.

"Ta," she said, triumphant.

She stood there in our den, smoking like a Divine. Practically speaking I couldn't do a thing about it. I was sitting on the Polaroid. I wasn't about to show a townie a thing like that; we'd never live it down. If I got up to leave, she'd see the photo. I had no choice but to sit there and wait till she'd gone. Without Skipper or the twins, I felt limbless and exposed. I began to sweat, the dampness spreading down my back.

The King Edmund smiled to herself and smoked with her arms crossed, leaning against the wall, blocking my way out, which felt like an act of aggression in itself. Her school tie was off and her loose hair, very smooth and pale blond, almost reached her buttocks. I forget exactly what she was wearing, probably the standard King Edmund's grey-white uniform, but I do remember that on her feet were wedge high heels, conspicuous for being particularly un-Divine.

"Chill out, I'm just waiting for my brother," she explained. "He works here, all right?"

Her brother, I guessed, was one of the muscles hired in for the day to help lug our empty school trunks off the Circle and stack them under the stage in the main hall where they remained till the end of term.

"Oh, well." I swallowed, feeling the photograph sticking to my thigh, my face growing hotter. "All right then, that's fine."

I nodded as if granting her permission.

She rolled her eyes at me. Then, examining the end of her cig-arette, she leant back against the wall. She was a little chubby in comparison to the Divine, though not overweight. Her face was round, a cluster of spots at the bottom corner of her lip she must have been picking. I had breakouts once in a while, too, but had had strict instructions from Skipper not to squeeze them. The King Edmund pushed her tongue against the inside of her lower cheek, and absently rubbed her finger over one of the scabs, her eyes moving round the decorations in our den, the wind chimes and the throws, the canopy we'd made to stop the rain coming in.

"Nice," she said, looking at the evil eye hanging from the branch and nudged it with her finger.

"Thanks."

"What happened to your face?"

I'd forgotten about the paper cut and put my hand to my cheek. My skin felt clammy, my cheeks flushed.

"Twig"—I pointed to the hedge—"climbing in."

I watched her cigarette as she brought it to her lips. She made a popping noise as she inhaled deeply. I smoked incessantly but never so professionally as this girl.

"You all right?" She peered down at me. "You look like you're going to puke or something."

I was sweating profusely now. My face had a numb and tin-gly feeling as if I was being drained of blood. Still I didn't move.

These days I'm not someone who embarrasses easily. But back then my threshold was much lower. I craved the approval of my peers, even a King Edmund. The thought that she might somehow catch me ogling a photo of an erect penis made me feel physically sick.

"Head rush." I nodded at the cigarette, before I remembered I never got round to lighting it myself.

She shrugged.

"So they just let you lot smoke in this place then or what?" the girl asked, gesturing to the can of cigarette butts on the floor.

"No," I had to admit, though this was something of a grey area.

Getting caught smoking on school property resulted in detention or, for repeat offenders, a gating. Gating was unbearably dull—two to four weeks of mind-numbing lock-down in which we were not permitted to step foot off school property. There were compulsory time-checks on the hour, every hour, from breakfast to lights off, carrying a small fold of paper down our bras for staff to sign. But the truth was that the sprawling shape of the grounds, which spanned the whole of town, including several off-site lacrosse fields and the orchard, made the no-smoking rule a joke, totally unenforceable. In addition, the average waistline of our housemistresses, many of whom were close to obese, meant they couldn't have squeezed inside our smoking den if they tried. Miss Graves, for example, my Brobdingnagian housemistress of the past five years, rarely left her armchair in the Egg. Typically she delegated the more physical side of our pastoral care to one of her deputies. These women survived no more than a year or two at most at the school, some just a matter of terms, and they were always jumpy-looking spinsters in their late twenties or thirties, whippet thin and lacking the necessary gravitas of a disciplinarian. We ran rings around them.

The teaching staff fared no better. I can only guess the sums of money these women must have been getting paid to work at our school. They were patronised and bullied. They probably thought they were selling their souls to the devil when they left the state sector, but what they got was far worse; it was Divine. If they grew a little tubby, we congratulated them on their pregnancies. We asked the old maids what their boyfriends were called. We splattered their backs with ink. When a teacher asked us to read something out loud or perform a task of some kind, we groaned and procrastinated and spoke in funny voices, or sometimes, such as in *The Doll's House* when Nora says, *I will brush my muff,* we outright laughed in their face.

Because we knew the tuition fees were staggering, we treated members of staff as exactly that. Staff. Under servitude. When we were bored with our lessons, we raised our lids and conversed behind our desks. The only teachers who garnered our respect were the ones that were so eccentric they defied categorisation. We had a history teacher who curled her hair into two ram horns either side of her head and when we spoke over the Treaty of Versailles she recited every monarch from 1066 onward until we were stultified into silence. Our maths teacher, Mr Chambers, one of the few men on staff, refused to learn any of our names and simply called us all Aggie. Desperate tactics, futile in the end, but at least they tried.

It seems amazing to me that more of us weren't expelled. We drank, we smoked, we snuck out at night through our bedroom windows. Everyone except Gerry Lake, who, afraid of heights, refused to so much as climb a gym rope. On a class trip to an Outward Bound centre—a day of scrambling around a muddy assault course in the rain, supposedly character building—Gerry had taken one look at the abseiling wall and marched straight back onto the school bus.

Why some of the more talented teachers stayed as long as they did I can't imagine. If they were hoping they'd encounter a better grade of student at a private school, they were wrong. I had always found academia relatively easy but the majority of Divines weren't in any way gifted, certainly no Wycombe Abbey or Cheltenham Ladies or Downe House. Our entrance exam was a joke. Some of the girls in my year, Skipper, for example, planned to take just one A-Level next year, something undemanding like Drama Studies or Food Technology. What the school had always prided itself on was producing a well-bred all-rounder, a glorified finishing school if you will, for ladies. The future wives of politicians and CEOs and chairmen.

The KE continued her interrogation.

"So you can smoke but you can't watch telly?"

"No. Yes," I said, suspicious now. This was the first proper conversation I'd ever had with a King Edmund, other than the insults they spat at us from the far side of the school wall. Why, I wondered, was a KE so interested in our rules? What did she want?

"And no, like, computers or Game Boys or Sega or anything?" she kept on.

"No."

"That's retarded." The KE stared at what was left of her fag.

I shrugged.

This lack of modern technology at St John's was another immovable fact of being Divine. In one classroom there was a row of ancient word processors where we learnt to type, deemed an essential skill for young ladies, yet we handwrote all our essays with fountain pens. We had restricted access to the single coin-fed phone installed in a booth in the middle of a corridor outside our rec room, the least private of all places. Outside of a few short hours in the evenings it was padlocked, to ensure that we didn't fritter our days speaking to boys. There were no mobile phones at all, though we briefly carried black pagers, which we clipped to our tweed skirts like emergency room physicians, until Fat Fran realised what they were and put a stop to it. We had no access to chatrooms. Facebook didn't exist, no likes or dislikes, no Google, Wiki, Instagram, Twitter, Snapchat, or Gmail. Total radio silence. Television was permitted at weekends in strictly policed portions, Miss Graves tugging the plugs from the walls as the allotted time expired, often mid-programme, swinging the cables in her hand like a baton. The kind of programmes we were permitted to watch were infantile, mindless drivel—*Blossom, Jerry Springer, Gladiators, Ricki Lake.*

"So, you're basically in prison," the KE mused.

She took one last drag on the cigarette then scratched it against the fence to put it out, tossed the butt into the can by my feet. It made a hiss as it hit damp tin.

"Actually"—she changed her mind—"my cousin Steve, he's banged up, and he has a telly in his cell."

I didn't believe her. I dabbed my sleeve on my sweaty top lip when she wasn't looking.

"What for?"

"To watch *Corrie*," she said, and fluttered her eyelids at her joke, which she thought was hysterical. Her eyelashes were as pale as her hair, almost invisible, which made her eyes seem watery and borderless.

"I meant, what's he in prison for?"

"This and that."

"Fine. Whatever," I said, trying to act as if I didn't care, though I'd never met anyone before with a relative in prison.

"You lot probably eat better food, though," she pondered.

I raised an eyebrow. Divines survived on fruit-flavoured bootlaces, squeezable cheese, instant noodles, and other kinds of high-salt, high-sugar, tuck box rubbish. It was amazing we had the bone density to walk. The exception was my dorm mate that term, Gerry Lake, who, due to the demands of a rigorous training schedule, ate like a pig, refectory food and all. Three times a week a beige Ford Escort made a brief stop in the Circle so that Gerry could jump into the rear seat where a middle-aged man wearing a red cap, possibly a trainer or a manager of some kind, drove her away to a nearby ice rink. Judging by the attention she paid to her clothes, the makeup she wore, we all assumed that Gerry had some sort of crush on this driver, a man old enough to be her father, that he was even her boyfriend. The same person deposited her back on school grounds four hours later in time for supper. After which she was allowed to skip the line, fill up her tray and scoff down plates piled with chicken vol-au-vent, cheese and crackers, chocolate pudding with a skin on its surrounding custard that was thick as a tectonic plate. The dinner ladies, sensing that she was more one of them than Divine, typically saved the coveted corner sections just for Gerry.

"So what do you do then"—the KE circled a finger in the direction of the boarding house across the road—"at weekends, or whatever?"

I turned my head, feeling where my shirt was slow to unpeel from my back, tacky with sweat. I was sure somehow she'd discover the photo, or worse, that one of my peers would catch me there alone, talking to a King Edmund. My feet were beginning to go numb. But I still didn't stand up. When was she going to leave?

"Isn't your brother waiting for you?" I asked pointedly.

"Nah." The KE shrugged. "So go on, what do you lot get up to?"

I felt it was an idiotic question. What did anyone our age actually do? We made mix tapes for each other and swapped clothes. We examined our underwhelming bodies in the narrow strip of mirror above each dorm door handle, standing on our desks and contorting our necks, or pressing our faces up against the speckled glass to probe at blackheads under magnification, pores craterous and oily as a tar pit. We smoked, of course, pierced each other's upper ears with a needle and cork, talked about moose, daydreamt about crossing over to the Other Side, bitched about other girls we knew, some of them former Divines who'd left for one reason or another and now attended day schools or co-eds where, the way we pictured it, there were boys on tap. Prolific letter writers, we spent hours crafting ten-, fifteen-, twenty-page shared missives to our pen pals, passing them from dorm to dorm like a religious scroll. These letters were a roll call of who had lost their virginity, or was about to.

"Not a lot really," I told the King Edmund.

"Shit." The KE adjusted her bag strap as if she was leaving finally. "No wonder."

"No wonder what?"

An all-girls school, we knew what the townies accused us of getting up to at night.

The KE girl stared intently at me, arms crossed, one thumb still running across the spotty patch on her lip. I was unconsciously pressing my finger into the sharp point of the Polaroid, spiking it into my skin. Just then we heard a voice yelling from the maintenance shed, a car horn chirped, then footsteps.

"Lauren," someone shouted.

"Yeah, what?"

A man pushed through the branches. He was dressed in the blue overalls of our maintenance men, folded down at the waist. Like the pinups that papered our dormitory walls that year—Brad and Leo and Johnny—his hair was a curtain, parted down the middle.

"Hurry the fuck up will you," he said, then stopped dead.

He looked me up and down—the baggy men's shirt I was wearing, a castoff from my father, the shoes my mother had forced me to polish—and his jaw stiffened. I sat awkwardly on the beanbag, hugging my knees.

"Lauren. Move it," he ordered.

Then he was gone.

Lauren rolled her eyes. She pulled her bag over her shoulder, her white hair swinging down her back.

"That's my brother, Stuart. See you around . . . what's your name?"

"Joe."

The townie rolled her eyes once again.

"Seriously, what's your actual name?"

Our habit of using boys' names was one of the peculiarities of the Divine that was to be heavily reported in the press later that summer. The tabloids in particular dedicated an entire page to the subject of our nicknames, lingering on the fact that in the three years Gerry spent at our school she never received nor gave herself an alternative moniker, pointing, or so they said, to social ostracism. The truth of the matter was Gerry already had a boyish name; she was one letter away from being a Jerry. Unlike my mother, say, whose Divine chums affectionately still call her Rod, it wouldn't have taken much for Gerry to play the game. But that was typical of her.

The KE made an impatient clicking noise with her tongue.

"Josephine," I conceded.

"See you around then, Josephine. I'm Lauren."

Laurence, I thought. *Larry. Len.*

She gave me a finger wave. I couldn't decide if she was being ironic. My mouth was so dry by then I could feel the corners sticking, and my legs throbbed from being hunched in the beanbag, foetuslike, knees to nose.

"Thanks for the fag. I'll pay you back."

"It's fine," I told her. It was just one cigarette. "Don't worry about it."

"I'm not a scab."

There was a brusqueness to her voice that made me stop whatever I was going to say next.

"You lot sleep in there, right?" She pointed at St Gertrude's.

I nodded.

"Lauren," her brother yelled, "come on!"

"Well, I know where to find you then, don't I. I won't forget."

There was a flurry of blossoms as she elbowed through the bushes, and I groaned, flopping back limply into the damp beanbag.

"By the way, *Josephine*"—her head poked back through the hole—"sick photo."

7

Cunth.

I can't get it out of my head.

I toss and turn the first night in the cottage, picturing the face of the woman in the red Mazda, lips curled in disgust, teeth bared, ready to spit in my face. I try to remember. To understand what kind of person I was back then. Why they hated us so much. What we were guilty of.

But in the morning Jürgen stands at the foot of the bed holding a breakfast tray. He promises to never say the word again. *Divine.*

"*Hand aufs Herz,*" he says.

Hand on heart.

Jürgen looks so earnest standing there, his hair parted like a Boy Scout, a smile flickers at the corner of my lips. I cover my head with the duvet so he won't see me laughing. He sets the tray down on the bed. Slips an arm under the covers, to test the water, the rest of him follows. The coffee goes cold, the eggs uneaten.

That afternoon we buy a fishing rod from a shop on the pier and I watch the way my husband whips the rod effortlessly over his shoulder, like a lasso. He'd make a good cowboy: the stubble shadowing his jaw, the denim shirts he likes to wear, his weather-worn hands, his habit of staring into the mid-distance when he's thinking about his work. When Jürgen catches a mackerel, on his first attempt no less, applause breaks out from a group of hikers on the dock. He unhooks the fish from the line and the mackerel thrashes helplessly on the concrete, wide eyed, sides heaving. I think he'll toss it back where it came from but, a country boy,

Jürgen takes off his boot without a second thought and slams it down hard, once, twice, red spattering the concrete. I gasp, horrified.

"Supper," Jürgen announces, his fly already arching over the water.

Later, in the cottage's tiny kitchen, I stand over the sink where Jürgen has been cleaning his catch. I look at their unblinking expressions, the emerald scales like sequins, bellies split, blood dribbling from behind the gills. Jürgen hums to himself. He slices a lemon, then sets the table. I stare and stare. *Cunth.*

All holiday Jürgen conspicuously avoids any further mention of my teenage years or the woman in the red car, hurling abuse. On our afternoon strolls past the village school he averts his eyes, staring out at sea so intently I have to stop myself giggling at his solemn expression. Finally, our last morning, he takes a final photo of the two of us standing in front of our holiday cottage, our heads pressed together, his arm outstretched, and then, loath to leave, we put the keys on the kitchen table, close the door behind us. I watch in the rearview mirror as the cottage slips from view, my stomach in knots. *Cunth.* I want to slam on the brakes, live out our days in this remote fishing village. Untouchable, anonymous, hidden from view.

"What are you daydreaming about?" Jürgen asks, touching my cheek.

Startled, the car swerves.

"Nothing," I say, eyes on the road. "Nothing."

A week after our honeymoon, I'm in the attic in my mother's cottage in Surrey, storing some boxes that won't fit in our London flat. Outside Jürgen helps Rod dig her vegetable patch. From the low gable window I can see his strong back ripple as he thrusts his spade into the sticky clod, turning it over with ease, as if it is butter. My mother, flustered by Jürgen's athleticism, reverts to old habits—flicking her hair, giggling. As far as I know she hasn't had another partner since my father died nine years ago. She walks along the flower beds pointing something out to Jürgen with a rake. An upturned yogurt pot blows off a cane, and she chases after it like a lacrosse player. I nose through a cabinet, take a file out. Rod, with her rosier view of her days as a Divine, has bundles of my correspondence, covertly rescued from the kitchen bin after I attempted to throw them away in a post-university purge. I dump them on the floorboards and sit down, surrounded by the memorabilia of my school days: letters and reports and year photos, a folder of clippings, on the front page of a yellowing newspaper, the headline: NIGHT OF TERROR.

From the pages of my old Bible, a letter slips out.

To my darling, my sweetheart, baby, I miss you like crazy, love, forever and eternity. I am shocked by the ardency. A girl whose face I can't even remember. Pressed flowers taped to the notepaper, pictures of hearts and lipstick kisses.

I stare at an unfamiliar picture of me with my arms draped around two girls from my boarding house. I am wearing a man's cardigan, black leggings, and my burgundy penny loafers. There is a leather choker around my neck with a blue scarab. My hair flops over half my face. I look conscientiously gloomy; Divines never smiled for photos. Holding the photo up to the window, I squint at the shoe tree in the background and then the tennis courts, and the ivy-clad backdrop of St Gertrude's and then—I see for the first time—there in the cross-hatched glass of our old dormitory window, the outline of Gerry Lake's head. Her snub nose, the jutting chin, the accusatory glare. One hand to her hip, the other giving me the finger.

8

Divines were committed oversharers by nature, the by-product of living cheek by jowl as we did, wearing criminally tight blue gym leotards and showering behind flimsy curtains. We had a school nurse who summoned us to the sanatorium by leaving notes on our year pin board. Each of these memos were torn from a thin papery pad so that key words—*acne, discharge, flaky, bleeding, cramps, boil, vaginal,* et cetera—could be read by any passing Divine, the overhead strip light perfectly illuminating her block handwriting each time the refectory door swung open.

What I did after I found the Polaroid was, therefore, not at all in the spirit of the Divine. I slid the photo down the back of my leggings and, while my peers were all busy unpacking, I crept into my new dorm, checking if Gerry was back at school, then I hid it before she could see. Who knows what instinct was driving me; I thought I was a little more institutionalised back then, something of a team player. Perhaps not.

When I had found a safe place, stuck to the reverse of a post-card I pinned on my bedroom wall, I finished unpacking and put up a few more posters on my side of the room, then lay on my bed with my Walkman, lights off, even though it was still early and as far as I could tell Gerry Lake hadn't even signed in yet.

Up and down the corridor, groups of Fifth Formers were going door to door, screaming, air kissing, spreading holiday gossip, admiring each other's interior decoration. Divines put a lot of effort into prettifying new dorms, hanging tie-dye sheets in windows, papering the walls floor to ceiling with posters, the content of which notably changed as we aged. First ponies, then pop bands, and finally hunks torn out from magazines—Brad, River, Leonardo, Johnny. Pseudo porn. Oily naked torsos and thumbs tucked into boxer shorts. Whole evenings were spent examining the two lean muscular lines that started either side of Stephen Dorff's belly button, the inguinal crease, moneymaker, angled slightly together so that, we speculated, they coalesced somewhere close to his pubic hair.

My door banged open, lights switched on. I winced.

Skipper. My best friend since I was eleven years old. Or my former best friend, I wasn't sure. For the past few months I had fretted endlessly about the status of our friendship. We had begun to drift, progressively hanging out less and less in each other's dorms or sharing cigarettes or even sitting together at break-fast. The daughter of a Greek shipping magnate and an English mother (also Divine, a contemporary of my own mother), Skipper had spent her four weeks of holiday in Athens. I had spent Easter in my parents' new house in Hong Kong. She had neither written back to me nor called during the entire break. This was the longest we had ever gone without speaking.

"Anyone home?" She knocked.

Her chestnut hair, of which she had a Botticellian amount, was piled up on the top of her head and fastened with a velvet scrunchie. The rest of her body was oddly hairless. Unlike the rest of us, Skipper never had to shave, not even her armpits. Her tanned legs had an imperceptible, iridescent layer of light fuzz that you could only see when, as on that first day of term, she stood backlit by the corridor light, dressed in nothing but a long Snoopy T-shirt. She was slightly stockier than I was, but her breasts were large and near-perfectly round. At that age I was mortified by how underdeveloped I was; the fact that I had pancake tits, bee stings as Skipper once called them, was a constant source of embarrassment to me. It was like they had forgotten to grow.

I raised a hand and gave Skipper a swift nautical salute from the bed, which had once been our greeting of choice, a private joke we had shared since first year, though suddenly the gesture felt juvenile, made more embarrassing when Skipper either didn't see the prompt or decided not to return it, and instead stood there in the doorway, balancing on one foot. She twisted a stray curl around her index finger. Her retainer clicked in and out of her mouth like a pair of dentures.

I pulled off my headphones.

"What's happening?" she asked.

"Jet lag." I pincered open my eyelids with my fingers. "Can't stay awake."

"Oh, right. Bad luck."

Skipper squinted around to see what I had done in the way of decoration. My half of the room was almost finished and a yin-yang sarong hung above my head. The other side of the room allocated to Gerry was still bare. A few remaining posters of mine were scattered around the desk below my bunk bed, some of them blown across the floor. I cast a look behind me at the postcard where the Polaroid was hidden but decided to wait to hear Skipper's news before I showed her.

Skipper walked across my room, treading on several clothes spewing from my overnight bag.

"Who's this?"

She was pointing to an effeminate-looking aftershave model I'd torn out of a magazine on the plane. Without waiting for an explanation Skipper climbed up on my desk, stepping over me so she could examine each of the new posters I'd carefully blu-tacked to the wall.

"Wicked," she said, pretending to stroke Matt Dillon's chest.

Skipper had a deep, rather masculine voice—I can still hear it now—plus all that thick hair, so both sonically and physically she took up a lot of space, which served her well on the lacrosse field where she was by far our best goalie. The ribbed thigh pads, chest protector, mouth guard, and grilled helmet virtually doubled her size. She was loud and quick witted, an expert skier and sailor, very confident. From the time our mothers pushed us together I was always rather in awe of her. Skipper had been the natural mouth of our duo and I the brains, tags that we capitalised on at first but had started to grow tedious as soon as we were teenagers. Reputations for being butch and brainy weren't going to get us boyfriends.

Skipper's legs were spread, her nightshirt hitched; I could see all the way up her thighs to her crotch, the only place, aside from her head, where she had any hair. I tried not to stare at the two tufts escaping from either side of her underwear elastic as well as the dangling string of a tampon. Long before I had started menstruating or grown breasts, Skipper had extremely heavy periods. In days gone by it had been my role to check the back of her skirt during the Sunday church service, avoiding the mortifying act of kneeling for Communion with blood seeping through her tights. In exchange I would exhale in her face so she could test for halitosis, bad breath being my own teenage neurosis.

Skipper moved along the top bunk looking at my posters, most of which were new, clicking her retainer against the roof of her mouth. She and I had probably shared twelve or so dorms in our time, our wall space typically split down an imaginary centre line. She favoured tennis hunks of the day, Andre Agassi and Pat Cash as I remember. I had a rotating collection of magazine front covers, *The Face* and *SKY*, most of which were ripped down and replaced each term except, for some reason, a signed photograph I had bought from a stall at Kensington Market, a pre-Bad-Seeds-era Nick Cave in which a very young, cocky Cave smoked and gazed mysteriously upwards through quizzical eyebrows. I don't know why his furrowed brow and pale skin appealed to me so much. Perhaps I thought it gave me credibility amongst my peers, or more likely a boy I had a crush on said he was a fan, I don't remember. On the whole, Divines had terrible taste in music. We couldn't have cared less about the rave scene or feminist punk or the underground. All of that passed us by. The tapes we blasted on our expensive boomboxes were whatever inane pop songs had made the top ten, novelty acts, and the slushy ballads we slow-danced to at school balls. Culturally immune, we wept over Kurt

Cobain when he died, not because we liked Nirvana or understood his lyrics, but because a beautiful boy had shot himself in the head.

Skipper was inching closer and closer to the postcard where the photo of the penis was hidden, the thought of which made me let out a nervous snort, like a horse exhaling. I quickly tried to cover it up with a laugh. Skipper looked down at me for a moment, finger curling her hair, as if she was trying to decide something, then she smiled and bounced down onto her bottom next to me.

"Very cool," Skipper said, twirling her finger at the walls. "I like what you've done. *Très bon.*"

I experienced a huge surge of relief. Whatever faux pas I had made earlier in the year clearly no longer mattered to her or had been forgotten over the Easter break. Probably it had just been my imagination. Riddled with insecurities, I had a propensity to read too much into a situation—if someone forgot to wait for me before crossing the bridge, for example, or if they hadn't saved me a space at the supper table, I brooded about it for days. I tortured myself over trivial comments, a flippant remark about my clothes or hair, analysing the exact wording for hidden criticisms, looping it in my head. Perhaps all teenagers live in this state of permanent paranoia, but I anxiously lived in fear of making a fool of myself in front of my peers, terrified I'd say something that would expose me as an imposter. I had persuaded myself that it was simply because our mothers pushed us together in those early years that Skipper and I became best friends. I was constantly expecting Skipper to realise we were only bound to each other by happenstance, that she'd tire of me, find someone funnier or sportier or more sophisticated to spend her time with, less of a bookworm, always waiting for the sword to fall. When it came down to it I had brains, not beauty, and I felt her loyalty to me was the only thing that saved me from being labelled a nerd.

I watched her waving at people as they put their head around my door, blowing them kisses, calling them darling.

Skipper's popularity seemed effortless; she just had to walk into a room and people turned to her like sunflowers. In comparison I was stilted and self-conscious, chewing on the inside of my cheek, my hair flopping over one eye. While I should have been jealous of Skipper, the precise opposite was true—in her company I instantly felt wittier and more likeable. Take that away and I felt I'd wilt, reverting to the pale, bookish misfit I believed myself to be, one of those ill-fated girls, like Gerry Lake, who had no one to share a dorm with, were doomed to eat alone, and had to ask a housemistress to order another Divine just to walk to Woolworths with them, some indignant classmate plucked at random from the refectory line or rec room. This was the future that awaited me without Skipper's friendship, I thought, looking over at Gerry Lake's empty bed.

I would have done almost anything to protect it.

Sitting on my bunk, Skipper's hairless legs formed a bridge over my own. There was a prolonged period of silence, unusual for us, which made me nervous. A year ago we had been close as sisters, and we never shut up. I became aware of the sound of my breathing; one of my nostrils was whistling, and I attempted to quiet it by pinching my nose. I racked my brain, trying to think of something clever or amusing to say to keep her interested. It was obvious. The moose. All I had to do was lean back a couple of inches and tug the photograph out of its hiding place. Her reaction would have been seismic. I pictured the high shrieks, first Skipper's, then other Divines stampeding into my room to find out the gossip, their hands covering their mouths in shock. Suddenly I realised the enormous power I had.

"Actually, I've got something to show you," I said, pulling out the photo.

But the door slammed open, thrust violently against my bunk.

"Well, look who it is." Skipper rolled her eyes, let out a sigh. "The Poison Dwarf."

9

Gerry Lake. Five feet one in skates, by far the shortest girl in our year, with lean, short limbs, doll-like in her proportions. She had a pert nose that turned slightly at the end, minuscule ears, cat eyes that seemed to be tugged by the severity of her high ponytail into two upwards slants, and a dark mole on her chin, a beauty spot that she covered with makeup. She glared at Skipper sitting on my top bunk, then, without comment, she unzipped the sports jacket she was wearing, made from a slick waterproof material with a number of team badges on it, and tossed it on her bed.

"Geraldine, love," we heard her father calling down the corridor.

I pushed the Polaroid photo back in place.

Mr Lake lumbered into our dorm after his daughter, wheeling a large zippered holdall with the name of Gerry's skating team on the outside.

"There you are," he said, and then, startled to catch us dressed in just our nightclothes, flushed with embarrassment.

"Sorry about that, girls. We'll get unpacked, won't we, Gerry, then I'll be out of your hair. This one's yours, is it, love?" and he gestured at the bed.

Mr Lake opened Gerry's wardrobe and began shovelling the contents of the bag onto shelves—sparkly beige tights, leotards, silk skirts. All the while his daughter looked on sullenly, not bothering to help. Her father pulled out a drawer, almost dislocating it completely from its socket, and when it was overflowing with Gerry's clothes, he bent over and began to pump its contents down with his fist as if he was plunging a blocked sink. To my vexation, girls in the corridor—hearing Mr Lake's groaning and the slamming of drawers—came to stick their heads around my door to see what was happening. Mr Lake was a stout man with a large gut who wore brightly coloured braces, a manager of some description, something to do with the sale of stationery, I think. Literally, a pen pusher. Each time he reached to pull out another drawer he grunted in discomfort, and when he stood up straight, he let out a loud gasp of breath as if surfacing from a long underwater dive. He placed two photos on Gerry's desk, one of her with the teammates we had never met—though in months to come we would see their bloodshot eyes and crumpled, puffy faces in all the newspapers—the second a family photo. Mrs Lake, Gerry's stepmother, was, in contrast to her husband, a thin tall woman, a nurse who had once, to our amusement and Gerry's disgust, come to give a sex education talk to our year. Mr Lake was loud, Mrs Lake was dour, neither of them at ease amongst the Divine.

Skipper nudged me with her toe and pulled a face at Mr Lake's back as he attempted to string his daughter's ice-skating costumes onto coat hangers, his large fingers working clumsily, stretching the fabric onto hooks. Off body, Gerry's leotards, bejewelled and sparkling, looked implausibly small. Tiny pelts. Gerry caught Skipper's look and narrowed her eyes at us, her arms crossed.

Finally Mr Lake plucked one or two of Gerry's stuffed toys from the holdall and climbed up the first rung of her bed to rest them on her pillow. He swore in frustration. The bed was stripped and unmade.

"Come on, love, lend a hand," he said to Gerry. "Daphne's waiting in the car."

Gerry's mouth, I remember, pinched together at the mention of her stepmother. She dumped her folded bedsheets in his arms then picked up her toiletry bag and pyjamas and stomped away in the direction of the bathrooms.

Mr Lake muttered something under his breath, then he smiled apologetically at Skipper and me. Climbing back up the ladder, he flapped the bedsheet, crawling on all fours over Gerry's bed, stabbing the corners of the sheet into place with his fingers. It was rare to see parents up in dormitories, let alone clambering around like an orangutan. Divines said their goodbyes at the foot of the shoe tree, a curt kiss to each cheek from their parents, a wave from the car window. Gerry, unsurprisingly, had always been babied by her parents. She was, her father would later say to the press, their *special girl,* their *princess,* their *gem.*

By the time he had finished making Gerry's bed Mr Lake was sweating in his suit, I remember, red all over, his shirtsleeves rolled up. Again, Skipper nudged me with her foot. Mr Lake, suddenly aware he was being scrutinised, glanced sideways, caught sight of our naked thighs, and turned an even deeper-coloured purple.

A bell sounded. Lights-out. Skipper spun her legs ninety degrees, rocked forward and back and jumped off my bed. Likewise Mr Lake scrambled down the ladder just as his daughter came back, dressed now in her pyjamas. He rolled down his sleeves and put his suit jacket back on, flustered, as if he'd been caught in the act. Gerry looked from her father to Skipper.

Outside girls were darting from room to room, trying to say their final good nights before the headmistress began her rounds. Skipper held the door open so that Mr Lake could pass through, wheeling Gerry's empty bag behind him.

"*Au revoir,*" Skipper said to me. "See you in the morning."

"Brill," I answered automatically, trying not to show how miserable I was to be left alone with Gerry. "*À tout à l'heure.*"

That was the way Divines spoke to one another, always truncating our language or speaking in French. *Merde,* we said when something went wrong. *C'est la vie.*

Skipper linked arms with Dickie Balfour, who was walking back along the corridor from the shower. I pictured the whispered conversations Skipper would have at night with the twins, the dorm gossip, the private jokes I wasn't party to and felt sick with anxiety. All my worst fears seemed to be coming true. I felt again how unfair it was that I was stuck with Gerry, in this term of all terms. Our last few weeks as juniors before we crossed to the Other Side. Or so we believed.

Skipper turned to Mr Lake.

"Marvellous to see you again, Mr Lake. Send our love to Daphne," she said, emphasising the word *Daphne* to a comical extent, a name so categorically unlike our own mothers'—Cecelias, Camillas, Charlottes.

Dickie snorted out loud. I held my breath, waiting to see what Gerry's father would say. Skipper sounded so insincere, so astonishingly fake, I couldn't believe she could get away with it.

"Oh, right," said Mr Lake, unaware he was the subject of a joke. "Yes, will do."

Gerry, however, was clearly livid. She stood completely still, one hand on her waist, her hip thrust out, a foot on pointe, the stance of a skater post-routine when they come to an abrupt stop on the ice, her back arching, head tilting back, staring at Skipper.

"I'll leave you girls to it," Mr Lake said. "Bye, love. Have fun."

He hugged his daughter briefly and was off down the corridor, dragging her empty bag behind him like a sledge.

Skipper turned and grinned at Gerry and me.

Her arm curled snugly beneath Dickie Balfour's elbow, their hips pressed together. I felt a knife slipping between my ribs.

"*Bonne nuit,* Geraldine," Dickie said, wiggling her fingers.

Gerry's face reddened.

"Go fuck ya mum."

Skipper let out a snort of delight.

"Fuck your mum," she repeated slowly. Impressed.

Within days the catchphrase caught on like wildfire. The trick, I remember, was to pronounce it just like Gerry.

"Fuck ya mum."

10

In our first year of marriage Jürgen and I grow increasingly no-
madic. First London, then Amsterdam, then Brighton and briefly
Berlin, rooming with people we know, or subletting underheated
industrial buildings, which double as Jürgen's studio. Unsurpris-
ing, given that when we first met for the magazine interview he
was still living in a tent. We move so often we never buy any furniture, our clothes and my laptop spread across the floor. I adapt
to this kind of low-level sparseness with surprising ease. While
Jürgen sketches, I work on my knees or I type up my stories on
my belly, squirming around on dusty wood. The nights we spend
at home, which are rare since, despite three years of compulsory
home economics lessons at St John's, I can't cook, we sit in bed
and eat cereal from two steel bowls Jürgen found in a Chinese
supermarket in Charlottenburg. I've never been happier. Come
laundry day I hang my damp knickers along the handles of his
various bikes. Subletting as we do, our bills are always in someone else's name, we are up and out at the drop of a hat, switching
homes, it occurs to me, as frequently as I once moved dorms.
Our newlywed tiff has been reduced to a joke, a silly anecdote
we bring up at supper parties to amuse our friends. How a crazy
woman spat in my face on our honeymoon and called me a cunt.

In America a bellhop wheels our life's possessions into our hotel
room on a brass trolley. We sit on the windowsill, robed, feeding
each other grapes like Romans. Far down at street level cars re-
shuffle themselves along Chicago's Magnificent Mile. Work is going surprisingly well for both of us. Jürgen, out of nowhere, has an
impressive new commission, a large installation in a public garden,

and I have been offered a feature by a Sunday supplement—an interview with a gymnast, one of several victims who have recently spoken out about their coach—a story that could make the cover.

In the morning Jürgen consults a doorman wearing white gloves and a cap who points us in the direction of Millennium Park.

"What's at the park?" I ask Jürgen.

"Wait and see," he says.

We crunch through the snow holding hands and staring up at the high-rises. We feel golden, laughing loudly at the yellow signs that announce the Damoclean possibility of falling ice shards. We stroll along the banks of Lake Michigan with the dog walkers and joggers with their foggy breath. Jürgen, standing sideways to the shoreline, tosses a handful of stones across the semi-frozen water, the arctic surface creaking and groaning, pebbles skittering across the crusty snow and plopping into the dark polynya beyond. His cheeks are red from cold.

He is so handsome that my cunt aches with desire for him; it actually throbs.

I tug him back in the direction of our hotel bed but Jürgen is insistent.

"Cover your eyes," he says.

He leads me across the park towards fairground music, my eyes blinkered.

"Surprise."

He peels back his gloved fingers from my eyes.

Jürgen looks delighted.

"Oh," I say.

An ice rink.

We drink gluhwein from matching porcelain boots and watch the skaters. Couples in rented boots shuffle on stiff legs, clinging to the edge. Hockey boys bump shoulders, trying to bowl their frat brothers over. Fathers tow long chains of children in padded ski suits and mittens. The pros cruise effortlessly in between, twisting and leaping. In the centre a girl in a purple leotard spins on one foot.

I wave as Jürgen steps onto the ice.

He beckons me over to the side.

"Come on, this is your day. I'll teach you," he yodels, "you'll love it."

I shake my head. I won't do it, not even for him.

He tries to take my hand and tug me onto the ice.

"No."

I go rigid.

I tell myself that this has nothing to do with Gerry Lake, that I have never liked the sensation of the earth slipping underfoot. I have a vision of falling and the skate blade slicing like a cheese knife through my fingers.

Jürgen pretends to be downcast.

"Go," I say, trying to make light of my nerves, "have fun. Go, go, go."

He waits for a chink in the crowd and pushes off seamlessly, his hands behind his back, rocking smoothly from foot to foot, one boot crossing the other, leaning into the curve. He is a natural of course. His blond hair smoothed to one side, a gentlemanly gait, sweeping gracefully around the more nervous skaters. When the young girl in a purple leotard falls, he holds out his hand and, skating backwards, tows her out of harm's way. She blushes. He bows and swims back into the shoal.

I watch the purple leotard make her way to the gate and stomp unhappily across the rubber carpet to where I am sitting. She unlaces her boots and slides a guard across each blade, zipping them into a padded case. Her hips are speckled with rhinestones. She must be twelve or thirteen, I guess, only a few years younger than Gerry Lake had been at the time of the scandal.

"You're very talented," I say.

The girl shrugs. She slides one arm then the next into her padded winter jacket. Sniffing.

"I fell."

"I saw. I'm sorry. Are you hurt?"

She shakes her head. Jürgen sweeps past, clowning, waving

at me, blowing kisses. The girl goes red. I know exactly how she feels; I can't believe he's mine. She wipes her nose with her sleeve, pushes her tiny feet into fleece boots.

"Is he your boyfriend?"

"Husband."

Her eyes follow Jürgen as he glides easily through the mass of skaters.

"He's good."

"Yes." I nod, hugging myself to keep warm.

"You don't want to skate?" she asks.

"No."

The girl shrugs, pulls a pair of gloves out of her pocket, red welts on her fingers like Gerry Lake, from years of tying boot-laces.

"I went to school with an ice skater," I say, as an afterthought.

"Cool."

"She was in competitions. She won trophies."

Why am I telling her this?

"I came sixth at Skate the Lake. But you don't get a trophy for that. Maybe I've heard of your friend. Is she famous?"

"No," I say.

"It's hard to make it to the top," the girl lets me know.

"She had an accident."

"Oh." The girl stares sadly at the rink. "That sucks."

"She fell," I say.

I picture Gerry on the ground. Her knee bent backwards, one arm raised, like a mannequin. Her dark hair pulled back in a bun.

The lake wind whips around us, making my eyes water.

"I'm really sorry," the girl says.

She is chewing on her lip, looking at me intently, as if she's about to ask me a question.

I rub my eyes, stand up quickly, scanning the crowd for my husband.

On the ice Jürgen circles and circles. He glides on one leg, arms spread, like Anteros.

11

Two weeks later the townie was waiting for me outside St Ger-trude's, leaning against the brick wall where her classmates had recently sneaked over the fence and spray-painted the word *CUCUMBERS* in large green bubble letters. This was a new one, cucumbers. It took a while for us to catch on. She was twisting the elastic on her school necktie around her wrist so that it left sharp red indentations on her skin like oven burns. Her hair, tied back in a thick plait, was even longer than I had remembered, skimming her waist.

"Surprise," Lauren said. "Bet you didn't think you'd see me again."

She was right.

"Well, are you going to invite me in or what?"

I looked at the door of my boarding house, horrified. She was a KE. A townie. Guests had to have written permission and be introduced to our housemistress on arrival. If I got caught with a townie in my room, boy or girl, I could be in serious trouble, hauled in front of Fat Fran, or gated. I could see that she wasn't going to move and, frightened one of my friends would catch me talking to a King Edmund, I ushered her into St Gertrude's and up to my bedroom before anyone could see. I was lucky that the house was unusually quiet; the tennis team had an away game that afternoon, and Gerry was training. Lauren shook out a fag from a pack of twenty and held it out for me to take.

"Here." She gave me two. "Call it interest."

I didn't really need her cigarettes but there wasn't any other option but to take them.

"Okay, thanks."

"That your mum and dad?"

She was examining the silver picture frames I had on my desk, first picking up the photo of the three of us on holiday in France, then pointing at the one of me jumping a pony.

"You're into riding, yeah?"

I made a noncommittal gesture of some kind when, in fact, growing up I had been horse obsessed. I was one of those girls who could recite all the points of a pony, fetlock to poll, and the endless pieces of tack it took to ride them, the bridles and bits, the numnahs and martingales.

Lauren put down the picture of the horse and smiled lewdly, flashing her eyebrows.

"Had any more special deliveries?"

I looked at her blankly.

"You know." She made a gesture in the air, curling her fingers and thumb into a penis-sized tunnel and shaking it back and forward.

I cringed, but I told her the truth.

"Yes, actually."

Unbeknownst to our housemistress, several more Polaroids had been deposited on school property since the first. Divines were manic, close to hysterical; this was the most interesting thing to happen to us all year. Eventually, after news of the third or fourth discovery, I slid the original photo out from behind the postcard where it was still hidden and carried it into Skipper's dorm, presenting it to my friends on an open palm. The twins screamed with horror and wouldn't touch it. George snatched the photo from my hand and marched over to the dorm window, tilting it forward and back in the light as if panning for gold. Skipper, sitting at her desk, crossed her arms, watching me. She could tell that I was lying about something but didn't know what.

"Where did you say you found it?" she checked.

"The smoking den," I said.

I described the camera flash, the footsteps on the tarmac. Almost, but not entirely truthful.

"Oh my god," Henry Peck squealed. "That's rank. He was literally just out there."

Skipper twisted the lid on her fountain pen, tapping it against her cheek.

"I thought you'd run out of cigarettes," she said.

Why was she looking at me so coldly? It could have been that Skipper was annoyed it was me who'd found a photo, that, for once, I was the centre of attention, or maybe she'd long suspected me of keeping secrets. I fumbled for an excuse, my face starting to burn. Before I could answer, Dickie Balfour had barged into the dorm, followed soon after by a gaggle of Divines, hands over their mouths, stifling screams, passing the penis from person to person, giddy with excitement.

Lauren, however, seemed unimpressed.

"So, do you know who it is then?" she asked, studying the posters on my wall.

"No," I had to admit.

The penises, or peni, or whatever their multiple is, seemed to exist in jaunty independence of the body they were a part of, or rather they were one and the same, synecdochical you might say, so we never really thought much of the man himself. Always erect, they appeared in places where we were likely to discover them before one of our teachers: in our smoking den, posted through a boarding house window, or on the bench in the orchard. It stood to reason the perpetrator was a man who knew his way around the school, a gardener perhaps, or one of the electricians. Perhaps we should have been scared of a predator lurking in the shadows but, deprived of male attention, if anything we felt flattered.

"It's probably my brother. He's a right perv," Lauren said, "or one of those dirty old men he works with. You should hear the way they talk about you lot."

She thumbed through the window where an elderly maintenance

man in blue overalls was stacking broken school chairs onto the back of a trailer. I didn't like to think about it.

Listening to make sure no one was walking along the corridor, I climbed up on my bunk bed with its desk beneath and plucked out the original photo I'd hidden beneath my postcard, plus the additional photos we'd found since, which I'd somehow become guardian of. There were maybe four or five we'd stumbled across by then, including the first.

"Here you go," I said.

"Fuckin' hell," she yelled, "look at the state of that."

I winced and put a finger to my lips, hushing her. I couldn't think of anything worse than someone catching me with a King Edmund, showing her these photos.

"So," I whispered, "what do you think?"

Lauren's smile dropped.

"What? I don't go 'round staring at my brother's knob, if that's what you're asking?"

She squinted at me, her white lashes flickering with annoyance. I felt heat rushing up my neck. She seemed to grow in height and angrily tossed the photos onto my desk. Her arms were rigid at her sides. One fist was balled up. I felt sick. Was she going to fight me? She was a KE, after all. But the next moment her shoulders sagged and she burst out laughing.

"Kidding," she said with a grin.

She gave me a shove.

"Fuck me, you should see your face."

"Very funny," I said, "ha ha."

But I *could* see my face, our reflections suspended in the tiny mirror on the back of the door. We were around the same height and age, but in all other regards I felt we couldn't have been more different. Lauren's plait swayed when she laughed; she seemed to be always moving, rocking from one foot to another, chewing on the side of her thumbnail, fluttering her long spidery eyelashes. When she laughed her whole face changed like a weather front; her cheeks lifted, her eyes gleamed, then in a snap the sun was chased to shadow, lightning flashed. She was meteoric. I was a corpse. My face seemed blank to me at that moment, utterly nondescript. I had flicked my hair so my head was tilted a little to the side, as per usual, most of my face tented so that I was looking at her with one eye, a symptom of the Divine. There was a pallor to my skin that made me look waxy and consumptive. My pubescent body, I remember, was a perpetual source of embarrassment to me—the pus and sweat and blood—something to be plugged with cotton, covered up, barely mentioned. At that age I had no understanding of what womanhood meant, the Hera-like power it could hold, the life-giving force. Even though Divines menstruated at the same time, our bathroom bins overflowing with sanitary towels, globules of blood left floating in the bottom of unflushed loos, I carried my tampons up my sleeve like a flick knife so that none of my peers would know where I was going. I wedged tissue into my underwear before double geography in case my period came early. We called it the Red Wave, Bloody Mary, the Curse. Worst of all, I had been told by Skipper that my face, when I daydreamt or watched television, looked particularly plain. A gormless openmouthed stare, my zombie face as she called it, something I never forgot. I began pinching my fingernail into my thumb to stop myself from drifting off in lessons, tightening my cheeks, trying not to let my face droop. Morning chapel was particularly painful. All the way through the tedious sequence of prayers and readings I kept my eyes open, peering at my contemporaries slumped over pews, their cheeks flattened against hymnals, mouths slack. Even now, after all this time, I've seen people meditating in yoga classes—serene, beatific looking—and wonder how they do it.

My mother should have taken me aside when I was a teenager and helped me do something about my unruly eyebrows and the long mousy hair that drowned my face. Perhaps she did try to get me to cut it, I can't remember. Probably I argued with her that I needed something to flick. Besides, she had bigger worries than my hair. Back then I was far too skinny; no matter how much I ate it didn't make a difference. Bulimia was rampant in boarding schools. I was forever having my lunch tray inspected or being weighed by the nurse. I wore a baggy grey cardigan to cover myself up, but that only made me look more emaciated.

"Are you sure you're eating?" she'd probe.

At sixteen I still had no hips. Despite the heroin-chic models that papered our walls, what I craved more than anything were breasts like Lauren and Skipper, something to fill out the front of my striped summer uniform, which sagged like an empty sack. To my horror, even Gerry Lake wore a bigger cup size than me. Formless as I was, I doubt if any Divines, other than Skipper and our small group, remember me at all. When I was at university my mother once handed a boyfriend my year photo and I waited to see if he could pick me out. Our intake had dwindled to the point it shouldn't have been hard. His finger worked the rows, left to right, but each time he skimmed right over me.

"Is this a trick?" he said.

Perhaps at that age we are all our own worst critics. I might not have been as plain then as I felt—the boys still seemed to like me, after all—but when you put me side by side like that with Lauren, I was invisible.

Lauren got out another cigarette and pointed it at the Polaroid. I felt a wave of panic that she was about to light up, there, in my dorm.

"For the record, it's not my brother."

"How can you tell?"

She scissored her fingers through the air.

"He's had the, you know, snip. Mum had him done when he was a baby. It's more hygienic."

I stared again at the photos on the bed. I wouldn't have known the difference between a circumcised or uncircumcised penis, of course.

"Right," I said, studiously.

She looked at me and let out a laugh.

"You're a bit of a weirdo, you know that?" she said and then she reached out, pressed her thumbs to my cheeks, and lifted my mouth, dragging it up at the corners into a clown's grin. I moved my head away but I couldn't help it, I started to smile for real.

"That's better."

She waggled the cigarette hanging from her mouth in the direction of the smoking den.

"Come on then," she said.

Just as I was sneaking her out of the boarding house, the blue school bus arrived back from the tennis match, and the team climbed wearily down and walked up the drive in their Aertex shirts and white pleated skirts, their rackets strapped across their backs like swords. I felt a stab of resentment when I saw Skipper laughing with Henry Peck, the two of them shoving each other affectionately, sharing a joke. When they reached the front of the boarding house Skipper saw me and stopped in her tracks. She stared at Lauren; her racket banged against her shin.

I acted as if nothing was out of the ordinary.

"How was the tournament?" I asked the Pecks.

Dave Peck answered.

"Bloody great, Henry crushed them."

"Brill," I said. "Wicked."

Skipper said nothing. She looked Lauren up and down. As a rule we were suspicious of outsiders. We closed ranks, kept our secrets to ourselves.

"Who's she?"

Lauren looked at me, waiting to see how I'd answer. I could feel where earlier she pressed my cheeks into a smile, her two thumbprints on my skin.

"We're going for a fag," I answered.

Skipper's legs were slightly spread, I remember, so that she seemed to be taking up more space than normal. A goalie through and through. She seemed annoyed that I had a new friend, a King Edmund no less. I felt a little rush of pleasure, so I stepped closer to Lauren and slipped a hand under her arm. As if she was Divine.

"She shouldn't be here," Skipper commented.

Amused, Lauren brushed past her.

"Come on, Josephine," she said.

There was nothing heroic or even liberating about what I did next; it wasn't an act of rebellion—I was a follower not a leader, after all. I was simply unhitching my carriage from one train and attaching it to the next. But forward or back, I had to choose.

"Excuse me," I said to Skipper.

She raised one eyebrow, then stepped aside.

It was easy as that.

12

For two hours every Wednesday we Divines were dispatched, dorm by dorm, to the homes of various old age pensioners around town, part of our headmistress's bid to ingratiate us with locals, a total failure, of course. We were patronising and rude, we stole cigarettes and loose change from their handbags, we ate them out of house and home. Now that I shared a room with Gerry Lake, to our mutual disgust we were forced to undertake these torturous visits together, perhaps the only time in the week we ever did anything as a pair.

Mrs Myrtle, or the Turtle as I thought of her, lived in an overheated bungalow with a Yorkshire terrier. Since she was neither incapacitated nor solitary there was confusion on the Turtle's part about what Gerry Lake and I were doing there. As we rang her doorbell we saw her craning around her sitting-room curtains, scowling, her head snapping back again. We heard a dog's frantic yapping in the hallway, the door tugging against the safety chain.

"Hello, Mrs Myrtle," I said, loud and obsequious. "Lovely to see you."

Gerry Lake rolled her eyes. She was in a particularly foul mood that day, I remember, returning late from training the night before, loose strands of hair tugged free from her bun, her makeup smudged. She stood now with her arms crossed, furious to be kept waiting.

There was further rattling and muttering. The Turtle opened the door.

"What happened to the other one?" she asked, looking around for Skipper. "Well, I suppose you'd better come in."

We followed her into her sitting room where *Countdown* was playing on the television.

"You interrupted my programme," said Mrs Myrtle, muting the television and looking us up and down, her mouth puckered like she was sucking on a boiled sweet.

"You'll be wanting tea, I suppose?"

Mrs Myrtle disappeared into the kitchen and came back carrying a pot wearing a woollen cosy. She poured milk into two floral cups and waited for the tea to steep. Meanwhile the dog, a bug-eyed Yorkie, jumped up on a chair by the window, pressed its nose to the glass and began yapping at the King Edmunds walking home from school. The electric heater was on full, the windows slowly misting. The room felt unbearably hot, the fake coals above the electric bars glowing a hellish orange. I found a seat on a stool, and Gerry was perched on the edge of Mrs Myrtle's sofa, straight backed, not bothering to make conversation. Even the way she sat seemed hostile. I was a habitual sloucher, something my mother (who had suffered years of mandatory deportment lessons as a Divine) frequently chided me about, needling her finger between my shoulder blades whenever I was home for school holidays. Gerry Lake had the posture of a Russian gymnast.

"If you want biscuits, you'll have to get them yourselves," the Turtle instructed and poured a third cup of tea for her dog to drink, resting the saucer on her lap. She switched the volume back up on the television.

The only biscuits left in her tin were a few stale pink wafers and digestive crumbs. The pink biscuit dissolved on my tongue, turning into paste. The dog lapped on its tea. I showed the empty biscuit tin to Mrs Myrtle.

"I could do some shopping for you if you'd like?" I offered, even though it was against the rules to venture into town on our own. But it was all I could think of to escape the Turtle and Gerry.

Gerry's head swivelled towards me, outraged.

Likewise, Mrs Myrtle looked at me incredulously and hacked into a handkerchief. She would rather have starved than hand over her pension to a Divine. For the duration of our visit she kept her handbag wedged beneath her armpit like a shotgun.

"I do my own shopping, thank you very much."

Mrs Myrtle's dog stared at us, panting, his bulging eyes fixed on me. I found little dogs repulsive, glorified rats. On the whole, the parents of the Divine favoured hunting breeds—German pointers, Labradors, spaniels—large, well-trained pedigree gundogs with names like Crumpet and Crumble.

"How about I take him for a walk, Mrs Myrtle?" I asked, desperate now to get out of the house.

Gerry Lake's back straightened even further, her jaw set hard, livid that I was planning to leave the two of them alone.

The Turtle pinched her lips together as she weighed my offer. This at least would get us girls out from under her feet. Then there was a kerfuffle as she dressed the dog in a checked jacket and, intentionally ignoring me, handed the leash to Gerry.

"Mind he does his business," she ordered.

Gerry Lake took the rope like it was a pair of soiled knickers, holding it between her finger and thumb, then she shoved past me, furious, yanking the dog out of the door in the direction of the duck pond.

"Well done," she hissed.

I trudged down the street after her, praying that none of my friends would see us together. The way Gerry Lake walked seemed ridiculous to me—her short arms rigid at her sides, hands curled into angry fists, her chin high, her small torso tilted forward. Maybe because of skating from such a young age, her joints were prone to hyperextension, her elbows in particular, so Gerry looked like a cheap plastic doll, I thought, dismembered, jammed back together incorrectly. Perhaps in the end, the only place she ever felt comfortable was on the ice.

The dog zigzagged around Gerry's ankles, sniffing, lifting a leg, tangling itself up in the lead, gagging and choking. Any time the terrier came close to her Gerry gave it a sharp kick with her toe. Her face was red, her eyes puffy from lack of sleep, or perhaps, I later speculated, she'd been crying. Who would have dared ask? Her lip curled up in a snarl so that I could see one of her fangs. She seemed dangerous, close to exploding. The thought of Gerry having one of her tantrums in public where anyone—Lauren, Skipper, the twins—could see us together was too awful to think about.

"Fuck's sake, you little shit," Gerry yelled when the terrier tried to jump up on her so that even I began to feel sorry for it.

At the duck pond, as if on demand, the dog crapped in the middle of the path. Gerry looked first at the dog and then at me as if she expected one of us to do something about the problem. She muttered under her breath at me and we left the pile there for someone else to scoop up or step in.

We were almost out of the park when another dog, a terrifying-looking pit bull belonging to some townies, lunged at us. Gerry Lake screamed and dropped the leash. I called the Turtle's dog to heel but the two animals—one thuggish and muscular, one tiny—both ignored me and ran away across the park, sniffing each other's arseholes, turning in circles, yapping loudly, tails wagging.

The townies smirked and exchanged looks with each other over their cigarettes, one of them mimicking the loud yelp Gerry had let out, raising his hands in the air and flailing them around, another clearly imitating the way I'd yelled out the dog's name—his voice shrill and histrionic. I cringed with embarrassment; was that really how I sounded? What did I care, I tried to tell myself, they were just drunks who hung out in the park all day, swigging White Lightning from the bottle. Gerry, on the other hand, was vibrating with fury, eyes narrowed, jaw pulsing. More than anything Gerry hated to be laughed at; she never could take a joke. She glowered at the men, then at me, outraged, as if the townies and I were conspiring against her. I shrugged my shoulders; it wasn't my fault she'd dropped the leash.

"Piss right off," she said, and stomped across the grass towards the dogs. The townies fell quiet, curious now, watching Gerry.

"Heel," she ordered.

The Yorkie trembled, its tail tucked under, small black eyes bulging with fear. When Gerry reached down to grab the leash, the dog skittered backwards. Fuming, she dived to grab it, but her sudden, angry movements only alarmed the dog more. Each time she got anywhere close the Yorkie ducked away. Eventually it ran for cover under a park bench. The yobs heckled loudly, cheering on the dog.

"Nice one, mate," they said.

"You show her."

Gerry stood for a moment, her face scrunched with rage, her small hands two tight knots.

Then she kicked the bench and let out a sudden, piercing screech.

The drunks laughed even harder, high-fiving each other.

"Time of the month, love?"

Horrified, I stood in the middle of the park watching Gerry explode, my mouth slack, completely immobile—the zombie stare I tried so hard to avoid.

I wanted to die.

"What's wrong with her?" I moaned to Skipper and the twins later that night, as we brushed our teeth. "Why can't she just be normal?" On Wednesdays, they visited a local retirement home, while I was stuck with Gerry. It was unbelievably unfair.

Dave and Henry exchanged a look in the mirror with Skipper. I felt my stomach knot. Was I boring them? Had I talked too much about Gerry, banging on and on? I had no idea what they said about me in the dorms, after lights-out. More and more I suspected I was being kept at arm's length, quarantined, my punishment for fraternising with a townie. Lately, when they went for a smoke, no one bothered to tell me. At breakfast they cleared their trays, getting up from the table before I'd even sat down. They slid down the pew in morning chapel, bunched together, gossiping behind their hymnals.

"Oh god, who cares about the bloody Poison Dwarf. Just ignore her," Skipper snapped.

I stood in front of the sink, humiliated, trying not to cry. My head tilted to one side, hair tenting my eyes, laughing at a joke Skipper told next, as if I found it funny. I brushed my teeth until my gums were raw. I smiled and smiled.

13

I cover the Chicago apartment we're subletting with photos of gymnasts, police reports, and headshots, plastering them to the wall like Hollywood hunks. Preparation for my interview. As more and more women speak out—three at first, then seven, then ten—an almost unthinkable number, I add them to the collage so it swells in all directions, a rising storm.

"My god," Jürgen says when he gets back from the studio, stamping his feet free of snow. "It's unbelievable."

He stands in his overalls, shaking his head.

"Right," I say.

I pour him a beer and he walks from picture to picture, looking at the pink cheeks and podium smiles, one of the girls so young she still has her baby teeth, a fact Jürgen finds so disturbing he raises his hand in the air to stop me midsentence.

"How on earth?" he asks.

The hours of training, the late-night returns from far-flung competitions, closed-door pep talks, the leg massages and costume adjustments. The teammates pitted against one another, made to vie for attention. We stand side by side, staring at the girls sitting on a beam—their high-cut leotards, cherry lips, medals around their necks.

He snuck me candy, one statement reads, *he took my mum to church. She totally loved him. One time he taught me how to drive in a parking lot. I sat on his lap and steered while he did the pedals.*

Four feet tall, nine years old, fifty-seven pounds. In her diary entries she repeatedly misspelled the word *vagina*.

He liked to snap our leos when he walked by, another gymnast says, the woman I am preparing to meet. *He flipped us onto the mat to tickle our tummies, fixed our uniforms to straighten the wrinkles. None of us wore underwear for training. That was the rule.*

Jürgen flinches as he reads, swigs his beer.

"*Verdammt,*" he mutters.

He faces the mug shot of the coach in question. A bulldog with a balding head and wrinkled brow. Jürgen shakes his head slowly, grimacing.

"The thing I just can't understand," my husband says later that night, undressing for bed. "The amount of time those girls spent together, why couldn't they talk to each other, that's what I want to know? Where were their parents, for god's sake? What about their sisters and friends?"

I shrug.

"They didn't know what he was doing was wrong? They thought it was just part of the job, like being stretched out or getting their bikini waxes. None of them wanted to get him in trouble. He was a con man. They adored him. He was their best friend."

Jürgen winces.

"Christ," he says, disturbed, and lies down next to me.

I gaze at the ceiling above our bed, at the layer of dust blanketing the motionless ceiling fan.

In a photo on Gerry Lake's desk she wore baby blue, sitting sideways on her trainer's lap, hugging a trophy. I think about how she came back after lights-out one night, shed her tracksuit, stripping down to her costume, and still as a statue—Galatea, milk white, sparkling—stood there in the dark for so long I thought she'd stopped breathing.

"Girls keep secrets," I say before I roll over. It's what we're good at.

Jürgen tugs the duvet over us, hooking me close.

"*Oh Gott,*" he says as he kisses my shoulder, "let's pray we have boys."

14

She would appear out of nowhere. After swimming, for example,
below the bridge as I crossed to the Other Side, a school bag slung
over her shoulder, picking at her nail varnish, examining her split
ends. Catching sight of Lauren beneath the bridge—her pale skin,
her long, almost silver-coloured hair, shimmering like a hologram
through the railings—my shoulders jolted in surprise. I stopped
dead, letting other girls flow around me. Lauren jutted her chin
hello and made a V sign in front of her lips, smoking an invisible
cigarette, then gestured at the churchyard.

We crawled into some bushes and sat on a grave. I watched
how she held the Menthol Light in her fingers as if it was an
extension of her hand, how she blew smoke from the corner of
her mouth, her habit of continually flicking the butt with her
thumbnail.

"You all right then?" she asked.

I nodded. My hair, wet from swimming, dripped down my
front, seeping through my striped summer dress, so I was afraid
that my bra might be visible—a small, childish crop top I barely
needed to wear—and I sat there with my elbows pressed together
awkwardly to cover my nonexistent cleavage. I had no idea what
she saw in me. Monosyllabic most of the time, I didn't have a clue
what to talk about. We hunched over our cigarettes, hugging our
knees. Crammed into a small hole in the bushes, Lauren seemed
somehow larger than before. Her school shirt, too tight for her
breasts, gaped open at the buttonholes and pinched her under the
armpits. Her cheap skirt, bobbled black polyester, was hitched up
her legs, the large plain of skin on the inside of her thigh, white

and mottled. Catching me staring at her knickers, she stuck out her tongue. My face burned. I blurted out the first thing that came to mind.

"One of the Sixth Form girls pierced her own belly button," I said. "And it got infected so they carted her off to hospital."

Lauren leant forward, interested. These seemed to be the kind of stories she wanted to hear.

"What with?"

"I don't know, a sewing needle?"

Encouraged, I told Lauren about the time George's hair caught fire in chemistry and how Dickie sneaked her boyfriend into St Gertrude's wearing a school cloak. When I ran out of anecdotes I fell silent again, sitting in the graveyard shivering in my damp summer dress. Quickly I scrambled around for something to ask her. Had she been up to anything fun? The minute I said it I realised how absurd I sounded—priggish, patronising, the kind of thing my mother might have asked.

Lauren snorted.

"Up to anything fun?" she mimicked.

I cringed at my plummy choice of words, the wooden way my face seemed to move, the stiff grin carved into my face like a totem.

"Fuck all," Lauren eventually answered.

She twisted her cigarette out on the name on the headstone on which she was sitting, stood up and walked off. I waited for a long time in the bushes with the dead bodies and beer cans and cigarette butts before I realised she wasn't coming back. Then I got up and left too.

Lauren's visits were like Lauren herself: unpredictable, volatile, disconcerting. On one occasion I heard a rap on my classroom window during prep time. I was reading a textbook, some dull piece of World War history, my cheek lying on my desk. Around me other girls were sleeping or writing letters instead of preparing for exams that were just weeks away. I gasped. Lauren's mouth sucked the window, her cheeks puffed out like a blowfish, her nostrils pressed sideways. Cackling, she unpeeled her face. There was a kiss on the glass, a greasy smudge where her nose had been. She gave me the finger and was gone. Once I found her waiting for me by the gates, holding her lighter to the corner of our school sign, studying the paint as it blistered and blackened.

Now that she considered me her friend, Lauren marched straight into my boarding house to look for me, despite the obvious death stares from my peers and mutterings of disapproval from Skipper in particular. Lauren's brother had recently been hired full-time as a maintenance man at the school and so there was something proprietary about the way she came and went that unsettled people. Like she thought she was Divine. Watching her roam around amongst us, I felt as if I'd let a wild animal out of its cage. Feline looking, she prowled the corridors of St Gertrude's until she came to a stop at our rec room door where, barred from leaving the boarding house after prep, we sat around doing nothing, sprawled across uncomfortable vinyl chairs, resting our heads in each other's laps, slumped on beanbags like golden retrievers. Despite the extortionate fees we paid, our boarding house had the feel of a hospital waiting room. It was tatty and utilitarian, scattered with debris from our tuck boxes and the crushed remains of biscuits we ate at elevenses, empty crisp packets and instant noodle packets wedged down the sides of our seats. Even before Divines began whispering and frowning, I knew Lauren was there, staring intently at me to get my attention. A tingle ran up the back of my neck. She put her fingers in her mouth and whistled.

"Oy, Josephine."

"For god's sake," Skipper said, outraged that a townie had the gall to come into our rec room, let alone whistle at us like we were dogs.

Ignoring her, I scrambled to my feet obediently and followed after Lauren.

Occasionally on these visits Lauren seemed sullen and bored, her arms crossed, barely staying more than a few minutes, as if she resented being there at all. Other times she clowned around in our smoking den till her brother finished work or the bell rang for supper. As a friend she was surprisingly generous. Often she brought me a present—a bag of crisps, a slice of her neighbour's birthday cake—which we ate together, hunched behind the boiler room, puffing on our cigarettes. Once she made me a bead necklace out of letters and shoelace. Another time she brought me a 3-D poster for my dorm—clusters of dots you had to stare at like the static on a television screen—the corners torn where she'd tugged it down from her brother's wall.

"Won't Stuart be cross?" I asked.

Lauren clicked her tongue. She unrolled the poster, spreading it wide between her arms.

"Go on then, you see it?"

I tried to relax, to make my vision go blurry, but I was too self-conscious to go cross-eyed in front of anyone, let alone Lauren.

A few days a week she had a job after school, repetitive factory work of some kind, and on those evenings, she told me, I could call her once her shift was over.

"Call you?" I checked. "At home?"

"No, at the fucking zoo, you div." She crossed her eyes.

She took out a Biro and tattooed her number on the inside of my arm.

The phone booth, a flimsy plywood box the size of a coffin with holes drilled in the side, sat in the entrance hall of our boarding house. The door was padlocked during the daytime to avoid distraction, except for a few hours each evening when our housemistress appeared after prep, plodding along the corridor with keys jangling at her hip like a prison warden. A crowd of girls stood around the booth, waiting to make calls. At times the phone would ring when the door was still locked, sad and unanswered. We'd press our nose to the glass, rattling the door, groaning about the love interest trying his luck out of hours, though it just as easily could have been our parents. Later, during the scandal, this padlocked pay phone became the focus of an investigation, the papers suggesting that there had been a critical delay in any girls alerting the emergency services to what had happened to Gerry (it was true that amid the drunken chaos of school dares Divines struggled to find an unlocked booth).

When it came to using the phone, priority was given to the handful of Divines, like Henry Peck, who had serious boyfriends. These girls were demigods. Through the strip of glass on the door we could see Henry sitting with her knees tucked neatly under her chin, knotting the cable around her finger as she giggled at the Moose, whom she was still calling long distance, murmuring indecipherably into the receiver, a string of yeses and nos and mmms, sometimes lifting her shoulders at us and shrugging, so that we could only guess at the X-rated words her tennis coach was whispering down the line—erotic poetry, pledges, declarations of love, heavy breathing. Inexperienced as I was, I had no clue what dirty talk entailed. Perhaps in the end they were only discussing her backswing.

Next in the pecking order were girls with brothers and cousins at nearby boarding schools: Radley, Pangbourne, Harrow, Charterhouse, Eton, Stowe; it didn't matter, any boy would do. Begrudgingly the brother hollered for his friends, classmates procured at random, boys we'd met in passing at a rugby match, say, or the Henley regatta, or with whom we'd exchanged salivary kisses at a winter ball. They grunted monosyllabic answers to our questions, we tittered and attempted to flirt, several of us crammed into the small wooden box at once, passing around the receiver like a baton until our charge cards ran out.

Afterwards, when we'd drifted back to our dorms, the phone was open to the rest of the year—homesick internationals like the Russians, two brooding girls, oligarchs' daughters, who wore cherry-coloured lipstick to lessons, trying their utmost to get expelled. Gerry Lake, though, as far as I could tell, couldn't have cared less about speaking to boys. The only calls she made were the rare times she spoke to her stepmother, Daphne Lake, who caused such a fuss when she hadn't heard from Gerry for more than two weeks that our housemistress escorted her from our dormitory to the booth herself. Gerry pouted through the conversation, hand on her hip, a foot on pointe as if she was on ice, not even bothering to close the door.

"Fine," she told her stepmother. "No. Yes. Stop asking that. I've got to go. You said that already, Daphne. Bye."

I waited until one of the Russian girls shuffled out of the phone box in house slippers, and while the rest of my year were brushing their teeth and scuttling between rooms, I slipped into the empty telephone box. I sat on the ripped waiting-room chair, leaning my head against the perforated wooden wall, sharp beams of light coming through the holes like a confessional. I felt strangely nervous, the handset slippery in my palm. What if Lauren had only been joking when she told me I could ring her? What if we had nothing to say? A man answered and I hung up. The next time I called, a woman picked up.

"Loz!" her mother shouted. "Phone."

I heard feet thumping downstairs.

"Yeah?"

"It's me," I said.

"Oh, right."

There was the grumble of a television set in the background, the clack of Lauren fiddling with her own shoelace necklace, sliding the lettered beads along the leather lace, rattling them like dice. She waited for me to talk. I felt blood pulsing in my neck, my throat tightening. I had a story prepared to tell Lauren, some derogatory anecdote about the Divine I thought she might find funny. Lauren's favourite pastime now was to hear about the senseless rituals that constituted the life of the Divine—the end-of-year dares we had already planned, the school motto, the boys' names, the hair flicking, the way we turned our Sunday chapel service into a fashion show, strutting down the aisle to take Communion as if it was a catwalk—she ate it up like celebrity gossip, sucking her teeth, snorting sarcastically. Now that I had her attention, the anecdote I had meant to tell her completely evaporated.

"How was work?" I blurted instead.

"Shit."

I didn't know the first thing about the factory floor, or assembly lines or packaging; I'd never had a paid job in my life. Silent, I stared at the doodles on the wall, the Biro hearts and boys' names, a cartoon of Fat Fran, with pendulous breasts and a Bible. One of us had written something about Gerry Lake and then scribbled it out.

"I saw you and your mate today," Lauren said. "The little one."

"What? Gerry? When?" I sat up.

"Down by the duck pond."

It was a Wednesday, my afternoon with the Turtle and Gerry. The thought that Lauren had seen us without me knowing was horrific. One of my greatest anxieties at that age was being caught in the act of doing something unflattering, picking a spot or sniffing my armpit or huffing into my palm to check for bad breath. Anything, in other words, that flashed open the curtain of adolescence to expose the awful ugliness of the person I thought I really was.

"Your mate looked like she had a right hump on," Lauren said.

"She's not my mate," I corrected her. The last thing I wanted was for Lauren to think I was friends with someone like Gerry. "We just share a room. We don't even speak to each other."

"Yeah?" Lauren's voice lifted with interest.

There was nothing she enjoyed more, I was beginning to learn, than to hear about our petty disagreements, the bitchy quarrels we entangled ourselves in, the cold shouldering and wrangling for popularity. I, on the other hand, knew next to nothing about her friends at King Edmunds. If I asked Lauren what KE girls talked about, what they did after school, what they ate for lunch, she never gave me an answer, deflecting the question or changing the subject. When I probed her about what KE boy she liked best, she sucked her teeth.

"Those prats. As if," she said, and, like now, turned the conversation back around to me.

"How come you share a room with that Gerry girl then?"

I picked at the synthetic padding of the chair through the rip, gouging little balls from the yellow foam, rolling them between my fingers and dropping them on the floor. I didn't reply. I pictured Gerry upstairs, sitting on her bunk bed, po-faced, massaging ointment into her dry ankles, disgusted by the thought of her mutated feet, the mangled toes, gnarled and twisted from years of skating. Or worse, the looks my peers gave each other as they passed our dorm—or was I just imagining it?—the whispers and giggling.

"Well, she looked like a moody cow if you ask me," Lauren tried again. "She got a stick shoved up her bum or what?"

"Yes," I burst out. "I hate her."

I meant it. I had never loathed anyone as much in my life as Gerry Lake.

On the other end of the telephone line there was silence. I heard Lauren rattling her necklace. Her voice lowered to a whisper.

"I can sort the bitch out for you if you want?"

A chill ran down my spine. I sat motionless in the booth, staring at the graffiti on the wall. Gerry Lake's name struck through with black felt-tip.

There was a sudden sharp click on the end of the line. A man's voice.

"Lauren, get off the bloody phone."

I yelped in surprise.

Lauren swore loudly at her brother, then she began to cackle.

"Oh my god, Josephine, you're so gullible."

"Oh," I exhaled.

"You two, stop fucking about, will you," her brother ordered, still on the line.

How long had he been listening to us?

"Nighty night, Josephine," Lauren said, still laughing.

The phone clicked dead.

15

January in Chicago and my husband is dressed in only his bath towel. I am wearing my quilted coat, hood still zipped up to my ears, fingers numb from carrying the plastic bags of damp laundry, still hanging from my hands. Melting ice trickles with uncertain, stop-start progress from my shoulders to my elbows, then patters onto the floor. The little tapping noise of my thawing arms is the only sound in our apartment.

"Jürgen? Jürgen, what happened?"

I gaze around the study.

Instead of packing for his trip, an art fair in Miami, he is leaning over my desk. My books lie strewn around my study in various stages of undress, their pages spread, jackets cast off. My desk drawers are wide open. The lights are dim. He stands in the eye of the storm, totally still. My first thought is that we have been burgled.

"Jürgen?" I repeat.

"*Ja*," he says, as if he's forgotten I am here.

"What the hell happened?"

He is silent for a while.

Then he answers.

"I was looking for my passport."

I believe him. Jürgen isn't someone who snoops through my drawers or goes looking for secrets. He isn't that kind of man. Outside I hear heavy boots crunching through salt up the front steps of our Chicago brownstone. A door slams overhead and there is the familiar elephantine thumping of one of the three men who occupy the top-floor apartment. Their television switches on immediately, after which comes a brief silence, which signals that their gaming system is loading. I hear the sound of the fridge being opened and slammed; what follows is the boom of bombs dropping, gun fire, apocalyptic screams, the *thup, thup, thup* of heavyweight artillery, which often goes on into the early hours. It is deeply unsettling. We live in a Chicago neighbourhood where kids ride around on their bikes with real handguns down their backs.

Our neighbours are currently the cause of a lot of tension. They are nice enough guys I'm sure, but one of them works downtown in security and his alarm wakes us at 5 a.m., and the other two flatmates tend bar. Collectively, therefore, they never sleep. At night, when they finish their various shifts, I hear the slam of the apartment door and immediately press a pillow over my head as I once did sharing a room with Gerry Lake. I listen to their cumbrous footsteps stomping overhead, a heavy clunking that sounds to me like they are pressing weights and then a repetitive mechanical whir as if they'd switched, for no reason at all, to shredding paper. Some nights I stand on a chair naked, muttering curses, trying to decipher the sounds. It has become an obsession. The man who has the room directly above our bedroom has a head shaped like a football; he is brawny with a huge buffalo-shaped back and an unbelievably thick neck. I wouldn't put it past him to bench-press in the early hours. But the shredding noise is a mystery.

Once I knocked on their door with a six-pack and begged them to take their shoes off or turn the television down. They are nice guys, as I say, and went straight over to find the remote. But in a couple of days they'd forgotten again and we were back to putting pillows over our heads, wishing them dead. From what I can deduce all three men are single. When they bring women home, stilettos detonate on the wood above us, chairs scrape, music rattles the walls. We know a great deal about their sexual techniques. The football head goes at it like a jackhammer, in sudden and erratic bursts, interspersed with moments of complete silence during which Jürgen and I lie side by side in the dark, wondering what the hell the man is waiting for. In those seconds I want to go up there with a crowbar, threaten to smash them in the head. Then the drilling takes up again, on off, on off, until it concludes with a loud, satisfied grunt. We all snatch some sleep after that but an hour or so later the security guard's alarm rings out and he begins showering and the radio turns on and that is that.

This sleeplessness is taking its toll. Jürgen and I are tired all the time, irritable, prone to snapping. Not our best selves. All the vigorous sexual antics that we hear going on overhead are a reminder that our own sex life is in danger of becoming somewhat automated now that we're trying, but failing, to have a baby. What was once effortless has become stilted and mechanical but we are too tired most nights to do anything to spice it up or make the whole endeavour seem less prosaic. Occasionally I wear the translucent chiffon slip Jürgen gave me on our honeymoon two years ago, and I have even shopped online for a toy, but the vibrating gold ring remains inside my drawer in the velvet display box it came in, like an enormous discarded wedding band.

Every few weeks, when I feel I can't take the noise any longer, I check myself into a single-floor motel under the pretense of a work trip, somewhere anonymous like Naperville or Joliet. I spend my supper vouchers at the adjoining diner, waited on by a Sally or Kathleen in their frilly aprons, a pen tapping their teeth as I scan the menu. Sometimes I float in my underwear in the Super 8 pool, my river of Lethe, then go back to my room, roll down the blackout blinds, flick through the channels till I find the right kind of porn. Afterwards I sleep like the dead.

This is my dirty little secret.

I look around the room, at the explosion of drawers, copies of old stories I've saved for posterity, now upended and scattered on the bed. The Sunday magazine with the gymnast on the cover tossed onto the floor.

"Jürgen, did you find it?" I ask.

"Find it?"

"Your passport."

"Yes," he says, nodding. "I found it."

He rubs his hand over his beard.

"I found a lot of things."

I look for my laptop but can't see it. Perhaps he's uncovered my embarrassing addiction to Facebook, noted the mindless hours I've spent nosing through the lives of my former school friends—Skipper, George, the twins—when I should have been working. My fruitless search for old stories about Gerry.

I come closer. Then I see them, the pictures of the erections, all of them lined on the desk, one slightly overlapping the next. I sneaked the Polaroids out of my mother's attic when I was last in England, afraid she might stumble upon them during one of her spring cleans. Why, I curse myself, didn't I just throw them straight in the rubbish bin? There is also the issue of the motel receipts, which I've kept for my tax return. Put them together, hard dicks and hotel beds, I can see what this looks like.

"Oh," I say. "Those."

"*Ja,*" Jürgen says, "those."

"Wait. I can explain. It's not what you think."

He raises an eyebrow.

"It never is."

"Please, Jürgen."

I try to think of a logical explanation, something that doesn't sound crazy.

"It's just something . . ."

"Don't say it." Jürgen groans, head in his hands. "Don't say it."

Suddenly I see the corner of his mouth twitching, the smile trying to escape. My husband finds the whole thing hilarious and is having his fun seeing me squirm. He doesn't for a second think I'm capable of lying and betrayal; if anything, he finds all this unexpected nostalgia endearing. He spins around, his towel drops, he wrestles me, laundry bags and all, down to the floor. Hard against my stomach, he unpeels me from my winter clothes.

"Don't say it," he taunts.
I arch my back, pretend to fight him off.
"Don't say it," he whispers softly into my ear.
"Don't say what?" I say, playing along.
"Don't say it."
"*Divine.*"

16

We were summoned to the rec room. So many of us had found
photos by then it was just a matter of time. Miss Graves, our
housemistress, sat on a chair with her deputy behind her, a lean,
fuzzy-haired young woman who knitted her own jumpers and
who had inadvertently stumbled across one of the so-called obscenities, perhaps the twelfth or thirteenth that were eventually
discovered on school property. The deputy, who had been making
her evening patrol of the orchard in an attempt to flush out smokers from the bushes, instead found a group of squealing Divines
inspecting the latest arrival.

"Step back," she ordered.

She covered her hand with a plastic bag, picked the photo up
and knotted the evidence like a mound of dog shit and carried
it off to the Egg where she deposited it on the desk of our headmistress.

That evening Fat Fran stood centre stage, though I also recall
that Padre and our school nurse, in charge of our spiritual and
physical well-being, respectively, hovered close to the door, ready
and waiting. Padre smiled at us sympathetically as we walked into
the rec room in single file. He was one of the few members of staff
we actually respected. We weren't religious in the slightest but that
didn't seem to matter to him. He listened to our petty troubles
and tolerated our bad language and, unlike our other teachers,
seemed to think us rather fun. Even when we went through our
occult phase and tried to summon Gerry Lake's mother from the
dead. (We weren't targeting Gerry in particular, at least not as far
as I remember. Gerry was the only one of us who had suffered

a close family bereavement, her mother having died when Gerry was eight or nine.)

Next to Padre was a member of the local police holding a series of brochures that we were handed before being ushered into our seats. We fanned ourselves and held our collective breath waiting for the first adult to say the word *penis*. Someone sniggered. Miss Graves glared at us.

"Girls," Fat Fran began, "I'm extremely disappointed."

Our headmistress had recently been ordained, one of the first women to enter the Anglican clergy, something of a pioneer, and she always had her fingers at her throat, straightening her new dog collar. Fat Fran was an unusually tall woman, even allowing for the exaggeration of memory over time, well over six feet. She was a mystery to us since she was heavily preoccupied with church matters and spent her days cloistered in her office, working, we presumed, on her Sunday sermons or other diocese business and had very little to do with the day-to-day life of the Divine other than our religious education (Fat Fran had made religious studies a mandatory part of our curriculum). She wore plain blue shirts and nondescript plaid skirts, tentlike in their structure due to her girth, beneath which her large feet splayed sideways. She was extremely fleshy. At her neckline several folds of jowl rippled over her dog collar. There was a flap of skin under her chin, like a pelican's, which hung to her throat.

That day I sat on a windowsill at the rear of the rec room, watching the curious way her gular pouch quavered as she waited for complete silence. She looked frazzled, her shoulders hunched with exhaustion. Like a blimp, partially deflated. Without question this was her annus horribilis, even before Gerry Lake. First of all there was the recently published *OFSTED* report, a damning assessment that had detailed the extent of St John's academic failings. The school inspectors insinuated that Fat Fran's staff were not in control, unable to confirm the whereabouts of pupils half the time, with girls scattered across the campus, smoking in bushes. To add to her woes there was the unfortunate matter of Chuck, a Sixth Former who had run off in the middle of the autumn term, with a man we knew as Disco Dave, the mobile DJ who performed at all our school dances.

As a consequence, intake had slowed radically at St John's—some alarmed parents even going so far as to remove their daughters—the bursar, a former army man, wringing his hands as our numbers swiftly dwindled, there being only fourteen new First Years that autumn instead of the usual fifty. Fourteen! Not enough to even play a decent game of lacrosse. There were rumours of mergers with another nearby private school or selling off some of our sacred sports grounds to a local developer to raise funds or, more horrifyingly, opening our doors to day girls. As my mother had commented more than once, the Divine were not what they once were.

Fat Fran, on the brink of disaster, stood in front of our entire year and prepared to deliver her lecture.

"My understanding is that several of you girls have already come across a number of lewd photos on our school property."

She held a bag aloft, the same plastic shopping bag our deputy had carried the photograph in.

"And that you attempted to conceal these"—she paused in disgust—"items from the staff, thereby endangering not just yourselves, but every single girl in this school."

The thought we might have been putting ourselves in jeopardy had never occurred to us until then. We didn't know anything about grooming or rings or sexual predators, even the word *paedophile* wasn't one we used, though we might have said *perverts* and *flashers*. We rarely read the newspaper or watched the news. We lived in an ivory tower, so when it came to men, we really had no sense of danger. Divines were boy crazy, and the thought of being assaulted simply never crossed our minds; if anything, we felt that *they*, the men, were the ones under threat. We ogled the gardeners and the delivery boys; hungry for attention, some of us even made eyes at Padre. Gerry Lake, if you believed the stories that circulated that term, had had several assignations with her trainer, the middle-aged man who we speculated was her boyfriend.

"I presume that all the photographs in question have now been handed in to either Miss Graves or another member of staff. If I have reason to believe otherwise, I will have no choice but to instruct Miss Graves to conduct daily dorm checks."

We let out a collective moan of discontent. A few Divines leant forward to whisper up and down the rows, elbowing one another and exchanging meaningful looks. I sat extremely still, chewing my cheek. Gerry Lake, as usual, sat bolt upright. She barely moved.

"Quiet," ordered Miss Graves. "You are Fifth Formers now. Some of you will be prefects next year, one of you will become head girl. I shouldn't have to remind you what it means to be Divine."

Memor amici.

I couldn't help but look at Skipper, whom people often referred to as head girl material, sitting on the windowsill across from me. Recently we'd barely spoken. Just as I'd feared, the unalterable fact that I was stuck in a double with Gerry Lake while Skipper was sharing a triple room with the twins meant that I was being kept at arm's length from my closest friends, no longer party to their dorm jokes, the whispered details of their latest crushes, the elaborate plans they had made for our end-of-year dares. Skipper, who was the nominal leader of this sacred Fifth Form tradition, seemed to be constantly huddled in furtive discussion with groups of girls, issuing instructions, arranging the purchase of the supplies we would need to carry out our pranks and where to hide them. (It was beholden to each successive Fifth Form to outdo the previous year's theatrics, the ritual growing increasingly more elaborate as the decades passed.) Since Gerry Lake had already made it clear that she wasn't remotely interested in the business of dares night, people grew increasingly suspicious of her motives, accusing her of leaking information to younger years or worse, sabotaging the whole endeavour by ratting us out to our headmistress (who had long threatened to put an end to the tradition for good). Whenever Gerry walked into the rec room, conversations would peter out to silence, Skipper and her attendants crossing their arms or pretending to discuss the most unlikely of subjects, GCSE exams. Once, I remember, Skipper was in the sports hall, bitching about Gerry and her refusal to take part in our dares, which she took as a personal attack. During this long vituperation she mimicked Gerry's accent perfectly—the dropped aitches and flattened vowels that made her sound so like a townie—before we realised Gerry was standing just a few feet away, getting undressed behind a nearby locker.

"Oh, hi there, Gerry," Skipper said with a fake smile. "You have something on your face."

She pointed at the dark mole on Gerry's chin.

Gerry made a hissing noise through her teeth and, seeming to single me out in particular, raised her middle finger and stormed out of the changing room.

"God, she's frightful," Skipper said, the first words she had spoken directly to me in days. "I don't know how you put up with it."

Watching Skipper, I was barely listening to our headmistress's lecture anymore.

"Should you come across anything like this in the future," she droned on, "or see anyone unusual or suspicious on or near school property, you are obliged to report it to a member of staff immediately."

Fat Fran held up a finger. The wattle on her upper arms fluttered.

"Immediately."

This time it was Skipper's turn to look at me. She raised an eyebrow, her standard I-told-you-so gesture. I pretended not to see, but as soon as we were dismissed I sidestepped past Padre and the nurse, trying not to draw attention to myself. First I went to my dorm and took out all the photos I had collected over the past few weeks, some four or five by then. I put them down the back of my underwear, pulled out one of my cigarettes and waited by the pay phone. Gerry was in the cubicle, muttering into the phone, her lips pinched, twisting the cord around her finger. When she saw me, she flushed red and slammed down the phone, barging past me as she left the booth. What did I care who she was talking to?

Lauren picked up after the second or third try. She sounded out of breath.

"I was in the bath," she said.

"Can you do me a favour?"

"Depends."

"I need you to look after something for me?"

"I don't know, what it is?"

"Please," I begged.

"Go on. You'll have to bring it here, though. I've got to cook our tea."

17

Lauren lived in a council house a short walk from the school, within sight of our lacrosse fields, and so had grown up with the sound of our hard rubber spikes clattering up and down the road as Divines marched past her window. A long army wielding sticks like bayonets, coloured bibs flapping across our chests, flicking our hair, our plummy voices carried in the breeze from the pitch, chanting and cheering. It must have been jarring.

I checked the address she'd given me. Hers was third in a long row of yellow brick houses. There was a narrow path between the gate and the front door with a low wall between her and each of her neighbours. In the tiny front gardens on either side were broken plastic toys, a couple of abandoned scooters, bikes, bins, barbecues, dumbbells, a damp mattress sagging against the back wall. Three windows along an England flag doubled as a bedroom curtain.

She'd been watching for me and opened the door before my finger could press the bell. She was wearing a tracksuit, the bottoms slung low on her hips. She pulled the door behind her and leant against the wall. Across the street an older man walking past shouted all right to her and she replied with an all right back, sheepish, as if she was embarrassed about me.

"You took your time," she said.

"Sorry," I said.

"I've got to eat and get ready for work, I can't hang about."

It was a Saturday afternoon. At the weekend she did an evening shift in a warehouse where she pressed small plastic letters and numbers into a frame, which had something to do with the side panel of a car. She pocketed fistfuls of these letters and made them into jewellery at home, including the shoelace necklace with my initials on it that I wore wrapped around my wrist.

"Oh, okay. Sorry."

I was always apologising for something or other back then.

"You're all right. What's so important?"

I was about to pull the envelope of photos out of my bag when a voice yelled from far back in the house.

"Who's that, Lauren love?"

"No one, Mum," Lauren called over her shoulder. "Just a friend."

"That's not no one, Loz. Don't make her stand out on the road."

"Fuck," I heard Lauren mutter, "you'd better come in then."

Lauren pulled the door open so that I could come into a corridor, flicked it shut behind me with her bare heel and I followed her down a carpeted hall to the back of the house. Her father used to be a jockey and on the papered walls were framed pictures of racehorses but I wasn't given time to look. In a small kitchen her mum was sitting at a table, her hands knitted round a mug of tea. She wore a dressing gown and slippers. Next to her was a woman holding a baby, and a toddler was crawling across the linoleum floor. The two women stopped midsentence and inspected me. I was wearing black leggings and penny loafers with a long shirt that belonged to my father. My hair was flipped over to one side.

"This is my mum," said Lauren. "And that's Sue. She lives next door."

Lauren gestured to the baby and then a toddler who was sitting by the back door, drumming the cat flap with a wooden spoon.

"Those two are Josh and Paul."

These were the owners of the toy trucks strewn around the adjoining front garden.

"Oy, Pauly, pack it in," the neighbour said.

"Pleased to meet you, Mrs McKibbin," I said. "I'm Josephine."

The two women nodded at me. I stood there, pretending to be interested in the baby as Lauren opened the oven door, shook an oven tray with a mitt and slammed it again. Lauren's mother was older than mine by a long way. Shockingly so. She had dark wispy hair, grey where her roots were showing. Her dressing gown was faded pink; underneath she wore a bobbled nightdress. Propped against her chair was a cane. There was a lazy Susan in the middle of the table with a china salt-and-pepper shaker set in the shape of two Siamese cats sitting amongst various orange-labelled pharmaceutical containers of varying heights like skyscrapers. Her mum spun the lazy Susan to reach for her cigarettes. She shook out a packet of Superkings and offered one to the neighbour. Lauren leant over to help herself but her mother slapped her hand.

"Buy your own," she said.

"Don't be a cow." Lauren snaked around her mother's neck and took the one from her mother's fingers. "You've had your two today anyway."

"You stopping, Joan?" the neighbour asked.

"Just cutting down," she answered as I followed Lauren upstairs.

"Oy," Lauren called back, "that's not what you told the doctor."

"Mind your beeswax" came the reply, then the baby began to cry and Lauren waved me into her room.

Her bedroom used to be her brother Stuart's and was still decorated for an eight-year-old boy. There were spaceships on the walls and glow stars and a bunk bed with faded Cabbage Patch stickers on it. I looked at a photo of her brother holding a football trophy. I recognised him from the maintenance staff. Sometimes I saw Stuart repairing broken chairs outside the boiler room or flattening our grass tennis courts with a roller. He liked to whistle. There were Lauren's schoolbooks and a desk for her to work at, but other than that she hadn't done anything to decorate her bedroom.

"I know, it's a shithole," she said, without looking at all bothered.

She kicked some clothes across the room and climbed onto the top bunk. The bottom bunk, which was neater, had a floral pillow and a folded blanket with an eye mask on top.

"Who sleeps down there?"

"My mum. She gets insomnia and nightmares and shit. Sometimes she comes in here to sleep. Or not sleep, I guess."

I looked at the spaceships.

"What about your brother?"

"Stuart? He's got his own place with his girlfriend and her kid. They're always at each other's throats. When he's had an earful, he kips on our sofa."

Like Gerry Lake, I was an only child and therefore filled with curiosity about what it meant to have a sibling, particularly a brother. My family was a small and remote island. I loved my parents, of course, and didn't resent them for sending me away to school. They were giving me what they believed to be the best possible start in life, a private education; it's not like they had thrown me to the wolves. My father was over fifteen years older than my mother and worked in international finance. I knew next to nothing about his office life, other than the grey-and-white pin-striped suits he wore to the bank and the mahogany briefcase he carried like an aegis. Above all, my father valued peace and quiet; he visibly winced when I spoke too loudly at breakfast, retreating into his study during half-terms and school holidays. My mother was the social one—extremely pretty, well bred, Divine—and therefore considered a catch. As far as I could tell, my parents were neither demonstrably in love nor out of it. In sixteen years I had never seen them yell or cry or even kiss on the lips. If they argued or—even more improbable to me—were overcome with sudden, violent desire, it was acted out behind their bedroom door, in a series of muffled whispers and coughs and sighs. Occasionally, when my father was in a particularly good mood, he would pat my mother on the hip as he passed her.

That was as much romance I saw at home. I had no idea what it was like to live, day in, day out, as part of a real family, one that squabbled and wept and hugged.

I was absorbed for a while in looking at the photos of Stuart in his football kit, hair spiked with gel.

"So what do you want to give me then?" Lauren asked.

I took out the envelope holding the photos and handed it to her. She fingered open the packet and shook her head violently.

"No way. I don't fucking want them."

"Just for a bit," I pleaded. "Just while they're doing dorm checks."

"Stick them in the rubbish then, torch them."

On the way to her house I'd had the same thought; I had even hovered beside a bin in the town rec grounds, but I couldn't bring myself to do it. I don't know why not. Maybe because my photo was the first to be found, and in an odd way I felt chosen. That's how desperate for male attention I was. At night I sometimes pulled the photos out from their hiding spots once Gerry was asleep and, under the cover of my duvet, studied them with a penlight, one hand between my legs. This had become something of a guilty secret. While Divines shared every detail of their romantic encounters with boys—limited as mine were—the topic of masturbation was strictly off-limits. I had no idea if Skipper and the twins pleasured themselves in the same way, or if the fact that I did made me a pervert. I could have asked Lauren, who wasn't squeamish in the slightest, but I was too nervous to say anything that I thought might jeopardise our friendship.

The truth was that Lauren and I had very little in common. I didn't know any of the boys she fancied, or the girls she sat next to at school, or any of her teachers. Her life felt infinitely more eventful than mine, more adult. Lauren had two jobs to help with the bills at home, the warehouse shift and Saturday mornings behind the till at Woolworths. I had never worked a day in my life. Occasionally my father paid me to hose down his car. Lauren's father was a retired jockey, but she had never ridden and wasn't remotely interested in horses like I was. Rather, she thought they were a waste of space. We liked some of the same music and books and television programmes, but I was always out of step with the latest episodes. Because I was paranoid she'd find me boring, I would save up funny anecdotes from school to tell her while we smoked, details of my ongoing feud with Gerry Lake. (Lauren took a particular interest in Gerry. Had I seen her skate? What about that boyfriend of hers, the older man? Wasn't he taking advantage?)

But for the most part the Divine life was insular, repetitive, trivial. Gerry and the photos gave me something to talk about. I wasn't ready to give them up.

"Please." I pushed them into her hand. "Just for a few days."

"All right, all right. Fucking hell." She wedged the envelope under her pillow. "But if my dad finds out, I'll never hear the fucking end of it."

Downstairs the front door banged shut.

"Shit," she said, looking alarmed. "That's him. Come on."

Mr McKibbin stood in the kitchen with the *Racing Post* rolled under his arm. He surveyed the various women in the room, his wife and neighbour, gripping their empty mugs, then last, Lauren and me as we jogged downstairs and she banged open the oven door and shook out their supper onto three floral plates.

"What is this, the flipping Women's Institute?" he asked.

He was a short, lean man, with a face that was ruddy and weathered from years of riding, lines radiating around his eyes, deep crescents either side of his mouth, pronounced bags. His eyes were so hooded that it gave the impression he was squinting. There was a white scar under his chin where he'd once been kicked by a horse.

Lauren took the first plate of food and put it on the table in front of her mother. It wasn't even six o'clock. I had never met a family who ate this early. Sue, the neighbour, hoisted her baby onto her hip and I noticed her squeeze Lauren's mum on the shoulder as she stood up.

"We'll be off then, Joan."

Lauren's mum reached for her cane, pushed her chair back. It screeched on the floor and the baby began howling.

"No, don't be silly," Sue said. "I'll see myself out."

Without waiting for us to leave, Lauren's father sat down and began to eat. He leant over his plate, stabbing one chip after another and forking them into his mouth. His leathered forearms were still hard and sinuous from riding. A thin gold disc, St Christopher, levitated on a chain over his food.

"Thanks so much for having me," I said. "Lovely to meet you all."

That was the obsequious way I spoke back then.

No one heard me over the wailing baby.

I raised a palm and left without anyone noticing I was gone.

18

It was one of those warm spring evenings in England when peo-
ple suddenly realise summer is around the corner. I should never
have been on my own, of course, but, instead of hurrying back
to school, I walked from Lauren's house through the public rec
grounds not far from where Gerry Lake had been jeered at by the
townies with the pit bull. There were semi-naked bodies scattered
across the park, absorbing the last of the sun. A group of boys
kicked a ball about. In the playground I saw the familiar gelled
high ponytails of three KE girls who sat atop a climbing frame,
swigging bottles of Hooch. They were drunk and taunting a man
pushing a baby on a swing. As I got closer I realised it was Lauren's brother they were heckling. Wolf whistling, trying to get
him to accept a drink. Stuart McKibbin—I recognised him from
school—leant against the swing, muscular, tall, totally indifferent
to their catcalls. He could have wheeled his girlfriend's baby elsewhere, but it seemed like all the attention entertained him. He
deposited the baby in the sandpit with a bucket and spade and
flopped on a bench with his arms spread out, legs splayed, his
groin jutting provocatively over the seat. He slid one hand beneath
his waistband and rearranged himself. Then he closed his eyes.
He wouldn't have looked twice at someone like me, I knew that,
but I felt something tugging, a kind of gravitational pull that made
me walk closer to the playground set.

"Stuart, stop taking the piss," the KE girls yelled.

Rejected, they turned their attention to me, their heads rotating slowly as I passed. White powdered faces and dark shark eyes.

"What she think she's looking at?"

I said nothing, put my head down, kept on walking.

"Who let the dogs out?" they called.

There was perhaps another three hundred metres or so before the gate. I just had to make it to the other side of the park, then I'd be almost back at school. The three girls swung down from their cage and followed after me slowly, making yapping and howling noises. I cursed myself for coming out alone.

"Oy, we're talking to you, posh twat."

My hands were clammy, I tried not to run or look over my shoulder, but they shoved past me and stood blocking the gate so that I had to be granted their permission to leave.

"Excuse me," I said.

They swigged from their bottles and smirked, swinging forward and back on the kissing gate.

"What's the magic word?"

"Please, just get off."

"Orff," they mimicked my accent. "Get orff."

"Seriously," I said.

"Seriously, seriously, seriously."

One of them held out her drink and then unclasped her grip around its neck, letting the bottle fall. There was a loud crack as it hit the tarmac.

"Look what you gone and done now?"

The others hissed with laughter.

"You owe me for that. You'd better go buy me another. Off you trot."

Even if I had looked old enough to get served, which I didn't, I couldn't have paid them. I emptied out my cardigan pockets to prove I wasn't carrying my wallet. All I had was the single cigarette I'd put in my pocket earlier. They seemed uncertain what to do next. The taller of the three girls peered down at her trainers where the tongues were sprayed with pink from the dropped bottle.

"They're ruined."

The others caught on.

"Yeah, look what she did. She's properly fucked your shoes up, Jade."

"Snap, snap." The leader clicked her fingers and pointed at her feet.

I stood there—utterly pathetic, weak—unsure of what exactly she expected of me. Why were they doing this? I felt a pulse in my throat and an unbelievable urge to urinate. If I wasn't holding my breath, I thought I'd wet myself. I cast my eyes around desperately, hoping to see another Divine out smoking in the park. I would have taken anyone in that moment, even Gerry Lake. Slowly, I crouched down on one knee and tugged my shirtsleeve over my fist. I began to rub.

"There you go, Princess Di, chop chop."

"Pack it in, you lot," I heard.

The KEs' heads snapped up. Lauren's brother stood behind us, one hand on the pushchair. I was mortified and relieved in equal measure.

"All right, Stu." They crossed their arms and pouted, totally impenitent, I remember, unassailable. I took my chance to stand and shuffle back a few steps, trying to make myself invisible.

"Jade, you heard me, get lost."

"Or what," she said.

She leant against the gate, rocking back and forth on her elbows. I watched to see what Stuart would do next.

He smiled, shook his head, and stepped in close to her, just millimeters apart, the other girls wolf whistling as though they were going to snog; I felt a stab of envy, but at the last minute he moved his mouth suddenly and whispered something into her ear. This KE, Jade, bit her lip, then she reddened, slammed both her hands into his chest and detonated.

"You dickhead," she said, spitting the words at him. "Twat, fucking knob."

Arms flailing, the other two had to drag her off him. Stuart held out an arm to keep her flapping at a distance and it seemed like she weighed nothing, a gnat or a fly.

"You're full of shit, Stuart McKibbin. Your mum's going to wind up in a fucking wheelchair, yeah, a spaz, you know," she yelled as the other two girls tugged her away. "I hope she shits herself."

"Nighty night, Jade." Stuart wiggled his fingers.

The girl was still screaming insults at him from the other side of the playground, fainter by now, snagged in the melody of the park, the radios and football games and the ice cream van, so that we only caught every other word.

"Girlfriend . . . sister . . . slag . . . lezzer."

Then they were gone, down the lane towards the duck pond, and it was just the two of us. Three, actually. The baby, ignored in the excitement, thrashed its legs violently, demanding attention. It tossed a sunhat on the ground.

"Here," Stuart said, "do us a favour and hold Kyle, will you."

He was talking to me, I realised. Shocked, I took the baby under its hot, fat arms. Stuart hoisted the pushchair easily over the fence and we crossed through the kissing gate, one at a time, where I stood on the pavement, watching as he strapped the baby back down and plugged its angry mouth with a dummy.

"You all right, yeah?" he asked, touching my arm.

I nodded. My hair fell, tenting my face, and without thinking I raised my hand and flicked.

"I'd stay out the park for a bit if I was you."

"Thanks very much," I eventually said, grimacing at how Divine I sounded, my voice particularly high.

He was facing into the last of the day's sun, his eyes squinting slightly so that I was reminded of his father, though they didn't particularly look alike. Nor did he bear much resemblance to Lauren, really, other than the colour of his hair, which was jaw length and shaved in an undercut at the back. He was his own man, I decided. Quite beautiful, very raw. Nothing like the boys I knew. I must have given the impression I was about to say something more because he raised his hand to his brow, waiting for me to speak.

I froze.

I had absolutely no idea how to talk to men. They might as well have been aliens. At our school dances, the only place we officially socialised with the opposite sex, Divines stood in tight clusters around the gym while boys pogo danced to the Prodigy and the Orb, thrashing violently, butting against one another, then came tumbling into us, unsubtle as peacocks. The darkened gym was dank with the sweat that sprayed from their floppy hair. There was no alcohol allowed, naturally, but by then we were already long drunk, downing bottles of Archers in our dorms as we wriggled into crushed velvet sheaths that barely skimmed our buttocks. Black chokers like girdles around our pale necks. We waited nervously under the shoe tree as batches of Harrovians or Amplefordians, transported to us in school coaches, cattle trucks if you will, rolled off the bus equally legless, their bow ties loose and shirts unbuttoned. When the slow dances played, there seemed to be some omnipotent force that arranged us into pairs, matching like for like on the unspoken scale of desirability and status. All except for Gerry Lake, who stood on the side with the teachers, her arms crossed. She had no interest in getting drunk or being groped. Without speaking a word these Henrys, Ruperts, Hugos clasped our lower backs to Meatloaf and pressed their chests against our nipples, shirts drenched, breathing heavily. When the staff weren't looking, couples peeled off into the darkness, crawled behind hedges, pressed against walls. Ears ringing from the music, we let their tongues circle our mouths. Once every fifteen minutes a deputy went from bush to bush with a cane, thrashing the undergrowth like a beater at a shoot. Undeterred, sweaty hands crawled under the waistbands of our tights, fingers inserted hastily. All this without sharing a single word. When the music stopped, we were finally flushed from the shrubbery, some of us draped in dinner jackets. Gerry sat on a gym bench with the teachers, her legs crossed primly. We snogged our conquests once more in front of our peers and sent them on their way.

I stared up at Stuart, my head tipped to one side in that

ludicrous flick, unbearably coy, growing more self-conscious by the second. I knew I had to say something.

"Sorry about what they said about your mother."

I knew from Lauren that Joan had MS. And then, because I had started and wasn't skilled enough to know where to stop, I held out my wrist with the shoelace bracelet on it.

"I'm friends with Lauren."

"Yeah, I know," he said, raising his eyebrows.

"My sister gets around these days, doesn't she? Moving up in the world."

People were leaving the park by now, shaking out blankets, dusting themselves off, though the footballers played deeper into the dusk, running and pointing, some of the players invisible against the bluing grass, a neon ball flashing between them as if it was levitating. The baby sucked noisily on his dummy. I supposed he was hungry and was annoyed that I was demanding Stuart's attention. We both ignored him.

"Shouldn't you be back in school?" he asked.

"Almost," I said, and then I remembered the cigarette I had brought with me, crumbling in my shirt pocket. I took it out.

"I'm going to smoke this first, I think."

I had something to prove, I suppose: I was a rebel, I didn't play by the Divine rules. I lit up, right there on the street, cupping the end with my hand. Then I held it out to Stuart. My offer took him aback for a moment. Had he been caught smoking with me he would have been in a lot of trouble. But he reached out to take it, keeping his eyes on me the whole time; our hands briefly touched as he inhaled and passed it back.

"Cheers."

Without saying anything else, he turned and began pushing the baby away down the street.

"If you see her first, tell my sister I'll drop by on Wednesday for my tea," he called once over his shoulder; there was a rattling noise of wheels as he crossed the street, the sound of him whistling.

"Will do," I shouted back but he probably didn't hear me.

I stood still, holding the cigarette exactly as he'd passed it to me, between my middle finger and thumb. It was damp with our saliva where our two mouths had pressed. I held my forearm, examining the exact place he had touched it, just below the elbow crease, but there was nothing to see. Slowly I upturned the cigarette, still smouldering, kissing it red against my skin.

19

The next few weeks, what became our last as Divine, we were hysterical, riddled with paranoia. Now that the photos were public knowledge, alleged sightings of the pervert ran as high as two or three a week. No one was above suspicion. This included an emergency plumber, a member of the Anglican clergy, and a school inspector. Even though our exams were just around the corner, we memorised license plates, reported townies that lingered near school grounds, crawled around in the undergrowth looking for clues. It was only a matter of time, I felt, before we'd begin to turn upon ourselves.

"It's got to be someone who knows the school really well," George Gordon-Warren argued. "An inside job."

We were in the pottery room, watching Dave work on a sculpture—a large, lifeless bust, Apollo perhaps, or Zeus—whose expression grew increasingly moribund the more she poked and scraped. I was ripping out photos at random from a stack of *National Geographic* magazines to stick in my portfolio. Neither of us were gifted artists, far from it; I could barely draw a bowl of fruit, but at least, I told myself, it was better than taking drama. Unlike Skipper, who considered herself something of a thespian, the idea of being called on by Padre to read at morning chapel, let alone perform a monologue, made me feel physically sick. At the start of GCSEs I was panic-stricken that Skipper and I hadn't chosen identical subjects, the first time in four years of friendship our timetables hadn't been in sync. Lately I found the art room—its loamy smell, the hearthlike warmth radiating from the kiln, the soft scratch of charcoal on paper—one of the few places

I could relax. Away from Skipper, my friends forgot they were meant to be giving me the cold shoulder and behaved like their old selves.

George began to make a dick out of surplus clay, a grotesque cartoon replica of the penis in the photos. The art teacher, Mr Rogowski, a softly spoken Polish man with absolutely no authority, shuffled around the room in a pair of rubber clogs, pretending not to notice.

George leant over and wiggled the penis by my ear.

"Bloody hell," I shrieked, batting it away with my notebook.

"Girls," the teacher complained, unconvincingly.

George crossed her arms, her feet up on an empty pottery wheel. She twisted the two ends of the penis like a corkscrew, studying our teacher.

"What about Rogowski?"

Mr Rogowski was the same age as my father. He wore thick corduroy trousers and home-knitted cardigans. His back was hunched and—the part that revolted us the most—his index finger was half missing, a deformity he used to his advantage, pressing the stump into clay eye sockets or using it to demonstrate a pinch pot.

"Rank," Dave said, without even looking up.

"For god's sake, who then?" George said and flung the dick onto the table.

So far our investigations had already ruled out the small handful of male teaching staff. They were pitifully asexual, neutered by decades of maltreatment at the hands of the Divine. We could hardly imagine they had penises, let alone posed naked with jaunty erections. Except for Stuart, the maintenance men seemed too fat or old, lacking in the necessary imagination. That left a French assistant (almost certainly gay), the baker who delivered our birthday cakes (too lanky), and one of the younger gardeners with learning difficulties who was always smiling and waving at us in class. All this fervent sleuthing worked in my favour because in between preparing for exams I could disappear, as I now frequently did, to smoke with Lauren and no one batted an eye. I saw her almost every day.

But, shortly after our headmistress's lecture, there were no more photos. We simply stopped finding them. Younger years unbuttoned their blue striped dresses down to their bras, they lay semi-clad in the orchard reading, one eye on their books, the other expectantly on the bushes. In May half-term came and went and eventually we had to concede that the danger was gone. Perhaps he'd been scared off by the sight of our deputies doing their rounds or found an easier way to get himself off.

"Maybe he died," Lauren said.

It was a Saturday afternoon. Lauren and I were sitting on a bench down by the old mill. She had just finished her shift at Woolworths, and her hair was tied back with a bandanna at the nape of her neck.

"Bet he wanked himself to death."

I had no idea if such a thing was even possible.

"Gross." We pretended to gag.

I rubbed the cigarette burn on my inner arm out of habit. It had bloomed into a taut yellow bud until it finally popped and was now a shiny pink scar because of my continued prodding and picking and stroking. I wanted to ask Lauren about her brother, but I couldn't work out how to do so without it being obvious that I was interested in him.

"Want to hear a good one?" I said instead.

"Go on."

"The Third Form set fire to Penfold."

"Who's Penfold?"

"Our lab technician; she sets up our chemistry experiments and stuff."

"They set her on fire?"

"Well, her skirt."

"What the fuck did she do to deserve that?"

I shrugged. "Nothing."

We crushed our cigarettes underfoot and walked along the brook that led past the flour mill, vaguely in the direction of school. I wasn't sure where Lauren was heading, but as always I followed along. The fact of the matter was that there wasn't much we *could* do in town. Other than St John's, which could hardly be considered an asset, the place had nothing going for it. A former brewing town, there were almost no jobs anymore. The cinema was on its last legs, and one by one the butcher's and the greengrocer's and the fishmonger had closed; all the townies shopped at Iceland. The only opportunities left were at the school: mopping our floors, peeling our potatoes, sweeping the tennis courts. No wonder they hated us.

A man on the path ahead of us sat on a bench with a bag of chips spread on his legs and a can of beer. Two kids ran back and forth to the bridge, tossing chips to the ducks.

"Oy, you prats," Lauren shouted and snagged one by the collar. "They don't fecking eat chips."

"Get off," the boy said, wriggling out of her grip.

The father took a slug from his can, looked up suddenly, and reddened.

"They'll kill the ducks if they feed them that," Lauren explained.

"Martin, Alan, get over here now," he ordered.

The man stood and emptied his entire chip bag over the water. There was a flurry of wings and snapping beaks, the water frothing, brown and green tails upturned.

"Now piss off," he snapped.

"Wanker," Lauren muttered; she gave him the finger and walked on. Totally in thrall, I trotted after.

On previous outings we had gone to the graveyard and walked about amongst the tilted headstones smoking; other times we sat in the town museum where there was a cheap café. Once Lauren climbed through the window of the wooden Girl Guide's hut where KEs supposedly went to lose their virginity, but there wasn't anything to see. She stole a packet of biscuits and we left again. That afternoon I remember we roamed the upper floors of the library, leafing through magazines while Lauren read her horoscopes. The fact that she was a Virgo, some kind of goddess, was supposedly significant to our friendship.

"When's your birthday again?" she wanted to know.

I didn't believe in star signs but I could see she wasn't going to drop it.

"Twenty-first of April."

The same, to my embarrassment, as Gerry Lake. It was bad enough I had to share a dorm with her, let alone a birthday.

I thought back to the second week of term. To celebrate, it was tradition that we congregate in the rec room to sing, crowding around a biscuit cake or tray of iced fingers—Sticky Willies as we called them—ordered from the local bakery. It was only after I had been given the birthday bumps, my peers grabbing me by the limbs, tossing me irreverently up and down in the air like a blanket, that we remembered.

Gerry.

Fuck.

There she was. In the doorway, just back from practice, her skating bag over her shoulder, arms crossed, that sour pout. Her dark hair was pulled back in the usual way. In her bun was a new bauble, a tacky-looking pin in the shape of a forget-me-not heart, a birthday present from her trainer Gerry let slip later. Which made me begin to wonder if there was some truth to the stories after all. Until then I had presumed it was just another rumour, one of many that circulated around Gerry.

A few girls began to sing happy birthday, rather feebly. Someone offered Gerry what was left of the cake. There were only a few crumbs. Gerry scowled, cat eyes, two green slits. If looks could kill, as they say. I felt her icy gaze fall on me. The singing of happy birthday petered out. Why was she singling me out like that? It wasn't my fault no one had waited. I was her dorm mate, not her mother. She always had to cause a scene.

"You cow," she had hissed and smacked the cake box to the ground.

"Taurus." Lauren tapped the pages of the horoscope.

As if that explained everything.

After the library we walked to the end of Mill Street, making a loop of town so that we arrived at the school by the back route, past the laundry where Divines deposited their bags of dirty clothes once a week, tossing their soiled underwear and clothes amongst the other towering piles to be washed, ironed and folded by our laundry ladies. It being a Saturday, First Years were busy polishing shoes outside St Hilda's and holding them out for inspection.

Lauren stood in the shadows, staring up at my large redbrick boarding house with its gables and ivy. There was the steady throb of the washing machines behind us, the soapy tang of detergent. Somewhere near the orchards I could hear clapping and cheering. We looked up at my dorm window on the third floor. It was slightly ajar, which made me think there was a chance Gerry was in there.

"Let's go," Lauren ordered.

She frequently invited herself into my boarding house but, except for her very first visit, had stuck to the ground floor.

"Actually, it might not be such a good time," I stalled.

I gestured to the deputy who sat on a chair outside the boarding house, wearing a drab floral shin-length skirt and a shirt with a knitted vest over the top. Like all the deputies she was a mousy, gaunt-looking woman, probably not more than thirty, but a single woman like that would have appeared to us as washed up, over the hill. We couldn't have imagined anything more pathetic. The deputy was reading, paying no attention at all to her wards, except for when they presented her with their leather lace-ups and penny loafers, at which point she raised her eyes wearily, gave either a nod or a shake, and went back to her novel. It would have taken no effort at all for Lauren and me to sneak past her. There were also the handful of First and Second Years to worry about, but they would have been too terrified to speak directly to me. There was a strict hierarchical order at play. Unless they were our siblings, we never conversed with these younger years who, in their blue-and-white-striped summer dresses, at least two sizes too large for them, were as amorphous as a shoal. Skinny, knock-kneed, and inane. A few of them attempted to copy the flick; the rest favoured enormous quiffs pinioned by Alice bands. They all wore scrunchies and friendship bracelets, which they spent hours weaving, around their wrists. A Fifth Former was God to them. They cowered when we passed, offered us their spot in the lunch queue, scrambled to make way for us in chapel. It was a great insult not to hold a door open for an older girl; I'd once seen a First Year lunge to catch a door with her fingers for Skipper, the new girl moving so fast she was in danger of tripping.

A couple of Second Years looked at us with curiosity as they buffed their shoes and quickly looked away.

"Don't be a pussy," Lauren taunted.

"All right, fine." I gave in. "Follow me and don't say anything."

Instantly I knew my mistake. This was the worst possible thing I could have said to someone like Lauren. She let out a derisive snort, curtsied.

"Yes, m'lady."

Instead of slipping quietly into the boarding house, Lauren tugged off her bandanna, raised her eyebrows, and marched straight towards the teacher.

"Lauren," I hissed. "Where are you going?"

She looked over her shoulder at me, wiggling her fingers.

"Wait," I said, panicking, and I sprinted to catch up, skidding to a halt in front of the entrance.

To my relief the deputy barely looked up from her book.

Perhaps she thought Lauren was a sister who was visiting or one of the Sixth Formers coming to deliver a note at the behest of a housemistress.

Lauren coughed.

"Good afternoon," she said, putting on a cut-glass accent not unlike my mother's. I winced. Did we really speak like that?

"Hello, girls," the deputy said flatly. "Don't forget to sign in."

I slipped one hand under Lauren's arm and tried to usher her away, but she shrugged me off.

"Okay, ya," Lauren mocked, swishing her hair over to one side. "Absolutely, will do."

This, at last, got the deputy's attention. She lowered her novel, trying to place the house to which Lauren belonged. Lauren's shoulder blades pulled back, her lips pinched into a fake smile, chin held high to express the kind of haughty disdain we were loathed for, her best impression of the Divine. For a moment I was struck by the brilliance of Lauren's transformation, the nymph-like way she could shape-shift, a better actress than Skipper by far.

The deputy frowned, flustered.

"Why aren't you girls at the match?"

That afternoon was the mother-daughter rounders game, a Fifth Form tradition that had been going almost as long as the school. Our mothers—most of them Old Girls—strode onto the pitch wielding bats or headed out to field and, hoisting their skirts above their knees, apologising for their rusty backswing, hooting with laughter as they swung for the ball, dashed like spaniels around our freshly mown lawn.

"I'm just getting my mother her hat," I told the deputy. A lie. My mother was six thousand miles away. At the yacht club, I guessed, on her second gin and tonic.

"Yes," Lauren chipped in. "Got to dash. Mummy's waiting."

The deputy squinted again at Lauren, her head tilted.

I held my breath, pressed my thumbnail into the burn mark on my arm.

"And who . . ." the deputy began to question, but just at that moment a Second Year thrust a pair of newly polished shoes under her nose.

"Come on," I hissed.

I pulled Lauren by the arm, up the steps and into the house. We took the curved oak staircase two at a time, along the corridor, ignoring a miserable-looking First Year who was wandering the corridor like a stray cat, and slammed into my dorm.

"Oh my god," I said, utterly in awe, chest heaving, giddy with relief. I couldn't believe we'd got away with it. "That was amazing."

Lauren flicked her hair, hand on one hip, still Divine.

"Ya," she said. "Bloody marvellous."

20

By Christmas I am pregnant and the matter of the Polaroid pho-
tos long forgotten. Jürgen sees them for what they are, distant
relics, mementos of the Divine.

My metamorphic body is a source of unexpected eroticism
for us both. My breasts grow first; finally I have the boobs I had
dreamt about in school. Plump, speckled brown areola, and nipples that react to the smallest of titillations: a tongue, the fridge,
the vibration of the "L" train as I'm circling the Loop. I am always wet. I ooze. I am constantly changing my underwear and
can come at the drop of the hat. This from someone who, no fault
of any of my bedfellows, orgasmed once or twice a year at best.
My labia is fat and juicy as a honeydew, its folds dark and volup-
tuous. I examine it by straddling my makeup mirror while Jürgen
is in the studio. My vulva is, I discover, positively O'Keeffe.

By summer I walk around our apartment with no clothes
on, emailing my editor copy while rubbing ice cubes behind my
neck and soaking my feet in buckets of cold water. The white
scar on my inner arm inexplicably begins to itch, turning a
dark shade of purple. My enormous stomach, however, eclipses
all thought of the Divine, of Gerry Lake. I give up googling
her name, looking for old stories. Instead I masturbate two or
three times a day, impatient for Jürgen to come home, my stomach hardening into a pyramid with each tingling spasm. I have
grown so large I become impossible for him to scale. Instead I
prop myself against the pillows and bring myself to climax just
by watching him. I find it incredibly erotic. The way his dick
nods gently against his pelvis, his fist oscillating, thighs spread,

a pose that replicates, not unintentionally, one or two of those old familiar photos.

Finally, the week before the baby is due, my libido recedes. My stomach is taut as a ripe pomegranate, and a brown welt runs from my belly button to my pubis, as if I am about to split open; my nipples leak. The thought of sex suddenly laughable, I wait until Jürgen is cycling, then I take out the Polaroids one last time. They are yellowing at the edges, the penises fading, dreamy looking, somehow less alarming. I inter them in a metal cash box I bought at a charity shop, along with all the other keepsakes I've taken from Rod's attic in England. My Pandora's box, if you will. A large bundle of letters, a school photo, a five-year diary I find too excruciating to read. Newspaper clippings, including the interview we gave shortly after the scandal, an attempt by the school to limit damage. I cringe at how pretentious we sound, our obsequious flattery of Gerry—her skill on ice, her pluck, her zest for life—so outrageously insincere, so overblown and phoney. I scratch my arm, add the clipping to the box.

Finally I sit on the bed with an old striped school scarf folded neatly on my lap. I stare at it for some time, chewing my cheek, hugging my stomach like a balloon. Then slowly I unwrap the scarf. There inside, just the same as I remember, the two halves of Gerry's broken hairpin, the little sapphire flowers, the sparkling heart made from rhinestones. Sweet sixteen.

I feel an unexpected wave of revulsion.

Toss the hairpin into the box, slam it shut.

Quick as I can, I heave myself up on a chair and, with difficulty, shove the cash box hard with a broom handle into the farthest recess of the wardrobe, on tiptoes—poking, prodding—until it's completely out of sight.

21

Lauren wandered around my dorm like a television detective, only the second time she'd been up there. She picked up the bottles on my countertop, the moisturisers and the spot cream, fingered through my toiletry bag, sniffed my bottle of perfume, turning in a circle and looking around at my walls.

"Look at the size of it, you couldn't swing a cat in here. The amount you lot pay. It's fucking criminal."

It was true. Gerry Lake and I shared a room no bigger than my parents' larder.

Lauren gestured to the other side of the room. "That where your mate Gerry sleeps then?"

I rolled my eyes.

Gerry's bunk bed ran in parallel with mine, either side of the window, slightly staggered to give us the illusion of privacy. Our desks were beneath our beds. We spent most of our time with our backs to each other. Likewise, there was an unspoken understanding between Gerry and me that we sleep foot to foot, as far away from each other as possible. Gerry's duvet was neatly made, her platoon of stuffed toys—mementos from her skating competitions—arranged with military precision on her pillow. An empty side table, which neither of us had claimed, was squeezed underneath the window.

Lauren undertook a similar forensic investigation of Gerry's possessions, nosing through Gerry's notebooks, examining each of her ice-skating trophies in turn, the medals and team photos. She swizzled Gerry's hairpin—her prized birthday present from her coach—rattling it like a cocktail stick against her teeth before she stuck it behind her ear. I wanted to ask her to put it back but I was worried she might make a scene and people would come running. Next she moved on to Gerry's wardrobe, where she levered the door open cautiously with a pencil, as if she thought it contained body parts. A boot tumbled out onto the floor. We both jumped.

"Oh my god," I screamed.

"That's all her skating kit then?"

I nodded and watched anxiously as Lauren began rifling through Gerry's clothes, listening for footsteps outside. She pulled out one sparkly costume after another, dangling them from her finger.

"What is she, a midget?"

"Pretty much," I mumbled.

I felt sick. What if we got caught, either by one of my friends returning from the rounders match or, worse, Gerry herself? The room felt increasingly small, the walls pressing down on us. I could hear the incessant footsteps of the First Year still pacing the corridor. I tugged at Lauren's arm.

"I'm bored," I said. "Let's go."

Lauren shook me off, her face lighting up. From the back of Gerry's wardrobe she pulled an outfit that was emerald green, off the shoulder. This was a trick of the light; the long sleeves were in fact a sheer, fleshy-coloured tan, to give the impression of naked skin. She lifted one foot and then another and attempted to wiggle the costume up over her jeans.

"Don't," I began to say. "Lauren, stop."

"How do I look?" she asked.

I snorted nervously. It was ridiculous, the gusset tugged stripper high, her T-shirt buckled underneath the nude sleeves. Lauren began to do a figure of eight seductively with her hips.

"Oh my god." I couldn't help myself, I laughed with fear. "Stop, stop. They'll hear us."

Lauren grinned and made a ponytail with her hair and began to twirl it, strutting up and down the room with the silky green costume riding up her crack. I was buckled, gripping the desk, trying to hold the laughter down so we wouldn't get caught. I could feel it clawing its way up my chest and into my throat.

"Seriously, Lauren, stop." I choked out the words.

She swung up onto the desk and then Gerry's bed, kicking long showgirl legs in the air. I crawled up onto my bed and buried my head under the pillow, rocking with hilarity, drunk on it, weeping with laughter, trying to get my breath back by taking long inhalations and exhalations through the mouth. My bed smelt of polish and wax and disinfectant. Suddenly Lauren went quiet. Outside I could hear the faint sound of Second Years squealing, playing a game of tag. Cheers from the rounders match. A maintenance man—Stuart, I daydreamt—was mowing the lawn. I lifted a corner of the pillow. Lauren was flat on her back, lying on Gerry's mattress in a death pose, her arms outstretched. Her hair was spread, Ophelia-like, in long silvery strands. Her eyes were open, staring at the yellow ceiling. She jiggled one toe.

"Why d'you lot hate her so much anyway?"

"I don't know."

"Yeah, you do."

When I said nothing further, she threw one of Gerry's teddy bears at my head.

"You're a shit liar, Josephine."

I looked across to see if she was joking. Lauren continued to stare at the ceiling, her lashes flickering, chasing a beam of light. I picked and picked at the scab on my inner arm. Why was it that Gerry was such an easy target? What was it about her that made us dislike her so much?

"How now brown cow," I said suddenly.

"Come again?" Lauren sat up.

"We used to get her to say it. Gerry. When she first came to school. How now brown cow."

"Why?"

"Just to hear the way she pronounced it."

"Which was?"

"Nothing. Just . . ."

Common, I almost said, but didn't.

"Different."

Lauren rolled her eyes.

"Bunch of stuck-up bitches." She jumped down from the bed, balled the green leotard, and tossed it thoughtlessly into the back of Gerry's wardrobe.

"I'm out of here."

I felt sick to my stomach. Why had I just told her that? She might never want to see me again. I looked down at the burn on my arm, wincing when I thought of her telling Stuart. I trailed Lauren out of the room, past the same morose First Year haunting the corridor and down the oak staircase. By the sports hall Lauren turned one way without saying goodbye, just a wave. I climbed the bridge, miserable, tugging myself arm over arm. But as Lauren reached the crossroads she stopped, turned and curtsied at me theatrically. Only then did I see the rhinestone pin still stuck behind her ear. Forget-me-not.

"Stop," I called after her. "Lauren, come back."

"Cheerio, old chum," she mocked, tipping an invisible hat.

22

I had fantasised about Lauren's brother so often and in so many forms, sexual and romantic, that when I saw Stuart McKibbin in the flesh again I thought he was a manifestation of all my nocturnal yearning, the nights spent lusting and sighing and flipping facedown on my bed after Gerry was asleep, my fingers down my pants. The morning after Lauren's visit I woke before my alarm, desperate for the loo, stumbled into the bathroom, ignoring the Out of Order sign, and did a double take. Stuart was belly to the shower room floor, loosening a blocked U-bend.

"Oh." I coughed, my voice thick with sleep.

I hadn't brushed my hair, my breath was rank, and I had hooded eyes, two puffy slits. I must have looked repulsive.

"Pass the bucket," he said.

Automatically I looked around and picked up a tub by the toolbox and handed it to him.

"This one?"

"Christ alive," he said, looking up. "Sorry, thought you were someone else."

His hair was tied back with a rubber band. I could see the fresh buzz of his undercut where the skin was whiter, one of the many parts of him I had fantasised about stroking, and the tanned back of his neck, a deep mahogany colour from the hours spent outside flattening our tennis courts and trimming the grass. He continued to loosen the pipe, one eye closed, trying to get purchase. Above him I caught sight of myself in the bathroom mirror and froze. It was worse than I thought. No one had showed me how to pluck my eyebrows back then, and they were as unwieldy as cats, extremely dark in comparison to the mousy hair on my head. That morning one brow had been crumpled in my sleep and plastered upright with what looked like drool. I licked my thumb without Stuart seeing and smoothed it out. I also combed my fingers through my hair to remove the tangles and tried not to breathe in his direction.

He grunted and heaved on the spanner and there was a sudden rush as the joint came loose and water thundered into the bucket. He stuck two fingers up inside the hole and circled them around. One eye on me. I found this gesture excruciatingly embarrassing. I could have moved to another bathroom along the corridor, but instead I stayed there, chewing on the end of my toothbrush, not knowing where to look.

"Can't get up high enough," he said.

He inserted a long plastic probe into the pipe and jabbed it a few times, thrusting and grunting. He could see the reaction on my face, the crippling embarrassment of it all, and continued to torture me further.

"Here she comes," he said, winking.

From out of the black pipe came a globule of hair, which he held aloft for me to see. It was grotesque, the size of a fist. The foul amalgam of all our flicking and preening in front of the mirror. I was as mortified as if I'd just given birth to the thing myself, right there on the bathroom floor. He tossed the hairball into the bucket, replaced the pipe with a few casual twists and stood up. His blue overalls were folded down at the waist, the sleeves knotted at his midriff.

"All yours," he said and began collecting his tools without even looking at me twice or asking about Lauren.

"Thanks very much."

I walked over to the sink but I certainly didn't want to brush my teeth in front of him, let alone urinate. He hummed to himself and emptied out the foul water in the shower stall as if I was invisible, and I realised, with a sickening blow, he didn't remember who I was. No doubt Divines all looked identical to him—Skipper, the Pecks, even Gerry Lake—we might as well have been clones. I had never felt more irrelevant. Miserable, my fingers picked at my old cigarette burn. I could hear some of my peers padding down the corridor, getting dressed or leaving for breakfast. Stuart hooked the bucket over his arm with his plunger in it and raised his chin as a goodbye.

"How's Kyle?" I asked quickly.

What good I thought it would do me, bringing up his girlfriend's baby, I don't know. But that was the best I could come up with. It stopped him in his tracks.

"What? Oh, yes." He pointed his finger at me. "I remember, from the park. You're Lauren's new"—he seemed to struggle to locate the right word—"mate?"

His face flashed with amusement. She was townie and I was Divine.

"Lauren says you work here," I said. "I mean, all the time now."

"Looks like it. My uncle knew someone." Stuart moved the bucket from one hand to the other. "He put in a word for me."

"Wicked," I said.

"Yeah, wicked." He raised both eyebrows.

Why couldn't I ever seem to speak normally to him?

"I mean, that's great."

As he gripped the bucket his biceps twitched.

"The money's all right," he conceded.

Outside on the lawn two men in blue were stacking chairs ready to be transported into the hall for the start of our exams.

"I better go and lend a hand."

"Of course."

There were rules, I suppose, about him fraternising with the Divine. Probably he wasn't meant to even be in the girls' shower on his own. But Stuart didn't move. He leant a hip against the shower tiles.

"What's your name again?"

"Joe," I said, and then corrected myself. "I mean, Josephine."

It sounded less Divine.

"Jo-sephine," he repeated; I could have listened to him say my name, separating the two halves out like that, all day.

"All right, Josephine, I hope you're not getting my sister into any kind of . . . trouble."

Again, the knowing smile that kicked up the corner of his lip. He rubbed his mouth with the heel of his wrist. I realised the view he had of me was quite different from the reality. He thought *I* was the troublemaker, the leader, the renegade. Lauren the sheep. He winked. I felt my heart clench.

"Um, excuse me" came a haughty voice from the corridor. "You can't be in here."

Skipper. Dressed in only a towel.

How much she had heard I wasn't sure.

Stuart picked up his toolkit, his eyes still on me, barely looking in Skipper's direction. Then came another wink as if we'd shared a private joke.

"Ladies first," he said but she'd already barged past Stuart towards the shower cubicles.

He bowed, exiting like a butler.

"Bye, Stuart," I said.

Skipper whipped the shower curtain shut.

There was only a thin skin of material slung between her naked body and me. I leant against the sink slowly brushing my teeth. Condensation hugged around me, the mirror misting slowly. I thought about Stuart, replaying our conversation. The smile. The wink. I didn't even care that Skipper had interrupted us; in fact, I was pleased. That I was talking to a boy, right there in our school bathroom, I was sure would impress her.

I continued to brush my teeth, waiting for Skipper to finish showering, when, above the hiss of the water, she shouted through the curtain.

"So what the hell were you talking to that pleb for?"

I froze, completely paralysed, my hand gripping my toothbrush.

"*Bye, Stuart,*" she mimicked.

I loathed Skipper in that moment. A girl who not long ago I would have done anything for: crawled over hot coals, lied, stolen, spilled my guts to. I thought about switching on all the cold taps so that scalding water eviscerated her skin. Or scaring her so that she slipped and hit her head. I squeezed the handle of my toothbrush like a switchblade.

"Shut up," I hissed quietly.

Skipper tugged back the curtain, steam billowing out; I could see everything, from her hairless legs to her dripping pubic hair.

"My god, darling," she snorted. "Oh please. A townie?"

23

There was only so long before Gerry Lake would realise that the hairpin, her precious lucky charm, was missing. I had to get it back. Lauren shrugged indifferently the next time I saw her, scrunching up her nose at first as if she couldn't remember what I was talking about.

"Oh my god," I moaned. "You haven't lost it, have you?"

"Chill out," Lauren said. "All that shitty plastic jewellery she's got, she won't even care."

It was true that at first Gerry seemed not to notice. Preparing for some important competition, she seemed even more preoc-cupied with training than normal. I saw very little of her during that period. She frequently arrived late, climbing out of the beige Ford Escort, waving goodbye to the driver in the red cap, often an hour after lights-out because training had run over. Later we questioned if Gerry was even on the ice at all.

A few minutes afterwards our door would open. If I was still up reading, Gerry would frown and say a terse hello, undress, and climb up onto her bunk bed. There she sat at the top of the ladder and began the gruesome ritual of massaging her feet, kneading her heels and ankles with ointment, bending her toes back so they doubled under, tugging on each one in turn, crack-ing them like chicken bones. Gerry's feet, disfigured from years of skating, were increasingly repellent to me. I baulked at the sight of her dry ankles, the ingrown toenails—yellowed and crusta-ceous looking—the blisters and bunions and corns. There were, I remember, small divots on Gerry's fingers from her habit of continually tugging her bootlaces tight, bruises the size of tennis balls on her hips and arms, which Gerry had sustained, or so we speculated, not from an accident but shagging her coach in the back of his Escort.

Once or twice at night I heard Gerry yelp in pain as she was tending to her feet, holding in a sob. Perhaps it wasn't her toes that were the problem; perhaps she had lost, or fallen, or the routine hadn't gone well. Maybe she'd had a fight with her sugar daddy. I didn't want to know. I could have asked Gerry what was the matter, offered her some words of comfort or advice; that would have been the charitable thing to do, I knew. But I was a teenager, self-obsessed, too caught up in my own narrative to care about anyone but myself.

Just a few days before the start of our GCSE examinations, when I had almost forgotten about the hairpin, Gerry Lake's step-mother put an end to the weeknight training. My first thought was that Daphne Lake must have caught wind of Gerry's infatuation with her coach and was trying to avert disaster. Or maybe it was our looming exams she was concerned about. Either way, Miss Graves appeared in our dorm one evening to announce the news.

"Just a temporary measure, dear," Miss Graves assured Gerry.

Gerry made a hissing noise, kicked back her chair, bulldozing past Miss Graves to call her parents. Those of us on the landing could hear, two floors away, the insults Gerry hurled down the phone at Daphne Lake—*vindictive bitch, jealous cow, evil twat*—before she demanded to speak to her father. When neither of her parents would capitulate, Gerry let out a high-pitched scream and (a fact people later dwelled on) publicly threatened to run away or throw herself out of a window.

"If only." Skipper rolled her eyes and returned to her dorm.

*The next three weeks Gerry was unbearable to be around. Sul*len, vicious, easily provoked. I sat hunched over a mountain of study notes while around me Gerry slammed cupboard doors, kicked shoes across the room, and tore sheets from her notebook, penning vitriolic letters home, the nib of her fountain pen scratching furiously across the page. When I asked her to please keep it down, she turned around and scowled, eyes cut to slits.

"Go fuck your mum."

By mid-June our exams were over. Gerry was allowed back on the ice. As tradition dictated, the entire year—all but Gerry Lake—gathered in bare feet in the Circle that day, our brown leather lace-ups knotted together and strung from our fingers. Skipper, the first to go, ran forward towards the shoe tree, her arm thrust behind her like a javelin thrower, tossing her shoes up into the weeping cedar. We whooped and cheered. Next Skipper called on Kwamboka, who tiptoed across the grass, jerked her arm, a tentative underarm throw into the lower branches. We applauded and she flitted back to the sideline. There was a great surge, a wave of blue as we all sprinted towards the tree. Euphoric, unshackled from textbooks and exams, we hurled our shoes up into the branches, side by side with the shoes of our mothers and grandmothers and great-grandmothers. We leaped and shrieked and hugged one another. Exhausted, the last shoes thrown, we came to a standstill. Our arms snaked around each other's hips, our heads resting on one another's shoulders, admiring our handiwork.

Then we heard it. A shriek like a scalded cat. Gerry Lake streaked out of our boarding house, her head down, exploding across the grass at Skipper, her leather training bag in her hand.

"Give it me," she yelled.

Skipper raised an eyebrow and looked down at Gerry. Even in bare feet Skipper loomed over her.

Skipper let out a dramatic sigh.

"Oh, for goodness' sake, here we go."

Skipper looked at the twins and rolled her eyes.

"Yes, Geraldine? What now?"

I kept my eyes down on the grass, arms crossed, my fingers picking at my inner arm. I noticed in the car park the beige Ford

Escort waiting to take Gerry to training. A man's arm dangled out of the open window, fingers drumming the side panel.

"Where is it?" Gerry hissed. "Give it me."

"Give it *to* me," Skipper corrected.

"You fucking cow," Gerry spat. "I want it back. *Now*."

Skipper stood looking down at my dorm mate, studying her as you might an animal in a zoo. Despite not having a clue what she was being accused of, Skipper must have seen that she had an opportunity to rile Gerry further. A thin smile was strung across her face. She stood back and gestured at the tree, its branches dripping with our shoes.

"Haven't you forgotten something?"

Gerry's fist bunched, her cat eyes small slits in the bright sun. The grip around the handle of her training bag tightened, strangling the life out of it. She flushed from her neck up to her cheeks, her lips knotting together. It was as if the air around her head was crackling. Recognising the signs of an imminent explosion—the hand on the hip, the sneer, the red cheeks—we watched, curious to see how this would end.

Gerry cast a look over towards the car park.

Then, to our surprise, she bent down and untied her shoes.

Who of us would have guessed Gerry Lake would give in so easily? Perhaps it was because she knew her coach was watching and didn't want to be seen in an unflattering light. Or that she was so desperate by then to return to training, she decided for once not to cause a scene. Or maybe, was it possible, Gerry wanted to be Divine all along?

"Jolly good," Skipper said, masking her amazement with a curt smile.

She stepped aside for Gerry to take her turn.

We quickly realised that despite her skill on the ice, Gerry Lake was a terrible thrower. Her first attempt, a dud, the lace-ups slid off a low drooping branch and fell to the ground in a brown puddle. I giggled with nerves. I wished I could throw them for her so that the whole stupid spectacle could be over. Gerry scowled at me and picked up her shoes for a second try. This time she aimed higher. One of the shoes snagged for a moment, then was pulled loose by its recalcitrant twin, the two shoes tumbling back to earth.

"Rotten luck," Skipper snorted.

Gerry chose a different side and ran a little way back on the concrete circle to gain some height, which must have unbalanced her somehow, because her toss was wildly off, thudding against the trunk. Divines whispered behind hands and sniggered.

I felt Henry Peck come up behind me.

"Oh my god," she said, giggling after Gerry's seventh or eighth attempt. "This is hilarious. Look at her face."

Gerry's cheeks had turned deep purple, her lips nipped together. In her fist was one single shoe, now uncoupled from its pair. Her head was bowed in defeat, and her chest puffed up and down. Despite Gerry's reputation for a quick temper, none of us could honestly say we had ever seen her cry. A hush fell over the group.

"C'est la vie," Skipper yawned, bored with the whole thing.

This time Gerry didn't miss. There was a hollow thud, the sound of a heel striking Skipper's temple, a yelp of pain.

"Fuck the lot of you," Gerry said.

We gasped in awe. Gerry marched across the car park and tossed her bag through the window of the Ford Escort, a final middle finger thrust in our direction.

24

My due date comes and goes and the only place I'm comfortable anymore is the water. I wade around the public pool, trying to avoid the lap swimmers, the neighbourhood kids, splashing and kicking, duck diving to stare at my grotesque belly, the pubic hair blooming from my bikini line like cotton candy. When my phone rings, getting out of the pool is no easy matter.

I lean over my towel, dripping.

Rod.

"Angel," she says. "Any news?"

This is her third call of the week.

"No," I snap, sounding brattish.

I'm exhausted. My back aches, I have shooting pains down one leg and, thanks to a heat wave, spent the last two days napping on the sofa, naked, draped in cold flannels. When I sleep I dream I've giving birth to an animal—something tailed and furry, a rat or a possum—that the midwife swiftly disposes of. Another time the baby slides right out of me in the middle of the supermarket, a red splatter on the floor, a squashed tomato. Mortified, I step neatly over the puddle, pushing the shopping trolley out of the shop as fast as I can before the guards catch me, practically running.

"Darling, did you get my email?" Rod checks.

"What?" I say, struggling to hear over the poolside screams, boys dive-bombing their teenage sisters, the lifeguard's whistle.

"My email," my mother repeats. "About putting the baby's name down."

"Name?"

I move towards the lifeguard tower where it is quieter, and pain fires down my leg like a lightning conductor.

"Fuck," I say, angling the phone away from my head, letting Rod do the speaking.

"I know it's rather early days, but I was talking to Charlie and she was saying that her first grandson had his name down yonks before he was born, so . . ."

None of this makes sense. I've missed half of what she's said.

"Down for what?"

"School, darling. Anyway, I've popped a few prospectuses in the post."

Trying not to overreact, I stare at my stomach, tight and waxy looking, a drum for my baby to pound. I squeeze my inner arm, dig my thumbnail into the scar just below my elbow. Even if Jürgen and I want to educate our child privately—which we don't—how on earth does my mother think we can afford it? She has no idea how much money a sculptor makes, let alone a freelance journalist.

"And don't worry about the fees," Rod says, reading my mind. "I've already set up a trust fund."

There's a second lightning strike down my leg. I gasp. Before I can react, my mother lays down her trump card.

"It's what your father would have wanted. Anyway, I'd better be off. Keep me posted."

By the time Jürgen cycles home at lunchtime to check on me, I'm pacing the apartment, livid, panting so hard he thinks the baby is finally coming.

"My bloody mother," I shout.

I rant and rail. Why would we ever think about sending our child away to a place like that? I remind him of the kind of girls I used to go to school with—supercilious and lazy, lacking any discernible ambition. The unbelievable snobbery, the bitchiness and backstabbing, how we ripped each other to shreds.

"I mean, a trust fund." I shake my head. "Fucking hell. What next, deportment lessons?"

At the mention of money Jürgen looks sheepish. We've already accepted, reluctantly, Rod's offer to pay for half the hospital costs, the portion that our inadequate insurance won't cover.

"Come here," he says, holding his hand out to me, like a jumper he's trying to talk off a bridge. He pulls me against his chest, smooths my hair back from my face, still damp from the pool. I can feel the baby, jammed between us.

"Breathe," Jürgen orders. I rest my ear against his chest. He smells of welding, burnt metal, and bike oil. "Don't worry about this, I'll call your mother."

Our standing joke is that Rod prefers talking to my husband more than her own daughter. He is, after all, easier to get along with. Never flies off the handle, is practical and level-headed and unflappable to the point of annoyance.

"We don't have to give her an answer right now. Let's just keep our options open, all right?" he soothes.

I begin to nod, then . . .

"Wait, what?"

I wriggle free from his chest.

He looks uncharacteristically defensive, avoiding eye contact.

"I'm just saying, who knows how we'll feel in a few years."

"Oh my god," I say, close to crying. Rod has already got to him. "You're such a hypocrite."

"Sephine."

He pauses, staring at the ceiling as he chooses his words. Directly above us I can hear the boys watching a Cubs game, pounding their feet on the floor like barbarians, hollering at the television screen.

"Just listen. When I was a kid I had to ride a bus for an hour and a half down the valley to get to the gymnasium, the secondary school. Most of the boys from my village didn't even graduate. What's so bad about wanting to give my child a decent education? Does that make me a monster?"

"But we agreed," I insist, my voice getting higher and higher.

I can't believe he's really considering accepting Rod's offer. What does it say about the kind of parents we'll make if we can't even agree on something as fundamental as this? My eyes start to burn, red from chlorine, the apartment stifling. The single air conditioner, an overworked and ageing window unit, lets out a death rattle; condensation drips from the grate, a puddle staining the wood like blood.

"Come on, we shouldn't be arguing," Jürgen says, reaching for the bump.

"Don't." I slap his hand aside. "I need some air." I grab my bag, head out of the door.

"*Verdammt*," Jürgen groans. "Sephine."

Outside it's a hundred degrees. I walk into the first place I can think of that's dark and cool—the dive bar on the corner—taking a seat in front of the beer taps. An old man, one of the regulars, sits beneath the television, eating pierogi from the Polish place on the corner, one eye on his dumplings, the other the baseball game. A drunk couple in the corner playing pool are dressed as if they've come from a funeral.

"Club soda, Coke?" the barkeeper asks. He's already dropped a slice of lime in a tall glass.

"Pabst," I say.

The barman's hand hovers over the tap uncertainly, looking at my stomach. My whole body aches, swollen and throbbing. My thighs burn where they meet in the middle, rubbed raw. My nipples ooze. All I want is a cold beer.

I give the barman a stiff, dangerous smile, eyebrows raised, defiant.

He's lucky I don't snatch the American Spirits out of his pocket and smoke one in his face.

"And some peanuts."

"You got it," he says.

I take the beer, ignoring the glass of water he's placed next to it on the counter, and carry it to the back of the room, next to the jukebox. Wriggling free from my sandals, I put my feet up in the booth. My legs stick out along the bench, fat and formless, ankles like badly moulded clay. I'm so tired I feel nauseated.

Resting my head against cracked leather, I immediately regret coming here. I stare up at the tobacco-stained ceiling and wish I was back on my own sofa instead of in a bar. I listen to the cheers of the Cubs game, the smack of pool balls, the drunk woman braying with laughter. Her husband goes to buy the next round, loosening his funeral tie as he walks, and the woman heads over to the jukebox, her black heels clacking on the floor. She casts a look as she passes by my table, then thumbs coins into the slot, standing on one leg as she chooses.

"Good on you, honey," she says when she's done. "I had Jack and Coke the whole way through mine and it never did none of my kids no harm."

I'm feeling too queasy to speak, but she leans against my booth and I can see that I'm stuck with her.

"You look about ready to pop. Boy or girl?" she asks.

"Boy," I say quickly, even though I have no idea. Jürgen made me swear we'd keep it a surprise, shielding his eyes during the ultrasound. The truth is the idea of a girl—a Gerry or a Skipper—horrifies me. I want a boy, a blond-haired, blue-eyed replica of Jürgen.

"You sure about that, hon?" the woman asks doubtfully.

She scans my midriff.

"I got three kids at home and my sister-in-law, she's had four. I'm telling you, I guessed right every time. Scooch on over."

This is what my body has become—public property—something to be stroked and patted and commented on. The waitress in our favourite restaurant, for example, wincing as she speculated about the baby's head size—enormous—or the gallery owner at an opening, a man I know only in passing, who rubbed my stomach like a poodle, squatted down and called into my belly button, *hello there*.

Without waiting for an invitation the drunk woman slips into the booth and begins fingering my ribs. I can smell the whiskey on her breath, see the crow's-feet, cracks plastered over with makeup, a paper tissue tucked down her cleavage.

"Girl," the woman says decisively. "I'm telling you."

I go rigid.

My belly tightens like a vice, the breath squeezed out of me.

"No," I say forcefully, practically shouting, spilling my drink.

She grabs a handful of napkins and tries to pat me dry but I'm already up, charging towards the bathroom. I lock myself in the single cubicle, sitting on the toilet, shaking. There's bloody mucus in my knickers.

"Shit," I gasp.

Knocking.

"Hon, everything okay in there?"

The baby elbows for freedom.

Done hanging around.

Head down, cramped and furious, ready to tear me open.

25

After our exams, I went up to London and didn't see Gerry Lake for another week. Her last as Divine. During that time I was staying with my godmother in Kensington. Each night after supper my godmother and her husband sat in front of the nine o'clock news and I went into their library where I poured myself a glass of sloe gin from a drinks cabinet and called Lauren. When she answered, I could hear her television playing loudly and her mother yelling from the kitchen.

"Who's phoning at this hour?"

"No one, Mum." Lauren pulled the phone into the corridor. "It's for me."

"Nice one, Josephine," Lauren said. "She probably thinks I've got a boyfriend or something."

"Sorry." I giggled. "Will your dad freak out?"

"He's down the pub."

"With your brother?" I asked as casually as I could.

"How the fuck should I know?"

I heard a rustle as she tucked the phone between her chin and shoulder. I pictured her sitting on the stairs, painting her toes.

"Did you get my letter?" I asked, thinking of the long memo I'd written her on *The Times* letterhead.

For one week of the summer term we Fifth Formers had been granted access to the real world, under the guise of work experience. This tradition was something of a misnomer, since the kind of professions we selected—private art galleries, party planning, interior decoration—seemed neither real nor worldly, the offices so plush it was hard to think of it as work. The majority of our placements were sourced by family friends, or well-connected relatives, as well as the small pool of alumni who had gone on to find an actual job. These Divine Old Girls, DOGs as we called them, let us stuff their envelopes and make their coffee and gave a knowing wink as we left at lunchtime to join our friends on the King's Road. For most it was a glorious week of holiday and gadding about Sloane Square. My godmother, on the other hand, knew an editor at *The Times* and had pulled some strings.

"Gosh," said the Pecks in unison when I told them where I was working. "Bad luck."

To my dismay the rest of my friends were all going to work for the same travel company—luxury safaris, Galapagos cruises—that belonged to Skipper's cousin. Despite how they'd been treating me, their cold-shouldering and whispering behind my back, I felt sickened by the thought of them spending the week together without me.

"Where's Wapping?" asked George.

It might as well have been outer Siberia.

Each day I was signed in by a receptionist at News International who gave me a plastic pouch with the word *VISITOR* on a tag that I clipped to my white shirt. I dressed like a middle-aged woman in an expensive Jaeger trouser suit my mother had bought for the occasion. The first morning I had waited for a long time, perhaps an hour or more, before my godmother's friend came out of her meeting and I was summoned into her glass box. She was ferociously intelligent, probably the first truly impressive woman I had ever met. I was utterly out of my depth.

"Tell me about yourself," she said with a smile.

I had never been asked this before. My mind went blank. I had absolutely no idea who I was outside of the Divine. My godmother, I knew, would have bragged about me being gifted. True, I was more academic than most of my peers, top of my year, but that didn't say much; the bar was set low. I had a useful knack for remembering facts by rote, regurgitating quotes from books, which is all that is required to do well in exams, but at the age of sixteen I had never had an independent thought, one that wasn't borrowed from the pages of a set text. Unlike Gerry Lake, I didn't have any real talents or skills. I had taken five years of piano lessons but wasn't a natural musician, I couldn't act or dance or paint, and I had no extracurricular activities to speak of, except, like all Divines, to drink and smoke. My politics, if I even had any, were inherited from my parents.

Perspiring in my suit, I scratched the scar on my forearm through the fabric. I felt the editor scrutinising me, her shoe tapping with impatience as a high heel swung from her other foot. I recited the A-Levels I planned to take next year, a story-writing prize I would be awarded at Speech Day, a recent holiday with my parents in Rome. I saw the editor's interest in me instantly extinguish—I was totally unremarkable. Her eyes slid sideways to her computer.

"Great," she said, barely noticing when I had finished. "Let me know if you need anything."

I never saw her again except for a curt wave through the glass shield of her office as I passed.

"She sounds like a right stuck-up bitch," Lauren yawned. "What else have you been doing?"

"Photocopying, checking facts, stuff like that."

The truth was the newsroom floor was the most thrilling place I had ever been. People moved with urgency between desks, sometimes they even ran; others hunched intently over their computers, like jockeys, fingers galloping on keyboards. Making news. Some of the very same journalists who just two weeks later went on to write about Gerry Lake. Buzzing around the gates, asking Divines questions.

I was in awe of almost everyone I met, particularly the sanguine men at the sports desks who took long boozy lunches and sat for hours, legs spread, gossiping and lobbing balls of paper at metal bins. I began to enjoy the feel of my suit as I walked around, its buttoned crispness that I thought suggested importance, the little pleat in the front of my trousers, which I hung up each night to preserve the fold. Every grown-up I knew back then—my parents and my parents' friends—they all read *The Times*. During my Easter holiday in Hong Kong my mother had bragged shamelessly to her friends at the yacht club about my placement, the strings my godmother had pulled to get me there, but I sat dangling my feet in the pool and shrugged as they congratulated me, sulking because I wasn't working at the travel company with Skipper. But now, describing my week to Lauren, I found myself name-dropping editors I'd met, the morning conference I had attended, the friendly assistant who'd bought me lunch.

"So will your name be in the paper then?" Lauren said, bored.

"No, I mean, it's not like they'd let me have my own byline."

I couldn't stop myself flashing my new vocabulary.

"Oh well, never mind, the money's all right, I bet."

I said nothing. Of course I wasn't getting paid. It was just something to put on my CV. Down the phone line there was a muffled sound as if Lauren was covering the receiver, and I heard the slow thud of a cane as Joan climbed the stairs to bed.

"School night, remember," Joan said. "Don't let your dad catch you up."

"Yeah, all right, night, Mum."

"Night, Loz."

There was silence for a while, and I could hear Lauren breathing, then the headset rustled as she switched it to her other cheek. I steeled myself to ask her about Gerry's hairpin.

"Um," I said, "I just wondered if you'd found that hairpin yet?"

Lauren clicked her tongue, annoyed.

"You're not on about that fucking thing again, are you? Give it a rest."

"Actually, I really . . ." I started to say but Lauren interrupted.

"Coz if you're going to nag me all weekend about that shite bit of plastic, you can forget about coming round mine."

My feet slipped off my godmother's desk. One elbow cracked against the dark oak top, hitting my funny bone. I winced, tears pooled.

"No," I almost shouted. "I mean, it's fine. Forget it."

All I had thought about all week was my night at Lauren's house. We had planned it meticulously: the train tickets, the sleeping arrangements, the lies to my godmother and the school. I knew that Lauren's brother often dropped around unannounced to have tea with Joan and thought there was a good chance of running into him. I had sat at my temporary office desk that week, smoking a pencil, rehearsing witty anecdotes about the world of journalism to tell around the kitchen table, deciding what I'd wear. Now I was in danger of being uninvited. I wished I'd never mentioned Gerry's pin.

"Everything's fine," I reassured Lauren.

"Yeah?"

"Totally."

"Okay, nice one." Lauren sounded excited now. "I'll see you Saturday then?"

"Yes, Saturday."

I took a sip of gin and winced.

"Don't knock, I'll meet you on the corner," Lauren reminded me.

"Brill," I said.

I heard her laugh, one of those strange openmouthed barks she often made whenever I said something Divine.

"Toodlepip," she teased and slammed down the phone.

26

*My train was late. At the station I stood in a long line for a mini-*cab, anxiously counting the number of people ahead of me, looking at my watch. When I got to the end of Lauren's road, I sat on the wall where we'd agreed to meet, hugging my leather overnight bag. I was extremely nervous, I remember, continually flicking my hair, checking my armpits for sweat, sucking on a polo mint so my breath wouldn't smell. It was long past our arranged meeting time and still Lauren wasn't there. I began to panic. What, I wondered, if she had changed her mind at the last minute or her parents had refused to have me in the house?

I waited for another twenty minutes, wringing my hands, and when she still didn't come, I walked a few metres up Lauren's road and loitered outside her house.

All the lights were off.

Next door I saw her neighbour sitting on the doorstep smoking while a toddler circled on a tricycle, ramming it into a line of dustbins, reversing, charging again. The neighbour watched me hovering on the pavement, craning my neck to look up at Lauren's window.

"They're out," she said.

"Oh." I felt my stomach turn.

"You're Lauren's friend, aren't you? The one from the other week."

I nodded. I could barely breathe.

"When will they be home, do you think?"

"Joan's gone to stay with her sister for a bit, that's all I know. They had a right old to-do earlier, her and Kevin."

This was out of the ordinary. I had never known Lauren's mother to leave the house. On a good day she sometimes went into the front garden to smoke, leaning against the wall with a mug of tea. As far as I knew, Lauren did the shopping and picked up her prescriptions. A health worker dropped by every other week.

I moved my Mulberry bag from one hand to the other, on the brink of crying. I had nowhere to sleep. I couldn't go back to school, it was an exeat—one of two weekends per term when Divines were released back into the care of their parents—and nobody except a few lone housemistresses would be there. I had lied to my godmother about returning early for a play rehearsal. It was too late by then to go back to London without it seeming suspicious. I had blown nearly all my allowance on the taxi from the station, I didn't have enough left in my account for a hotel, nor could I have called my parents even if I wanted to, because it was the middle of the night in Hong Kong.

There was a loud boom as the toddler crashed his bike into the bin again and laughed demonically.

"Paul," Sue snapped, "give it a rest will you. You're doing my head in."

"Um, do you know if Lauren went with her mum by any chance?"

"No idea, love, sorry."

"And what about Mr McKibbin, he's not home?"

She rolled her eyes.

"Back down the pub, I should think. Or the bookie's."

"Right," I said, squeezing my arm, trying not to sob.

I was completely clueless about what to do next, where to go, how to fend for myself in the world. I was totally naïve. Terrified to be on my own. I pictured myself wandering the canal all night without Lauren, sleeping on a park bench.

The toddler backpedalled, ready for another charge at the bin.

"You could try her brother," the neighbour suggested, taking pity on me. "Expect Lauren went round there. Like I said, Joan and Kev had a proper barney earlier."

"Her brother. Okay," I said, uncertainly.

This at least was something. But I had no idea where Stuart lived. I lifted my bag over my shoulder, staying where I was.

"Round the corner, love." Sue pointed towards the park.

"They're in one of those new builds on Charlton. Nasty piece of work if you ask me, that Kerry girl. No manners. I don't know why Stuart puts up with it."

I stared in the direction the neighbour was pointing. I didn't have any real sense of the geography of the town, other than marching to the lacrosse field and back.

Suddenly the toddler, cornering too fast on the tricycle, toppled midattack, the bin rolled sideways, split bags of rubbish emptying into the front garden. There was a moment of silence, then an unearthly howl. Sue tugged the boy up by the wrist and dusted him off with angry swipes.

"I told you, didn't I? Look what you've done. Look at that."

Inside the house, a baby started crying.

I hopped over the wall, righted the bin, and began tossing what I could into the container. Above the wails my own voice raised in my panic, becoming higher, more Divine.

"So, it's not far, Stuart's house?"

Sue hoisted the boy onto her hip, his face greased with snot and tears.

"Left after the post office," she snapped. "It's one of the new houses on the right."

"Thanks so much," I said.

"Pauly, put a sock in it, will you," Sue ordered the toddler and carried him inside.

The door slapped shut.

I was on my own.

As I walked towards the housing estate, the weight of my bag seemed heavier than before, cutting into my shoulder; the new shoes I was wearing grated against my heels. When a car slowed to a crawl beside me, the driver rolling down his window—a middle-aged man with a moustache—I let out a yelp of surprise.

"Need a lift, love?" he asked.

I shook my head, walked faster.

"Come on, I won't bite, get in," he said, cajoling.

He patted the seat beside him, a chunky gold bracelet jangling on his wrist.

"No," I said, almost shouting, my voice quavering. "No, thank you."

He looked me up and down, shrugged.

"Suit yourself."

The car rolled away.

I started to run. Through the park, past the post office, pausing for breath only once I'd reached the pub, but as soon as I put my bag down two drunk women came tumbling out of the door, slapping each other, clawing and screaming, careering into a table.

By the time Stuart's girlfriend answered the door I was close to hysteria. Hers was perhaps the third or fourth house I tried. Tiny and very pale with dark eye makeup, she had little black ticks at the corner of each eye, long spiky lashes. Her black hair was pulled back tight. A seam of gold studs ran up her ears.

"Yeah?"

She glared at me. She was wearing a crop top and big baggy trousers with pockets, which hung from angular hips so that I could see the men's jockey shorts she was wearing beneath. Stuart's I supposed. Her stomach was concave, a diamond stud in her belly button. It seemed impossible that a baby could have come out of anyone so petite.

"Sorry, are you Kerry?"

"Who wants to know?"

In my new suit I looked like a social worker. Or a Jehovah.

"I'm a friend of Lauren's."

"Fuck's sake," Kerry said.

She turned and walked along the corridor, leaving me on the doorstep.

"Oy, Lauren," I heard her yell. "Your girlfriend's here."

Kerry turned briefly back to look me up and down.

"The posh one."

Lauren was there. I was faint with relief. I saw Stuart thumping down the steps in bare feet. I smiled, raised a hand hello. Kerry's lips pursed.

"Lauren's taking the piss, Stu," she hissed.

She pointed to my overnight bag.

"What does your sister think this is, a fucking hotel?"

Stuart's thumbs were tucked into the waistband of his football shorts.

"All right, Josephine," he said.

Behind Kerry's back he quirked his eyebrows at me, an amused smile. He thumbed in the direction of the sitting room.

"Lauren's in there."

It didn't matter to me that we were in his girlfriend's house, that she was standing right there between us with her hands on her hips, or that he even had a girlfriend at all. He had smiled when he saw me. I felt like I was levitating.

"In there?" I checked.

Stuart slid past his girlfriend and took the Mulberry bag from me.

"Go on."

Lauren was sitting on the sofa with her knees tucked underneath her, smoking and eating chips. The TV was playing *Stars in Their Eyes*. Her eyes were swollen, porcine looking, her lashes damp. Her thumbnail picked at something in her fist. She barely looked up from the screen.

"Oh, right," she said flatly. "I thought you'd bottled it."

"My train was late. That's all."

Lauren didn't seem to care that I'd been wandering the streets looking for her, that a pervert had tried to lure me into his car, that I'd been caught up in a catfight. She switched the television over to a different channel and then back to the music. She made no indication if she wanted me to stay or go. I'd never seen her like this before. Her thumb picking at the thing in her hand, a fish and chips fork perhaps. She was wearing no makeup, her skin a raw pink colour, pale lashes now virtually invisible. I could see a cold sore on her bottom lip. It was like catching her naked. All her guards were down, none of the familiar bravado there.

"Your neighbour, Sue, she thought you might be here," I said by way of explanation.

"Nosy bitch," Lauren muttered. "Bet she loved sticking her beak in. She told you about my mum leaving then?"

I didn't answer.

"Can't keep her gob shut, that one."

"Are you okay?"

"Yeah, ta." She stubbed out her cigarette and picked at a bag of chips by her side. "Happens all the time. My dad went and blew all our disability again."

"He didn't, like, hit you or Joan or anything then?"

"No." Lauren's head snapped around fast. "Fucking hell, did Sue tell you that?"

I don't know where I got the idea that her father was abusive. Perhaps I made it up. Mr McKibbin was a short and wiry man and something of a drinker, but not a drunk. No more than my parents anyway. Though I remember that there had been one incident; when I was shopping in town, I had seen Lauren's dad coming out of the bookie's and another man catching him on the shoulder by accident as he came through the door. Mr McKibbin's craggy face reddened, and he had sworn, stabbing the stranger once on the chest with his rolled paper. It left me with the impression that he was a volatile man, prone to bouts of unexpected violence.

"No," I said. "I don't know why I said it."

Through the wall we could hear Kerry's shrill voice growing louder and Stuart muttering the odd reply. Lauren rolled her eyes.

"Moody cow," she said.

Then Kerry's feet pounded down the corridor, the door flung open as if she was trying to catch us out.

"You can stay"—she pointed at Lauren—"but your *friend* here's got to go. This isn't a bloody rave."

Alarmed, I looked at Lauren, but she ignored Kerry and tapped another cigarette out of her packet. A slight smile curled at the corner of her mouth fleetingly, then evaporated. I was astonished. Once I had told Lauren how we gave Gerry Lake the silent treatment, acting as if she were invisible, pretending not to hear a word she said—putting her in Coventry as we called it, a speciality of the Divine—and Lauren had scrunched her face and accused us of bullying. But now I could see how much she was enjoying using the tactic on Kerry.

"Lauren, did you hear me or what?" Kerry said.

Stuart's girlfriend walked across and switched off the television. Lauren uncurled her legs and leant along the sofa to offer me a drag from her cigarette.

"Fuck me," she said and gagged. "You smell like shit."

I looked down at my Jaeger suit. It was a Saturday. There wasn't any reason for me to still be wearing a suit but I wanted, I think, to impress Lauren with my new outfit, to give the impression I'd been called away from a pressing task. To show her that I was experienced, that I could negotiate the real world, that I was a professional. Now the suit was wrinkled, there was a dark unidentifiable dribble on my sleeve, which I sniffed, and a smear on the leg.

"Oh my god," I remembered. "Sue's bin fell over."

Lauren grinned.

"Nice one."

I had almost forgotten about Kerry, who was standing in front of the blank television screen, her hands on her bare hips. I could see an angry red line running along her waistband where they'd cut her baby out of her. I wondered where Stuart was.

"Are you two fucking deaf or what?" Kerry said.

Again, the corner of Lauren's mouth twitched.

She offered me a chip from her paper.

"You hungry?" Lauren asked me, continuing the game. "There's probably some scampi in the kitchen."

I didn't know what to say. I was in fact starving. Except for polo mints, I had barely eaten, nervous about the possibility of seeing Stuart. My godmother, thinking I had period pains or was hungover, had even given me a glass of water and some paracetamol the night before and encouraged me to go to bed early.

"Go on, help yourself." Lauren shook her chip bag under my nose.

Kerry's face was frozen in disbelief. Her tiny body stiffened, kohl eyes narrowing into two thick, black lines. I couldn't help but think of Gerry Lake, one hand on her hip, a recalcitrant pout. Standing by the shoe tree Gerry had actually spat with anger; a little froth had come out of her mouth and dangled on a thread down her chin.

I waited to see if Kerry would detonate in the same way.

She made a sucking noise through her front teeth.

"You two think this is funny?"

Lauren stared right through Kerry as if the television was still playing *Stars in Their Eyes* and began to hum . . . *strumming my pain with his fingers*. She chewed noisily on a chip.

"Fugees are right racists," she announced. "You've heard that thing Lauryn Hill said, about she'd rather eat a black baby than a white person bought her record?"

"Totally," I agreed, even though I wasn't sure she'd got the story right exactly.

Lauren started to belt out the song.

That did it. I watched Stuart's girlfriend explode. She smacked the bag of chips out of Lauren's hand. Screamed, kicked the sofa so hard that it shook.

"Get the fuck out of my house. You, too, Hooray Henrietta. Now!"

Lauren laughed loudly, shrugged, and got up slowly, raising her arms above her head. As she stretched I could see the thing in her hand wasn't a chip fork at all. Gerry's hairpin. My mouth opened.

"We didn't want to kip here anyway, you gyppo," Lauren fired at Kerry. "Did we, Josephine? We'd catch something."

Stuart came in and stood on the threshold of the front room looking at his sister and me. His hair was loose, the fringe flopping forward. He ran one hand through it wearily.

"Don't start," Lauren said. She shoved Gerry's pin in her jeans pocket, ducked under his arm and walked out of the house.

"For fuck's sake, Stu. Are you just going to stand there and let your sister speak to me like that?" Kerry demanded.

Stuart didn't have an answer for that. I remember my leather overnight bag was sitting in the corridor and he carried it to the front door for me. He was a gentleman, I could see.

"You'll make sure Lauren gets home, yeah?" he said as he passed the bag, hooking it over my shoulder.

"Okay," I said. I felt my skin tingle where our hands had touched.

"But what about your dad?" I remembered.

"Don't worry about him. I'll sort it."

Lauren, waiting for me on the street, stuck two middle fingers up at Kerry, who was watching from behind the sitting room curtain.

"Give it a rest, Loz," Stuart said, groaning.

Pikey, Lauren mouthed.

Kerry thumped on the window.

"You can talk, you filthy bitch. I know all about you."

"Fuck off."

"*You* fuck off, and take your girlfriend with you."

A skateboarder on the corner ground to a halt, flipping his board upright. A man squinting into his open car bonnet under the last of the day's light lifted his head as Lauren steamed past, a long train of obscenities flowing from her mouth. "Slag, tramp, slut, minger." One or two neighbours came out of their front doors to tut. I chased gracelessly down the road after her in my fitted suit and square wedge heels, my bag thumping my back. Lauren wasn't wearing any bra, I remember, just one of Stuart's old football T-shirts tucked into her jeans. But she didn't care; in fact, I could see she was enjoying it, her breasts jiggling, people staring

and heckling. Two men drinking in picnic chairs beside a barbecue wolf whistled.

When I'd caught up with her, she draped her arm around my
shoulder as if we were Divine, provoking catcalls, one man stamping his boots on the ground with excitement.

"Fancy a threesome, girls?"

"In your dreams," she taunted, "in your dreams."

27

There is nothing divine, I discover, about giving birth. The contractions have barely begun and I puke and shit and swear and am prone to loud, crapulous fits of belching, which I direct at the boys in the flat above. When the real pains start, I lurch around the apartment like a belligerent wino looking for a fight. I rant and rage and drip blood.

Jürgen ushers me through the early stages of labour as best he can. We don't mention the fight, that I staggered home clutching my stomach, reeking of beer and peanuts, my trousers sodden. He rubs my shoulders and feeds me a bowl of pasta, and when I am on my knees, cursing and rocking and weeping, he slides aside the furniture as you would for an epileptic to stop them hurting themselves. When the time comes, he drives me to the hospital, bringing with us a copy of our birthing plan, which he hands to a nurse on duty. In this document we have stressed the importance to us of going natural. Old school. This was the way our mothers did it.

The midwife, on being handed this birthing plan, makes a cursory glance at the header that reads, "PLEASE do NOT offer me any pain medication," and gives me what I take to be a withering look. Clearly she doesn't think I am up to it.

"Don't let that bitch anywhere near me," I hiss to Jürgen.

I am convinced that the whole floor is out to get me. I'm being punished. They put us in a darkened room where I pace in circles for hours, I lose all sense of time, demented, howling in unimaginable agony, speaking gibberish. Eventually, when I am still not dilating, Jürgen leads me out into the corridor where I grip a handrail and stagger up and down like an agoraphobe, gasping in horror whenever a contraction comes on. I am going to die. I actually believe this. When I see an empty trolley in the corridor, I am overcome by an urge to ask for forgiveness, to unburden myself. I cling to Jürgen, sobbing.

"I'm sorry," I say. "I'm sorry."

He strokes my hair.

"For what?"

And then, just like that, I can't bear to be touched by him. The nurse is right, I don't have it in me to endure this much pain. Am I crazy? I summon back the obstetrician.

"I change my mind, I want the drugs," I say.

She looks at Jürgen.

"Don't fucking look at him." I snatch her wrist. "I want the epidural."

Jürgen, who hasn't slept in nearly a day and a half, nods, and when the anaesthetist arrives, my husband backs out of the room guiltily, in search of something to eat. I doze for a while in pain-free serenity, and when the time comes I push and pant and perform all the tricks our birthing instructor has taught us.

"How now brown cow," I say.

The words come out of nowhere.

"What?" Jürgen's brow creases.

"How. Now. Brown. Cow." I groan.

The doctor lifts her head up from between my thighs.

"That's a new one on me," she says with a smile. "Okay, I'm going to give you a little cut to help things along."

I clench my jaw as if I am trying to shit.

"How now brown cow. How now brown cow. How now brown cow. How now brown cow."

One small flick of the doctor's knife, one big push, and it's over.

A harpy's wail and . . .

"Baby girl," the doctor announces.

A team of nurses move into action, bustling around the

room, weighing and measuring, then they deposit the baby on my chest.

"Girl," I repeat, dazed.

I look down at my daughter.

Purple faced, fists like a boxer, head thrust back, screaming bloody murder.

28

That night Lauren dragged me around the town for a long time, furious, looking for trouble. When she got to the rec grounds the gates were locked, and Lauren shook the chain and kicked the wall and for a moment I thought she might start to cry again, or even hit me.

"Let's just go back to yours," I said.

"Yeah, all right."

But before we got to her road, Lauren took a sudden left turn up a mud track towards my school sports fields, towing me after her. I was hobbling in my new wedge heels to keep up, my bag banging against my thigh.

"I thought we were going home."

"Shortcut."

"I'm really hungry," I moaned.

"Don't be a pussy," she said.

She swung a leg over the five-bar fence with the Private Property notice bearing our school crest and ran off into the dark.

"Lauren, wait."

I tossed my bag over, tugged up the legs of my suit, and, after hesitating for a moment, followed her.

The lacrosse fields, I remember, had been mown and rolled and lined into an athletics track ready for Sports Day by Stuart and the other maintenance men. There was a chalky white triangle marked on the ground for throwing shot put and an area we used for the long jump where Lauren now stood in the moonlight, kicking the sand with her jeans rolled up, like she was at the beach. I wanted to ask for Gerry's pin back. Instead I stooped to pick up one of the grey balls, tucked it under my chin, turned, and swung. Such was my upper body strength back then it thudded a few pathetic metres into the dark.

"Nice one," Lauren snorted.

Divines were famous for their athletic underachievement, consistently bottom of every interschool competition. Other, more accomplished schools—Ascot or Calne or Cheltenham Ladies' College—actually cheered when they saw our blue bus rattling up their leafy drives. We simply didn't take competition seriously or have the focus or determination required to foster a sense of rivalry. During the annual cross-country race we set off at a sprint, then slowed to a trot once we were out of sight, clambering through the hedge looking for places we could smoke. Henry Peck, it was true, had been a first-rate tennis player. She could hold her own at a county level. But after the Moose relocated to Brunei, she spent less time on court. When he stopped replying to her letters that term, her serve grew sloppier, she barely made any effort to run for the ball, and her returns limped over the net. Out of sympathy we had stopped using the word *moose*.

"This is shit," Lauren said. "Come on."

She stepped over a wooden stile, onto the public footpath. In a paddock two horses stood under a tree, nose to flank. Their shadows stretched, stilt legged, across the path. One was a thoroughbred, the other a smaller pony. Lauren climbed up on the fence near a streetlamp, studying them, her jaw set hard. She lit up a cigarette. The pony flicked its ears, interested, watching the flame. I rested my arms on the top rung, wondering what Lauren was up to. I didn't like the way she was staring at the animals, chewing her lip, her shoulders hunched. It occurred to me that she might try to hurt them in some way. I thought of the time she'd melted the school sign with her lighter, watching it blister and burn.

"I'm actually pretty tired," I said. "Let's go back."

"In a bit," she hushed me and made a clicking noise with her tongue.

"Here, boy."

The pony came first, docile looking and round as a barrel. She flattened her hand and it took nips of her empty palm. Disappointed, it plodded over to me and tried the same trick, nudging my arm and leaving a trail of green saliva on my shoulder. I pulled a clump of long grass from the path and fed it that.

"Seriously, Lauren," I tried again. "I'm starving."

My voice kicked up high.

"Seriously?" Lauren mimicked, using one of her voices.

She slid off the fence and walked over to the gate where two headcollars were hooked over a fence post.

"Lauren, what are you doing?" I hissed.

She took one headcollar in her hand, swung it in a circle like a hammer thrower, then launched it into the bushes. Then she did the same with the second, startling the horses.

"Ha ha," she sniggered.

The large mare leaped forward from the shadows, her tail held high, then came to a sudden stop, ears upright. I still had no idea what Lauren was doing. She had told me her father had connections from his racing days and that on the side he sometimes worked with yearlings and horses with bad habits, training them for their owners. Maybe the expensive-looking horse was one of these and Lauren was trying to punish her father. Or maybe it was any old horse, I couldn't say; a meaningless act of vandalism wouldn't have been out of character for Lauren. Something completely pointless.

"Very funny, Loz," I said. "I'm bored. Can we please go?"

She looked at me, her arms crossed defensively, chewing on her lip.

"Sorry. I thought you were well into horses and that," she said. "That photo in your room."

It dawned on me then that the whole moment—bringing me to the paddock, showing me the thoroughbred, hiding the headcollars—was all for my benefit. The idea that Lauren might want to impress me as much as I did her had never occurred to me until then. Realising this, I forgave her everything.

"I am. I love to ride."

I walked right into it. Lauren's expression instantly changed, her pout was gone, she grinned at me.

"Well, what are you waiting for then?"

Confused, I looked at the pony. It was grazing calmly by then, taking small steps, nibbling the ground.

"No, you twat." She pointed at the thoroughbred. "That one."

"No way," I spluttered.

"Why not?"

I giggled with nerves. The horse was over fifteen hands, we didn't know anything about it, there was no tack. She couldn't honestly expect me to ride it—I could break my neck. Lauren continued to stare at me, a silent challenge, her head tilted to the side, her thumbs hooked in her waistline. Our whole friendship seemed to hang on this one idiotic act.

"Okay." I gave in. "Fine."

I put down my bag, climbed over the fence, and began walking towards the trough where the mare was drinking. She eyed me with suspicion, water dripping from her bristled chin, the whites of her eyes rolling. I remembered the polo mints I had in my pocket and held a few in my palm, making a kissing noise. The mare hesitated, then craned forward, neck stretched.

"Not so fast," I said.

I made her come to me, then I uncurled my fist and fed her one. After that I stroked down her neck and leant my weight against her shoulder, like the boys at our school discos. She sidestepped two or three paces, close enough to the water trough that I thought I might be able to use it as a mounting block. I fed her a second mint.

"Good girl," I said.

I took a fist of mane, stepped on the trough and slowly, bit by bit, winched myself upwards, gradually putting more weight on her back. She pirouetted, her rump swung suddenly around but by then I was already on.

"All right, all right, all right," I shushed.

She gave a small jolt, as if electrocuted. I twisted my fingers into her mane. As her hindquarters went up a second time my pubic bone slammed down into the withers, ramming the hard rocky ridge at the base of her mane. I gasped and slid heavily to one side.

"Jesus," I heard Lauren shout. "Watch yourself."

The mare began to reverse like a dumper truck, fast, tail tucked under. I could feel my chest tightening, a dull white hiss in my ears. At any moment she could throw me off, snap my bones on the hard ground, trample me underfoot. I began to talk to the horse, whispering up her neck, telling her how beautiful she was, what a good job she was doing. *Please, please, please,* I begged. All of a sudden the mare stopped crab-stepping and bucking and stood there listening to me. Her ears, which had been pinned tightly against her head, started to flicker as she relaxed. She let out one last, disgruntled snort and the fight was over. I couldn't believe it, I'd done it. My fingers, knotted with fright, began to come back to life. The ringing in my head quieted. I started to laugh, a form of nervous hysteria, and I looked over at Lauren, who was grinning back, hands clapping.

"Fuck me, Josephine. I thought you were a goner," she shouted, impressed.

"Me too."

"My turn," Lauren said and she marched towards me where the pony was chomping long grass around the trough. Before the pony knew what had happened, Lauren had vaulted up off the ground and swung a leg over its back. Her feet dangled ridiculously either side of his wide, barrelled stomach.

"Giddy-up," she ordered. "Go."

The pony dug its heels in and refused to move.

"It won't fucking budge."

"You have to show it who's boss," I said.

Something came over me. Without warning I leant down and gave her pony a sharp smack in the hindquarters. It lurched forward in surprise, charging off across the moonlit paddock. Lauren wobbled on top, her long legs flapping, joggling up and down. I remember her long pale hair fluttering against her back and the sound of her laughing hysterically as she was bouncing up and down. Braless, her breasts jiggled under her football shirt. All at once the pony must have decided enough was enough and came to a standstill, then dropped a shoulder, switching directions. The pony went one way, Lauren went the other. She slammed onto the grass, rolling a few times.

"Ow," she screamed.

"Oh my god," I yelled, sliding off the thoroughbred. "Are you all right? Don't move!"

I ran to her, stroking the hair out of her eyes, cleaning grass from her mouth.

"Tell me where it hurts." I looked for blood. "Is anything broken?" I shouted.

"Yes," she said and let out a long moan.

I felt sick. I'd done this. This was my fault.

"My bum," she said, "I think I've broken my bloody bum."

Then she rolled on her side clutching her bottom, laughing so hard she couldn't speak.

"Oh my god, you bitch," I screamed. "I thought you were really hurt."

Lauren howled even louder.

"Seriously," she gasped, struggling for breath. "You're going to have to get me up."

I held out a hand and helped her hobble towards the gate, where she lay on her stomach still laughing. We chain-smoked one cigarette after another, bragging about what we'd just done. I remembered that I had taken a bottle from my godmother's house and pulled it out of my bag.

"What *is* this?" Lauren peered at the handwritten label.

"Sloe gin."

She took a sip and gagged.

"Tastes like cough syrup to me."

"It's medicinal."

She downed the cup I poured. I yawned, got up, dusting down my suit that was probably ruined, a fact I'd have to explain to my mother. I had two mints left in the roll in my pocket. I lined them up on the fence for the horses to find later. I helped Lauren to her feet, hoisted my bag over her shoulder and offered her my arm to hold. She leant in close to me.

"You're a right nutjob, you know that?" she said.

She made a pincer with her middle and thumb, sent her cigarette butt arching over the fence.

"Nutter," she shouted.

The horses were asleep. They snorted, shook their heads, then dozed back into standing slumber. We hobbled back to Lauren's house, arms around each other, drunk and giggling.

29

Thanks to the number of times we changed dorms—a carousel of rooms and beds and bodies—Divines could sleep anywhere. On our desks, in chapel, through exams and plays and public lectures. But that night, while Lauren snored, I lay awake and stared at the old football stickers and Cabbage Patch cards stuck to the wall. Above me Lauren's arm dangled down from the top bunk like a vine. My stomach made a series of whining and gurgling noises, akin to a draining sink, and I crawled out of the lower bunk, which had once belonged to Stuart.

"Lauren," I hissed.

I stood waiting for her to move, shoving the bed so that her arm swayed, but she grunted incoherently, rolled over, went back to sleep facing the wall. Her jeans were lying in a puddle on the floor where she'd shed them before crawling into bed. Silently I patted the pockets for Gerry's pin but it wasn't there.

I rattled the bed again.

"Lauren, I'm really hungry," I pleaded.

No answer.

I made my way gingerly down the stairs, pausing on the bottom step to check there wasn't anyone home. Joan was staying with her sister after the fight, but who knew about Mr McKibbin. I had a Hadean view of Lauren's father. Sullen and inhospitable, he had spoken to me in words of one syllable the few times I had run into him, sometimes just a nod as I came through the front door, flashing the white scar under his chin. I was rather scared of him.

"Hello," I called out, even though it was the middle of the night.

There was nothing but the sound of a clock from the sitting room ticking. Along the wall running down the stairs were pictures of racehorses and a clip frame of McKibbin family photos. I spent some time examining each of them, picking out Stuart's face as an adolescent, buried up to his neck in sand, holding a football trophy or one from when he was four or five, all ears and teeth.

I padded into the kitchen where I unearthed a loaf of Mighty White from a bread bin and chewed two whole slices at once, balling them into my mouth. Then I stood at the fridge and found some Hellmann's and individually wrapped squares of cheese and a jar of strawberry jam and I shook the pink jam on top of the mayo and flattened the cheese right on top of that, which as a combination tasted surprisingly good I remember. At that age I was perpetually hungry, oblivious to calories or fat, desperately trying to grow some hips.

The clock blinked two twenty-one.

Carrying a second sandwich on my palm, I went in search of more photos of Stuart. Hidden in this house where he had grown up were small clues to imbibe, something that would help me unlock him. In reality I expect he wasn't a particularly complex individual—I don't know what secrets I imagined he had hidden—but I wanted to know everything about him. Even though he had a girlfriend and they lived together and that girlfriend had a child, Kyle, who wasn't his, but still, one could argue that he was a parent. Despite all of that, I had decided that the two of us were destined to be together. This was the first genuine crush I had ever had. I had been pawed during school balls, boys cupping my buttocks as we swayed through the slow numbers. And for a short period I was pen pals with an Etonian—the son of my father's oldest friend—until our parents insisted we get Scottish dancing lessons together one Christmas. Humphrey's hands were small and clammy, his breath rank, and he dressed, to my horror, in a velvet waistcoat and tartan trousers; we skipped to "The Dashing White Sergeant." I never wrote to him again.

Compared to these boys Stuart was an Adonis—superhuman, a colossus carved from stone. I was obsessed.

I elbowed open the door of what they called their front room, which was extremely neat, barely used since Joan and Lauren watched television in the kitchen and Mr McKibbin was always at the pub. According to Lauren, the only person to go in there was her brother after he'd had a fight with his girlfriend and needed somewhere to sleep. For that reason I felt like this room belonged to Stuart. There was the floral sofa with white lace doilies on each arm and embroidered cushions where I imagined he laid his head. Light cut through from the streetlamp outside and I lifted the cushion to look for a strand of his hair or some other sign of him being there. I may, I think, have even sniffed it. Hugging the cushion under one arm, I walked around in the dark, squinting at the nest of three lacquered tables decorated with roses, and an anniversary clock under a glass jar with little balls swinging hypnotically, glinting in the yellow streetlight. Opposite the door was a dresser on which various china ornaments were arranged, mostly animals, mice and hedgehogs, and one blue Dutch-looking milkmaid, though the majority were horses. I weighed a Shire in my hands and stroked his glazed tail, licking my fingers free of jam and mayo before I did so. On the top shelf were racing trophies and faded rosettes, which didn't interest me much since they were Mr McKibbin's, but when I opened the bottom cupboard I hit the jackpot. Three or four shoeboxes at least, full of yellow Kodak envelopes. Here, surely, was everything I needed to know about Stuart.

As I thumbed open the first packet I left a greasy print on the top photo.

"Oh shit."

I wiped my palm on my bare leg.

"Naughty, naughty, Goldilocks," a voice said in the darkness.

I screamed. My arm jerked in fright, photos fanning to the floor like playing cards.

30

We name our daughter after Jürgen's grandmother. It is not my first or even my second choice. But a week goes by without deciding, then another, and another, and a baby can only go nameless for so long. What I would give to be like Skipper who, at age thirteen, kept a list at the back of her diary: two pencilled columns, boys and girls.

From the minute we bring our daughter home everyone comments on how alike she and I look: our paediatrician, our friends, our landlord even, a chain-smoking Armenian man who holds her under one arm like a loaf of matnakash, looking at me and then the baby, wiggling his finger between us.

"Same, same," he says.

I nod, even though I have no idea what he's talking about. The baby looks like a baby. Still, Jürgen hangs over the Moses basket, examining our daughter's physiognomy, trying to identify a piece of himself amongst my genetics.

"Fine, Magdalena," I surrender, feeling sorry for him. "Let's call her that."

His face lights up.

"Really?"

It could be worse. There are women in his family called Gerwalta and Valborga and Edeltraud.

"Hallo, Magda," he tests. "Maggie, Maggie, Maggie."

"Lena," I say, watching the way her minute bird mouth opens and shuts, her tongue flicking. Hungry. A furious red-faced scowl not unlike Gerry Lake.

"*Ja,*" Jürgen says. "Lena."

We are moving again. This time to Los Angeles where Jürgen has been offered free studio space and a teaching job. But instead of packing for California, I sit amongst cardboard boxes in the living room, unable to begin. I pick up one of Lena's blankets, stare at it, then put it down again. For once she isn't howling. She's passed out on her back, arms splayed like a drunk, eyelashes twitching. I should make the most of this lull in the storm—shower, brush my teeth, make supper—but that would require me to get up off the floor. I sit and stare at the front door, trying to remember where Jürgen has gone. The hardware store, the bank, the studio? He told me and I've forgotten, have no idea. I picture Jürgen breezing out of the apartment earlier, whistling as if it was nothing, jingling his keys. How I had the overwhelming urge to dive for his ankles, to knock my husband to the floor, fell him like a tree.

My phone vibrates. A message.

Long line. Sorry. How's the packing?

I get up and hurry into the bedroom throwing clothes into cases without even taking them off their hangers, empty our shoe rack, tip out drawers of underwear. Next I make a pile of toys, presents from my mother that Lena's clearly too young to play with. A felt shopping basket filled with pretend food, knitted radishes and tomatoes, a cardboard can of baked beans. WARNING, the label reads. For play purposes only, no real food inside. Shit. I remember the fridge is empty; I've forgotten to buy anything for supper.

I text Jürgen, but by then the baby is already awake. Affronted to find herself alone on the floor, she lets out a series of earsplitting wails. I rush into the room, bra unclipped, and offer her my breast like a courtier. As she sucks on my nipple her small, sharp fingernails dig into my skin. She drains one side, then the other, pushing me away when she's done. I change her and put her in the middle of the bed while I finish packing up the bedroom. On the top shelf of the cupboard, shoved all the way to the back, the cash box. I take it down, holding it delicately by the handle as if it's dangerous, Medusa's head.

I rest it on the bed, next to Lena.

The baby. The box.

We really don't have time for this now. I should be packing or entertaining my daughter. Anything but opening the lid. Lena, bored already, starts to whimper. I make faces to stop her frowning, blow a raspberry on her belly. But the truth is Jürgen's the one who sings as he changes a nappy, *alle meine Entchen*, making duckling sounds, flapping his wings. I can barely summon the energy for a peekaboo. Lena's fists tighten, her face scrunches, angrier by the second.

"What do you want?" I ask her. "Seriously, what?"

She's fed and dry, my tits are empty, I have nothing left to give. My daughter flails her arms and legs. She makes a noise I've never heard before, a little growl, in the back of her throat. Like a wolf pup.

"Fine," I say.

I open the box.

Holding up a copy of the school magazine, I begin to announce, in alphabetical order, the list of prizewinners of 1996. Lena stops wriggling, listens, surprisingly attentive. Next I read aloud the headmistress's report, chapel notes, and a poem by a First Year entitled "The Lonely Tramp." Lena gurgles with pleasure. A bedtime story. I turn the page. Lacrosse results, Duke of Edinburgh Awards, an account of a Fourth Year geography field trip to Swanage. And there, I turn the page, a picture of Gerry, the same one they later replicated in all the papers. Chin high, shoulders thrust back, holding up a gold medal. Beneath, a description of her performance. My daughter rubs her eyes. I yawn and curl up next to her on the bed and keep reading. Quieter and more softly, until I'm nothing but a whisper. My arm wilting, the magazine slowly fluttering to the bed.

The front door slams. Lena is howling, her nappy sodden. I must have been asleep. Jürgen stands in the corridor, peering into the bedroom. He sees my waxy pale face, the baby crying, thrashing her arms, perilously close to the end of the bed.

"Sephine, are you sick?"

He scoops Lena up, pressing her to his chest, rushes to check my forehead for a fever. Then he sees the box, open, the pile of letters and a year photo. Confused, he picks up the magazine and looks at the cover.

"St John?" His face tilts to one side. "Sephine?"

Blinking, still half asleep, I shrug defensively, like an alcoholic caught with a bottle.

"But I don't get it. This place. You hated it. Why do you still have all this stuff? You're obsessed."

"I'm not obsessed," I say, defensively. "I was just . . ."

Unable to explain myself, I scratch at my inner arm, just below the elbow crease.

Jürgen sits down on the bed next to me, trying to understand.

"They were awful, right? Those girls. Why keep digging it up? It's not healthy."

He gazes at the state of the bedroom—the unpacked boxes, the curdled milk bottles on the side, the dirty breast pump left out since the morning, the bucket overflowing with nappies.

What am I supposed to tell him? That, since becoming a mother, I exist in a state of perpetual unease. That the world seems to me overwhelmingly dangerous and chaotic. How of all the multitudinous threats posed to him and the baby— earthquakes, rising sea levels, drunk drivers, melanomas, pandemics, zealots with semiautomatics—it's something else I'm most afraid of. The past, slowly coiling around us, the snake in the crib.

"No more, okay?" he says and flips shut the lid of the box. "Enough."

"I was just clearing it out," I lie. "It's going in the bin."

"Good," he says.

He tugs me towards him, swaying side to side to stop the baby crying, making the clicking noise with his tongue that Lena likes.

"Promise?"

"Promise."

31

Naughty, naughty, Goldilocks.

Stuart McKibbin was sitting out of sight, hidden behind the open door.

"Oh my god," I said, tugging down on my nightgown, paralysed with embarrassment. "I'm so sorry, I was just . . ."

I remembered how I'd sniffed the cushion and wanted to die.

"Yes?" Stuart asked and raised both eyebrows. The way he spoke, I remember, was very cold, almost mechanical. His head was tilted to one side, his hair falling in a smooth curtain, his jaw set hard, a dangerous expression on his face, arms crossed. He was a townie. I was Divine.

My heart was pounding. I could barely breathe. He leant back, nodding, waiting for me to explain myself.

"Go on. I'm listening. You were just . . ."

"I . . ."

Then with a loud explosion of laughter, rocking forward and back, he slapped the side of the sofa he was sitting on.

"Ha, ha, ha! Loz said you were an easy touch. Jesus, look at the face on you. I'm just winding you up."

I exhaled, my heart still thumping. My body went slack with relief, arms dropping to my sides like a puppet. Stuart wiped his eyes, still hooting.

"Fuck me," he chuckled, patting his pockets clumsily as if he was looking for something, and took out a pouch of tobacco and some papers and held them up. I saw now there was a beer can between his thighs, another couple of empties on the floor.

"You want one?"

I couldn't speak.

There was a click and a hiss as he opened the can. He slid over to make space on the sofa beside him and rolled a cigarette.

"Come on, Goldilocks. Don't get the hump. Sit down."

Stuart thrust his hips upwards to raise his bottom and fished a Zippo from his back pocket. He lit one cigarette and passed it to me, and then rolled another for himself, spilling tobacco everywhere, brushing down his thigh afterwards. I sat on the sofa, pulling my nightie down over my knees.

"Good one," Stuart said as he chuckled, elbowing me. "I had you there."

Stuart's breath smelt of lager. I realised he was incredibly drunk. Probably he'd been down the pub with his friends and come back to Joan's to sleep it off. Or maybe he'd been waiting up for his father, standing guard, protecting Lauren and me. When he inhaled, I stole a look at the small indent in his top lip, the slope of his nose, the way his hair fell forward from behind his ears, the shaved undercut.

"Nice pyjamas," Stuart said.

I felt naked. Poking out from under the hem of my Garfield nightie, my legs looked pale and veined, shapeless as garden canes. To my horror I noticed my nipples needled through the thin T-shirt material. I crossed one arm across my breasts. I was so flat-chested I doubt Stuart even noticed. He had closed his eyes and was rubbing his face. I wondered what he was thinking about. Perhaps he was worried about his parents, or he had another fight with Kerry? Or maybe he was just drunk and tired and he wasn't thinking of anything. All he wanted was his sofa to sleep on.

I took a drag on my cigarette but all I sucked was air. It had gone out. Stuart fished his Zippo out of his pocket again and sparked the flame. Then he smoothed his hair behind his ears and tilted back on the sofa as if to size me up.

"Couldn't sleep then?" he asked.

I shook my head.

"So what trouble did you and my sister get into tonight?" he probed.

"Nothing," I said, inhaling quickly.

Stuart's eyebrows climbed up his forehead.

"Bollocks. Come on, I won't blab," he said and tapped his nose. "Mum's the word."

There was something confessional about the dark room with the yellow streetlight coming through the net curtains. Like being in church. I could tell him anything, I felt.

"We rode horses."

"What horses?"

"I'm not sure, just a horse in a field."

"Lauren dared you to ride it, did she?"

I nodded.

"Jesus," Stuart snorted. "My sister."

He cracked open another can of beer. One unsteady finger waggled in the air as he spoke.

"She's always had her own way that one. Don't let Loz push you around. You stand up for yourself, Josephine, yeah. Wear the trousers as they say."

He patted me on the leg as if I was a puppy. I realised now that was how he had really thought of me all along, Lauren's little pet, a pathetic playfellow that followed her around. A toy. I sat there next to him, chewing on my lip unhappily.

"Come on, I was only teasing." He reached over and gave me another nudge with his arm. "You've got to take a bit of rough with the smooth with us McKibbins. Don't look like that."

He put his arm around my shoulder and pulled me in towards his chest, patting my shoulder a few times. When I closed my eyes, I could smell the pub on him, the smoke and the beer and the musty smell of aftershave. Even though he was very drunk, I let myself imagine that he was my boyfriend. His palm was rubbing me gently on the back, in smooth circular motions. I pressed slowly into him and he continued to rub me. My head was nestled under his chin. I lay it against his chest. Gaining confidence, I took the beer out from between his thighs and took a sip, lifting my chin so our faces were just a few inches apart.

I can see now the kind of impression I must have made. The neckline of my nightie had slipped so that one shoulder was showing. My face—coy looking, tilted to one side—staring up at him through long lashes. The rim of the beer can pressed suggestively against my bottom lip. Working at the school Stuart must have been told stories by the other maintenance men, heard the foulmouthed way we discussed boys, endured our wolf whistles and heckles.

My fingers were trembling, my heart thumping so loudly I thought he must be able to hear it. I inched closer to muffle the sound.

Stuart's hands stopped rubbing. He cleared his throat.

"You're Lauren's . . ." he started to say.

"It's fine," I whispered.

"Yeah?" Stuart said, surprised, tilting his head.

He studied me for a moment, uncertain. I reached out and put my hand on his cheek, our lips pressed together, and all of a sudden he moved very fast, tugging his belt, hitching his hips so he could pull down his trousers. He flopped back on the sofa, his gaze resting on the patch of light on the ceiling as if he expected me to know what to do next.

I was clueless of course.

Despite our promiscuous reputations I knew next to nothing about my own body. For a long time the only way I knew I had a clitoris was sliding down a gymnastic rope.

Stuart's eyes fluttered open.

"Here," he said in a strange, rasping voice. He took my hand and moved it onto the bulge in his boxer shorts. His other hand came to rest in an encouraging way on the top of my head, like the blessings that Padre offered during Holy Communion. I bowed forward, parted my lips. My mouth was so wide I thought my jaw might split.

"Christ," Stuart muttered with pleasure, pushing me deeper.

When I gagged and pulled away, my front teeth grazed over his skin. Stuart groaned. I sat up, terrified I'd hurt him.

"What? You hear someone?" Stuart looked panicked for a moment. Perhaps he thought it was Kerry, lurking in the shadows. The last thing I wanted was for him to think of his girlfriend.

"No," I said quickly. "Sorry, there's no one."

"Well then," he said, and he lay back on the sofa and opened his arms and patted his chest. "Get over here."

I climbed in next to him, my head beneath his armpit, my feet reaching to his ankles.

"You're a sly one, aren't you? It's always the quiet ones you've got to watch," he said, and he slid a hand up inside my nightie.

His thumb made clumsy circles around my left nipple then the right. How rigid I must have seemed to him, a plank, the rough surface of his thumb sanding my breasts. He tugged my knickers, pushing them below my knees with his foot and pinged them onto the floor. I could see the white school nametape sticking out of my underwear in blue letters. He rolled on top of me, his elbows either side of my head, and he snaked down the sofa so that his head was between my thighs. I was horrified. I hadn't taken a shower since early the previous morning. I could only imagine how terrible it smelt down there, so close to where I did my business. He parted my pubic hair and tongued me a few times, bottom to top. At the top of each one he glanced up at me. He reminded me of a cat cleaning itself. Very pleased with itself. I could barely look at him I was so embarrassed.

"Relax," he said. "No one's there."

I let my head flop back, watched the orbs of the anniversary clock turning like golden apples. I tried to forget about Lauren, sleeping in the bedroom just above us. Stuart persisted between my legs using the same little cat licks. Then his finger slid suddenly inside me. I jerked in surprise, let out a yelp. He laughed, taking this as a signal. Then there was the soft patting of his palm on the floor searching for his jeans, the Velcro sound of his wallet opening as he looked for a condom.

"This okay?" he checked, holding it up.

Fear flickered through me, my throat felt very tight.

"Yes," I managed to say.

He hunched over—simian looking, I thought, grunting—and rolled the condom on.

"Shit," he said.

"What?"

He held up the split condom.

"Fucking hell." He let out a groan of frustration and bowed his head, resting on top of me. "That's that then."

There was the smell of his aftershave. His stubble prickling my shoulder. I could feel him start to soften, his body slipping away. Soon, I knew, Stuart would sober up, get dressed, go back to Kerry. I felt a stab of jealousy and dug my fingers into his back.

"It's fine," I said.

"What?"

"We can still, you know."

I nudged closer. Lifted my hips a little.

"Honestly, it's okay."

"Really?"

"I'm on the pill."

How easily the lie came out.

"Oh right? You are?"

He hovered uncertainly in between my legs. I wasn't sure if he believed me. Perhaps then he remembered all the rumours he'd heard.

I nodded again, looped my arms around his neck as if I knew what I was doing, pulled him towards me.

"Nice one," he said.

I felt a sharp pain, like a graze, as if I'd skinned my knee. I bit my lip. Stuart began to move mechanically in and out of me. How many nights I'd spent picturing this moment. The flowers and candles, the declarations of love, the transformation I thought would occur. It was nothing like the descriptions in women's magazines. I felt none of the sensations Henry Peck had raved about. While he worked up a sweat, I lay there, completely super-fluous. I might as well have been picking my nose.

Stuart's jaw clenched, his lips curled over his teeth, he let out a strange mewl. I remember the weight of him as he collapsed, my arm trapped beneath my back, a dripped sensation between my thighs.

"Shit, sorry," Stuart said and rolled off.

He wiped between his legs with his underwear and offered it to me like a napkin. Then he gave me a pat on the hip and rolled onto his side, his arms crossed over for warmth. I was pinned in the small space between his body and the backrest. My vagina was throbbing, a pain akin to a toothache or twisted ankle. How I yearned to be held. I would have swapped being a virgin again in an instant for just one sign of affection.

"Stuart?" I tried to rouse him.

"Hmm."

He began to snore.

32

I woke to the sound of a kettle boiling in the kitchen, the clink of a teaspoon in a mug. Stuart whistling. The smell of a cigarette already on the go. I crept upstairs, treading towards the bathroom silently along the corridor edge where the boards wouldn't creak. I winced as I peed. On my knickers was a crust of dried blood like brick dust. I looked under the sink for a sanitary towel but couldn't find one, so I wrapped my hand in loo roll, wedging it down my pants. My face looked ghoulish, mascara flaking beneath my eyes, my skin pale and greasy looking. I brushed my hair with my fingers as quickly as I could, tried to do the best I could with the makeup I found lying on the windowsill.

Halfway down the stairs I heard the jingle of keys in the lock and the front door opened. Joan. She was carrying two plastic bags of shopping and stopped dead when she saw me, her lips pressed together.

"You're here, are you? Where's Lauren?"

I began to sweat, fixated on the wedge of loo roll stuck down my pants. All I wanted was to sneak out of the house unnoticed. I couldn't face talking to any of them, not Stuart or his mother, especially not Lauren.

"She's asleep," I said.

Joan nodded, a slight tremor in her body I could see, exhausted by the weight of the bags.

"Make yourself useful, will you, and hold these while I get my coat off."

She handed me the shopping bags. I stood there looking at her dumbly as she set aside her cane and shook rain from her parka.

"You can put those in the kitchen."

"Okay," I said, and I carried the bags along the corridor. My heart began to thud.

When I walked into the room, there was Lauren, sitting beside her brother.

"Oh," I said. She must have woken up while I was in the bathroom.

The siblings glanced up at the same time. So alike in that sudden turn of the head. Stuart looked quickly back down at the table, staring awkwardly into his beige swirl of tea, hair tenting his face. Lauren squinted at me, then him, then back to me. Cogs turning.

I didn't know whether to stand or sit.

"Your mum's home," I said.

I couldn't look at either of them. I saw that the box of Belgian truffles I'd bought at Paddington Station—a thank-you to Joan for having me to stay—was open on the counter. Lauren picked at them, taking three or four in a row.

"Pig," Stuart said.

"Yeah, well. Someone ate all the sodding bread, didn't they." She nudged the box towards me.

"Here you go. I'm hungover as fuck," she said.

"Actually, I don't think I can stay," I mumbled. I glanced at Stuart as I said this, waiting for him to look at me—a wink or a nod—but he barely acknowledged I was in the room.

"What?" Lauren's head snapped up.

I felt my cheeks burn.

"I have something at school."

She stared at me.

"I forgot, sorry," I muttered.

"Suit yourself." She shrugged, clearly annoyed.

"I'd better go and pack my stuff."

I put Joan's shopping down on the counter and went up to get my overnight bag, wondering if Stuart might follow me. He sat very quietly, nursing his tea. Upstairs I stuffed my suit into my overnight bag, zipped it up, kicked through Lauren's dirty clothes on the floor for my missing sock, slid open her drawer for a fresh pair. There, tucked between her clean clothes, was a flash of blue. Gerry's pin. Relieved, I quickly put it into my bag and went back down to the kitchen.

The siblings fell silent.

"I'm off," I said.

I glanced at Stuart as I said this. His head was still down over his cup of tea, barely registering.

"Um, well, bye then," I said, my voice reedy, very high.

My eyes began to prickle. I felt the humiliation of standing by the table, waiting for him to throw me a scrap. Lauren looked up at her brother, and then at me, and I could see her lips crumpled together censoriously. She let out a mean snort.

"Toodle-oo, Josephine," she said. "Tally ho."

"Pack it in, Loz," Stuart said.

He got to his feet.

"I'll walk you out. Come on."

He took my elbow and led me into the hall where we saw Joan, standing in the doorway of the front room, her hands on her hips. She gestured at the mess on the floor, the cans, the half-eaten sandwich, the overflowing ashtray, photos everywhere, the ruffled cushions, her china ornaments in disarray.

"Oh, hi, Stuart. You're here, too, are you? Look at the state of this room," she muttered. "I'll kill your father."

I stared at the sofa where I could see a smear of blood.

"Leave it, Mum, I'll sort it." Stuart slid between his mother and the room.

He gave Joan a squeeze around the shoulders, then picked up my leather bag and carried it to the front door.

"Bye, Joan. Thanks for having me."

"Fine," she said.

Stuart closed the front door behind us. He stood on the front step in his bare feet, his jeans very baggy, slipping down his hips. He had no underwear on.

"You got everything then, yeah?"

I was standing on the step beneath him, one leg twisted around the other, squeezing my thighs together so the roll of paper wouldn't fall out, a dull throbbing in my vagina. It was drizzling. He put his hand on my arm and started to say something, but a girl in a purple tracksuit pushing a buggy up the road slowed and waved. Her toddler held a plastic umbrella and wore green boots with yellow crocodile eyes.

"Bollocks," Stuart muttered.

He was embarrassed to have been caught talking to me. I knew from the abrupt way he pulled back into the doorway, the speed with which he removed his arm. His eyes darting about, looking at the air around me instead of at me. This was what it felt like to be Gerry Lake.

"All right, Stu?" the mother called.

"Yeah, you?"

"Not bad."

On the girl rolled into the park, turning once or twice to see if we were still standing there. Stuart stared after her in the direction of the playground, rocking from foot to foot with his hands in his pockets.

"Fuck," he swore loudly.

One of Kerry's friends, I guessed.

"Um, look," Stuart said, rubbing his forehead, squinting a little at the white sky. "I was a bit pissed last night. You know, after the pub."

"Oh."

"Off my face, to be honest with you."

I stared at his feet. They were very wide, large toes with big knuckles.

"Absolutely. Me, too," I said, exaggerating how drunk I'd been.

Stuart looked relieved at that. He tucked his fringe behind his ears and smiled.

"I think you're fit, don't get me wrong, you're great, but you know, Loz is my sister. And, you know, I work at the school and what with Kerry and everything . . ."

"Yes," I said.

"So, it's cool then? We're cool?"

I felt my stomach cave in. I smiled, I flicked my hair.

"Yes," I said. "Totally, no problem, of course."

"Good girl." He gave my chin a little nudge.

Reeling, I picked up my bag and turned. Stuart doffed an invisible cap and took a step back inside the house. When I tripped on a paving slab, he pretended not to see. I turned to wave but the door was already closed.

33

It was only ten o'clock. Sunday morning. Church bells and football cheers. Hours before the school gates would be open. I sat in the bus shelter at the top of the road as if I had somewhere to go. I was shivering, my teeth rattling with misery. When the drizzle stopped, I walked down to the mill stream and found an unoccupied bench where I tried my best to read the only book that happened to be in my bag—*A Streetcar Named Desire,* a set text I had studied for my exams. My eyes skimmed over the words, not taking anything in. Every time anyone walked by my heart raced and I looked up, willing it to be Stuart. I had a series of very long, romanticised daydreams as I sat there, about him chasing around town trying to find me, slamming open the door of the chip shop and the tea house, standing on the streets in bare feet like Stanley Kowalski, shouting my name. Of course, this was complete fantasy—he never came. Everything ached, inside and out. I felt very dirty and bruised. Still bleeding. At eleven o'clock the Regent screened two children's films back to back, a short cartoon and *Babe,* the one with the talking pig. It was a parochial cinema; the films they showed were always months out of date. I ate a bucket of popcorn—my breakfast and lunch—and when they were over I watched a third film, *Jerry Maguire* this time. Then it was time for me to go back to school.

All the housemistresses were sitting in the Egg, I remember, despotic looking in their wingback chairs, dogs at their sides. Their hands resting on their enormous domed stomachs like Henry VIII. I looked down the row of my classmates' names for a friend—George or the twins or Skipper—if they were still my friends, I wasn't sure. But I was the first girl to sign in.

"Good afternoon, Josephine," Miss Graves said. "How was your work experience?"

One of the two golden retrievers that belonged to a housemistress sat up, wagging its tail. It padded over and stuck its snout in my groin. I was sure that the roll of paper wedged in my underwear, now stiff with blood, would fall down my trouser leg.

"Sit," the housemistresses ordered the dog. "I said *sit*."

Back in my dorm I ran to shower. I smelt rancid. A day-old fish. I washed, scrubbing hard at the terracotta line of dried blood inside my thigh until it was gone. It was only then, sluicing water between my groin, that I fully realised the recklessness of what I had done.

"Oh my god," I said out loud, banging my head against the cold tiles.

I turned the temperature as high as I could stand and sprayed between my legs. I wasn't under any illusion—I knew that you couldn't stop yourself getting pregnant like that, or wash away diseases—but still, I tried. When I emerged, the shower room was thick with steam. I felt extremely faint. I hobbled back to my room and, even though it was still only the afternoon, I put on my pyjamas and climbed into bed, lying with a hand on my stomach.

Little by little I heard my peers return, the shrieks, the darlings, and the air kisses. Gerry Lake marched through the door just as the bell went. This was the first time I had seen her since the incident by the shoe tree. She was wearing her team tracksuit, her hair pulled tight in a bun. The lurid makeup she wore for competitions—pale face, red lips, peacock-coloured eye shadow, fake lashes—made her look like a concubine. She frowned at me.

"What's wrong with you?"

When I didn't answer, she kicked her training bag into the back of her wardrobe.

"Suit yourself," she said and went off to the bathroom to change.

Later the deputy did her rounds. Divines scuttled to their rooms and our lights went out. Gerry and I hadn't exchanged a single word. Once in a while a loo flushed or there was a giggle from friends illicitly sneaking into each other's dorms. Even at fifteen and sixteen we weren't above such things as midnight feasts and nighttime pranks.

I curled into a ball. How could I have been so stupid, so cavalier about my own body? I was not a risk taker by any means; I hated heights and needles and horror films, and I was diligent when it came to studying. Unlike Skipper or the twins, I had never winged an exam in my life. When I closed my eyes, I pictured Stuart juddering inside me. I wanted to shriek, to pull my hair out. I pressed my fist into my stomach, bit the pillow. Stupid, stupid, stupid! I imagined the shame of telling my mother and father, their shock and disappointment. As parents they were pragmatic but deeply prudish people. *Sex* was not a word any of us would have willingly uttered out loud. The birds and bees, as my mother called it, was something one discussed with friends or learnt in biology lessons.

I thought then of the talk Gerry's stepmother had given, held one evening in the rec room. How Daphne Lake, dressed in her nurse's uniform, had laid out various props and switched on the overhead projector. She was not a natural speaker. She was thin-wristed, timid, inaudibly quiet, and before she even said the word *banana* Skipper and I were doubled over on the floor laughing.

"Gerry," I whispered. "Gerry, are you awake?"

Slowly Gerry rolled over and put a hand to her forehead.

"What?" she snapped.

She loathed me, I realised; it was hopeless.

"Nothing," I said. "Never mind. Go to sleep."

I wished I could call Lauren. Gerry sat up and blinked. The gap between our two bunks seemed a dark, impassable crevasse.

She fumbled around then shone a torch at me. I stared back at her, not moving, caught in her beam.

"What?" she ordered.

My mouth opened. I shook my head. A sob rose up to choke me. I stuffed my hand into my mouth and bit down hard on my knuckles.

"Sorry," I gagged. "Sorry."

34

There is such a thing as boarding school syndrome. According to Jürgen, this is a real condition. He heard it on one of the podcasts he listens to driving to class. I look it up online and find he is right. There are survivors' groups and trained trauma therapists. Specialists in the sudden and traumatic abandonment of one's childhood self. I find an article about it online to forward to Rod. She video-calls me as I am feeding Lena her breakfast. I turn the screen so that Lena, seated in her high chair, can babble indecipherably at her grandmother.

"Poppycock," my mother says, offended by the article. "What utter nonsense. To be honest, darling, I didn't even bother to finish reading it."

Lena squeezes a banana, pulverising it in her fist. *Dod,* she says, trying to get Rod's attention. *Dod, dod, dod.* I repeat the symptoms out loud to my mother.

"Difficulties in relationships and parenting, workaholism, inability to relax, isolation, highly experienced as a bully, substance abuse, a sense of failure, as well as physical, sleep, and sexual problems."

Rod raises an eyebrow.

"Nonsense, I sleep like a log. Always have. And you have friends, lots of them."

This is not true. Since we've moved to Los Angeles I've made a total of one new friend, Audrey, a tall redheaded woman I met at Lena's toddler group who raised both eyebrows during the group sing-along, locking eyes with me across the room, and above the head of her eighteen-month-old son mouthed the words, *Kill me.*

The other mothers frowned. They bent into spouts, tipping themselves over, pouring themselves out.

On the screen Rod covers her eyes with her hands, then flaps them open.

"Peekaboo."

Lena grins. She wiggles her arms. Blobs of banana splatter onto the floor. I can tell from my mother's tone that she doesn't want to discuss the matter any further. Hurt by the implied criticism.

"With the adoption of a strategic survival personality—a disguise, a front, a mask—the true identity of the person remains hidden. This pattern distorts intimate relationships and may continue into adult life."

"Oh, for goodness' sake, please. What a lot of whiners. Your father and I were very content. And look at you and Jürgen, you're happy, aren't you?"

I don't give her an answer. Lately, with the baby and Jürgen's new teaching job, our primary source of communication has become the Post-it note pad left out on the kitchen counter. We haven't had sex in months. I look at my face on the screen, my finger trailing my puffy, inflamed skin, peppered with spots. I had a better complexion at school.

"It's hormones, darling," my mother reassures me. "Did you try that cream I sent you?"

Rod is a firm believer in self-maintenance, beauty regimes and expensive lotions and potions. It's so easy after having children, she tells me, to let oneself go. Go *where*? I think. Wistful.

I haven't worked since Lena was born. On a freelance wage, who could afford a nanny? When Jürgen comes home early, he kisses us on the head—the baby first, then me—and asks us what we've been up to. I stare at him blankly. Sometimes I pass an entire day without speaking to another adult. During naps, I sit beside Lena's crib, aimlessly scrolling through Facebook or, once or twice, looking up Gerry's former skate club. Just last week I lost an entire afternoon to pictures of Dickie Balfour's wedding.

It is then that I remember the camaraderie of school life. The sensation of having my knee tickled, my hair stroked, the weight of an arm linked through my own. The complete indifference to the outside world. The jokes, the rumours, the secrets.

This morning I found myself in front of the garage, where, buried deep in a pile of storage boxes, hidden amongst old baby clothes and winter coats, is the metal tin. Lena on one hip, a knife in my hand. Deciding.

On the screen my mother starts to look worried.

I force a smile.

"I'm just tired," I say.

Rod sucks in her cheeks, looking her most Divine.

"Of course you're tired. You're a mother. Oink, oink," she snorts at Lena.

Lena blows a raspberry back, spraying me with food. I wipe banana from my shirt.

"Anyway"—she changes the subject—"I mustn't keep you."

"From what?" I say.

"Toodlepip." She waves, already gone.

35

Gerry Lake took me to the San. The school nurse, a gaunt and malnourished-looking woman, who lanced our boils and deloused our heads and checked our feet for verrucas, asked what kind of symptoms I had. I stood there, picking my inner arm. Gerry stepped forward and said in a scathing voice it was a personal women's matter and that I needed a doctor's appointment immediately.

I stared at Gerry, amazed.

The nurse sighed and nodded. Then she opened a locked desk drawer and wrote something in my file. We each had one of these identical beige folders with details of our various allergies and ailments, and I wondered whether the nurse took the Hippocratic oath like a doctor, or if this was the kind of anecdote teachers tittered about in the staff room during their cigarette breaks.

Next Gerry escorted me to the doctor's, marching ahead along the road, her small arm swinging, her hand in a fist. I had a stitch, a pain in my side like a knife wound. I wished Gerry was Lauren.

"Slow down," I pleaded.

Gerry stopped, surprised, looking at my arm wrapped around my ribs. We walked awkwardly together the rest of the way, side by side, not speaking.

In the surgery, she and I sat for a long time in the plastic blue waiting chairs amongst elderly couples, coughing into their handkerchiefs, and townies with snotty, bawling babies. When the receptionist called my name, I wanted to crawl under a rock.

"Go on," Gerry said.

I stood up.

"Tell her it broke," Gerry advised.

"What broke?"

"The condom."

"Oh, right. Thanks."

I knocked and saw that it was Dr Hadfield. Dr Hadfield had come to school over the years and given us all our diphtheria vaccinations. He had very large flared nostrils and was hairless and polished looking. A pair of glasses, which he used as he was making notes, were strung on a chain around his neck.

"Oh," I said and backed out. "Is there a female doctor I could talk to instead?"

"Not today. Take me or leave me," Dr Hadfield said without looking up.

I didn't know anything about contraception or what rights I had. I presumed the morning-after pill meant just that. I closed the door and sat down.

"I'll be with you in a moment, young lady."

After some time the doctor turned to me, took off his glasses, and asked me how he could help. My hands were sweating, I could feel my heart thumping, I picked at my arm.

"I think I need the morning-after pill," I said and stared over his shoulder at an anatomical heart.

"You think you do?" Dr Hadfield frowned.

Dr Hadfield was a particularly fastidious man, pedantic about the application of grammar. A person who frequently tutted at our "likes" and "ums," lecturing Divines on our various solecisms while he was administering our jabs.

"I mean, I do," I corrected myself.

"You had unprotected sex?"

"No." I flushed.

My hands were pressed under my thighs to stop them shaking. I knotted my fingers together.

"The condom broke," I lied.

"During penetration?"

"Yes."

He put on his glasses and began taking notes.

"And approximately how long ago was that?"

"Saturday," I fumbled. "I mean, early Sunday morning."

"I see. And how many sexual partners have you had, would you say?"

He peered at me over the top of his spectacles.

"One."

"I see. And would you say you are in a monogamous relationship with this person?"

"Monogamous?"

"Is he your boyfriend? Does he have other partners?"

I looked at the floor then, picking the edge of the scab I had made with my fingernail so that it flapped completely open. I felt humiliated, chastened.

"No," I choked out, "he has a girlfriend."

The doctor clicked the end of his pen, slid off his glasses and looked at me sternly.

"A girlfriend? That doesn't sound like a very promising start now, does it? You might want to think about choosing your partner more wisely next time."

I nodded, too ashamed to reply.

"Well, in any case, young lady, you'll need to come back in a week for a few tests."

"Okay," I said and wiped my nose with my sleeve.

Dr Hadfield handed me a box of tissues.

"You'll know better next time, I expect."

He wrote out a prescription for the morning-after pill.

Gerry looked at my puffy eyes as I walked out to the waiting room and seemed embarrassed. Unexpectedly, she slipped her arm under mine, holding it stiffly, as if it was set in a cast. She led me to the pharmacy and as soon as we returned to our dorm she got me a glass of water to swallow it down with and that was that.

"Whatever you do don't puke or it won't work."

"Did that happen to you?"

Gerry acted as if she hadn't heard. I thought of the hairy arm hanging from the window of the beige Ford Escort. The slow drumming of fingers against the door panel, the sobs at night I'd never bothered to comfort her over. I realised I knew almost nothing about Gerry's life outside of the Divine. I felt a sudden respect for her.

"Get into bed," Gerry ordered.

I did as she said, still fully dressed, and watched Gerry get ready for lessons. Despite the fact our exams were over, there were still two pointless weeks of classes ahead of us before Prize Giving and the end of term. Gerry checked herself in the mirror on the back of our door. She pulled tight the immaculate bun she always wore, smoothing the bumps. She speared stray strands in place with hairgrips.

"Doesn't that give you a headache?" I asked.

"You get used to it."

Gerry glanced at the timetable on her desk and slid a folder into the blue canvas tote bag we lugged around school.

"Thanks," I said quietly.

"It's all right."

"I'll make sure you get your hairpin back," I promised. "You know, the one you got for your birthday."

I didn't tell her that it was inside my desk drawer. At any time I could have climbed down from my bunk and given it to her then and there. But I didn't. I was too much of a coward. If I waited a few days, I thought I could sneak it back onto her desk while she was out, avoiding further drama. Gerry's reflection froze, a hairgrip hanging from her mouth. She bit down on it, her eyes narrowed.

"That fucking cow, I knew it," she said. Meaning Skipper. Then: "Thanks."

She shouldered the book bag and headed out of the door.

"Wait, what will you tell everyone?" I asked.

Gerry stopped, one hand on her waist, her hip jutting out. Her chin tipped up like a cat, blinking. After all that she had endured, she should have revelled in seeing me like this: pathetic, weak, in need of her help. She must have known that if the shoe had been on the other foot, our teasing would have been relentless.

She nudged the rubbish bin closer to my side of the room with her foot.

"I'll say you *ate* something funny."

This was Gerry's attempt at a joke, I realised, the first I'd ever heard her tell. She looked at me nervously, checking my response.

"Ha ha."

When she came back after lunch to check on me I was groaning to myself, swallowing, licking my lips like a poisoned dog.

"I want to die," I said, gagging.

"Did you puke?" Gerry inspected the rubbish bin.

"No."

I rocked from side to side, pulled my knees up to my chest, anything to stop the nausea.

"Can I get you anything?"

I shook my head weakly. How could one small pill make you feel so bad? Why did women have to go through this when all a man had to do was wipe himself down, roll over, fall asleep?

"This is the worst bit. Try and rest. You'll feel better when you wake up," Gerry said.

I didn't want her to leave me on my own but I closed my eyes, knotted myself into a ball. I felt my stomach churn. I was in a storm, trapped belowdecks, rolling this way and that, clinging to a bucket. Every now and again I heard the door creak open.

"Gerry?" I moaned.

There was the shush of feet on the carpet, a fresh glass of water, and once, though it's possible I dreamt it, a hand gently rubbing my back.

36

It was dusk when I woke and oddly hushed. The hollow quiet of empty dorms and silent corridors. Gerry had left a cup of tea on my desk—long gone cold—a piece of toast, and some magazines to read. I sat up, feeling better. I chewed a corner of toast, flicked through *Just Seventeen*. Along the corridor was the sound of a phone going unanswered. It stopped, then, after a short pause, began ringing again. The idea suddenly came to me that it was Stuart trying to reach me. Had he changed his mind about the two of us? Perhaps he'd had another fight with Kerry. I kicked down the bedcovers and rushed to the communal phone. When I got to the booth, the door was locked. I pressed my nose against the perforated plastic glass, listening to the phone warbling to itself.

"Shit," I said. Where was everyone?

I went into the empty rec room and I checked a few dorms, all of them unoccupied, books open on desks as if people had got up in a hurry. I racked my brains, trying to think what day it was.

I went outside to the steps of the boarding house. It was exceptionally quiet. On any given summer evening Divines would be out on the grass courts, thumping tennis balls back and forth into the gloom till they were summoned inside. There would normally be squealed laughter from dorm windows, music from our stereos, bells that announced the start and end of lessons or prep. That evening, though, I remember the tennis courts were silent, no music played. I considered going to see Lauren, since there was no one there to stop me, but I remembered how her eyes had narrowed, sliding between her brother and me. A look of utter disdain.

Inside the phone began to ring again.

I shivered, dressed in just my shirt and leggings, and went inside to retrieve my grey cardigan. There was a single cigarette and a lighter in the pocket. Smoking seemed like as good an idea as any. I put on my penny loafers and as I set off to the orchard, I heard the low ominous rumble of thunder. I folded myself into my enormous cardigan and examined the sky. The lights were on in the chapel, I noticed, each of the thin pencil-shaped windows of the sanctuary illuminated, the stained glass glowing brimstone orange. There had to be an evensong service I had forgotten about or some other school gathering. Often there were end-of-year performances by our drama club or motivational speakers or a touring Shakespeare production. If I timed it right, I could join the mass of girls as they were leaving, so that it would appear to the housemistresses as if I'd been there all along. No one would ever know what had happened.

I climbed the bridge, walked through the labyrinth of corridors and swing doors that led towards the school chapel and waited in the Egg, sitting in one of the empty wingback chairs normally reserved for my housemistress. I heard the same thunderous vibration I'd heard before, the sound of stamping followed by a loud booing, none of which was particularly unusual behavior for the Divine. We were a tough audience to please, prone to heckling and loud theatrical yawns.

"Girls, please, settle down," I heard Fat Fran shouting. "Sixth Formers, stay in your seats. Girls, I said *sit*."

They stormed out of the chapel, arm in arm, utterly defiant. First the older girls in home clothes, then my own year, then the Fourth Form and so on down the ranks. They were swearing, shaking their heads in disbelief, the younger girls near hysterical, ashen, some of them barely able to walk, others running as if from a disaster.

"What happened?" I pulled aside a Third Year. "What's going on?"

"Oh my god," she said again and again. "Oh my god. I can't believe it."

She was beside herself. In shock. I wondered whether I should slap her.

A calamity had occurred, I realised, the death of a favourite member of staff or a parent. From time to time catastrophes like that befell the school; an older girl was once thrown from a bus in her gap year. Another was diagnosed with an inoperable brain tumour. A group of my own year stumbled past, clinging to one another. I saw Skipper with her arm around the twins, and I pushed through the crowd towards them.

"What's happened?"

"It's a fucking joke," Skipper said.

"What is?"

"The school's gone down the bloody drain. No more dosh. Fuck, I knew I should have gone to Marlborough."

"We're closing?"

"Worse. Merging."

She named a local boarding school, a long-standing rival of ours with a reputation for producing straitlaced, priggish girls, not at all Divine. Our buildings would go up for sale to generate revenue, and the staff and the few remaining girls would be absorbed by this other school.

It took a while for me to realise the enormity of what she was saying. We had been sold off like cattle. No more morning chapel, no more school dances or end-of-year pranks. I thought of the shoe tree, a hundred-year-old tradition, felled, chopped up for firewood. Our boarding house flattened, our tennis courts turned into a car park or a shopping centre. My ears began to ring. I saw Gerry quietly pushing her way through the crowd with a strange determined look on her face, elbowing her way past sobbing girls.

"Where were you all day, anyway?" Skipper asked coldly.

"I was feeling ill," I bluffed.

I knew she didn't believe me.

"Well, everyone's meeting in the orchard to talk about what to do about dares."

"Brill," I said.

As Gerry drew closer I held my breath, waiting to see if she would come over to me. I was suddenly filled with panic that she might confront Skipper directly, demand her pin back, so that I would be forced to explain my lies in front of the whole year. Gerry stopped at the edge of our group, staring at Skipper. Her face was a mask—pale and unreadable. I had no idea if she was as shocked about the closure as we were or if she simply thought we had got what we deserved.

"Are you even listening?" Skipper nudged me.

"What? Yes," I said, keeping my eye on Gerry. "Orchard. Dares."

"Okay, girls," Skipper boomed. "Listen, we'd better bloody think of something big, that's all I can say. Everyone agree? Let's go out with a bang."

There were mutterings of agreement all around us. *Cheers. Hear! Hear!*

I saw the corner of Gerry Lake's mouth flicker. She raised two pistol fingers, aiming them through the crowd at Skipper. Our eyes met across the room. Her lips parted.

Bang, she mouthed.

37

Jürgen and Lena go to Costco to buy nappies and come back with a dog. My husband opens the door of our bungalow and Lena—muscular like her father, even at two and a half—pushes the dog in a plastic carrier over the threshold as if it is a shopping trolley, her back hunched.

"What's this?" I ask.

"Puppy," Lena says, "puppy, puppy, puppy."

Jürgen jogs in from the street carrying a new dog bed and bowl and before I can make eye contact, he runs back down the steps to the car, returning with a sack of dry dog food on his shoulder.

"A dog?"

He gives me a sheepish look and unlatches the door of the cage. The dog tumbles free, paws splayed on the wooden floor. It is incredibly ugly, no discernible breeding—half this, half that—with the face of an imbecile. When its tongue lolls out, I think of Mrs Myrtle and her Yorkie.

"Jesus, Jürgen, you're going to Venice next week. What am I meant to do with a dog?"

"I know, I know," he admits. "The timing's not great. But he was sitting there in the pen, right outside the store. No one wanted to even pet him. Look at him."

We study the dog—the wrinkled pink snout, the curled tongue, the large bat ears, hair that is greasy and lank. Those animal shelter people know a soft touch when they meet one. Only Jürgen could fall for a dog like that.

Jürgen thumbs in the direction of Lena's bedroom.

"You should see them together."

Lena reappears wearing bumblebee wings and carrying a tray of coloured plastic teacups.

"What are you doing?"

"Tea party," she says and is gone again for extra provisions.

Jürgen beams.

"See."

I say nothing.

I picture the Turtle and her Yorkie sharing a slice of Battenberg from the same plate.

"Look, the people from the shelter said that if you really, really don't like him, or if it isn't a good fit, then, you know, then we can always take him back."

"Like a pair of shoes?"

"*Ja*, exactly." Jürgen gets down on his hands and knees. I can see how happy he is. The dog licks his face; he actually lets it slobber on his chin and cheeks and even, I notice, curl its brown tongue up inside one of his nostrils. I grimace. I am no Mrs Myrtle.

"He'll keep Lena busy," Jürgen calls after me as I head out to the car to get the rest of the shopping. "You'll finally get some work done. She'll play with him all the time. All the time."

At this point I have been underemployed for over two years. Occasionally I pitch an article to a former colleague, a man I used to consider a peer, now the editor of a magazine. I volunteer at Lena's preschool, do some copywriting for my friend Audrey, a brand director, tutor the occasional student, but the cost of childcare makes a mockery of the term *freelance*. I know what I've become. Domesticated. Humdrum. Utterly Divine.

I stare into the black mouth of the car boot for a while, thinking about this, then I shoulder a box of nappies and a giant vessel of olive oil and head back into the house.

"All right," I agree. "The dog can stay."

The next morning I set my alarm as if I am on a deadline. I sleepwalk to the kitchen, switch the light on, and let out a scream.

Yellow puddles leach across the floor, paw prints track over a new sofa, shredded cushions, feathers. The dog thrashes his tail and curls his lips in pleasure, overjoyed to see me. His purple tongue lolls from the corner of his mouth; he gives my ankle a rough lick. I stare around me in disbelief. Undeterred, I drag the dog into his metal jail and move the cage, dog and all, outside onto the porch.

He lets out a series of pathetic yaps.

"Shussh," I hush him. "Shut the fuck up."

I pick up the pile of half-chewed letters and spray the floor with disinfectant to mask the smell, tossing newspaper to soak up the puddles for Jürgen to clear up later. His dog, his mess. Then I make a desk for myself in the corner of the sitting room, brew some coffee and get to work. I research four or five pitches to send to a magazine, but none of them interest me much. Anyway, it will probably cost me more in babysitting fees than I'll get paid for each one. I search through some job listings, consider an internship in a cactus shop, text my friend Audrey about asking for more work, flip back to my blank page. Outside the puppy claws at the lock, throwing itself against the metal cell walls. I put a pair of headphones on. Still nothing. I make another pot of coffee and stare at the empty screen. Eventually, out of desperation, I sift through the pile of mail. Car insurance, credit card statements, a second or third reminder from the gynaecologist, and last, a thick embossed envelope forwarded by my mother, heavier than all the others, edged in gold. I slice it open with my thumbnail.

Dear Alumni.

Twenty years since we burned our books, tore our dresses to shreds, flung our shoes into a tree. Since Gerry made headline news.

I prop the invitation against the wall. Then I open my browser and trawl the internet again for Divines, clicking from follower to follower. Some are blonder, some leaner or ruddier, others unaccountably unchanged. Wedding photos, Labradors, shoots in

Scotland, christenings, memorials. In these photos, my old friends hook their arms together like days of yore, flicking their hair for the camera. Even now, decades older, indisputably Divine.

I read and read, hunched over the keyboard, in a trance, barely aware of my own body. The dog gives up whining and goes to sleep. I don't even notice Jürgen is awake until he pads into the kitchen, dressed in just his towel, his arm covering his nose.

"*Wah! Mein Gott,* what happened? Where's the dog?"

"Outside," I say, quickly snapping shut the computer screen.

"You're working," Jürgen says, delighted.

He leans over my shoulder, dripping, kisses me on the neck. "See?"

38

In the days after the announcement of the school's merger we became completely intractable. We ignored our teachers, skipped our lessons, were even more haughty and rude. When a heatwave set in, we insisted our classes be moved outside. At first the staff, stunned as us by the news, were often seen whispering to one another in nervous clusters about who would stay and who would go, fanning themselves with our unmarked prep. But then, as the shock wore off, they became increasingly Laodicean about the whole thing, even jolly, particularly the younger teachers. What did they care in the end what happened to the Divine?

They'd shoulder their handbags and escort us outside. No one did any work, of course. Our exams were over. All we did was sunbathe. When Gerry skipped out of class early to go to practice, the teachers shrugged phlegmatically at one another across the rose garden. We could, as it turned out, get away with murder. Before a lesson was over, we stood in unison, dusted off our legs and drifted off across the grass.

We waved our fingers, toodlepip. They could hardly expel us. We were above punishment. Untouchable. Immortal.

The only thing anyone really cared about now was the planning of school dares. While these end-of-year pranks had always been good-natured—food fights and stink bombs, the kind of lighthearted tomfoolery that our teachers found funny, though they couldn't admit it—our nightly meetings held under torchlight had the zealous enthusiasm of a terrorist cell. Anger consumed us like a fever. Fat Fran had betrayed us all, it was agreed, sold us down the river, and had to pay. Gradually the stunts we planned slipped from comic, to absurd and then to outright malicious. We would, Skipper announced, shred all the Bibles in the school, burn them on the tennis courts or set fire to them in our headmistress's office. We'd strut around like strippers in Fat Fran's vestments, the cassocks and stoles, pen a fake letter of resignation to the diocese. Finally we agreed we'd bundle our headmistress into the back of a van with a sack over her head and hold her ransom. Tie her to a chair, interrogate her until she confessed to what she had done, until she broke down and wept. But the logistics of kidnap—the lack of a getaway vehicle, Fat Fran's gargantuan weight, the location of a safe house—proved too complex a stunt for us to pull off.

"We could put laxatives in the Communion wine," someone offered as an alternative.

"Yawn," said Skipper, who seemed to take the closure of the school more personally than the rest of us. The head girl that never was. "Next."

As dares night grew closer Skipper issued us each a shopping list of supplies, divided up dorm by dorm to make it less obvious to the school staff and shopkeepers what we were up to. Paint, glue, clocks, balls of string and lighter fluid, surgical gloves, vast quantities of sugar. Alcohol and cigarettes of course.

"Don't get busted," Skipper ordered as she handed them out. We tucked the lists inside our underwear.

Later that afternoon, as instructed, I went to town with the twins, where we bought bottles of bleach, an alarm clock and a litre of vodka from the man at the corner shop who had been selling us our contraband for years. He slid our fake IDs across the counter without looking up from his newspaper and signalled to us with his eyes to take our alcohol and go. We walked back to school together through the town square. Either side of me the twins were bickering about something. I wasn't paying attention. Nervous, I stayed in the middle of them and kept my head down, eyes on the cobbles in case I saw one of the McKibbins. Out of habit, the twins and I linked arms, and I felt the comforting sensation of their bodies walking in step with mine, our hips pressed together. Since Fat Fran's announcement I had noticed a gradual shift in my friends' behaviour towards me. A thawing. The school was in jeopardy after all, under attack; we were in this together.

Lauren had telephoned every day since I'd slept at her house a week ago. Each time I made an excuse to not come to the phone, dreading whatever it was she had to say. Skipper looked at me curiously, but made no snide, sarcastic comment.

At the sight of a pair of blue overalls coming down the corridor at school I held my breath until the maintenance men had passed, staring at my shoes. Whenever I thought of Stuart, I felt crippled by shame, turned inside out. I replayed what we had done over and over. How he couldn't even look at me in the morning, how he rushed me out of the door, let it slam in my face. Once I ran into him as he was standing outside the boiler room, laughing with a couple of other workmen. I saw his body stiffen as I walked by, worried I might cause a scene, embarrass him in front of his colleagues, try to get him in trouble. His hand moving through his hair, he turned his back to me, carried on talking as if I was invisible. Humiliated, I scrambled into the smoking den, sobbing.

Back in my dorm Gerry Lake scowled at the bags of supplies I was carrying. I tucked them under my bed and then, when there was no more room in my cupboards, I asked her to let me hide some of it on her side of the room.

"No fucking way."

"It's just for a couple of days," I pleaded. "Please, Gerry."

She stood with her arms crossed in the old way, her chin jutting out, on the brink of a tantrum. Gerry had made it clear that she found the tradition of dares—the covert meetings, the codes, the cloaks and hoods—utterly puerile. She was right, of course. But if you stripped the Divine of its rituals, took away the shoe tree or the hair flicking, one had to wonder, like the Queen or the pope, what you'd have left.

"Pretty please," I tried again, pressing my palms together.

No one had ever begged her for anything or even asked for a favour. I watched her surprised expression, the strange backwards bend of her arm as she pulled on her elbow. Her face, I thought, began to soften.

"Fine," Gerry said, giving in. "Whatever."

That evening I climbed out of my bunk and pressed my ear to the door, listening for the sound of our housemistress doing her rounds. Gerry was on her bunk, writing in my leavers book. After GCSEs it was customary for Divines to buy a blank book that our friends inscribed with sentimental notes, reminiscences about the past five years, as well as parting messages from those who were moving on to other schools for A-Levels. Pages garnished with Xs and Os. We cut strands of our hair and stuck them to the paper, we sliced our fingers and signed our names in blood. *To my darling, my sweet, I'll never forget, masses and masses of love, forever and a day.* No one, I knew, would write in Gerry's leavers book, except Kwamboka, who was equally kind to everyone. I stood with the door cracked open. I watched Gerry doodle.

"It's the last meeting," I said. "So . . ."

Gerry's pencil hovered over the page.

"So what?"

"You should come."

Her chin snapped up, she squinted at me, shocked.

I blushed, embarrassed. The offer wasn't genuine. Even as I said it I knew that Gerry wouldn't accept. She had a competition the next day; her green feathered costume was hanging from the edge of her bunk, her skates zippered inside her boot bag, the blades tightened, the leather polished.

"Never mind," I quickly said, obviously relieved.

Gerry scowled.

"Fine." She set my leavers book to one side and climbed down her bunk. "If it's such a big deal, I'll come."

"Oh."

It was too late to take it back.

"What?" Gerry asked.

Her jaw was set hard, her lips pinched together. I knew that there was no point trying to dissuade her.

"Nothing," I said. "Brill."

We walked in single file along the corridor to Skipper's dorm. I hadn't hung out in Skipper's dorm or exchanged more than a few words with my former best friend since our exchange in the shower room. Now I'd be arriving with Gerry, the least popular girl in our school, the one person Skipper couldn't abide. With my nervousness I forgot the code I was meant to use, a series of elaborate knocks. Divines lunged under duvet covers and behind curtains, elbows and feet sticking out, bodies hidden under desks and beds like cadavers.

"It's just me," I said.

There was a collective exhalation.

"Bloody hell, Joe," the Peck twins groaned.

Skipper sat up in bed, her knees tucked under her chin. Her lip curled in distaste when she saw Gerry coming in after me. Her eyebrow arched.

"Marvellous. You brought the Poison Dwarf."

For a moment Gerry said nothing. Then her fists bunched. She hissed.

"Which one of you cows has my hairpin?"

Skipper let out a loud yawn.

"Oh, lorks, here we go again."

Gerry scowled. I knew this time she wasn't going to leave without it. She turned to me and nodded, waiting for me to back her up.

"Go on."

"Um," I said.

I remember how the attention of the whole room shifted in that moment. There was the sound of a pipe clanking. The air in my lungs seemed to be pressed out of me, as if there was something standing on my chest. My mouth opened, nothing came out.

"I don't really know . . ." I started to backtrack.

Gerry stared at me. Her eyes were slits, her mouth pinched together hard.

"Oh, go fuck yourself," Gerry said.

She pushed me backwards, a hard thump in the chest.

"Get out of my way."

We heard her feet running down the corridor, our room door slamming shut.

The room was silent. I stood in the middle of the group. I squeezed my arm till I could feel it go numb. Skipper began to clap slowly.

"Bravo, Joe." Her voice dripped with sarcasm. "Well done."

"She followed me out," I mumbled, the first lie of many I would tell about Gerry.

"Please. From what I hear, you two are quite chummy these days. Best of friends. Skipping arm in arm through town. Very jolly."

A few girls laughed. The twins sneaked a look at each other. I bit my lip, knotting my fingers together. They must have seen me with Gerry on our way back from the doctor's and ratted me out to Skipper. Even though they'd been friendly to my face, chatting to me in the art room, smiling at me when Skipper's back was turned, when it came down to it, their loyalty lay with her, not me. I felt sick; I wished I were dead.

"We were just going to the doctor," I said.

Skipper rolled her eyes.

"What for, a lobotomy?"

I paused for a moment. I squeezed my arm even harder, pinching my skin.

"The morning-after pill," I said quietly, my face burning, remembering the lecture from Dr Hadfield.

"Gerry Lake," Dickie shrieked. "Gerry?"

I said nothing.

"Oh my god," another girl yelled. "Who the hell would shag Gerry?"

I could have corrected the mistake but I didn't.

"Come on, Joe, just tell us."

I became aware that the mood in the room had shifted. There was an invisible hierarchy at work in which I had been suddenly and dramatically elevated. I noticed the sympathetic smiles, the tendentious outrage my friends seemed to feel on my behalf for the predicament Gerry had put me in by asking me to cover for her.

Slowly I began to describe a middle-aged man, Gerry's trainer, his hairy arm and thick meaty-looking fingers. Lies tumbled like dominoes, one after another. I alluded to the secretive way Gerry was always dropped by him near the school gates, their late-night assignations, the after-competition rendezvous, the gifts. George Gordon-Warren pretended to gag.

"I knew it. What a slut."

"Isn't he, like, a million years old? Rank."

"Ghastly."

"Oh my god, you poor thing," Dave Peck said, offering me a kiss.

Another girl hugged me. I only realised then how ostracised I had felt that term, spending all my time with Lauren, shunned by my peers. Now, I had never felt more popular. The only one not to leap to embrace me was Skipper. She crossed her legs on the top bunk.

"Fine. But how do we know your little chum won't blab?"

She pointed at the pile of supplies in the middle of the dorm.

"She won't," I said.

"How do you *know*?"

"I have the pin," I confessed. "The one he gave to her."

This part at least was true.

"Who?"

"The trainer. Her boyfriend."

"Oh my god," snorted George Gordon-Warren. "You've got it?"

I nodded.

"We could use it as a ransom," I suggested.

"Hats off," George said.

Skipper finally seemed placated. Impressed even. She tapped her fingers to her forehead and gave me a salute.

Someone made space next to her on the bed so I could climb up on the top bunk. I hugged my knees, then after a while Skipper rested her head on my shoulder. She tickled my arm in the old way. I was forgiven. A bottle of peach schnapps circulated. Someone told a joke. Skipper laughed so hard the whole bed shook. We shushed her, batted her with a pillow. In the end her laughter spluttered out like a car engine. She wiped her eyes.

"Remember that time we got busted at the rec grounds?"

We all nodded. There came a flurry of stories: boys we'd snogged, the detentions, the expulsions. We interrupted each other, finished each other's sentences, doubled in hysterics.

"What about the pervert?" someone squealed, as if this was something that had happened decades ago, and not a matter of weeks.

"Oh my god, the photos!"

Some of us were crying with laughter, we realised, while others by then were crying for real. Suddenly we were sombre. Divines could be cruel, conceited, arcane, but we were faithful to the end. We sobbed and hugged one another. *Forever,* we promised, *always.* Nothing could break us apart, proving in the end how much we underestimated Gerry. We swore on our lives. We crossed our hearts.

39

Gerry Lake got up at dawn. This was not unusual for her on the morning of an important competition. Instead of doing her exercises she knocked on Miss Graves's door and didn't come out till breakfast. The last some of us would see of her. After chapel—from which Gerry was notably absent—Padre instructed the Fifth Form to remain in our seats. He smiled at us regretfully, rocking in the pulpit. Along the back wall we noticed a line of teachers like riot police, instructed to prevent us leaving.

"Outrageous," we shouted.

We threatened to call our parents and our parents' lawyers.

"You can't do this. It's against the law," we cried, citing the Children Act.

Meanwhile Fat Fran, with a number of deputies, ruthlessly tore apart our dorms—upturning mattresses, shaking out laundry bags, ransacking our tuck boxes—until the vast mountain of supplies we had accrued had been uncovered. A team of maintenance men were sent in to bag the evidence, hoisting it over their shoulders and tossing it into a skip.

When the raid was over we were escorted from the school chapel to the Circle, walking like convicts in crocodile formation. Fat Fran awaited us flanked by our housemistress and deputy. Gerry Lake was nowhere to be seen. Fat Fran held a bottle of vodka in one hand, a packet of Marlboros in the other. First she upturned the bottle, then she crushed the cigarettes in her large, hammerlike fist and emptied them on the ground, crushing the remains underfoot.

"If even half of what I understand you had planned is true,

well, it's beyond words. Flabbergasting, in fact. No better than animals. Animals! When I think of everything you girls have been given, the kind of opportunities you've had. You disgust me."

We stared at the vodka as it bubbled into the earth, the tobacco flattened under Fat Fran's heel.

"I'm going to kill bloody Gerry Lake," Skipper hissed.

"Enough. Let this be the end of it," Fat Fran added. "Or else."

Or else what?

This was a question she hadn't thought of.

"Quiet," shouted Fat Fran. "Think of your poor mothers."

In trying to humiliate us, she inadvertently provoked just the opposite effect.

Who were we if not our mothers' daughters?

We linked arms, flicked our hair, marched away in unison across the lawn.

40

Lena likes to dress the dog in the frilly knickers that belong to her doll, and when it shreds them to pieces, she gives it a ferocious scowl and squats on stout legs, her heels flat to the floor.

"Bad baby."

He should be used to it by now, but the dog cowers in alarm, bug-eyed. He wears the same doleful expression no matter what you say or do. It is the sort of animal you're always tripping over. Whenever I go near him his tail thrashes uncontrollably with pleasure, and he writhes and curls up his gums as if he is trying to smile. He pisses with excitement all over my feet.

"Darling!" I shout. "No."

Jürgen is lying on his back doing exercises his physiotherapist prescribed for a bad back. He lifts one leg in the air slowly and lowers it. Then the other. Craning them up and down.

"My god," he complains. "Darling. I still can't believe we let her name him that. It's ridiculous."

"You were the one who said Lena could call the dog whatever she wanted."

I give him my best I-told-you-so expression.

"True."

I sit on the arm of the sofa watching Jürgen as he embarks on a sequence of crunches, his arms tugging on a resistance band as if he is rowing a boat. Each time his chest rises up from the ground he grimaces. He has gained a little weight since he fell off his bike, an accident on the way back from the studio, yet Jürgen is more attractive than ever. Same chiselled chin, perfectly straight nose, muscular buttocks. A Grecian statue—Achilles—toppled to the floor.

"Sephine, stop staring at my paunch," he says and sits up.

"Fat belly, fat belly, fat belly," Lena cries, running towards her father, body slamming him back to the ground.

"Ouch," Jürgen grunts.

Outside Darling begins yapping. I get out the leash and the roll of poop bags.

"We're going to meet Audrey at the lake," I tell him. "I'll take the dog."

"Have fun," Jürgen shouts after us. "Darling."

At the park I take Darling off the lead and watch him scuttle from tree to tree, cocking his bowlegs and nose-diving the man who sells plastic children's toys laid out on a blanket.

"I need to go potty." Lena suddenly grabs her crotch, twisting one leg around the other.

"To the loo," I correct without thinking. "We say, loo."

"I'm going to go, I'm going to go," Lena screams.

I pick her up and carry her behind one of the trees, hoist her under her armpits as she squats, a spray of yellow froth soaking her underwear and my feet.

"I peed on you." Lena giggles.

"I can see that, thank you." I strip her of her knickers and put them into one of the blue plastic poop bags.

"Swing," Lena suddenly shouts and dashes across the playground barefoot while I wash our sandals in the water fountain, calling for the dog.

"Darling," I bellow. "Darling, Darling, Darling," yelling louder and louder.

Other parents in the park look alarmed on my behalf. I shrug and sit on one of the concrete benches, waiting for Audrey to arrive. She's the only friend I made at Lena's weekly playgroup, which, to my relief, we've long since given up. A tall, redheaded New Yorker, Audrey arrives bent over her double pushchair. Her eldest son is technically too old to ride in it, but she crams the two boys in together to avoid any unnecessary dawdling on trips to the park. There is a takeaway coffee cup in each of the pockets. Reaching the playground, her youngest, Theo, escapes the pushchair as fast as he can and clambers the wrong way up the slide to the climbing frame where Lena, at the top, sits crosslegged, claiming ownership of the tower. She is wearing no knickers, I suddenly remember, her naked bottom pressed, like a fetishist, through the rope floor.

"Lena," I call up to her. "Cover your . . ."

Here I get stuck. Jürgen and I have struggled to find a word for our daughter's genitalia that doesn't sound utterly ridiculous.

"Fanny," I say.

Audrey turns around on the bench slowly, both hands cast in the air.

"You're kidding me, right?" she asks. "You Brits. What the fuck is wrong with you? It's a vagina. Call it a vagina."

"Vagina," I repeat, trying not to wrinkle my face, thinking of Daphne Lake.

"Jesus Christ, yes, repeat after me, penis, vagina. Stop looking like you ate a lemon."

"Vagina," I try again, forcing myself to say it out loud.

"That's better, here, drink your coffee."

She sits with her long legs stretched out in front of her, crossed at the ankles, her eyes eclipsed by large circular sunglasses. She has wide shoulders and a solid jaw, her hair tied back in a tight bun with a crisp side parting. In all our school plays she would have been cast as a man.

"So what's new?" Audrey asks.

"Not much," I say.

Audrey is one of the few people I don't bother to inflate my depressingly nonexistent career to.

"I started getting up early in the morning to work."

"On what?"

"Nothing really. Some pitches. They're all shit."

"Please. What about that story you wrote about the gymnasts? I read that, it was great."

It's true my article had attracted a lot of attention when it was first published—thousands of shares and comments—but over time the story has been eclipsed by even bigger scandals. Decades of abuse. Hundreds of girls. Gyms, pools, Scout troops, ice rinks, Sunday school classrooms. How, everyone wants to know, could we have let this happen right under our noses? I think of Gerry Lake, the Polaroids, the beige Ford Escort.

Audrey fishes her phone out of the pushchair pocket, finds my article and holds the screen up to me as proof.

"That was years ago," I mumble. "Before Lena. I've forgotten how to write."

Audrey turns her whole body now to look at me sternly, one eyebrow raised, incredulous. She was back at work three weeks after she gave birth to Theo. She finds the notion of baby brain insulting.

"Seriously, it took me an hour to reply to a school reunion the other day," I confess. "An hour!"

"God, those things are awful," she says. "You're not going, are you?"

I scratch my inner arm. Despite Rod's constant nagging, I've been procrastinating for months, the RSVP still on my desk, waiting to be posted. Who would fly five thousand miles to be with a group of people you've spent twenty years avoiding?

"My mother's giving me a guilt trip about not going. It's the most exciting thing that's happened to her all year."

I describe the Divine, making light of the whole business—our ridiculous uniforms, the rituals, the pageantry—turning it into a joke.

"Boarding school?" Audrey says slowly, sliding her sunglasses down her nose. "Wow."

"All girls." I cringe.

"Urgh," Audrey says, giving a ghoulish judder. "I'm so glad I had boys. Girls are vicious. No offense."

I look at Lena balancing at the crest of the slide, knees tucked under her chin, rocking on her heels like Gerry Lake on the windowsill.

"Yes," I say.

I scratch my arm.

"Vicious."

41

We dressed in silence, black school cloaks and school stockings tugged over our heads, the empty legs dangling behind us like the ears of cartoon rabbits.

Our first stop was the chapel where we tiptoed between pews, laying traps. Next we broke into the vestry and stole one of Padre's outfits—a black cassock, a surplice, and a stole—which we draped over the head of the body we'd hidden beneath the altar, a large and busty scarecrow, sewn from pillowcases and pieces of old clothing, limb by limb, like Frankenstein's monster.

Between us we carried the effigy we had made to the top of the bridge, heaving it over the railing. This was quite a challenge, dressed as Fat Fran was, in a dog collar and vestments, a gym rope looped around her neck. For a moment her enormous padded feet kicked girlishly in the evening breeze. Then the seam along her chest split open and handfuls of shredded paper and cotton wool spewed like innards onto the road below. Cars honked their horns. A man came with a disposable camera and took several grainy photos of us clinging from the rail and whooping, which he later sold to the tabloids.

NIGHT OF TERROR.
The Belles of St Jo.
Blue Murder.

The spark that had been lit inside each of us began to smoulder. We walked about the school, cloaks flapping, looking for trouble. Stripped of our arsenal of supplies, we fashioned homemade ammunition from what was lying around: art room paint, laundry detergent, sanitary towels. First we drenched the Egg in honey, then we sprinkled it with cornflakes. Fat Fran's office was doused in glue and a Hitler moustache added to her portrait. The bloody contents of a bathroom bin we upended on her large oak desk, where soiled tampons and clumps of hair stuck to her Sunday sermon. A number of Fifth Formers broke into the swimming pool and dive-bombed each other in the dark. A flour fight began in the refectory, spilling out into classrooms and corridors, a white cumulus of dust that billowed into the Circle. We went from doorknob to doorknob, smearing them with Vaseline. Growing increasingly reckless, we screamed and whooped and tore apart the staff room, spitting in the teachers' instant coffee, smoking their cigarettes, nosing through their private belongings.

Eventually, running out of steam, we congregated in the orchard. Tired and at a loss as to what to do next, we drifted lethargically about the trees, lacking any real intent. Branches fluttered with tissue paper garlands. There were a few screams in the dark, a paint bomb thrown. After a while we peeled off the stockings from our heads. Dissatisfied, we sat on the grass, smoked, played loud music on a boombox. There was nothing particularly daring about that.

"How tedious," Skipper said with a yawn.

I nodded, wrapped myself in my cloak.

"What a flop," someone said.

It wasn't even midnight.

"Well, that's that then."

The Pecks sat side by side on the grass, their knees tucked under their chins, striking identical poses.

"Wait, who's that over there?"

A posse of staff had formed beneath the bridge—deputies and some of the support staff, the French and German assistants who shared an apartment—and began moving towards the orchard, wearing head torches, a metre or so apart from one another. Their arms were spread outwards to give the impression of an unbroken line. This was unnecessarily heavy-handed. The worst of our antics were over. If they'd left us to it, eventually we would have got cold and drifted inside to bed. What came next might have been avoided.

"Right. Up, everyone!" Skipper shouted.

We scrambled to our feet, blinking into the light. There was some furtive scurrying as we repositioned our beige tights over our heads and linked arms, battle ready. We held our breaths, waiting. A number of eggs were thrown, halfheartedly, intentionally missing their targets. The teachers seemed to jostle marginally in and out of line, as if they were on horseback. There was a discussion going on between some of them. They appeared to hold their positions, waiting for a signal.

"What's happening? Can you see?" I asked Henry Peck.

"Nothing yet. No, wait, look."

Fat Fran crossed the road with a megaphone in her hand, a loudspeaker reserved for Sports Day and the annual school photo. She paused in the middle of the street to look up at the bridge where her effigy was hanging, then soldiered on towards the orchard.

We were circled, corralled into the top corner of the orchard. Fat Fran stepped forward to address us. Her legs were splayed like a Roman, shoulders drawn back; she raised the megaphone to her lips. Something was wrong with it, none of us could hear her.

"What's she saying?"

"Shh."

We craned to hear.

"Something about ladies."

In response an egg splattered at Fat Fran's feet. The megaphone let out an angry whine, then the buzz of her response. Another egg.

"Disgrace," we heard, "consequences."

"Traitor," we began to chant, "trai-tor, trai-tor, trai-tor."

"Just who do you girls think you are?" Fat Fran demanded.

That was a mistake. We knew exactly who we were. Divine.

From one of the junior houses a girl let out a long, high-pitched howl of support. We heard it and began to cheer. There was another howl from another dorm, then another and another. Some girls threw their heads out of the window and barked; they whined and yowled and yelped.

The teachers, unnerved, began to break rank, tentatively backing away, covering their heads. We were long past the point of being ordered or bribed or cajoled.

"One, two, three," we all counted.

Skipper took my hand.

"Charge."

We rushed at them, cloaks flapping. Fat Fran, who stood her ground, was shoved aside; with one shoulder knocked suddenly back, then the other, she spun like a weathervane.

"Enough," she yelled into the megaphone.

There was nothing she could do. We pounded over the bridge and into the main building, smashing and tearing and stamping on anything that was in our way. We were a hurricane. We stormed inside the science lab and piles of green worksheets fluttered out through the window and onto the ground. Then came textbooks, Bunsen burners, lab coats, and test tubes that tinkled to the floor like Christmas baubles. Other years looked on in admiration. Wasn't this, in their heart of hearts, what they all wanted to do?

"Come on." Skipper tugged me towards the main hall where girls were gouging out the names of former head girls, embossed in gold on a wooden plaque. *Memor Amici*. Remember Friends. Our building was being sold from underneath us, torn apart, our friends parcelled off to another school. Soon we'd switch our old traditions for new ones, the shoe tree would hang empty, no one would care about being Divine. We'd be consumed by another matriarchy. The Queen is dead, long live the Queen.

"Here, take this." Someone put a lacrosse stick into my hand.

We went outside into the rose garden, picked up stones from the path, put them in our nets and launched them at the refectory.

There was a satisfying pop as they sailed through the tall windows. Like squeezing a zit. I thought then of Lauren, who would have delighted in this more than any one of us.

"What next?" Skipper asked, breathless.

We strolled to the Egg. There were no teachers in sight; we were totally unchecked. We had never felt so free. It was exhilarating. All around us was the flutter of books falling to the ground like bats from the top of stairs, posters being torn from bedroom walls, uniforms shredded. We launched more stones through internal windows and tore down some curtains. A carnival spirit prevailed. In the refectory, euphoric younger years were throwing food at one another, skidding through puddles of spilt milk, squishing handfuls of tuna salad in each other's hair. Girls who'd broken the lock on the drama cupboard wardrobe sported elaborate costumes—a donkey head, bodices, towering wigs, tottering on high heels like courtesans.

We came to the Circle, where the housemistresses and their deputies were cowering under the shoe tree for shelter, and some had locked themselves in their cars. Padre silently stood beside Fat Fran, holding the large school Bible under his arm, bewildered. This was the only time we felt any guilt. Padre was fond of us girls, one of the few champions of the Divine. He smiled when he saw us; then, noticing our lacrosse sticks, his face fell and he looked very glum. Miss Graves stood in shock, dressed in only a white flannel nightgown.

A number of maintenance men who had been called in for backup stood waiting for instruction.

"Headmistress?" they asked.

A look of righteous resignation came over Fat Fran's face. She had expected this of us all along. Privileged, arrogant, beyond salvation. She crossed her arms.

"Call the police."

42

We ran, scattering like field mice. Into classrooms, under benches, behind the ha-ha, pressed between the mossy gap between the science block and a maintenance shed. Some of us dashed for the main hall, where we dived behind the curtains or dropped beneath the stage, motionless as corpses inside empty trunks. Skipper and I covered our heads with our cloaks, held hands and bolted for the boarding house. Gasping for air, dizzy with excitement, we made a charge for my dorm.

There we found the window thrust wide open. The curtains were flapping.

"Well, well," Skipper said. "Look who it is."

Framed in the open window, small, birdlike, dressed in sparkles and feathers. Despite her fear of heights, Gerry was perched on the very edge of the sill. Her hair was gelled and rolled tightly in a perfect bun, her lips were painted a garish red, lashes curled, clumped together in glittered chunks. She was sitting very still except for one finger, which had worked a hole into her flesh-coloured tights, worming its way through to skin.

"Piss off," Gerry said.

She barely turned her head. There were, I saw, two long charcoal streaks running down her cheeks, cutting through the thick layer of stage makeup she applied before competitions.

"What, no medal?" Skipper said, pretending to pout. "Rotten luck."

Gerry said nothing. Her finger continued to pick at her tights, nagging at the small hole till it was as wide as her knee.

Later the press made much of Gerry's competition. How,

seemingly distracted, Gerry had fumbled a simple combination, spun off axis, toppling to the ground. Instead of continuing the routine she lay on her back for a moment, prostrate on the ice, ignoring a decade of training. Then, watched by her trainer and fellow teammates, she got up and exited the rink. It was the last time she ever wore skates.

"Poor little Geraldine," Skipper said, adopting a babyish voice.

She picked up one of Gerry's white boots that was resting at the top of a kit bag. She jiggled it by the laces directly in front of Gerry's nose, as if teasing a cat. Gerry's gaze drifted towards the chapel spire. She barely blinked.

We had grown so accustomed to Gerry's terrible temper—the swearing, the violent explosions, the slamming of doors—that this sudden indifference came as a surprise. Flustered, Skipper dropped the ice skate out of the open window, then picked up the second boot and threw that too.

"Oops," she said, smirking at me.

Gerry leant out to look, not even bothering to secure herself in any way by holding on to the frame, I remember. She considered the white skates down on the grass as one might a painting in a gallery—silent, impassive, head tilted to the side—then curled back into herself, her knees tucked under her chin.

Skipper, too, seemed lost for words. Her legs were set apart as if she was standing in goal, her jaw clamped together. She scanned the dormitory, searching for something else she could throw. When her eyes lighted on the three-tiered jewellery box that housed all Gerry's cheap baubles, one eyebrow arched and her lips curled into a cruel smile. She walked over casually and rested her hip against Gerry's desk.

The knot in my stomach tightened.

Beneath the heavy folds of my cloak I squeezed my arm.

Skipper drummed the box lid with her fingers.

"Poor old Gerry," she said. "Did you have a little fight with your sugar daddy?" She pretended to gasp. "Wait, did he dump you?"

Gerry's eyes were oddly glazed; it was hard to tell if she was even listening. She barely blinked. Her pale stage makeup gave her the lifeless complexion of a china doll. I could tell that she really couldn't care less what we did or said. She stared at the tip of the shoe tree, bending slightly this way and that in the breeze. My throat pulsed with anxiety. The world seemed suddenly a menacing, uncertain place. I had no idea what Gerry was about to do next, what she might say. She could have burst into laughter or pulled a gun from beneath her feathers and I wouldn't have been surprised.

Skipper seemed oblivious. She covered her mouth as if shocked.

"Oh no," she gasped. "Oh my god, your boyfriend didn't get you pregnant again, did he? Chop, chop, Joe. Time for Gerry to take another trip to Dr Hadfield."

This, finally, was what got Gerry's attention.

She blinked as if woken from deep sleep.

"That's what you told them, was it?" she said flatly.

Skipper glanced quizzically in my direction. I pretended not to notice.

My cheeks burned. I wished Gerry Lake had never been born. I prayed an invisible hand would reach out and shove her through the open window. That some Stymphalian bird would swoop down and pluck her in its claw.

Skipper let out a large sigh and went to sit on the edge of the desk where she flipped open the lid of Gerry's jewellery box. She picked up a pair of cheap gold hoops and held them to her ears.

"Such a shame about that little pin that went missing, of course," she said.

"Cunt," said Gerry.

"Now, now. No need for foul language."

"Why can't you just leave me alone? Get out of my room," Gerry said and thrust her chin at the door. "Fuck off."

Gerry's back was to the open window now. Behind her I could see the zigzag of torches as teachers scoured the orchard, flushing girls from the bushes. A whistle blew, a scream, some figures with powdered white hair streaming behind them, cloaks flapping.

"Tell her to get the fuck out," Gerry said to me. "Or I'll . . ."

"Or you'll what?" Skipper asked, curious.

Gerry gave me a dangerous look. Her eyes were two small dark holes. I felt a knot in my chest pull tighter and tighter. I wanted to put my hands around her throat to silence her, squeeze so hard the words couldn't come out.

"For god's sake," I hissed, unable to bear it any longer.

I went to my desk and took out the blue pin.

"Here."

Gerry looked at my palm. Her mouth widened. I could see one of her two fangs, stained red with lipstick.

"*You*? You *cow*."

She lunged forward from the windowsill to grab the pin but Skipper, faster on her feet, got there first. She snatched the hairpin from my palm and held it high in the air.

"Give it me," Gerry hissed.

She became very still.

"I said, give it me."

Skipper smiled and slid the end of the pin between her teeth, testing the gold.

"It's not even real. Look," Skipper said, and she took it between her fingers and thumbs and began to press.

"No."

There was a snap like a chicken bone.

"Oh shit," Skipper said, looking sheepish. She giggled with nerves. "Terribly sorry."

Gerry let out a shriek.

Skipper darted forward and put a hand over Gerry's mouth to quiet her. Gerry began to flail in all directions, to kick and claw and bite, her lips curled, her teeth stained red. The pin dropped to the floor. I scrambled after it, reaching for the two separate halves, hoping to fix it. But the small blue petals were crooked, the stem itself snapped completely in half. Gerry hissed and thrashed, fighting free from Skipper's grip. She stood on the side table under the window, then she leant over to my desk and picked up a framed photo of my parents and hurled it like a lightning bolt to the floor near where I crouched. Then a book, then a tennis racket, then a stapler, till the desk was empty. When I stood up, the pin in my fist, Gerry was wielding one of her skating trophies, her arm thrust high above me as if she was about to swipe my head. Skipper bellowed loudly. For a horrific second I saw my face distorted in the chalice—bloodshot eyes, hair glued in knots, a nest of snakes, an ugly, saturnine expression—and, disgusted, I flung Gerry's broken pin out of the window.

The trophy fell.

Skipper lunged towards us. Her arm raised, shielded by her cloak, an aegis protecting her from blows.

Or was it me who moved first, flinging myself forward, landing heavily against the table—Unintentionally? Intentionally?—causing it to tip?

Memor amici.

Remember.

How the table rocked.

Gerry's "oh" of surprise.

The curtains parting.

Feathers.

Sequins.

How she toppled backwards, curtsied through the open window like it was part of a performance, a final bow.

43

I can't sleep. Two or three hours a night at most, while just next to me Jürgen snores like a bear, turning in his dreams, pawing his chest. Sometimes his arm thrashes out, accidentally hitting my head or chest. I know it is childish but when this happens I kick him hard, heeling him in the thigh with all my strength. I thump him in the shoulder, like a school bully, or circle his upper arm as if I am throttling it.

"Ow!"

"You hit me."

"Sorry."

In the end I give up and get out of bed. I pour some whiskey into a mug, pick up my laptop and head outside to the garage where I make a desk for myself amongst Jürgen's wrenches and chain lube and the other surgical-looking bike tools gathering dust on his workbench. I pull out a packet of cigarettes stashed inside my old cash box. The Pandora's box. I have started smoking again, just one or two a day, hiding the evidence from my family, brushing my teeth at odd hours, sneaking around like a teenager.

I rub out my fag butt on the garage wall, open my computer and prowl the web, looking for god knows what anymore. A ghost?

But as far as the internet is concerned, it's like Gerry Lake never existed.

I sip the whiskey, letting it roll around my mouth, light another cigarette.

There is a Lake Gerry, I discover, in Chenango County, New

York, coincidentally nestled between the towns of Guilford, Oxford, and Norwich, population 1,905. I come across a Dr Geraldine Lake in Sydney, Australia—no relation—a specialist in palliative care and what her website calls end-of-life issues.

Eventually I return to the Old Girls Facebook group, set up by some well-meaning DOGs to ensure that "the name and the memories live on." *Memor Amici.* There are notices about holiday homes in Provence, and private ski instruction in Courcheval, and an obituary for a former maths teacher who, despite his treatment by the Divine, lived to be an octogenarian, a shining light in the town production of *The Pirates of Penzance*.

Leavers of 97, I write, using a fake profile. Who remembers Gerry Lake?

I sit on Jürgen's workshop stool checking the message board, scratching my arm, waiting for a response, even though in England they're probably just eating their breakfast. I refresh and refresh, but no one except me is thinking about Gerry Lake at 2:07 a.m.

To pass the time I watch videos of young skaters performing routines. Some of them are five or six years old and wear lipstick, have fuchsia-blushed cheeks, and wiggle their hips to Mariah Carey. By thirteen and fourteen they are nymphs, long-legged shapeshifters flitting over the ice. Even when Gerry brought back medals and trophies we never acknowledged that she had a genuine talent. Her costumes were cheap and sluttish, we bitched, her eye makeup gaudy, her routines obscene.

From outside, a wary cough.

Startled, I almost fall off my stool.

Jürgen squints into the garage, face creased from the pillow, eyes puffy.

"What are you doing out here?" he asks from the doorway, almost but not quite crossing the line, as if he feels he needs to be invited to come in.

"I couldn't sleep," I say, sliding the packet of cigarettes into my robe pocket.

In the video a figure skater makes a perfect "p" with her body and performs what the commentator calls a Biellmann spin.

"What's that you're watching?"

"Research."

As far as Jürgen is concerned I've been working on my résumé all these weeks, sending out more pitches.

"How's it going?" Jürgen asks.

"It's going," I say, a little too quickly.

He yawns loudly, stretches, then comes to stand behind me and rubs my shoulders. The quicker you speak, the guiltier you sound. No one ever lies slowly; the tongue runs and runs like it's racing on thin ice.

"Come to bed."

"I will," I promise. "Soon; go back to sleep."

All I can think about is checking the screen to see if anyone has responded to my question. The skater, dressed in red, crouches on the ice, turning slowly at first, then faster and faster, a blur, furiously spinning. A tornado. Tisiphone, rising from the underworld, come to avenge the dead.

"Don't be long," Jürgen says, kissing the nape of my neck.

"I won't," I say.

As he leaves he catches sight of the cash box, sitting on the top of an old crate. He scratches his chin, as if something about it is familiar, then he yawns again and pads back into the house.

As soon as the coast is clear I click back to the Old Girls page.

Comments: One.

I scramble for my packet of cigarettes, light up, inhale deeply, then read:

Geraldine Lake? That Fifth Year who fell out of the window? Good lord. As if one could forget.

A second message appears.

> Oh my god. Gerry Lake! We thought the whole thing was a dare.
> All part of the pranks. One feels rather awful when you think
> about it.

Another and another.

> We spent half our life climbing in and out of windows remember? We
> used to sit on our ledges and chain smoke. Once we tied our bed sheets
> together and abseiled down St Hilda's. What a hoot.

Someone else agrees.

> OMG. Yes. Hilarious!

Gerry Lake didn't smoke a day in her life, I type. She was an athlete. Amongst other things, she was afraid of heights.

There is a pause. I imagine these women sitting at large oak desks, in libraries and studies, a Labrador by their feet, surrounded by silver-framed photos of their children.

Gerry did take her skating terribly seriously, someone remembers. A funny old stick. Lorks, she must have thought we were such heathens! Her year did rather enjoy winding her up. And some of those Fifth Formers were quite terrifying, naming no names, but that one who wore the cardigan, she scared me silly.

I picture a group of Second Years scurrying to hold a door open for us, darting like fish.

We mimicked Gerry's accent, I reply quickly. We rifled through her desk. Hid her skates before training. We called her the Poison Dwarf.

Outside I can hear one of the raccoons who live beneath the garage, rummaging around in the bins. A bottle smashes.

Oh, Gerry Lake never could take a joke. Rather a spoilt madam. One has to blame the parents of course for what happened. Awful people. Very pushy. No wonder she jumped.

I think of Mr Lake. Almost unrecognisable in the photos in the papers at the time, hollowed cheeks and wispy hair, barely visible next to his lawyer.

The parents? I write, stubbing out my cigarette.

I stare out into the darkness, pinching my arm. There's a whine from the dog standing guard in the house, the Santa Ana winds, palm leaves clattering like bones. I uncurl my fingers.

Jumped?

44

Our parents were called, some arriving as early as that very morning, after which we were summoned to the headmistress's office in groups of four or five, ashen and unwashed, eggshell and flour still in our hair. The rest of us were confined to the rec room while we waited to be interviewed. No one would tell us what had happened to Gerry. We had no idea if she was alive or dead.

Prisoners, we sat by the window, jostling for space. The maintenance men piled a heap of broken furniture on the lawn, desks and chairs, as if building a pyre. News spread of our disgrace. One by one, the townspeople came—a dog walker, two old women pushing shopping trolleys, the librarian, the pub landlord, a delivery man, the cinema projectionist, the owner of the tea shop, the Woolworths manager, perhaps even Lauren—hands on hips, tutting. Bit by bit they shuffled closer, onto school property, seeing that no one was stopping them. Both curious and vitriolic.

They crunched over broken glass, shredded books, the plastic bones of a laboratory skeleton. Our faces were pressed against the rec room windows.

"Shameful," they said, shaking their heads, at us. "Disgusting. Pack of wild animals. Hooligans. Ungrateful so-and-sos."

When the cleaners and the kitchen staff arrived for work, there was a loud rumble of dissent.

"Forget it," they said and put their coats back on. They gestured at us. "Let them clean this mess up themselves. Those la-di-das can sort their own breakfast for once, I'll thank you very much."

The Third Years made jam sandwiches, which they delivered

to us on brown plastic trays with a glass of milk, dispensed from three four-litre jugs. Other years who'd participated in the rebellion had been given brooms and sponges and mops, their hair tied up with handkerchiefs, like the women of the Blitz. Teachers stood watch as they swept and scrubbed. A wartime spirit seemed to prevail—make do and mend. They spent a lot of time arranging the bandannas in their hair. They whistled and sang.

"This is so unfair," moaned George, flopping onto a beanbag next to me. "It's not like we're criminals."

There were mutters of agreement.

I pressed my thumbnail into the soft skin of my arm and said nothing. Across the rec room Skipper was talking quietly to Henry Peck, their heads pressed together, whispering. She stared at me once, then looked away.

The townies came and went, their numbers growing minute by minute. There was a loud murmur of excitement whenever a new parent arrived.

"If one of mine had done all that, I'd beat her black and blue," they heckled. "I'd wring her blooming neck."

Some parents, shocked by the level of destruction, must have made the decision to pull their daughters out of school then, a week before the term ended. The maintenance men tossed trunks into car boots, carelessly swinging. Our friends waved pitifully at us through the rec room window, slid into the back seats of BMWs and Volvos, lying flat as their parents drove round the Circle past the townies.

"Good riddance to bad rubbish."

"Buzz off."

"Get lost."

A gang of King Edmunds leant against our school wall in the spot where Lauren used to wait, giving each car the finger and hurling empty cans of Coke.

By lunch our numbers had dwindled to just a handful. George sat with her legs wrapped around Henry, plaiting her hair. We slept or grazed from unguarded tuck boxes or doodled in each other's leavers notebooks. I stared out of the window. It was Dave, or possibly George, who thought to compare the various messages we'd been left by Gerry.

"Good luck with your GCSEs," George read first, holding her book up so we could see where Gerry had signed her name with a large G to cover the empty white page.

"Good luck with your exams," Dave read out next.

"Good luck with everything," Henry said, yawning

"Good luck," someone else read out.

"Good luck."

I watched as George went around the rec room comparing notes, every message more or less identical. I nudged my book beneath my seat, not wanting them to see where, beneath the large swirling G, Gerry had written her address in bubble letters, doodled round the edges. As if she believed we'd stay in touch over the summer, write to each other, visit. That we were friends.

George squatted down and retrieved my book from beneath the seat, thumbing through to the end pages.

"Oh my god," she said.

Her face paled. She shuffled with embarrassment.

"What?"

When Skipper peered over George's shoulder to read, her mouth dropped open then quickly snapped shut. She snorted and let out a small, "Ha."

"Let me see." I snatched the notebook.

The address was gone, painted over with layers of Tipp-Ex.

Instead, in thick block letters:

YOU BITCH.

45

My mother, I remember, was seated in our headmistress's office next to Skipper's parents. Standing behind them, as if posing for a school photo, were the Pecks and the Gordon-Warrens. The school nurse—ghostly looking, painfully thin—hovered in the corner with her arms crossed, there to deal with sudden cases of faintness or hysteria. Divines were famed for their dramatics. Against the wall stood two uniformed policemen.

My mother sighed loudly as we filed into the headmistress's office and raised her eyebrows at the other parents. Disgruntled, they considered this whole process pointless, unnecessarily heavy-handed. Rod, in particular, seemed notably put out. My mother had arrived from Hong Kong a week earlier to visit old friends, her various lunches and dinner plans now disrupted. More than once that day I saw her check her watch or yawn, giving a sense of what she must have been like as a student. Her eyes roamed over the bookshelf, visibly flinching at the Bible and prayer books. She, like most parents, considered Fat Fran intolerably pious.

"A very silly woman," I overheard her once saying. "Not at all Divine."

"Isn't this rather a waste of everybody's time?" one of the fathers grumbled.

The policemen glanced at one another. Townies.

"All the same," the taller of them said.

"Girls," Fat Fran instructed. "Sit down."

There was a prolonged silence. The large oak bureau on which she wrote all her sermons was notably missing, replaced by a flimsy folding table. Likewise her portrait had been removed, a picture light illuminating a blank wall. The carpet, cleaned of glue and feathers, was still tacky underfoot. Fat Fran herself wore a look of smug self-satisfaction, her chin resting atop her interlinked fingers. All the crimes she had long suspected us of— snobbery, cruelty, a propensity for violence—had proven to be true.

"For goodness' sake," my mother said. "Let's get this over with. Darling, just tell them whatever it is they want to know."

One of the policemen kept his hands in his pockets, studying the five of us. The other rocked from foot to foot.

"What I know," I echoed.

"About Geraldine Lake," the more serious policeman clarified. "Friends, boyfriends, unusual behaviour. Anything that seemed out of the ordinary."

The school nurse looked at me. I slid my hands inside my cloak and gripped Gerry's broken pin, which I had picked up from the grass. Skipper's knee began to jiggle, her heel drumming the floor as she was prone to do in moments of pressure: school exams for example, speech days, the sidelines of a lacrosse match. A single feather drifted down from the top of a bookshelf.

"Girls?" Fat Fran pressed her hands together and tilted forward.

I watched the feather fall, rocking to and fro.

The twins and George glanced at Skipper, then me.

They shook their heads.

"Nothing," they agreed.

What were Divine if not loyal?

My mother stood up and dusted down her skirt, notably relieved.

"There we have it."

She tapped me on the shoulder and I got up and followed her out.

"Absolutely ridiculous," she muttered under her breath.

In the tea shop in town she instructed me to order whatever I wanted.

"Special treat," she said. As if in some way I'd earned it.

A surly waitress did her best to ignore my mother's attempts to get her attention, a finger raised in the air. When our food arrived, the teapot and cake were dumped on our table without ceremony, our cutlery dropped in a pile. The Victoria sponge was dry and crumbly. The waitress scowled the entirety of the meal—or perhaps I was imagining this—and eyeballed me accusingly from her seat at the counter. My mother ate nothing as usual, sipping a cup of black tea.

"You're looking rather pale, darling."

I pushed the cake around the plate, pressing the slice with the back of my fork, jam oozing, congealing on the prongs. For the first time, my mother seemed concerned. She moved aside her teapot and the vase of plastic flowers on the table and bent towards me.

"One mustn't let it get you down," she said.

These were, it struck me, the same words she'd uttered shortly before the kennelman put a bullet through the brain of my first pony—an ancient, much loved Dartmoor—and fed him to the hounds.

I nodded, trying not to cry in the tea shop, my head cradled in my hands, staring down at the white tablecloth. I felt Gerry's hairpin burning in my pocket. My mother reached out and for a moment it seemed she was about to stroke my cheek. I willed her to cradle me in her arms, to rub my back, smooth my hair, to tell me everything was going to be all right. But she wasn't that kind of mother.

"Elbows," my mother said, tapping me on the arm instead, raising an eyebrow at the offending body parts till I removed them from the table.

"The school has rather been on the rocks. Nothing one can do about it now. All that money we donated to the new sports hall though. Your father will have a fit."

This was what Rod cared about, the school merger.

On the subject of Gerry Lake herself, who she knew not to be part of my inner circle, she said almost nothing, resorting in the end to schoolgirl French.

"*Tant pis*," she said with a sigh as she drank from her teacup. Too bad.

Then she signalled for the bill.

We walked back to my mother's car, parked underneath the shoe tree, and got in. I watched as she reached across the seat and, to my surprise, took out a packet of Marlboros from the glove compartment. Using the red coil from the car lighter, she lit it, sank back into the driving seat and sighed with pleasure.

Seeing my expression, she offered me the packet.

This was the first time I had ever smoked in front of an adult.

"Go on. You've had a rough night, I suppose. Just don't tell your father."

I took one and wound down my window.

The cleanup was still under way. Maintenance men, including Stuart McKibbin, were carting broken laboratory equipment towards the skips. Stools, a microscope, specimen jars. I saw him make a crude gesture with a preserved sheep's head, thrusting it at his groin, laughing coarsely. I slid down in my seat out of view.

"Oh god, I remember him," my mother said of the sheep, as if discussing an old friend.

The men tossed a human skeleton into the skip. At the sight of the body, a bag of bones hanging limply over the side of the skip, my teeth began to chatter. A feeling of dread flooded through me. My heart began to pound. My eyes stung. I thought I might vomit. I threw the cigarette out of the window.

"Please, Mummy, can't I just come with you now?" I begged. There was only a week left until the end of term, exams were over, what was the point, I argued, in me staying.

My mother, who never believed in pandering to homesickness, patted me a few times on the knee. The chapel bell rang. A line of First Years climbed the bridge like ants, followed by the older years. I saw Skipper and the twins hovering underneath the shoe tree, watching our car. Feeling increasingly desperate, I imagined holding the sharp end of Gerry's pin that was still in my pocket to my mother's neck, ordering her to drive. But that was the kind of thing Lauren would do, someone spontaneous and plucky, not a coward like me.

"Chin up, angel," my mother said, oblivious, and she gave me a kiss on the head and stretched across me to open the car door. She smelt, I remember, of smoke and mothballs. "See you in a week."

In chapel that afternoon the other girls, older and younger, craned their necks to look at us, their heads hung upside down from the choir stalls. They whispered behind their hymnbooks, watching as one by one we slid grimly along the wooden pews and waited for an announcement.

"Girls, I am sad to report that last night . . ." Fat Fran began, but she was interrupted by the chime of an alarm clock.

"Oh fuck," said George.

We knew what was happening but were powerless to stop it. We didn't even try. Fat Fran ignored the bell and continued.

"I have some . . ."

Another chime began. A chirp from the small Braun clock we'd hidden the previous night beneath the white folds of the altar, timed to go off during evensong. Fat Fran frowned, looked briefly over her shoulder, and began again.

"As you know, one of our Fifth Year . . ."

A third alarm went off, louder this time, this one coming from underneath a pew. Girls began to giggle. Fat Fran gripped the pulpit, tilted forward a little, and raised her voice.

"Last night I was informed by . . ."

The fourth clock sounded somewhere in the sanctuary, then a fifth up by the organ, then a sixth, then a seventh, then an eighth in near perfect succession, pealing like church bells. Appalled, Fat Fran's mouth fell open, the many folds in her neck buckled.

"Whoever is . . . ," she tried to shout, but by then it was impossible to hear anything above the incessant ringing. How many had we hidden, tens, hundreds, we couldn't remember. At first we sat, our heads slightly bowed, some of us wincing with embarrassment or chewing our nails, pretending we couldn't hear it. How could we have predicted what was going to happen to Gerry?

"Intolerable." Fat Fran slammed her hymnal on the pulpit. A starting pistol. All around me girls sprang into action; they leapt from the pews and scrambled around the chapel trying to muffle as many clocks as they could find. In the vestry, the pews, behind the kneelers, high up on the crucifix, resting in the crook above Jesus's shoulder. Pandemonium. Younger years were squealing in excitement, stamping their feet and laughing.

No one was bothered that Gerry Lake was in a coma, her life hanging by a thread. That her pelvis was broken. That, as we'd later read in the papers, she had sustained significant trauma, lacerations to the liver and spleen, possible spinal cord damage. No one cared if she died or not. No one thought of her at all.

46

I look like a crone. Grey haired, haggard, barely functioning after weeks of not sleeping. My friend Audrey offers me her therapist's details, but I squirm with embarrassment at the word *shrink.*

"Don't be so fucking British," she tells me and texts me a number.

When I ask Jürgen if he thinks I need to get my head examined, he looks around shiftily and tugs on his beard, a man who cannot lie.

"Fine," I give in.

Instead of contacting Audrey's woman, I opt for a different therapist I find online, someone anonymous, a man called Dr Jason. Whether that is his first or last name is unclear. A secretary responds within the hour with an appointment time, attaching a long questionnaire.

Are you currently experiencing anxiety or panic attacks or having any problems sleeping?

I chew my cheek, rattling my fingers on the keypad. I think of my inability to concentrate, the constant dwelling in the past, the irritability, the sudden flashes of violence, the time, for example, I kicked the dog for no reason, or how just this morning, when Lena refused to get dressed, I pinned her to the bed, pressing so hard with my palm that I momentarily left a handprint.

Do you consider yourself to be spiritual or religious? Were your parents present during your entire childhood, yes or no? Which of the following describes your childhood family experience:

It was an outstanding home environment.
It was an orderly home environment.
It was a chaotic home environment.

As I drive along Sunset Boulevard, I begin to regret finding a therapist on Google or even seeing anyone at all. Suddenly I don't feel like spreading myself out on a rock to have my liver pecked apart. What was I thinking? I pull up in front of the office, which is on the second floor of a mini-mall, between a dispensary and a beauty salon. I'd be better off getting my nails done. I email the receptionist from the car, hunched low behind the wheel, citing a family emergency.

When I get home, Jürgen is standing in front of the garage scrubbing his bike.

"So? How was it?"

"It wasn't. I got a pedicure."

Jürgen squints at my toes quizzically, wondering if this is a joke.

"Where's Lena?"

He thumbs towards the garage.

"Mama," calls Lena. "Come, come."

She is sitting crosslegged on the floor with my cash box. The box is empty, the contents—cigarettes, letters, cuttings, the Polaroid photos—neatly ordered around her as if she's setting up shop.

I shriek. My face pales, my legs seem to empty of blood, I can't seem to run there fast enough.

"What is it?" Jürgen says and rushes after me into the garage.

Lena holds up a photo of a penis.

"Hundred dollars, please."

"*Mein Gott!*"

Jürgen shakes his head at me in disbelief. A vein between his eye and his temple bulges. This is the angriest I've ever seen him.

"I can't believe this. Sephine!"

Then he is down on the floor, snatching up the pictures, ramming them back in the cash box.

"*Scheiße*, Sephine, what the hell, are you crazy? You told me you threw these fucking things away. You ripped them up. You actually used those words. What's wrong with you?"

"I know. I know. I only kept them because . . ." I stumble over my words, trying to come up with a rational explanation.

Jürgen groans. He draws his hand down his chin, squatting on the garage floor, staring down at the concrete between his knees.

"Enough," he says quietly. "Enough now."

He carries the cash box under his arm to the barbecue, empties it upside down, and douses it with lighter fuel. Lena screams as she watches her entire shop's inventory go up in flames, flailing her arms, yanking on Jürgen's shirt.

"Stop it, Daddy, stop it!" Lena cries.

Something in Lena's hair glints. Gerry's pin, which my daughter has stuck back together with duct tape. I snatch it from behind her ear and slide it into my pocket.

"Ow, Mama hurt me," Lena screams. She glares accusingly, her hands on her hips. Stealer. Thief.

47

We were gated, kept under lock and key, like princesses in a cas-
tle, Hera on her golden throne. No leaving the school grounds
under any circumstances, escorted to meals, under constant sur-
veillance, no telephone contact or visits from the outside world.
But by then I hadn't seen Lauren in over a week and she had long
given up calling. After the clock incident in the chapel, I returned
to my dormitory briefly, instructed to take only the possessions I
needed for those last remaining days of school. A weepy-looking
deputy stood in the corridor as I packed. Someone had thought to
lock the window by then; the floral curtain was hanging lifelessly,
the table turned upright. According to newspaper reports—an
anonymous source—this was an accident waiting to happen,
the window opening three times the legal limit, ample space for
someone as petite as Gerry to drop through. I tried not to look
at Gerry's neatly made bed, the indent on her pillow, her stuffed
toys, the photos of her teammates. As quickly as I could I filled
an empty duvet cover and dragged it a few feet along the corridor to the single room, traditionally reserved for French exchange
students.

We read about Gerry in the tabloids—the life support machine, the coma, the dwindling prospect of recovery, the trainer
who'd been taken in for questioning, his collection of Polaroid
photos—crowding around a single copy in the San, the only place
in school to which we had unlimited access.

"He took the photos? That was him? Rank," George
Gordon-Warren screeched and threw the paper to the floor.
"That gorilla?"

I thought of the hairy arm I had seen dangling from an open car window on days he had come to collect Gerry.

"Told you so," announced Skipper, though she'd never once mentioned the trainer. "Gerry was probably in on the whole thing."

The twins made gagging sounds at each other and rolled around on the San floor.

The school nurse observed girls for signs of trauma or depression, putting her palm to our foreheads, scrutinising our behaviour. As if what Gerry had might be contagious. I avoided looking the nurse in the eye. I shrunk from her as she fluttered around us, recoiled from the reach of her clammy hands.

Before long we became restless. While for the rest of the school, lessons went on as normal, we were trapped inside the grounds with nothing to do except tidy our school desks and write letters of apology to horrified benefactors. The end-of-year celebrations had all been revoked, the leavers ball and school outings cancelled, replaced instead with community service. Painting classroom walls, scrubbing the chapel clean, varnishing pews.

"Oh my god," George said after we'd tugged free all the loo roll from the apple trees, flopping on her back in the orchard. "If they keep us locked up any longer, I'll do a Gerry."

The phrase spread like wildfire that week, taking over from the pistol-fingers-to-the-head gesture, or pencil fingers up the nose. *Fucking hell,* girls said as they sighed dramatically, flicking their hair, slumping down onto their bunk beds, hands cast over their brows, *I'm so bored I'm going to do a Gerry.* If we were late for lunch, or our cigarettes finally ran out, or when Dave noticed the period stain on the back of my thin summer dress as I was sweeping the rec room floor, she shoved me in the ribs, *don't do a Gerry.* Hollow feeling, mechanical, I forced my cheeks into a stiff smile. Even though I was back amongst my old friends, I felt like an imposter. Skipper looked at me from across the room. She, in particular, was always watching me, judging, a constant reminder of Gerry. As much as possible I tried to make sure she and I were never alone. I showered late at night or in the early morning. I ate my breakfast with Dickie Balfour.

The final weekend of the Divine—the very last time our school gates would be open—we were banned from taking the bus to Oxford. We summoned boys from a nearby boarding school instead. They arrived by taxi on Saturday afternoon, already drunk, quarter bottles of vodka hidden in their blazers, whistling for us to sneak them over the fence in broad daylight. Our housemistress and her deputy were, for once, nowhere to be seen, finally beyond caring. We smoked and flicked our hair and one by one couples disappeared into the laundry room or behind the sports hall or the maintenance shed. The last boy left was a short, stout-looking Rupert with a lisp, his bottom lip fat and bee-stung. I was only interested in his vodka. He kissed me sloppily before he prodded his finger inside my pants, circling it around like he was stirring a cup of tea with a pencil. I laughed in his face, an ugly cackle.

"I thought you liked me," he whined.

"Grow up," I said.

After Stuart I couldn't have cared less about a boy like him.

I didn't care about anything.

"Frigid," he hissed as I climbed out of the bushes, taking his bottle with me. "Hey, where are you going?"

I climbed the bridge. I wanted to smash something, to tear it to pieces, to yell and shout and scream. I dropped the bottle off the bridge. Saw it explode like a firework on the road below. A car swerved, the driver spouting expletives.

"What the bloody hell do you think you're playing at?"

I slunk off the bridge.

Down the school drive.

Out of the gates.

I, myself, didn't know until I was across the park and walking down Lauren's street.

I thumped on her door, hammering so hard my knuckles burned.

"All right, all right. Keep your bloody hair on," I heard her shouting and the thud of feet on the stairs.

The door yanked open.

"Oh," said Lauren, her face soured. She sucked in her cheeks, crossed her arms and blocked the doorway.

"What the fuck do you want? I'm getting ready for work. If you've come here for that fucking pin, I've lost it, all right?"

I opened my mouth but nothing came out, a lump in my throat as if I'd swallowed a large stone. She looked me up and down distrustfully, taking in the red eyes, the bitten lip, the bruised knuckles. Her lip curled up at the edges with scorn. I shook my head.

"Sorry," I said. "Never mind."

Stiffly, I turned to leave.

"Jesus Christ, Josephine." Lauren clicked her tongue.

She nudged the front door open with her heel.

"Where d'ya think you're going?"

48

Lauren's father was drinking tea at the kitchen table, the news-
paper spread open in front of him. The racing was playing loudly
on the portable radio. He watched me over his cup as I came in
and didn't say anything to either of us except for when Lauren
switched channels.

"Turn it back."

Lauren rolled her eyes but did as he said. She filled the kettle,
took out the instant coffee, fished around in the sink for some
mugs, drying them on her T-shirt. I stood very still in the corner
of the room trying not to draw attention to myself. I looked at the
white scar under his chin.

Mr McKibbin grunted at me, rolled his paper under his arm
and got up.

We heard the door slam.

"Wanker," Lauren said.

Upstairs we sat on her bedroom floor with our cups of coffee. I was on one side of the room, Lauren on the other. Her legs
were curled beneath her like a cat—guarded, distrustful—as she
waited for me to say something.

"You all right then?" she eventually asked.

"Fine," I mumbled, though it must have been obvious this
was far from true. I was even skinnier than normal. My hair was
greasy and limp, my shoulders hunched. I was drunk and miserable.

Lauren sipped her coffee in silence looking at me, but in the
end she couldn't help herself.

"Talked to my brother lately?"

"No," I said.

This at least was true.

Lauren narrowed her eyes, trying to decide if she believed me. Then she stuck out her tongue and blew a raspberry.

"Stuart's a right slag. Don't waste your breath on him. Here," she said, and crawled beneath the bed and pulled out a bottle of Bell's, sloshing it into my coffee. She licked her arm where the drink had splattered and filled her own. Lauren was trying to make me feel better, but her words had the opposite effect. I hadn't meant anything to Stuart, I wasn't special at all. I felt the whisky burn the length of my throat, scalding, clawing my insides. I held out my cup for more.

"You hungry?" Lauren asked.

I hadn't eaten properly in days, only picking at my school meals, tossing the contents in the scrap buckets before everyone else had barely begun.

"Not particularly," I said.

"Well, I'm fucking starving." Lauren got up and pulled my arm.

I followed Lauren downstairs where she looked into the fridge, and when there was nothing there that seemed to satisfy her, she made me walk with her to the fish and chip shop. We sat there with the fish spread out on the table between us. Lauren salted the chips.

"Red sauce?"

I nodded.

The smell of the chip fat, the hiss of baskets as they plunged into simmering oil, the great big slabs of fish, all made me nauseated.

The man at the table next to us was reading a copy of the local newspaper, the headline fanned out towards our table. Lauren glanced at it and shuffled a chip around the white paper, nervous, or was it only my imagination, reluctant to look me in the eye. I turned and stared out of the window. Outside the sky looked curdled, the sun a sickly yellow. The chippy was unbearably hot; I remember there was a light overhead humming, and my head ached. When the first specks of rain began to hiss on the hot pavement, townies ran for cover, and the door began to jingle nonstop. Men jogged to the bookmaker's across the street with newspapers over their heads. Two girls with g-strings showing raced their pushchairs. A large posse of King Edmunds, shrieking loudly at a thunderclap, came ducking in through the doorway, Kappa jackets over their heads, tight ponytails, wide shiny foreheads. Lauren pretended that she hadn't seen them. Her jaw jutted out, she speared a chip but didn't eat it. Some of the King Edmund's girls turned to look at us in the corner and began sniggering and elbowing the boys they were with, who turned around to look at us too. Lauren's hair was loose, a long white cape down her back. I was deathly pale, grim looking. We made a ghoulish pair, I suppose. An easy target.

One of the group, I recognised, was the girl from the park who had ordered me to get down on my knees and polish her shoes.

"Jade Dockett," muttered Lauren under her breath. "Slut."

The KE girls sucked their teeth.

"Jade, did you hear what that minger just called you?"

"Fucking cheek of it."

"Nasty little bitch."

"Cucumbers," another shouted, which I presumed was meant for me. "Lezzers."

The boys snapped their fingers in the air and fell about laughing.

"Just ignore them," I said.

I scrunched up our leftovers and tossed them in the bin.

I pulled Lauren to her feet and slipped my arm under hers, as if she was Divine. The boys, dressed in tracksuits and big baggy jeans, stamped their legs under the table, red-faced toddlers with their trousers nearly falling down. I felt something vicious and ugly hammering inside my rib cage, clawing to get out. Silently I dared one of them to do something. *Go on, try it.* When we walked past, I stared unflinchingly at their table, but no one spat in my face or shoved me or tripped me up.

"Oy, McKibbin," one of the boys shouted.

He made a V with his fingers and lizard flicked his tongue at us, which made the girls all squeal in disgust. The girl from the park sniggered loudly.

I slipped free of Lauren, marched back to the table, singling her out in particular.

"Bugger off," I said and sent her Coke flying.

She screamed and leapt to her feet. The boys stamped their feet even harder; we could hear them snapping their fingers and howling hysterically as Lauren and I walked arm in arm out of the door.

Lauren stopped in the road.

"I can't believe you just did that. To *Jade Dockett*."

"What?"

"Bugger orff," she mimicked.

I lifted my shoulders as if it was nothing. As if my heart wasn't pounding. As if my fists weren't knotted in balls.

She repeated it again, in awe.

"Bugger orff."

She gave me a peck on the cheek to thank me.

"Gayer," I joked.

She shoved me hard in the hip. I smiled. She reached her arm around my waist and hooked me back in.

"Let's get pissed."

49

We got drunk on a cheap bottle of vodka and a pint of milk from the corner shop, bought with the last of my allowance money. The man at the till looked at Lauren's boobs and didn't bother asking for an ID. From a phone box she called her boss at Woolworths and told him she was too poorly to work. Sitting cross-legged in the park bandstand, Lauren emptied out half the milk and topped it up with vodka, shaking it like a cocktail waitress.

"White Russians," she said with a shrug when she saw my expression.

She passed me the carton, chin glistening, wiping it on her sleeve.

I told her about the school merging, how we'd all be moving to the new campus, thirty miles away.

"So, what, you're not coming back here then?"

"We could write to each other?" I suggested. "I could visit?"

"Yeah, whatever," she said, sounding insulted. "I mean, it's not like I'm going to live in this shithole forever."

In the past when I'd asked Lauren what she'd do after she left school she didn't have an answer. She was probably far brighter than most Divines, but university was out of the question.

"Brighton," she said now, swirling the milk in the carton. "I'll probably move to Brighton or something. Or Bournemouth."

"What's in Bournemouth?"

"I dunno, never been, sounds good, though. The sea and that," she said and tossed the empty vodka bottle into the bushes.

On the way home Lauren picked a route, intentionally or not, that led us down Kerry's street. As we neared her house I kept my eyes forward, pretending not to recognise it, but Lauren slipped her arm free of mine and sashayed into their front garden.

"Lauren, please," I begged.

The last person I wanted to see was Stuart's girlfriend.

"Oy, get out here, you pikey," Lauren shouted, banging on the door, but to my relief no one answered.

She glared through the letterbox.

I had never understood why Lauren hated Kerry so much. Whenever I asked Lauren, she rolled her eyes as if it was obvious. A former King Edmund, Kerry perhaps had been the school bully, cornered Lauren in the playground, spat on her, pulled her hair, mimicked her the way Skipper had Gerry. Or maybe her only crime was that she'd stolen Lauren's brother.

A few neighbours were peering out of their front doors to see what the commotion was about.

"Oy, keep it down, will you," a man said over the wall.

"Lauren, come on, they're not even home," I pleaded. "What's the point?"

Lauren snorted in defiance, sloshing milk through the mail slot.

This seemed to give her inspiration.

She turned to the rubbish bins and flipped the lids open. It didn't take her long to find the ammunition she was looking for. She waggled a soiled nappy in the air, triumphant, and before I could do anything to stop her, smeared it on Kerry's door handle. Appalled, all I could do was stand and watch.

Across the road a neighbour was threatening to call the police.

What would my parents say if I was arrested for throwing shit at someone's house? I pictured their reaction—my mother summoned from London, her weekend plans ruined; my father pacing his office, placing calls with connections he had, attempting to keep it out of the papers—and felt instantly sober.

"Please," I hissed. "Stop."

But Lauren just cackled.

"Just wait until your father hears about this," shouted the

neighbour, reading my mind, and she rushed inside her house as if she was about to summon Mr McKibbin.

This, finally, got Lauren's attention.

"Nosy old bag," she complained and dumped the nappy onto the street. "Let's go."

I hesitated. Lauren was still drunk, buzzing with adrenaline, a loaded gun. I had no idea what trouble she had planned next, what she might do, where she might lead me. But when I thought about going back to school, holed up in the rec room with Skipper and the twins, or sitting in my empty dormitory with nothing but a small wooden crucifix on the wall to look at, I wanted to sob.

"Go where?" I asked Lauren tentatively.

"I dunno. Home," she said and wiped her hands on the wall.

"What about Joan?"

"Out. Gone to the pictures with Sue."

"Okay," I finally agreed. "But just for a bit."

The house was as we'd left it—dark and empty, dirty plates still sitting in the sink. We stole two beers from the fridge. After a while I stopped thinking about Stuart or Skipper, or even Gerry, and began to relax. Lauren turned up the stereo full volume in the sitting room. I demonstrated to Lauren how the boys danced at our school parties, pogo bouncing, thrashing my head. I flopped on the sofa next to her, too dizzy to stand.

"God, you're a skinny bitch," Lauren said, comparing our bodies.

I looked down. Knock-knees, thighs no bigger than my calves, legs like pipe cleaners. I felt a sudden wave of misery wash over me again. Lauren was right, I was hideous, a walking skeleton. I tried to cover myself up.

"Oy, don't get the hump; I didn't mean it like that."

I downed my can.

"I hate my body," I confessed.

"You what?"

"I hate my legs and, like, my whole face."

"Shut up." Lauren looked genuinely surprised. "You're so pretty."

I knew this wasn't true. I waited for her to laugh sarcastically but she didn't. This was the first real compliment she had ever given me. I was so needy, so ravenous for someone's approval by then, like a dog waiting for scraps from the table, I almost whimpered.

"My nose is enormous," I said, covering it with my hand.

"Shut up, you're just posh. All posh people have big noses."

I elbowed her.

"I fucking hate my hair," she admitted, swigging from her can.

"What?"

I couldn't believe it. Her hair wasn't mousy like mine, it didn't frizz when it got wet. It was smooth, silvery, ethereal looking.

"But it's amazing," I said, reaching out to touch it.

It ran through my fingers like water.

"Fuck off. I only keep it like this because of my mum. She's always wanted this proper girly girl, not a tomboy."

I helped Lauren to twist it behind her neck to see what it would look like short.

She stared at herself in the mirror. "My dad would go mental."

"You look really good with long hair, too," I said, trying to make her feel better.

Her face stiffened and she walked out of the room.

"What are you doing?" I called after her.

When she came back down the stairs, she was armed with an electric razor and a large pair of kitchen scissors.

"No way," I said.

"Pussy."

She took a fist of hair and snipped. Half a curtain was gone.

I let out a scream.

"Oh my god."

She sawed another chunk from the back, close to her scalp. Then she handed me the razor.

"You going to just stand there like a lemon or what?"

She knelt on the floor and closed her eyes. I took a few deep breaths. I hesitated, then I cleared one straight line over the crown of her head to the nape of her neck. There was something powerful about the action, God-like.

"Chin down," I ordered.

I made half-moons around each ear.

I licked short her sideburns and the forelock at the very top of her head. After all her hair was gone, I told her to keep her eyes closed and led her back to the mirror.

"Three, two, one," I said.

Lauren's eyes opened.

"Fuck," she said and stroked her head in circles. "It's so weird. It's like looking at . . ."

"Stuart," we said at the same time.

The anniversary clock in the sitting room chimed six. I had already missed three check-ins. I wasn't even supposed to be out of my dorm.

"Shit, we'd better tidy this crap up before my mum gets home," said Lauren.

We brushed up the chunks of blond hair from the floor and hid the empty cans at the bottom of the bin. When Lauren went for a shower, I waited in her bedroom to say goodbye. This might be, I realised, the last time I'd see her. In less than a week I'd be back in Hong Kong. I thought briefly about inviting Lauren to stay with me that summer but I knew it was impossible. Despite what she'd claimed in the bandstand, I knew Lauren would probably never leave the town. Her job would be to take care of Joan as she grew more incapacitated, manage the house, pay the rent.

Thinking about this, I played with the collection of necklaces on her dressing table for the final time, letting the beads clack through my fingers, tried some of her lip gloss, opened and closed the drawers. The envelope of Polaroids. My stomach lurched. I took them out and laid them flat on the bottom bunk. My head danced and swirled from the vodka and beer. Lauren came back with just a towel wrapped around her.

"Lightweight," she mocked, nudging my toe that was on the floor to stop the room from spinning.

I wriggled upright.

"Feel," she said.

She sat next to me and took my hand in hers and rubbed it gently over her shaved head. One way bristled, the other felt like velvet. I closed my eyes. It felt very comforting, like stroking a cat or a dog. I didn't want to cry in front of her, but suddenly tears ran down my nose and pattered to the floor, seeping slowly into the carpet.

"Shit. You want to talk about it?"

"What?"

Lauren glanced at the photos.

"You know. Gerry."

I tried to speak, but the words caught in my throat like I'd swallowed something whole. I shook my head. Felt the floor dropping out from under me. I lurched forward to the bin, on my knees; a river gushed out of me. Still I couldn't get the words out. I gagged and wept, choking on my own bile. When I was finally empty, I slumped down on the floor, hunched on all fours like a dog.

Lauren lay down next to me on the carpet. A hand on my back, rubbing me gently between the shoulder blades. *Shh, shh.* She smelt so clean, I remember, of talcum powder and toothpaste.

I tried to sit up.

"I'm disgusting." A saliva thread hung like a cobweb between my chin and the floor. I wiped my hand across my mouth.

"No, you're not. Don't say that."

"I am," I insisted.

"Shut the fuck up."

She came closer to prove it, nose to nose, inhaled.

"See."

"Freak," I said.

"Yeah," she said quietly. "Probably."

She stared at my mouth.

Then she kissed me.

50

At the airport Jürgen puts my luggage on the scales and slides two passports to the agent at the check-in desk as if he is the one going somewhere. The agent hands my documents back to Jürgen, who puts the boarding card inside the passports, takes Lena's hand, and walks us to Departures where he stoops on one knee, as if proposing. Lena sits down on it. They whisper in each other's ears and I feel the old sting of being cold-shouldered, left out of the conversation, not privy to their secrets. I tell Lena we have to go.

"Why isn't Dada coming?"

Jürgen looks at me as if he, too, wants to hear the answer. After what happened in the garage, I haven't dared tell him about the possibility of attending the reunion. I've blamed this trip—booked hastily and in the middle of the night—on one of my mother's guilt trips about how little she sees of her only grand-daughter.

"Daddy has to work," I say.

She clings to his leg, refusing to let go.

"I want Dada."

"Be nice to Mummy, all right," Jürgen warns when he finally unpeels her.

As we say goodbye Jürgen holds me on either side of my head, cupping my ears, the closest we've been since he set fire to the photos. Everything Jürgen says at the airport sounds as if it is coming from a long way above me, on the far surface of the water. Something, something, something, I hear.

"Agreed?"

I nod.

"*Gut.* Now go, or you'll miss your flight," he says and pretends to boot Lena in the bottom, walking towards the car park without looking back.

Standing in the security line, I turn and I see him there, behind the newsstand. Blinking at the ceiling, his fists knotted behind his back, jaw pulsing. *It's fine,* he had said. *I forgive you. Let's just move on.* Now, looking at him, I am not so sure. I take off my shoes and hold my hands up above my head in the body scanner. It beeps. An officer moves me to one side and begins a pat-down. Lena, quietly curious, watches from a studious distance, as if her mother might be a criminal.

"Ma'am," the man in uniform asks, "is there something in your pocket?"

I put my hand in.

Uncurl my palm.

Lena's mouth drops open with recognition.

The hairpin.

"Next," the uniform calls.

On the walk through the terminal Lena trots happily beside me, holding on to my bag strap.

"I'm going to be nice like Dada said."

"Okay, that's good."

Her hand slips inside my pocket, feeling for the pin.

"Can I have it?"

"No," I say.

"We share it?"

"Sorry, but no."

Lena stops abruptly on the travelator. Passengers with wheelie bags tumble into one another, muttering, craning their heads. A suit sashays around us, holding his coffee aloft.

"Lena, walk, please. There are people behind us."

Her jaw trembles, tears spilling over.

"No," she whimpers. "Not fair."

"I'm sorry."

"Why?"

"It doesn't belong to me. I'm taking it back."

She thinks about this, the two of us sliding side by side on the travelator like driftwood down a river.

"Where?" She sniffs. "How?"

"I don't know. Sorry."

I stroke away her tears with my thumb. When I scoop her up, she snakes her legs and arms around me, sobbing into my hair. I close my eyes and rock.

"Shh, shh," I whisper into my daughter's ear, squeezing her tightly as we draw near the edge of the travelator, closer and closer, about to tumble.

"Mummy," Lena howls, "Mummy, stop it. That hurts."

51

Her kisses were soft. Cool and minty, vaguely medicinal.

I stayed still.

I didn't move.

What surprised me most—more shocking even than the kiss itself—was that a girl could be more expert at it than a boy, more tender and responsive. Despite what townies wrote on our boundary wall, I was incredibly naïve about what women did in bed together. No section for it existed in our biology textbooks, or any other book I'd read for that matter. The prudish picture I had in my head back then was of two girls, fully dressed, awkwardly knocking their hips together, butting like goats.

As far as I knew, no Divine had ever confessed to liking girls. Back then we used the word *gay* frequently, uttering it with loud, disgusted gratification, a dirty word. *Don't be so gay,* we said to Gerry when she had one of her tantrums, or if the refectory had run out of coffee, or the fire alarm went off, *that's so gay,* oblivious to how bigoted we sounded.

And once we tried experimenting with poppers in the rec grounds. Skipper held out a vial that her older cousin had given her and told us to inhale it. Someone told a story then about "poofs" using it to relax their sphincters. When I heard the word *poof* I thought of the round leather stool my mother used to rest her feet on at home. Everyone always seemed to know more than I did. I held the glass tube under my nose suspiciously.

"Stop being such a gayer," Skipper had said, without irony.

I felt the weight of Lauren's forehead resting against my shoulder. As if all that kissing had exhausted her. Still I didn't move.

I thought of the boy in the chip shop, flicking his lizard tongue. *Cucumbers, lezzer, dyke.* I heard him snapping his fingers in the air, falling off his chair, laughing and laughing.

I grew hotter, my skin burned.

It all made sense—the smirks, the nudges, the leers, the sniggering, the knowing looks.

Stuart saying—eyebrows raised, a quizzical smile—*you're Lauren's . . . ?*

"No," I shouted.

I slapped her.

A blow so hard it sent her sprawling onto her back.

Towel thrown open.

Legs in the air.

The Polaroid photos scattered on the floor.

I stared at the mound between Lauren's thighs, transfixed by the parted folds, the garish pinkness.

Downstairs I heard the front door slam shut. Keys jingling. Lauren's mother.

"Oh my god," I said.

"Loz?" Joan called. "Why aren't you at work?"

I jumped up but Lauren didn't move. There was loud muttering as Joan climbed the stairs, the sound of one leg dragging behind the other. The bedroom door swung open.

"Oh, it's you, is it?" Joan's lips pursed together as soon as she saw me, an iron stare. "Lauren, what's going on here?"

She barged past me into the bedroom with her cane, gasped at her daughter's shaved head, the slap mark, the photos.

"What the bleeding hell have you done?" Joan barked at me.

Lauren made a dismal noise, a wail. She squeezed tight a fist and struck the side of her own head. She began to pummel—her thighs, her chest, her temple.

"Loz, don't. Stop it. Stop it!" Joan said and seesawed painfully down onto the floor. "Stop that now. What's happened to you?"

Lauren let out a sob.

She curled up in her mother's lap.

Her mother rocked her, stroked her head, and whispered into Lauren's ear. I tried to find a blanket to cover them.

"Get out," ordered her mother bitterly.

"Please," I begged. I scrambled to pick up the photos.

Joan lashed out with her cane.

"You stay away from us, do you hear? If you lay another hand on my daughter, I'm calling the police. Same goes for our Stuart."

Joan widened her eyes at the Polaroids in my hand.

"Jesus. I don't know what you're playing at . . ."

I picked up my shoes and backed towards the door.

"You're a nasty piece of work, Josephine, you know that? I always thought it."

Her mouth pinched. She spat at my feet.

"Now fuck off or I'll scream the house down."

Outside on the street, two neighbours stood in the middle of the road, arms crossed, eyeballing me, muttering to each other. Another man stopped working on his motorbike and watched, a spanner in his fist.

I put my head down.

Kept on walking.

Never looking them in the eye.

They were townies. I was Divine.

52

Lena is in the garden with my mother. From the window in the attic I can see the two of them ambling up and down the lawn in deep philosophic discussion, their hands knotted behind their backs. Next time I look out they are standing at the base of the apple tree gazing up; then before I know it they are outside the toolshed. Moving like a flip book. I hear the grating sound of a ladder being dragged across gravel, Lena's end skimming the floor, and when I come outside to join them, my daughter is standing at the base of the ladder, catching the apples as they fall. Nesting them delicately in a basket.

When she sees me coming, she points a finger at me and wags it.

"Go away, Mama."

She doesn't want me interrupting their little game. Or am I still not forgiven for refusing to give her the hairpin? Horrible Mummy. A baddy. A thief.

I take an apple from the basket, rub it on my thigh and sit down on the grass.

"Hello, darling," my mother says from the top of the tree. She makes a point of not commenting on the notebook by my side. My old leavers book, the pages yellowed and speckled with mould, the messages barely legible. Despite Rod's constant probing about the school reunion, the guilt trips and dropping of hints, I still haven't given her an answer.

"Taking a break from work?" Rod asks.

"Yes," I say.

That morning I carved a desk space for myself in my mother's attic, amongst the boxes of old reports, art projects and address books. I sat at her writing bureau with its enormous PC that my mother uses for the sole task of corresponding with fellow DOGs. I read and reread Gerry's message in my leavers book, rubbing it like braille, picking at the layer of Tipp-Ex. At the bottom of my school trunk were pages of old newspapers with their glaring headlines: TEENAGER, 16, PLUMMETS FROM WINDOW. BOARDING SCHOOL GIRL, LEFT IN COMA. Underneath the pile was the bead necklace that Lauren gave me. I worked it through my fingers like a rosary, rubbing each letter in turn. Then, on a whim, I called her number, two decades too late, barely looking at my old address book, reciting the number by heart. The voice at the end of the line suspicious sounding, brusque.

"Lauren?" I asked.

"Who? No. Wrong number."

"Lauren McKibbin," I said, before the woman could put the phone down. "The McKibbins."

"Who's asking?"

"We were friends," I said. "At school."

I heard the woman snort with contempt and knew instantly. Kerry. She and Stuart must have stuck it out, against all odds. Good for them.

"School friends?" Kerry repeated, incredulous.

"Yes. I mean, no. We just used to hang out together. Has she moved?"

There was a moment of silence. I pictured Kerry, her small, beaklike nose, eyes narrowed, a smirk on her lips, enjoying this brief moment of power.

"Please," I said. "I'd really like to get in touch with her."

"Yeah, well, Lauren hasn't lived here for years. Not since Joan passed."

So Joan had died. I thought of her cane, hanging on the back of her kitchen chair, the tubes of pills turning on the lazy Susan. And of Lauren, curled in her mother's lap on the floor that day, naked, sobbing.

"Do you have her address or a number?"

An angry tut at the end of the line.

"Who do you think I am, her bleeding secretary?"

"Did she go to Bournemouth?" I tried, remembering something Lauren once said.

But Kerry hadn't changed. She was still catty sounding, spiteful.

"She fucked off after the funeral, didn't she. Good riddance."

I saw Lauren packing her bags, still dressed in black, stuffing clothes into one of Stuart's old sports bags, slamming the door behind her, shoes clicking away up the street, free.

"Maybe Stuart knows?"

Kerry sighed dramatically, was quiet for a moment, then at last she said, "Who did you say you were again? An ex?"

"A friend," I said quietly.

"Yeah, well, last I heard she's a hairdresser. At some salon in Brighton."

"Thank you," I said.

"Whatever."

"Can I leave my number?" I asked.

"Suit yourself."

I recited my mother's number, but for all I knew Kerry was checking her split ends, examining her fingernails, writing the digits in the air.

Afterwards I sat for a long time at Rod's desk; the lettered beads rolled through my fingers, clicking against one another. I thought about the fact that Kerry and Stuart were still together, twenty years on, probably even married. I imagined my own husband, thousands of miles away, working on his bike in the garage or slumped on our sofa with the dog, eating from a tub of peanut butter. I had never missed him so much. In twenty years' time, I wondered, would we still be together? I pictured coming home to an empty house, one without Jürgen, and felt a jolt of panic, shook my head. Through the window I watched Lena. How she took a bite of an apple like it was a hunk of meat, savage looking, juice dribbling down her chin. Her father's daughter. Wild, wickedly funny. Though she has the propensity in certain situations—at birthday parties or playdates—to seem unfriendly. Her head tilted to the side, just like mine, arms crossed, a deadpan face, while other girls skip and prance. *Der Gevatter Tod,* Jürgen teases, our little Grim Reaper. Watching Lena from the attic window, inspecting her apple core intently, I yearned to lift my daughter in my arms, feel the weight of her small, muscular body, her legs wrapping around me. Quickly I picked up the leavers book and rushed out into the garden, only to be greeted by her disapproving scowl, the wagging finger.

Rod has taken off her gloves now and is sitting on the top step of the ladder, looking down at me. I know she's going to bring up the reunion again. I scratch my arm, avoiding her stare.

"How's poor Jürgen getting on without you?" she asks, as if she can read my mind.

"Fine," I say. "I think."

This is the longest we have ever gone without speaking. Several times a day I turn to the map on my phone that shows a small orange bubble where Jürgen is sleeping. Floating above our house. When it is time for my husband to cycle to his studio, I see this same orange balloon gliding south along the LA River, then ten hours or so later, checking at two or three in the morning when I can't sleep, it makes the same journey in reverse. I feel a certain kind of calmness, watching over him like this, a Zeus-like omnipotence, noticing the clockwork precision of my husband's day, the predictability of his routine, the tidal ebb and flow of his journey across the city. Although when Jürgen falls off the grid—Location Not Available—when his phone has run out of battery power or when he makes an unusual journey, to a downtown bar, say, or a cinema or an unknown restaurant on the other side of town, anything out of the norm, an excruciating sense of panic comes over me. I find myself refreshing my phone every thirty seconds or so, my heart thumping, unable to sleep, holding it above my head like a candle in the early hours to test my connectivity.

Rod studies me from the top of her ladder, scratching my arm.

"You sure you're all right, darling?"

"Yes."

She points her pair of secateurs at my leavers book.

"You're not still worrying about that silly article you sent me ages ago, are you? Boarding school what-not?"

"Syndrome," I say.

My fingernail digs into my skin.

I shake my head.

"Utter drivel," she says and starts picking again. "And do stop clawing your arm, you'll make yourself bleed."

Later we carry the basket of apples between us into the kitchen. My mother sees me staring down at my telephone for the umpteenth time and wrinkles her brow. She still has a somewhat Divine view of modern technology. She takes out one apple at a time, inspecting them for blemishes.

Lena, with her magpie eye, grabs the phone from my hand.

"Dada," she screeches.

"No phones at the table," my mother tuts.

"It's my daddy."

"Just Daddy," I say. "You don't have to say 'my.'"

"I want to call Dada."

It is a Saturday, around nine in the morning in Los Angeles. The bubble is floating above the dog park.

"Okay." I start the video call for her. "Take it into the sitting room."

Lena cradles the phone in both hands and skips out of the room.

"Dada, Dada, Dada," she sings.

My mother frowns at me again, an apple in her hand, then turns to the sink and carries on peeling. I wonder how long we can go on without discussing what I'm doing here on my own. Why my husband hasn't called me, why I'm spending my days hiding away in the attic.

I sit in the kitchen, watching my mother peeling fruit over the sink and squinting through the window at her garden where a squirrel is ambushing a bird feeder. Each mottled apple skin unfurls from her palm in a long, continuous spiral. She passes one of these golden curls back for me to chew as she used to when I was a child, then carries on peeling.

"Your father once rather took a shine to one of the girls from his office," she tells me out of nowhere, her back still turned to me.

"What? When?"

"I forget. Donkey's years ago. Hong Kong, I think. Or maybe Singapore."

"What happened?"

"Oh, nothing, darling. It was just one of his silly ideas."

She thumps on the window to scare away the squirrel.

"And your grandfather's commanding officer wrote a stern letter to my mother, after the war, saying your grandfather was about to make a fool out of himself with some major's wife, so she hopped on a train to Nuremberg—this was during the trials— with three babies. And that put a stop to that."

Whatever domestic problem she thinks I'm having, it's clear that she assumes I am the wronged party. The cheated on, not the cheater. I should be offended but when one looks at Jürgen— golden haired, blue eyed—I can see that this makes sense. The truth is I was the one with the secrets. The incriminating photos. The other women.

My mother puts her paring knife down and wipes her hands on her apron. She turns around to look at me. I stop myself scratching my scar.

"Darling," she says, "chin up, these things happen. You just have to tough it out."

When I say nothing, she begins searching around the paperwork in her kitchen, rifling through the various baskets of seed catalogues and *Home & Garden*. She lays down an invitation in front of me, heavy and embossed, identical to my own.

"I know you're rather sniffy about school these days, but at my age I really do dread driving on my own at night. I know you don't want to go, darling, but, well . . ."

Rod looks flustered, folding and unfolding a tea towel. She hates to ask me for anything.

"Memor amici," I say.

"Exactly."

53

Our dorms were empty, stripped of hangings and mementos.
Our trunks were packed. Instead of sleeping in our own beds we
decided to spend the last evening together. One by one we dragged
our horsehair mattresses from our dorms and along the corridor
to the rec room, thumping them down the stairs like dead bodies.

Our deputy housemistress opened her door a crack, watched
for a while—utterly indifferent—and closed the door.

The twins and George played a game of lacrosse along the
corridor with broken sticks and a pair of socks rolled into a ball.
We grazed on whatever we found in our tuck boxes. Some girls
were crying, I remember; others—the exchange students—were
already asleep. Skipper pushed up the rec room window and sat
on the sill staring out at the Circle. A few figures, maintenance
men, stood smoking by the school gate talking to some townies.
Skipper let out a loud self-pitying sigh. Her plans to be head girl
forever thwarted. She curled a finger in her hair.

"*C'est ça,*" she said. "*La fin.*"

I came up behind her.

Did I already know that I'd never speak to her again? Or any
Divine. That their letters and calls that summer would go unanswered. That the following term I'd persuade my parents to let me
go to an international school in Hong Kong, make new friends,
though none I was ever particularly close to. That I'd call myself
Sephine. Lose my accent, flattening my vowels to sound less pretentious. Never ask a single question about Gerry. Never search
for her obituary in the papers. Refuse to read my mother's round
robin letters, ignoring the Old Girls' gossip. Never attend a single

wedding, christening, or reunion. That—until my honeymoon, fourteen years later—I'd pretend I was never Divine.

Quietly, I moved in close to Skipper, palms flat, as if I was going to push.

"Don't do a Gerry."

Skipper's eyes widened, and she squealed and grabbed the window frame.

"Oh my god," she said, grabbing her chest. "Oh my god. Bloody hell . . ."

She held her hand to her heart, openmouthed, hyperventilating. She looked around the room to see who'd noticed.

A smirk twitched across my lips.

"Oh ha, ha." Skipper let out a fake laugh. "Very amusing."

I could tell that she was furious with me. She swung her legs back inside, barged past me to the bathroom to brush her teeth, and when we all went to bed she and the twins took a mattress on the floor as far away from me as possible. There was no arm tickling, no reminiscing, no final whispered words. The sisterhood was over.

I sat for a long time, propped upright with my head close to the window. I watched as sleeping bags rose and fell, listened to the sighs and snores, the slow grinding of teeth.

When I drifted off, I dreamt of Gerry. Standing in the centre of the rink, smiling for the judges. Her chin held high, long swan neck, perfect white feathers, neat and unruffled. Gerry looked at me. A dark stain slowly spread across her costume. I screamed for an ambulance. I ran from judge to judge yelling, *She's bleeding, she's bleeding.* They continued their deliberations, nodding and whispering, making notes. I bellowed at the audience, her coach, the fellow skaters, hitting them, showering them with punches. *Please,* I shouted, *can't you see? She's bleeding.*

I jerked awake.

"Get up." Someone shook me. "Something's happening."

Dazed, I saw that Skipper and the twins had crawled out of their sleeping bags and were peering under the curtain.

"Oh my god," they hissed. "Quick, look."

I went over to see for myself.

The townies were back.

First a group of boys jammed open a prep room window and climbed out, lugging a large television between them. They returned a few minutes later for the VHS.

A few figures came up the drive and rattled the sports hall doors, waiting for security to stop them. No one did. There was, at most, one maintenance man on night duty. He came out of his shed and shook hands with a townie. They laughed and patted each other on the back. We watched as they pointed at the top branches of the shoe tree, then they kicked the base a few times, as if testing its strength.

Boys ran back and forth with objects under their arms. Typewriters, projectors, a bronze bust of our founder. A team of three pushed a harp. It played a disjointed tune as it rattled over cobbles.

"Plebs," Skipper said, returning to her mattress.

Any one of us could have sounded the alarm but, by then, what did it matter? When there was a dull thud and a crash and the icy scrape of something very heavy being slid across concrete, we lay back down, closed our eyes, waiting for it to be over.

54

At the reunion we stand side by side, Rod and I, sipping from plastic goblets, our respective years, '96 and '73, pinned to our chests. I have no idea what I'm doing here, why I let Rod bully me into coming or arranging the sitter. Jürgen was right all along: the past should stay where it is, dead and buried. I want to rip off my name badge and run for the door. Beg my husband to forgive me.

"Lawks, darling," my mother says, looking down at her lapel, practically giddy. "I'm vintage. Chateau Margaux."

I chew on my empty glass, watching trays of homemade sandwiches circulate. A hundred or more DOGs are crammed into the place we once called the Egg—now the communal entrance hall of twenty or so split-level maisonettes. The occupants, members of a shared ownership scheme, have been bribed into letting us poke around their abodes in carefully escorted groups, no more than five or six at a time.

My mother has forgotten her reading glasses. While we wait for our turn, she peers unashamedly at the breasts of the women who pass. First name, pseudonym, surname.

"I don't recognise anyone," Rod says, frowning.

Her enthusiasm wanes, and she nervously puts her hand to her throat, swallowing. Back-to-school jitters.

"I'm sure they'll be here soon, Mummy."

She redirects the conversation. "It's rather a poor show from your lot, isn't it? I suppose things had rather gone to pot by the end. Your year never did quite gel in the way we did."

This is, I think, one of her greatest understatements.

I glance around the room, playing with the hairpin in my

pocket. The Egg is eerily unchanged, the original tiled fireplace is framed by four matching wingback chairs, remarkably like the leather thrones our gargantuan housemistresses once inhabited. The mahogany chest where we collected our post each morning has been replaced by a long sleek glass table, similarly used as a dumping ground for junk mail, takeaway menus, and oversized parcels that won't fit through the small pigeonholes assigned to residents.

I think of the morning after the dares and am overcome by a feeling of dread that I haven't felt in two decades or more. I hear the bell ringing, Divines streaming in one long blue river to chapel, arms knotted together, flicking their hair. I sweat uncontrollably, fear knotting my stomach, and gnaw deeper on my plastic cup.

"Gosh, what on earth's wrong with you?" my mother tuts. "You look like a hamster. Don't you feel well?"

"Nothing. I'm fine. It's hot in here."

I take off my cardigan and drape it around my shoulders.

Everyone here seems older than me by more than a decade except for a small group of women in the corner who whisper to one another and intermittently glance over in my direction. They wear tight, brightly coloured jeans, V-neck jumpers, long equestrian-looking leather boots. They gossip amongst themselves for a while, and when my mother drifts off to read a display board, two or three of them stride across to speak to me.

"We had to find out; it's Joe, isn't it?"

I give a thin smile. I was so unremarkable at school, I tell them, I find it hard to believe they remember me.

"Oh, my goodness," one woman says with a snort. "We were all absolutely terrified of you."

They must have me confused with someone else. Skipper perhaps.

"I really doubt it," I say.

They all begin to talk at once.

"We thought you were so sophisticated. That thing you did with your hair."

"Oh my god, totally, and that cardigan she used to wear, remember? We all wanted one just like it."

I picture the cardigan they're talking about. Rescued from my mother's Oxfam pile after the moths had got to it. Grey, down to my knees, holes in the sleeves I poked my thumb through in winter to keep my fingers warm.

They squeal.

"That's it, we First Years all snipped little holes in our jumpers. That was a whole trend for a while. And that death stare you had. Oh my god, absolutely brutal."

"Death stare?"

Giggling, they try to replicate the expression. Faces blank as mannequins, utterly vacant, their heads dipped to one side.

"What a hoot." They laugh and bounce back to life, skipping off to update their friends.

I am dazed by their description of me. I suddenly feel very dizzy. A tray of drinks levitates past me and I switch my empty glass of wine for a new one. The room is unbelievably loud. Cacophonous. Grown women yapping with delight, jumping up and down, hugging and squealing. Worried I might pass out, I signal to Rod that I'm leaving.

"I need some fresh air."

"Hang on a sec, darling." She grabs my arm. "Speech."

A ruddy-looking woman, the chairlady of the Old Girls Association, whistles and stands on a stool to address us. Franella "Frank" Burwood-Carter.

"Hello all." She claps a few times to get our attention. "Absolutely wonderful to see so many of you here. A big thanks to all the DOGs who pitched in with food. Particularly you, Mike, for supplying the vino."

I see that we are sticking to our traditional names. No matter what I do, I am Joe again. My mother, Rod.

A few DOGs chortle. The speaker lets out her own chuckle. Frank has wide shoulders, hands that are as big as plates, and a deep androgynous voice whose loudness makes me wince.

"Shh." My mother puts a finger to her lips when I try to tell her I feel unwell, that this whole thing is pointless, that I urgently need to call Jürgen.

The chairwoman embarks on a speech. A long elegy about girlhood friendships that stand the test of time. I watch this woman's enormous hands gesticulate as she holds forth. I feel increasingly sick. I tug at the neck of my shirt. But eventually she finishes with a quote—George Eliot: *Every limit is a beginning as well as an ending*—and wobbles down from her wooden stool.

"We're off," my mother says and nudges me.

I'm trapped in the centre of the mob, pressed on all sides, as the chairwoman leads the charge into Fat Fran's office, now a ground-floor studio apartment. The vestibule where Fat Fran's various blue cassocks once hung has been replaced by a tiny kitchen of glass and chrome. There is a small dining table for one, angled to best see an enormous television, a window at street level, car wheels hissing past behind lace curtains, one small sofa, a single bed, neatly made with a decorative cushion, a few empty photo frames.

"It's rather sad, isn't it," my mother whispers.

She and her peers had once, famously, broken into the headmistress's office and switched around the furniture piece by piece, and every pen, trophy and crucifix, to make an exact mirror image.

"Mm," I murmur.

"Darling, are you all right? You look rather woozy. Sit down."

I slump onto the bed. DOGs mooch around the small apartment making polite noises, though there is very little to see.

Frank claps her hands and I think I can make an escape but my mother, who is excited now to be back amongst the Divine, is already off, following our leader, who holds a printed sign above her head bearing our old crest. We troop, two by two, out onto the street in the autumn drizzle and back through the dentist's, which used to be our chapel. Everyone stares up at the domed ceiling and the organ. The last time I was here it was my honeymoon six years ago and someone called me a cunt. It would be nice, I think, to sit down on one of the pews and get my bearings, but a disgruntled receptionist asks us to make way for patients.

Now Frank is on the move again. Umbrellas open. She marches up the road towards St Gertrude, our former junior boarding house. Swimming pool gone, sports hall flattened, the bridge long since dismantled. An ugly low-cost housing scheme, which has swallowed up the heart of our old school, triggers a round of scandalised muttering—*hideous, shocking, terribly naff*—until finally, Frank's pièce de résistance, she turns an abrupt left into a modern cul-de-sac in the centre of which still stands, we can't believe it, our shoe tree.

There is a collective gasp.

"How extraordinary," my mother says.

We circle around the trunk like a pack of hyenas.

On the upper branches of the tree remain, unbelievably, a few pairs of our leather lace-ups, tongues stiff and weathered, dry as pelts. We crane to look at them, heads tipped back, openmouthed. Suddenly there is an outburst of noise. Across the grass comes a handful of stray DOGs, hooting with laughter and apologising dramatically for their lateness. Frank has her hands on her hips, huffing and puffing, handing out badges and striking their names off her list.

"Sorry, sorry," they cry.

"Oh look, it's Charlotte." My mother's face breaks into a huge smile as she waves her arms. "Thank god. Charlie, over here."

"Rod," they cheer.

I watch as my mother dashes towards her friends with surprising athleticism, four or five women, all in their late sixties, air-kissing, squeezing hands. They genuinely love one another.

"Josephine, darling, look who it is."

"Hi, Charlie." I wave. "Good to see you."

"No, no." My mother beams.

She has arranged a surprise for me.

"Look!" she says.

Out from behind her mother steps Skipper.

55

We face each other across a pub table, my former best friend and I, with two pints of shandy, lemon crescents floating up and down in the bubbles like dead fish. We contemplate our drinks awkwardly, nothing to say. Skipper looks around with bemusement at the White Horse, at the cracked leather seats and polished brass.

"God, it feels small, doesn't it?"

"Hmm, yes."

We fall silent again. I try to remember what it was we used to talk about all those nights in our dorms for hours and hours. It's hard to believe this is the same girl who used to tickle me on the arm, leave me funny notes under my pillow, wrap my hair with coloured threads while I sat nestled between her thighs. I see two old men standing outside, puffing in the drizzle. When I ask Skipper if she has any cigarettes, she looks at me aghast.

"Oh, I haven't done that in years."

I go up to the bar and order a bag of peanuts and some Scampi Fries. There is a guy at the bar, young looking, in a paint-splattered T-shirt and work boots.

"Cheers," he says to no one in particular and takes one long thirsty tug on his beer, then wipes his chin with his arm.

When I get back to the table, I rip both snacks open and spread them on the table. Skipper wrinkles her nose.

"Can you believe we used to live on this kind of junk. We were so skinny back then we never cared about what was in our tuck boxes, all that lacrosse and tennis. Now I just have to look at a crisp and I go up a dress size."

It is true, she is stockier than I remember her, certainly much more weathered looking than the photos she posts online. She is wearing an unforgiving pair of navy trousers and a striped shirt that gapes open at the breasts whenever she reaches for her drink. Her jaw is square, a thick layer of foundation spread across her face. She has a matronly way of folding her arms that I don't recognise, her shawl resting neatly across her knee. I notice she has her handbag next to her on the floor with the strap looped around her ankle in case of pickpockets. Only her hair is unchanged, enormously curly and untamable; a few strands of grey but that is it.

She picks up a peanut and sucks on it like a mint. I check my phone for messages from Jürgen or the babysitter. Skipper does the same.

"Husband?" I ask.

"Yes. Number two actually. The first was a bit of a shit."

"Kids?"

"Three. All boys, for my sins. The oldest goes off to Harrow next year. You?"

"One girl. Lena. She doesn't start school for another year."

A neighbourhood school, despite my mother's protestations, a short walk from our house, close enough I can hear the bell at recess. A collection of small pink buildings with a chain-link fence. No hymns, no prayers, no morning sermons. All the same, when I imagine Lena in kindergarten—the stifling classrooms, the spelling tests and homework, the mean girls on the playground, the picking of teams, being left on the sideline—it's as if I'm being slowly strangled.

"A daughter?" Skipper smiles. "That's funny."

"Why?"

"You hated babies. You used to glower at them in Woolworths to try and scare them. It was hysterical."

Did I?

"The rest of us just wanted to get married and pop out sprogs—none of us were terribly ambitious I suppose—except for you. You had that whole thing about it being cruel to bring a child into the world. You were rather right on back then, weren't you? A real *feminist*," she says, dabbing quotation marks in the air with her fingers.

I can't remember any of this. I don't think I expressed a strong opinion about children one way or another back then, at least, no more or less than any other teenage girl with a healthy fear of falling pregnant. They were about as interesting to me as a cat or a dog.

"Was I?"

"Oh, it was probably just a stage. We always had some fad or other, didn't we?"

I pry free a peanut from the roof of my mouth with my tongue, trying to decide which fad Skipper is talking about. Was it our occult phase, when we spoke to the dead on a Ouija board, claiming to have summoned Gerry Lake's mother? Or the time, out of boredom, we pierced each other's ear cartilage with sewing needles? Or our brief flirtation with drugs?

"Drugs?" Skipper lets out an incredulous snort and shakes her head when I remind her of the time at the rec grounds. "I don't think so. That must have been someone else. I'm a bit of a prude when it comes to that sort of thing."

Why would she forget this? She was the instigator—*stop being such a gayer*—the rest of us following her lead. I try to jog her memory.

"Poppers. You got them from your cousin Milo I think."

"Milo? How strange. He and George Gordon-Warren got married, did you hear? Super wedding."

It annoys me that she is trying to change the subject.

"They live in Putney. He works for some bank or other. She has a rather nice gallery in Holland Park."

I vaguely remember my mother telling me that she'd been up to London for a gallery opening, but I'm not prepared to let go of the previous conversation.

"Skipper, seriously, I can't believe you don't remember that day at the rec grounds."

I can hear the shrill tone of my voice as it grows more pedantic.

"We had splitting headaches? Henry Peck had to lie down in our dorm with a cold flannel on her head?"

Skipper's shoulders rise and drop in embarrassment. She gives a noncommittal shake of the head, a little laugh.

"I don't think I was ever that worldly; I don't know the first thing about drugs. I mean, we were rather in our little bubble at school, weren't we? I don't know if I read one newspaper the whole time I was Divine. We smoked like chimneys, of course."

She admits to that at least. I pick up a handful of peanuts. Fire them into my mouth, one after the other. Now that Skipper has begun reminiscing it's as if she can't stop, recounting the names of boys we kissed, the class outings and school plays, the secret trips to the pub, the gating and suspensions, every little misdemeanor.

"Oh god, remember when Freddy threw up during Communion, right into the chalice? Probably still blotto from the night before. All that incense wafting about didn't help. Padre did like his bells and smells."

"Freddy who?" I say.

I have no memory of this person. But Skipper's already moved on.

"Such a shame we never made it to the Other Side. You'd have been head girl, of course."

"Me?" I say, incredulous, spitting out my shandy.

"Without a doubt," Skipper says. "Who else?"

She smooths straight the cashmere shawl on her lap, stroking it like a cat.

"You," I say, stating the obvious.

"Oh god, no. Hardly. I was far too immature. You were the one everyone looked up to. Such poise. So self-assured compared to the rest of us. And all the teachers loved you, naturally. Brain box."

Poise? Self-assured?

Who is she talking about? Nothing about her description of me is familiar at all.

Disoriented, not even bothering to correct her, I stare at myself in the pub mirror, hollow eyed from lack of sleep, greasy skin and frizzy hair, sweaty looking and dishevelled. In the reflection I see that the young workman at the bar has been joined by another much older man, his grandfather perhaps. The grandfather is skinny, bowlegged, wearing a tweed coat. He carries a paper under his arm. He pats his pockets looking for his lighter, then the two of them, one tall, the other very short, leave their drinks on the bar and go outside to smoke.

I would kill, I realise, for a cigarette and stare at the space on the pub wall where a vending machine used to be.

"Should I ask someone for a fag?" I suggest.

"Oh god," Skipper says, groaning. "My husband would murder me. He's a surgical oncologist."

She goes on to bore me about the details of her husband's job, the women he has treated, the lives saved. All the time she speaks I stare at the men outside with longing. I slip my hand into my pocket and press Gerry's pin into my thumb.

"Look, it's stopped raining," I interrupt Skipper abruptly. "We could take a walk around town before we go back?"

"Top idea," Skipper says, oblivious to how Divine she still sounds. "See some old haunts."

She wraps herself in her shawl. I put on the winter coat I have borrowed from my mother. I'm not used to the English autumn, the damp chill, pewter skies. I feel amazed that we used to run around in winter in just our pleated lacrosse skirts. Or is that another thing I've made up?

"One sec," I say to Skipper as we step outside. I approach the two men smoking.

"Excuse me, sorry to interrupt, do either of you have a spare cigarette we could have?"

The men look at each other. The younger of them, the grandson, holds out a packet of tobacco for me to roll my own.

"Put that shite away, Kyle. I've got one, love," the elderly man says as he hands his grandson his newspaper and begins patting his sides again. It takes a long time for him to find his cigarettes, but eventually he passes me a packet and a flimsy pack of matches.

"Keep the matches," he says.

The old man lifts his head and I see the white scar under his chin—a lightning bolt running through his stubble—and I know exactly who he is. Mr McKibbin. He gives me a watery stare. His face is extremely wrinkled, deep pouches under each eye. There is an unkempt look about his clothes, a missing button on his shirt, a crust at the corner of his mouth, the musty smell of wood shavings or hay. Around his neck the same thin gold chain he always wore.

"Thank you," I mumble.

I stare at him and then the grandson. The boy, sullen looking, wants to get back inside to his drink. Kyle, I think, Kerry's son, all grown up.

"How's Lauren?" I say. But the old man doesn't hear me and raises a hand to his ear.

"Sorry?"

"Never mind. Thank you for the cigarette."

As I walk back towards Skipper, a third man passes me coming up the road. Head down against the cold, hands in his pockets. But I would recognise the walk anywhere, even now. A certain swagger. Jack the Lad. His blond hair is shorter, the curtains gone, the gold stud he wore in one ear removed. He's more solid than I remember, almost thickset, his skin unseasonably tanned. Creased at the neck, older but just as cocky, whistling to himself as he always used to. Stuart gives me the once-over as he goes by and my skin prickles. No flicker of recognition. Not even a smile. Brushing right past me.

"All right, Dad," Kyle says. It's hard to believe he's the baby from the park.

"Who's that you were chatting up?" I hear Stuart ask, ruffling Kyle on the head. "Bit old for you, isn't she, son?"

"Her? No one, just some posh bird who wanted a ciggie."

"You coming in then?"

"Yeah."

They stamp on their butts, thump each other on the back, make a joke. And as he follows after them, he can't help himself, Stuart steals a final look at Skipper and me over his shoulder.

"Afternoon, ladies," he calls as he opens the door.

Tilting his head to one side, giving us a wink.

56

From the looks of it, St Gertrude's, our former boarding house, has been converted into a treatment facility, a halfway home. According to my mother the town is rife with addicts. I have no idea where she sources her information. Patients buzz in and out using a keypad, staring up into the eye of a security camera as they do. In what was once our rec room there is a woman in a purple medical tunic, holding a cup of tea. The upper windows all have bars.

"How depressing," Skipper says, looking up at the ivy-clad walls.

We duck down the side of the building, next to what used to be a boiler room, pushing through the shrubbery and hawthorn, slipping on the red berries underfoot. Twigs snag my coat and claw my hair. Skipper stops abruptly so that, bent double over as we are, I almost run into her.

"Oh my god." I hear Skipper gasp. "I don't believe it."

She pushes through the final web of foliage, and I come slithering out behind her into our old den like afterbirth.

"Look."

Our sofa is still there, protected in part by the overhang from the boiler room roof. There are the same wide pub ashtrays, slime filled, piled with leaves and rank with stagnant water, a couple of crates. What might be the damp remains of a tie-dye sheet hangs from a branch, threadbare, mostly colourless.

"Henry Peck helped us drag this hideous thing in here." Skipper kicks the sofa. She wipes the mud off her shoe.

"How is she?"

"Henry? Oh, she's done very well. She married Freddie Brice. We took the boys shooting at their place in Scotland last year."

I feel my skin prickle when she says this, something hot needling my chest, not immune it seems—despite all my protestations—to the sensation of being snubbed, uninvited, forgotten about.

"What about Dave?" I ask.

"Oh my god, didn't you hear? Dave joined a cult. Seriously, she's totally off the radar. She and Henry are barely speaking. Fell in with a weird crowd at university and that was that. It's awfully sad. Apparently she's given away her inheritance, absolutely everything, the London flat, all her clothes. Not a penny to her name. Literally sackcloth and ashes. Can you imagine?"

Of the twins I always liked Dave the best.

I offer Skipper the cigarette, but she waves it away and sits down on the sofa arm. She names all the other girls we went to school with, the living and the dead. Their husbands and babies, various cancer scares, a fatal riding accident, a particularly nasty divorce. Her anecdotes run on and on, seemingly endless. She has turned, I think, into a bore.

Inside the treatment centre someone is singing to the radio. A bell rings, perhaps the same system used for our former morning wake-up call, and the music turns off. The building gives off the same faintly medicinal smell it always did. I strike a match and hold out the lit cigarette to Skipper. She looks over her shoulder suspiciously, waiting for someone to bust us.

"Oh, all right then. Sod it. Just a puff."

She lets out a sigh of delight as she exhales. Two plumes waterfall from her nose.

"Divine."

I stand with my arm wrapped around my middle for warmth. There is a long silence neither of us knows how to fill now that Skipper has finished her roll call. She shrugs and hands the cigarette back to me.

"That's everyone, I think, the whole year."

Can she really have forgotten or is she just being coy?

"Not quite."

"Really?"

Skipper unzips her handbag and consults a small leather address book, skimming down the alphabet.

"Gerry," I remind her. "Gerry Lake."

Skipper's finger freezes. She adjusts the scarf around her neck. Snaps shut the address book, drops it inside. The heel of her right foot taps.

"Oh, her. Well, she was always a bit of an odd bod, she never really made any effort to fit in. Not exactly PLU."

People Like Us.

"God, do you remember that hideous sex talk her mother gave us?"

I nod. I remember.

"The bananas!" Skipper shrieks. "I thought Gerry was going to spew with embarrassment. Awful woman. Very nouveau."

She is talking too fast, touching her neck, shoe clicking.

"Stepmother," I remind Skipper. "Not mother."

"Well, you'd know best."

"What?"

"Nothing, forget it."

Skipper seems uncomfortable, she still won't say Gerry's name, fiddling with her bag, incessantly checking her phone. Her foot starts tapping again.

"No, go on," I say. "Please, I want to know."

Memor amici.

Skipper gives me an odd look.

"You were rather touchy about Gerry, that's all."

In my pocket I can feel my phone vibrating. I ignore it.

"I was?"

"Well, I mean, Gerry was a complete drama queen," Skipper goes on, trying to make me feel better. "The papers banged on about her wonderful skating career cut short, but who knows how talented she really was. I'm sure half of her stories weren't true. She used to stamp her feet if she didn't get her way. Terribly spoilt."

Skipper hasn't told me anything I don't already know. The den is very quiet. Her heel dances on the ground.

"And she was such an attention seeker, always trying to show off about her so-called boyfriend. Bragging to you about the presents he'd given her. And remember how she wouldn't join the dares that night? She was in a foul mood about losing some silly competition. Vile. Absolutely screaming the house down. Threatening you. I suppose we should never have stooped to her level, but gosh, all that fuss over some lucky charm."

Skipper gives a nervous chortle.

"Honestly, we were sick to death of her."

I look up quickly, and my fingers inside my pocket press against Gerry's pin. Skipper's hand goes to her throat, loosening her scarf. She seems to regret her choice of words.

"Oh, I didn't mean it like that! I was talking about throwing her skates out of the window. Everyone knew her fall was an accident. It's not our fault Gerry was such a pill."

I stare at her, not saying anything.

"Come on. This is rather silly. Stop acting like you don't know what I'm talking about. You were there, too."

There it is, she finally admits it.

She lets out a short, dry laugh, rather like Gerry Lake.

"Please, it was your dormitory, after all," Skipper protests. "Why else would we have gone back up there?"

"I don't know," I say honestly.

Why did we go back up there that night? Why didn't we hide under the stage or behind the boiler room like everyone else?

The cigarette twitches in my fingers.

I remember the police sirens, the flashing lights, how we sprinted across the Circle, cloaks flapping. Had we looked up, we'd have seen Gerry, knees tucked under, small and feathered, perched on the window ledge.

"This is ridiculous." Skipper sniggers nervously. "I'm starting to feel like I'm on trial."

She sits primly on the edge of the sofa, legs pressed together, back rigid. Her cardigan is buttoned up to her neck. She is hugging her handbag tightly to her chest, like a pile of schoolbooks. Who would have believed twenty years ago that my best friend would grow up to be so dreary, dress like her mother?

"Accidents happen," she mutters.

"Accident?"

Skipper's eyes dart this way and that, around the den, down at the handbag, at my shoes and my hands, the cigarette butt crushed underfoot. I take my fist out of my pocket and she sees the rhinestone pin in my palm, the forget-me-not hearts, the fake sapphires. Her mouth turns into a wide O before she snaps it shut. She seems about to say something but changes her mind.

"Oh, for goodness' sake. It was such a long time ago, who even remembers? I'm sure if you asked the whole year, any one of us, we'd probably all have totally different stories about that night."

"Like the poppers," I point out.

"Exactly. No. Oh for god's sake."

Skipper stares at me. Her eyes are watery from the cold. Her nose red. She loosens her grip on her bag and sniffs.

"You haven't changed a bit," she says sourly.

My mobile begins to vibrate again in my pocket. The babysitter, I think. Or my mother. Rod and I have arranged to meet up for a late lunch with the others. She must be wondering where we both are. But when I take out my phone, I see Jürgen's name.

I clasp my mobile, stare at the screen, unable to breathe.

"Sephine?" I hear Jürgen calling, his voice gravelly, distant sounding, but still, I could cry with relief. "Hallo? Sephine, can you hear me?"

"It's my husband," I explain quickly. "I have to take this."

Skipper waves me away with her hand, sulking, throwing evil looks in my direction. My phone is at my ear, I'm scrambling to get out of the den, when Skipper begins muttering to herself.

"Ridiculous. I don't know why you're grilling me about any of this. For goodness' sake, if you're so obsessed, just ask her yourself."

The ground turns to liquid under my feet.

"Sephine?"

My hand drops.

I turn around, claw back to her through the long grass and brambles.

"Sephine. Hallo, hallo?"

"Ask who?"

Skipper's lips pinch together, her heel taps, her fingers clench the strap of her bag. I think I'm going to have to wring it out of her. But in the end she raises an eyebrow pointedly.

"Gerry, of course. Who else?"

57

In the end it isn't hard to find her. Once I know what I'm looking for—a person, not a ghost—it doesn't take long at all. A few calls, a stilted conversation with her stepmother, who, after some persuasion, agrees to pass on my details. Then, shortly after I return to Los Angeles, an email from Gerry herself.

We agree to meet at the airport. It is two weeks before Christmas and Gerry is flying home to England from a conference on the other side of the world. A stopover of just a few hours. I have to go to New York to interview a young pop star, a girl I'd never paid much attention to until my editor gave me the job, after months of pestering him for work. I'll take anything, I said, and he gave me the petulant teenager. I book my flight so it coincides with Gerry's.

In our various emails back and forth, I offer to show Gerry something of my city if she's able to land a few hours earlier. The Hollywood sign, the Observatory, a trip to the beach, the holiday ice rink even.

God no! Gerry writes back, naming a restaurant inside the airport. She has work to do before the long flight home. Some housekeeping to finish before Christmas. Thanks to my repeated requests to meet in person without any explanation, I sense I have been sublimated to an item on Gerry's checklist. An irritating task to complete, a chore.

I check in hours earlier than necessary, ride the shuttle to her terminal, take a seat in the restaurant. Not at the high counter of the bar, my preferred choice when travelling without Lena, but one of the tables nearer the concourse. A spot with enough space for a wheelchair to access. No unwieldy pot plants or book displays. Nothing to knock into. No tricky corners.

While I wait I try to distract myself with work, researching the pop star, her swift rise to fame, the predictable burnout, the reinvention. I order one item after another to keep the waitress happy. Coffees, a sandwich, then, eventually, gin and tonic. My eyes flit between my screen and the crowded concourse. As the time gets closer I take out a small blue box from my hand luggage and arrange it neatly beside my laptop.

When a woman at the bar takes off her glasses and raises a tentative hand, it takes me a while to realise it's me she's signalling. I look over my shoulder, then back down at my work.

The woman slips nimbly off her stool and walks over to my table.

"Hello there," she says, as if she knows me. "I suppose we both had the same idea."

The stranger gestures to her computer.

"My flight landed early. I thought I'd catch up on emails."

Her hair is short, a neat bob. Chestnut brown. A minimal amount of makeup. No wheelchair, no limp, not even a cane. She wears jeans, a silk shirt, petite, but nowhere near as short as I remember. Not even close. This woman can't possibly be Gerry. But before I can speak, she's off again.

"I'll get my stuff, wait a sec," she says.

She weaves back through the busy restaurant and returns with a smart leather case in one hand, her glass of wine in the other. Slides into the chair across from me. In spite of enduring a fourteen-hour flight, her makeup is flawless, skin that's velvety looking, her hair tucked neatly behind her ears, a perfectly placed beauty mark.

"So," she says, pausing to take a sip of wine. "Lovely to see you again. Thanks for getting in touch. What a surprise."

There must, I think, be some mistake.

"Gerry? Gerry Lake?"

"Yes, well, Clements now. I'm married."

Dr Geraldine Clements. Child psychologist, specialist in eating disorders and childhood trauma. Published author, a media spokesperson on anorexia in the prepubescent, sought-after presenter and keynote speaker. All facts I have mined from the biography page on the conference website. Dr Clements herself has no Twitter page or Instagram feed, or any other online presence I could find, despite hours of searching.

"God, don't you hate all that social media nonsense. I mean, who has time for Facebook? I literally have no idea." Gerry shakes her head, bemused.

She's not being facetious. This is a genuine question.

Her face is smooth, unwrinkled, strikingly youthful given that we are both nearing forty. The only imperfection I can see is a small scar, a red stripe running into her hairline above her ear. We used to, I remember, call Gerry Lake 'baby cheeks,' suck our thumbs, push out our bottom lips in an attempt to rile her.

"So, how about you?" she asks after she's described her conference, the title of her keynote speech alone running so long I forget where it started. "What are you up to these days?"

She tilts her head at the mess of scribbled notes and printouts on the table beside me. On the top sheet is an unflattering tabloid snap of the pop star. A dishevelled-looking teenager, shielding her eyes from the lights of paparazzi. I stuff my notebook into my bag, conscious that Gerry herself was once front-page news.

"Not much," I say and mention a few of the magazines I've worked for in the past.

The truth is that if Gerry's googled me already—and why would she not—she'll already know that there is nothing particularly meaningful about the kind of work I've done of late. Hotel reviews, top ten lists, "must haves" for summer. Dull advertorials in airline magazines. Stories that you skim as you wait for the in-flight entertainment to start. There's a slim chance, if she's delved back far enough, she's found my feature on the gymnastics scandal.

"Freelance. Sounds fun," Gerry says diplomatically. "How

fantastic to be able to work from home. On your own clock. I'm jealous."

She is composed, eloquent, polite to the point of emotionless. Her accent sounds polished, almost plummy. No more dropped aitches and flattened vowels. These days she sounds more Divine than I do.

"I think I always imagined you'd end up in a suit," Gerry says, leaning back in her chair and crossing her arms as she looks at me. "A barrister. Banking perhaps. Good on you. You have an actual life. Bravo."

A backhanded compliment. I raise both eyebrows, neither agreeing nor disagreeing, and signal to the waitress for another gin and tonic.

"I barely see my children," Gerry complains.

"Children?"

It is my turn to be surprised.

"As good as. Stepchildren. Two girls. Seven and fourteen. I can bore you with photos if you like?"

I nod.

Gerry shows me pictures of her family—her wife, her children, even her dogs, grinning like maniacs at the camera—unequivocally proud.

"They're Julie's, from a previous relationship," she explains. "It's not as complicated as it might sound. I've known them since they were babies."

I hand the phone back and ask her if she thinks they'll have more.

Gerry grimaces—a white flash of canines—and for a moment she looks like an approximation of the girl I remember.

"Nappies, night feeds, god no. I can barely keep up with the girls' lives as it is. And now we've got an adolescent in the house, bloody hell, that's enough to put anyone off." She rolls her eyes at the ceiling as we used to during Padre's Sunday sermon. "Teenagers. God help us."

I feel my face stiffen, and my thumbnail presses into the fleshy part of my palm. I am about to say something when the waitress delivers my drink. I try again, switching the conversation in a different direction.

"Do you still skate?" I ask.

In another world Gerry might have continued to compete, I think, gone on to be a professional, won medals.

She snorts.

"A lifetime of bunions and in-grown toenails. All that training. No thanks. I couldn't wait to give it up."

I look down, not sure what to say next.

"They turned the chapel into a dental surgery," I offer.

"The what?" Gerry asks. "Oh, the school chapel. A dentist's? How bizarre."

For a moment I think of the clocks. The overture of bells, one after another, almost melodious. Our frantic scramble under pews, in the choir stalls, beneath the altar skirt, while Gerry slipped into a coma.

"And St Gertrude's is a rehab unit of sorts. For addicts." I keep going, studying Gerry's face for a reaction. Her expression remains the same, smiling politely, one leg crossed over the other, a casual raise of her eyebrows, untroubled.

"That seems apt," she says.

"Bars on all the upper windows," I say.

Still nothing.

Gerry glances at her lap, turning her inner arm discreetly so she can see the face of her gold wristwatch. About to make her excuses.

"The shoe tree," I say before she can speak, "that's still there too. In the middle of all these new builds. It was a big hit at the reunion. Everyone wanted their photo taken in front of it."

Gerry nods, still smiling.

"I can imagine," she says, and then, even though I haven't asked her the question, she says, "I was busy that day. Working or, no, my daughter had a concert. Something or other, I forget. You know how it is. My eldest plays the saxophone, she's in two orchestras, so it's nonstop rehearsals, or a competition or a master class, absolutely endless."

Just like that Gerry shifts the conversation back to safe ground—her children, unfinished Christmas shopping, a recent visit from her in-laws. She asks if we'll be in Los Angeles for the holidays and I tell her no, that we're going to spend it in England with my mother.

"Oh, fuck," she says suddenly. "Presents. I forgot to get the girls anything from Sydney. I'd better pick up something before my flight."

This is the most rattled I've seen her so far.

She scribbles in the air in the direction of the waitress.

"It's been nice to see you again, Joe."

She stands up quickly, tucks her silk shirt neatly in place and hooks her bag over her shoulder. She can't get away fast enough.

I feel the moment slithering away from me.

"Wait," I say, rocking the table as I stand, grabbing her arm. "Gerry, I have something to say first. Please."

Gerry stands with her hand in her pocket, her elbow jutting out, legs bent slightly backwards as they always used to. She looks down at my hand and flinches—perhaps I'm imagining it—and I let go of her sleeve. The frown evaporates. She dons the same serene, indecipherable expression as before and nods.

"I'm sorry, of course. Go on."

Gerry sits and puts her bag down, resting it by her neatly crossed ankles, as if she has all the time in the world, regarding me, I think, as she might one of her young patients. My eyes gravitate towards her scar, the crack in her hairline like a piece of broken china.

"I want to say I'm sorry."

Gerry's nose wrinkles, at a loss to know how to respond.

"Okay," she says.

"For the way we used to treat you. The things we did. Dares night."

The taunting, the snobbery, the social ostracisation.

Gerry leans forward as she listens, her arms on the table, and twists her wedding band thoughtfully, as if she's cracking a safe. We sit in silence.

"Well, for a start," she begins, "I wasn't exactly the easiest person to get along with. There was a lot going on that year that I didn't talk to anyone about. I wasn't"—she reaches for the right words—"I wasn't very happy in my own skin."

Who is? I want to ask her. Even now. Is she?

"It's very sweet of you to apologise."

Sweet? I wince.

"But to be honest, I haven't thought about any of that stuff in years. I didn't particularly enjoy school, of course, but it's not something I dwell on. I wasn't in with the cool crowd, not like you, and let's face it, most girls can be pretty horrible to each other, can't they? But I don't think I was particularly singled out. I wouldn't say that. No more than anyone else. And I can't even remember much about dares night. Sorry to have wasted your time, but it's really not a big deal in my life. I moved on."

Her voice is light and breezy, as if she finds the whole thing humorous, a smile at the end of each sentence. I stare at her, baffled. Can this really be how she remembers her schooldays? Harmless joshing?

"God, you should see what my daughters have to contend with," Gerry continues. "The vile things teenagers post about one another these days, the comments online, it's enough to make your toes curl." She shakes her head and a strand of hair slips out from behind her ear, covering her scar. She tucks it back in place again. "You've got that to look forward to, I suppose."

A muffled announcement comes over the airport intercom. Gerry strains to listen. She squints at the departures board. Checks her watch. We only have a few moments left. I slide the blue box from my side of the table to Gerry's.

"What's this?" she asks.

"It's yours."

"I don't understand."

She opens the case and stares at the forget-me-not pin, re-stored as best the shop in the jewellery district could manage—the missing gems replaced, the two broken halves somehow welded together—the cost of the repairs probably far exceeding the value of the ornament itself. Gerry peers closer.

"This was mine?"

She seems bemused.

"Yes."

"Are you sure?"

"Yes."

"Gosh."

Finally she takes it out, twisting the pin between her fingers. It's as if she's seeing it for the first time. It's clear she doesn't re-member. Then she places it back in the box.

"Strange," she says. "But thank you."

A large group outside the restaurant is waiting to be seated. The waitress stares meaningfully in our direction. We get up. Gerry walks ahead of me to the exit, eager to have this meeting over with. When I stuff my notes and laptop into my bag, I see that she has forgotten to pick up the jewellery box from the table. I carry it over.

"Silly me," she says, patting her pockets as if she doesn't have anywhere to put it. This, too, is an inconvenience.

We say our goodbye in the middle of the terminal, amongst the wheelie bags and sprawled bodies and heads hunched over phones. No hug or handshake. No request to stay in touch or a false promise to meet again the next time I'm back in England. Gerry raises a palm and smiles, that's it. She has nothing more to say to me. She'll board her plane, order a Bloody Mary, flip open her laptop without a second thought. I doubt she will even bother to tell her wife and kids about our meeting, a detail forgotten as soon as she walks through the door, lost in the welcome home hugs and shouts of excitement. Skipper and I have no place in her narrative. Not even as a footnote. We have been written out, painted over like the message in my leavers book, banished from the pages. In making light of my apology, she's refusing to play the victim, to seem in the least bit tragic. And why not? Who are we, after all, if not the author of our own story?

A happy ending then. It could be worse, I know, but instead of catharsis, I feel the opposite. Despondent, strangely hollow. What would I prefer—eternal damnation? For Gerry to scream in my face, chain me to a rock, flay me alive, pummel me with accusations?

Instead I stand there in the middle of the concourse feeling small and inconsequential, like something you might brush off your coat, still holding the jewellery box.

"Gerry," I call after her.

She ignores me at first.

But then, halfway to her gate, I see her hesitate.

She loops back around, swimming awkwardly the wrong way through the crowd and comes to a standstill in front of me, a hand on her hip.

"Actually, I do have one question. I'm curious. No hospital visits or calls. No get-well cards, not a single one from any of you. Twenty years. Why now?"

There is no point in lying.

"I thought you were dead," I say.

Gerry's mouth widens.

She lets out a screech.

People crane their necks to look.

"Dead?"

Her lips pinch into a beak, shoulders thrust back, one knee bent.

"You wish," she hisses.

She claws the jewellery box from my hand.

Turns on her heel.

My last view of Gerry, or any other Divine. Marching across the polished floor towards a bin, dodging frantic travellers. No second look, no equivocation. A snap of the wrist. She tosses the blue box, barely stopping to see it land, and vanishes into the crowd.

ACKNOWLEDGMENTS

Thank you to my brilliant, unflappable agent, Julia Kenny, for her passion, humour, and cautious optimism; Veronique Baxter in the UK; and everyone at Dunow, Carlson & Lerner.

Thank you also to Liz Stein, my extraordinary editor, for her razor-sharp notes and the care she's taken with this book; Vedika Khanna, Mumtaz Mustafa, Eliza Rosenberry, and the rest of the incredible team at William Morrow, for helping to usher it into the world; and Beth Hoeckel for her stunning artwork. In the UK, thanks to Kate Howard and everyone at Hodder & Stoughton.

I owe a great deal to poet Kate Llewellyn, for setting me on this path in the first place and teaching me about rope; Sir Andrew Motion and my cohorts from Royal Holloway, in particular Sarah Perry, whose long-distance friendship, bolstering emails, and early championing of the book have kept me sane.

Thanks to the Kerouac Project and the Writers in Prison Network whose residencies gave me space and time to write.

For reading and rereading versions of this and earlier books, thank you to Patrick Hussey, Ivo Watts-Russell, Jeff Capshew, Tempany Deckert, Emma Finn, and Alexandra Calamari. Thanks to Karin Casparian for, amongst other things, patiently answering all my questions about Austrian German idioms. Special thanks to Holly O'Neill, for her immeasurable editorial skills and wit, and not least for inadvertently helping sow the seed that would grow into *The Divines*.

Lastly, thank you to my family. To my parents, Jennie and Julian, for their unwavering support, and to my sister, Kythe, 90s fact-checker, survivor of the green velvet minidress, kindest of all people.

And above all, for everything, always, thank you to Tom and Iris. Here we go.

THE
DIVINES

THE
DIVINES

ELLIE EATON

**HODDER &
STOUGHTON**

First published in Great Britain in 2021 by Hodder & Stoughton
An Hachette UK company

1

Copyright © Eleanor Eaton 2021

A CIP catalogue record for this title is available from the British Library

Hardback ISBN 978 1 529 34012 9
Trade Paperback ISBN 978 1 529 34013 6
eBook ISBN 978 1 529 34014 3
Audio ISBN 978 1 529 34016 7

Printed and bound in Great Britain by Clays Ltd, Elcograf S.p.A.

Hodder & Stoughton policy is to use papers that are natural, renewable
and recyclable products and made from wood grown in sustainable forests.
The logging and manufacturing processes are expected to conform to the
environmental regulations of the country of origin.

Hodder & Stoughton Ltd
Carmelite House
50 Victoria Embankment
London EC4Y 0DZ

www.hodder.co.uk

FOR TOM AND IRIS

γνῶθι σ᾽εαυτόν